The Western Story
FACT, FICTION, AND MYTH

Edited by
PHILIP DURHAM and EVERETT L. JONES
University of California, Los Angeles

The Western Story

FACT, FICTION, AND MYTH

HARCOURT BRACE JOVANOVICH, INC.

New York   Chicago   San Francisco   Atlanta

ISBN: 0-15-595316-8

Library of Congress Catalog Card Number: 74-27765

Printed in the United States of America

COVER: from the Erwin E. Smith Collection
in the Library of Congress—
photographs of cattle ranching and cowboy life
made 1905–1915 by Erwin E. Smith
of Bonham, Texas, himself a cowboy.

Copyrights and Acknowledgments

THE AMERICAN SCHOLAR for "The Olympian Cowboy" by Harry Schein. Reprinted from *The American Scholar*, Volume 24, Number 3, Summer 1955. Copyright © 1955 by the United Chapters of Phi Beta Kappa. By permission of the publishers.

ALLAN R. BOSWORTH for permission to reprint his "Stampede." Copyright 1950 by *The Saturday Evening Post*.

KNOX BURGER ASSOCIATES, LTD., for "The Tin Star" by John M. Cunningham. Copyright 1947, 1973. Reprinted by permission of the author and Knox Burger Associates, Ltd.

Page 369 constitutes a continuation of the copyright page.

PREFACE

The Western Story: Fact, Fiction, and Myth deals with a form of popular art that is uniquely American in its settings, conflicts, and resolutions. Yet it is also the one genre of American popular fiction that has seized the imagination of almost all the rest of the world. The Western hero, with his sturdy independence, his faithful horse, and his prominently displayed gun, has become the exemplar of American manhood, idealism, and courage. He has also represented a glorification of lawlessness, aggression, and violence. Always he has exercised a peculiar attraction for nearly all readers or viewers.

Western stories have been dismissed by a few critics as mere adventure stories, indistinguishable from the dime novels that preceded them, and just as ephemeral. But their popularity has endured, though it has waxed or waned from year to year in every decade of the twentieth century. They have established a body of conventions, stereotypes, and clichés known to virtually every citizen of the Western world.

This book presents brief samples of the sources, the variety, and the great range of interpretations of the Western story. It recognizes that Western stories are historical fictions. They exploit the history of the cattle country and the Pacific Coast during the last half of the nineteenth century, but as fiction they draw on the international literary traditions of the pastoral, the epic, and the romance. Although they may sometimes seem simple, that very simplicity gives them qualities of universality similar to those of older epics, sagas, and romances.

The stories and essays collected here are representative selections from the literature of the West. Part One reprints several factual descriptions of the cattlemen's West, beginning with an account by Theodore Roosevelt, who was a rancher and hunter years before he became President of the United States. Part Two presents sixteen examples of the fiction of the West, beginning with early stories by Bret Harte and Jack London and ending with Western stories by contemporary authors. Part Three offers a sampling of the large outpouring of critical interpretations of Westerns that have been produced by literary scholars, journalists, sociologists, psychologists, historians, theologians, political scientists, and writers of Western stories themselves.

For classroom study and discussion, the Western story has unique advantages. It enables students to examine critically the core values of American society and to study our national self-image in one of its most attractive and compelling forms. It is a kind of fiction and drama with which all students have some familiarity and about which they can talk with some sophistication. And its implicit value systems bear on contemporary issues: the traditional roles of the sexes, attitudes toward national and racial minorities in American society, the attraction and legitimacy of violence, and man's place in the natural world.

It must be admitted that many Western stories are less than "literary," the creations of entertainers who scoff at pretenses to art. But their entertainments are unusually accessible and interesting for students, and examination of the limitations and traditions of even the commercial Western story can be a valuable preparation for later study of more complex and demanding literature.

In preparing the introductions and exercise materials for this volume, we have drawn freely from papers we have read before meetings of the Western History Association, the Los Angeles Historical Society, the 1974 Oregon State University Conference on Western History and Myth, and colloquiums at UCLA. We are also indebted to our fellow members of Western Writers of America for expressions of provocative and frequently conflicting attitudes toward the Western story. And finally we are grateful to William A. Pullin, a patient and persistent editor who has encouraged us in all our work.

PHILIP DURHAM
EVERETT L. JONES

CONTENTS

Part Two
FICTION
61

Part Three
MYTH
305

The Western Story
FACT, FICTION, AND MYTH

INTRODUCTION

The Western story is a special kind of popular literature that always commands a large audience. Western novels are regularly published in both hard and paper covers, and classics like *The Virginian* and *Nevada* have sold millions of copies throughout the world. The vogue of Western stories in motion pictures, radio, or television may wax or wane from year to year, but their durability as a form of popular entertainment seems assured.

Stories of the American West have interested a worldwide audience never reached by other kinds of frontier literature. Novels set in the Argentine Pampas or the Australian Outback may win critical acclaim, but they do not capture the attention of the millions of readers and viewers of Western stories. A single author like Edgar Rice Burroughs may achieve great success with a character like Tarzan, but that success does not result in a flood of jungle stories comparable to the seemingly endless outpouring of American Westerns.

Western stories ordinarily describe a part of the comparatively recent past, a time that lies somewhere between the Civil War and the invention of the automobile. Most Westerns (except for a few that involve their characters in "real" historical events like the Custer defeat or the Lincoln County War) resolutely avoid any more specific dating. Consequently the West becomes a land without time, distant yet paradoxically so close that it seems almost a part of the present. This illusion is so compelling that many Asians and Africans, and even some Europeans and Americans, think Western stories dramatize aspects of the contemporary United States. Thus, in the words of Archibald MacLeish, "The West is a country in the mind, and so eternal."

This country in the mind is the land of pastoral—a country landscape—little complicated by civilization. It is eternal because its simplicity, in the words of Oscar Wilde, can be "the last refuge of the complex." As early as the third century B.C., highly educated and urbane men wrote celebrations of the simple rustic life—almost always life in a distant country and a remote time. Theocritus sat in Alexandria and wrote of Sicilian goatherds, and Virgil lived in Imperial Rome and wrote of shepherds in far-off Arcadia. Neither writer was realistically describing rural agricultural life; both were criticizing the vices, hypocrisies, and vanities of sophisticated society by writing of men and women in an ideally innocent and pure environment. The writers of Western stories, similarly, describe a remote country that is, like Arcadia, a place of simple truths and eternal verities, free of most of the complications and vices of civilization. Though the West may sometimes be arid and unfriendly, full of spiked cactus, inhabited by tarantulas and rattlesnakes, and as lonely as the serenades of its howling coyotes, still it presumably strips its hero of all that is inessential, false, and corrupt.

Then it gives him a mission. Sometimes the task is epic: the hero must open up the country, lead a wagon train from the Mississippi River to Oregon, or drive a herd of cattle from Texas to Kansas. In these actions, he is a part of the history of the nation; he can be compared to an Odysseus, Aeneas, or Roland. At other times, the task is smaller: the hero must protect the ranch, save the heroine, or merely defend his honor. Now he becomes a hero of romance, living by a code very similar to that of Lancelot or Sir Gawain, riding over the countryside to rescue a fair lady or avenge a wrong. At still other times, the hero may be little more than an adolescent, and the plot of his story may be his initiation into manhood—with armed conflict becoming his rite of passage. Or he may be an old man, living and dying by the code or expiating his failure to conquer his passions, his weaknesses, or his changing environment. The Western story is thus a bottle into which almost any wine can be poured; the variety of its plots is nearly inexhaustible.

The setting is constant, as the name "Western story" implies. But frequently the story is vague about exact place; its action unfolds on deserts or ranges that might be anywhere between Texas and Montana, and its hero can ride through mountain passes that might be in the Oregon Cascades, the Colorado Rockies, or the California Sierra Nevada. Its isolated town may be in Wyoming or Arizona, and its lonely wind often howls in some nameless part of the vast West. This lack of specific setting gives a universality to the action, emphasizing the almost mythic quality of the characters and setting many Western stories apart from merely provincial or local-color fiction. Vagueness about exact place in Western stories has, incidentally, also been useful to Hollywood producers, who have filmed hundreds of Westerns just outside the suburbs of Los Angeles and thousands without going more than 250 miles from Beverly Hills.

Though the Western story is vague about both time and place, it also claims to be "true." Almost every writer of range romance has vigorously defended the historicity of his stories, their fidelity to the spirit—if not the letter—of Western history. Writers of all kinds of fiction attempt to achieve verisimilitude, to describe persons and places that can be believed while their stories are read. But Western story writers have almost always insisted that their characters are more than merely believable—that they are typical of our immediate forebears, of the Americans who pioneered in the cattleman's West. These writers achieve an almost Virgilian melancholy in mourning the passing of giants, the recent end of a period of simplicity, innocence, and heroism. From the earliest dime novelists to Owen Wister, from Zane Grey to Jack Schaefer, authors of Westerns have in this spirit maintained that their narratives are essentially true—true of times and places that have only recently passed away or changed.

The rich mixture of history and nostalgia in the work of these authors, together with a debt to centuries of literary tradition in pastoral, epic, and romance, helps to account for the continuing popularity of the Western story. For the combination is a perfect vehicle for the elaboration of myth and legend. It helps to transmute the stories of Wild Bill Hickok, Sam Bass, Wyatt Earp, and Billy the Kid (to name only a few) into legends; and it gives us the nearly mythic story of the simple, noble, and courageous American who helped to "build the country" and to defend the young, the beautiful, and the helpless from attack. He is a strong folk hero, frequently nameless. (The Virginian has no other name; the Lone Ranger even wears a mask; and Jack Schaefer's famous hero says only, "Call me Shane.") He is the apotheosis of the American common man, an embodiment of his culture's traditional values.

The cowboy has long been the hero not only of fiction but also of radio, motion pictures, and television. Before Western programs began to take over much of prime television viewing time in the 1950s, Western films accounted for nearly a quarter of the total production of the motion picture industry. From the time of "The Great Train Robbery," heroes and villains have been photographed riding thisaway and thataway, sometimes on location in Wyoming, Colorado, or Mexico, more frequently over the well-worn trails of the San Fernando Valley or the Mojave Desert. The product has been standardized and expertly packaged, and it has found a market in most of the world.

Only the Soviet Union—where "cowboy" is a term of abuse— and the Peoples Republic of China have barred their people from the pleasures of horse opera. A good Western picture will ordinarily realize half its gross receipts in Europe, and it will play to audiences in Egypt, South Africa, and Nigeria, as well as in Central and South America. The plot and dialogue of ranch and range lose little in translation, dubbing, or unmodified screening.

Along with the durable vogue of Western novels and films in other parts of the world have gone all the accessory interests and activities so familiar in the United States. Children wear paper

Stetsons and toy pistols to play cowboys and Indians in South America, Japan, and Western Europe. Some of their fathers, older and fatter, wear elaborate Western regalia and gather in clubs to drink beer or wine and practice the fast draw. In Munich or in Rome a man in complete Western costume occasions no great surprise, and crowds flock to the bare-skin entertainments of the Paris Crazy Horse Saloon. In the West Indies there are groups of black "cowboys" who dress their parts and act out Western skits as part of Christmas celebrations. More serious scholars, fascinated by Western lore and history, have organized themselves into groups of "Westerners," with "Corrals" in England, France, West Germany, and Sweden.

All of this, however, is only an exotic reflection of the cult of the West in the United States; for it was here, of course, that the whole thing started. Here millions of people sit in darkened theaters or living rooms to watch almost ritualistic confrontations of good and evil. In Los Angeles, for instance, a family could at one time view Westerns on television during almost twenty hours of prime time each week. The vastly greater number of daytime and late evening hours given to television reruns and old Western films varies from week to week, but a day without some of them is very rare.

Any large city always has some theaters that are playing new Westerns or reruns of old ones. The single theater of a small town, particularly if it is West of the Mississippi, ordinarily books every Western it can get. New paperback Western stories (original or reprint) appear almost daily in drugstores, liquor stores, and supermarkets. Shelves of Westerns are maintained in nearly every public library, with this subgenre carefully segregated from other forms of popular fiction.

The Western has become the basis of ballet in *Rodeo* and *Billy the Kid.* David Belasco's play *The Girl of the Golden West* became the libretto of Puccini's opera. Western scenes and heroes were first drawn by Frederic Remington and other illustrators for *Harper's Weekly,* and their tradition has been carried on by a host of illustrators for books and magazines. Much of this artwork is endlessly reproduced on postcards, prints, and souvenirs sold in museums, national parks, and almost every Western town.

Rodeos have become one of the great American spectator sports, drawing crowds that rival those of baseball, and rodeo champions have become affluent popular heroes, with their saddles, spurs, and trophies eventually displayed in the Oklahoma City Cowboy Hall of Fame. Dude ranches—some with cattle, some without—have multiplied throughout the West, and even in the Catskill Mountains of New York.

In Eastern cities small boys wear Western costumes, complete with holsters and toy guns, while surprising numbers of their parents go out in the evenings appropriately dressed for Western square dances. In the West and Southwest, of course, druggists, filling station attendants, and even doctors and lawyers wear Western boots and Stetsons. In Texas, particularly, a wealthy oilman or successful politician hastens to acquire a ranch and cattle, the ultimate status symbols.

Towns like Tombstone, Abilene, and Dodge City, once ashamed of their wild reputations as cattle or mining towns, now celebrate their romantic past and construct replicas of their old Front Streets and boardwalks. During the summers they stage mock shoot-outs three times a day, and Abilene is not unique in hiring high-school girls to dance the cancan in a "saloon" where only soft drinks are sold. In Los Angeles, the home of the Western motion picture, tourists are invited to visit Frontierland in Disneyland, to ride the stagecoaches at Knott's Berry Farm, to watch a brawl between stuntmen on a Universal Pictures soundstage, or to visit one of the "movie ranches" in or near the San Fernando Valley. And throughout the West almost every city or town celebrates at least one "Frontier Day" or "Stampede" each year.

All of these activities are outgrowths of the Western story and its glamorization of Western history. No other popular fiction produces the same kinds of activity; no other fictions are so truly mythic in describing what their audiences believe to be the antecedents, the admirable qualities, and the heroic mission of Americans. No other period of American history has so penetrated the folklore and leisure activities of almost all Americans. Although inns and houses along the Atlantic Seaboard boast that George Washington slept there, and Williamsburg successfully marries antiquarianism with show business, these are regional rather than national celebrations. Gettysburg, Pennsylvania, is similarly a cemetery and military park, even a national shrine, but it generates no continual celebration of Civil War history. Only the cowboys ride indefatigably through our fiction and over our screens to celebrate our past and to establish our national self-image.

It is significant that no other part of our history becomes part of the play of children. Although simulated coonskin caps were once briefly sold to exploit the ephemeral popularity of a single Davy Crockett television series, they were quickly discarded. No child buys tricornered hats or Civil War costumes. Only pint-size Stetsons and toy six-shooters are perennial costuming staples in our toy shops.

No other part of our economy or history has so affected the language of adults. Even on Madison Avenue people buy cigarettes in red boxes that come from Marlboro Country, and advertising executives sometimes rustle or corral other agencies' accounts, round up material to cinch a deal, enjoy reputations as straight shooters, and try to avoid four-flushers. Once they escape Manhattan, they may drive their Mavericks or Pintos like cowboys. As one of the most famous of old automobile advertisements said, the best cars are designed for a girl who lives "somewhere west of Laramie."

The mythic quality of the cowboy is undeniable and is manifested in the telling and retelling of his history, in its dramatic reenactments, in its use as metaphor and American self-image, and in its ramifications of costume, ritual, and language. The potency of the Western myth, like that of all myth, lies in its linking of the present to the Titans of a vanished Golden Age.

The myths of any culture usually exalt the values of an age more barbaric than its present, and a complex civilization can find its myths not only anachronistic but also embarrassing or dangerous. Thus the stories of Siegfried made beautiful opera, but they also helped to rationalize an insane German attempt to establish "Aryan" supremacy. The ancient Sammurai of Japan are magnificent in motion pictures, but they would be monsters in the modern world. And the myth of the cowboy, with all his independence, manliness, bravery, and violence, glorifies attitudes that may help to aggravate the troubles of our populous urban civilization.

The independence and freedom of the Western hero, for instance, help him to "tame the wilderness," but even in 1902, when Owen Wister published *The Virginian*, that kind of freedom was beginning to damage the environment. Wister described the false fronts of the buildings in Medicine Bow, Wyoming, as "rearing their pitiful masquerade amid the fringe of old tin cans." The independence and freedom of the West have all too frequently become the freedom to litter, to ravage, and to destroy. Freedom has been the cry of those who would overgraze and cut down national forests, destroy the land itself with hydraulic dredging and pit mining, or exploit and rob the Indians who remain on pitifully restricted reservations. In the name of freedom our cattlemen and cowboys have nearly exterminated the mountain lions, eagles, and coyotes of the West.

The manliness of our cowboy myth-hero has been maintained at the expense of women. One of the oldest American clichés describes the West as a place where "men are men, and women are glad of it." Another describes the West as being "hell on women and horses." And the Western story is unique in popular literature in making prostitution glamorous. The hero spends his leisure in saloons with whores or "dancing girls," open hearted ladies who understand that "a man's gotta do what a man's gotta do." Even "Gunsmoke"—the most long-lived, carefully edited, and cunningly produced of television series—made the only permanent female member of its cast the owner of a saloon, happily neglecting the historical fact that no respectable woman in the real Dodge City ever entered, let alone owned, such an establishment. The fictional cowboy hero is usually uncomfortable with a "good girl," who would curb his freedom and deplore his violence. Marriage to her may be his reward, but it also is usually the end of his story. And almost never, of course, does he meet an intelligent, adult woman who could both complicate and enrich his life.

The hero's manliness is also associated with incorrigible provincialism. The East is almost always seen as the home of decadent corruption and feminine weakness. Its manners are believed to be insincere and pretentious, and its concern with art, literature, and even decent cuisine is believed to be effeminate. (Europe is considered to be as bad as the East—if not worse.) Only in the West, says the myth, are men open, candid, and generous.

But only to other white men. For Western fiction has been even more racist than the society whose values it has celebrated. Until very recently, Western heroes held that the only good Indians were dead Indians and that most blacks and Mexicans were ignorant, cowardly, or treacherous. Only occasional exceptions were made for an Uncle Tom or an Uncle Tonto, a faithful companion who held the hero's horse or bound his wounds. Occasionally a Cisco Kid emerged as a "proud Spanish American of the Southwest"—but only occasionally. And only in the recent self-conscious times have Western heroes stopped praising their comrades by saying, "That's damned white of you."

Finally, of course, the hero is above the law, dispensing his own violent justice and punishment. Only the Western story has persistently glorified not only a kind of code duello but also vigilante terror and lynch law. Other forms of popular literature may exploit violence and death, but only in the Western myth is it approved and applauded by almost the whole community. Occasionally the "good girl" may naively oppose or condemn the hero's actions, but she falls into his arms after the final shoot-out.

It is true that these kinds of racism, sexism, and violent lawlessness have their antecedents in our history. But they hardly need the extenuation and glorification they receive in the daily rehearsal of the Western myth. Perhaps we should agree with the late Mody Boatright, a distinguished student of Western folklore and literature. "We may yet regret," he said, "that in a time of greater complexity and greater insecurity than [Owen] Wister lived to see, the cowboy with his six-shooter, his simple ethics, and his facility for direct action is our leading folk hero."

Whatever the shortcomings of the Western hero, however, he is a precious part of our history, our mythology, and our self-image. Reading Western history, Western stories, and critical analyses of Western fiction can present fascinating and puzzling questions. It can involve us in quandary and paradox, confusion and conflicting loyalties. But most important of all, as generations of readers have known, it can involve us in great adventure, great fun, and the challenge of life in a broad land under a big sky.

PART ONE

FACT

Late nineteenth- and early twentieth-century journalism did as much to shape the Western story as did the earlier fictions of James Fenimore Cooper and sensational dime novelists. All visitors of the cattleman's West—even those who lived there for some time, as Theodore Roosevelt did—saw it as remote, exotic, and unique. And always they saw it as a country constantly changing.

Thus Roosevelt, who spent years as a rancher in the Dakota Territory before he became head of the New York City Police Board, candidate for mayor of New York, and later Vice President and President of the United States, wrote about the West as a place that was growing and slowly becoming civilized. But the historical West that he knew was the one that later became fixed as the timeless West of fiction—an area still not fully settled, not firmly governed, not yet tamed. It still was occupied by buffalo hunters, wolfers, trappers, muleskinners, cattlemen, and cowboys; and its frail peace was occasionally threatened or guaranteed by individual force or lynch law.

Only a few years later, at the turn of the century, Emerson Hough wrote about the cattle country and sounded the note of nostalgia that became characteristic of almost all later writing about the West. Already the range was being fenced, and cowboys were beginning to carry pliers as well as guns; already they were dismounting to help with harvesting hay or repairing windmills.

By the 1920s, when Douglas Branch described the trail drives from Texas, he was writing history of a long-vanished past. The old drives had ended, blocked by the homesteading of Kansas and made unnecessary by the building of railroads to nearly every part of the cattle country. In concluding his book on the cowboy, Branch wrote, "Already a sweet sentimental haze is overlying the great spectacle of the range, the long trail from the heart of Texas to the cowtowns of Kansas, and beyond to the edge of the mountains of Montana; the drive to Kansas is becoming confused with the caravan to Cathay. . . ."

Jack Schaefer and Donald Jackson are contemporaries who have written articles describing the modern cattle business and the few old-time cowboys who still live in the twentieth century. The business is now complicated by science and technology; modern ranchers care more about genetics and feed-grain costs than about roundups and cattle drives. And the few remaining old-time cowboys are lonely, sometimes embittered men who have outlived the days that still survive in our fiction.

THEODORE ROOSEVELT

THE CATTLE COUNTRY OF
THE FAR WEST

The great grazing-lands of the West lie in what is known as the arid belt, which stretches from British America on the north to Mexico on the south, through the middle of the United States. It includes New Mexico, part of Arizona, Colorado, Wyoming, Montana, and the western portion of Texas, Kansas, Nebraska, and Dakota. It must not be understood by this that more cattle are to be found here than elsewhere, for the contrary is true, it being a fact often lost sight of that the number of cattle raised on the small, thick-lying farms of the fertile Eastern States is actually many times greater than that of those scattered over the vast, barren ranches of the far West; for stock will always be most plentiful in districts where corn and other winter food can be grown. But in this arid belt, and in this arid belt only—save in a few similar tracts on the Pacific slope—stock-raising is almost the sole industry, except in the mountain districts where there is mining. The whole region is one vast stretch of grazing country, with only here and there spots of farm land, in most places there being nothing more like agriculture than is implied in the cutting of some tons of wild hay or the planting of a garden-patch for home use. This is especially true of the northern portion of the region, which comprises the basin of the upper Missouri, and with which alone I am familiar. Here there are no fences to speak of, and all the land north of the Black Hills and the Bighorn Mountains and between the Rockies and the Dakota wheat-fields might be spoken of as one gigantic, unbroken pasture, where cowboys and branding-irons take the place of fences.

The country throughout this great upper Missouri basin has a wonderful sameness of character; and the rest of the arid belt, lying to the southward, is closely akin to it in its main features. A traveller seeing it for the first time is especially struck by its look of parched, barren desolation; he can with difficulty believe that it will support cattle at all. It is a region of light rainfall; the grass is short and comparatively scanty; there is no timber except along the beds of the streams, and in many places there are alkali deserts where nothing grows but sage-brush and cactus. Now the land stretches out into

level, seemingly endless plains or into rolling prairies; again it is
broken by abrupt hills and deep, winding valleys; or else it is crossed
by chains of buttes, usually bare, but often clad with a dense growth
of dwarfed pines or gnarled, stunted cedars. The muddy rivers run in
broad, shallow beds, which after heavy rainfalls are filled to the brim
by the swollen torrents, while in droughts the larger streams dwindle
into sluggish trickles of clearer water and the smaller ones dry up
entirely save in occasional deep pools.

All through the region, except on the great Indian reservations,
there has been a scanty and sparse settlement, quite peculiar in its
character. In the forest the woodchopper comes first; on the fertile
prairies the granger is the pioneer; but on the long, stretching uplands
of the far West it is the men who guard and follow the horned herds
that prepare the way for the settlers who come after. The high plains
of the upper Missouri and its tributary rivers were first opened and are
still held by the stockmen, and the whole civilization of the region has
received the stamp of their marked and individual characteristics.
They were from the South, not from the East, although many men
from the latter region came out along the great transcontinental
railway lines and joined them in their northern migration.

They were not dwellers in towns, and from the nature of their
industry lived as far apart from each other as possible. In choosing
new ranges, old cow-hands, who are also seasoned plainsmen, are
invariably sent ahead, perhaps a year in advance, to spy out the land
and pick the best places. One of these may go by himself, or more
often, especially if they have to penetrate little known or entirely
unknown tracts, two or three will go together, the owner or manager
of the herd himself being one of them. Perhaps their herds may
already be on the border of the wild and uninhabited country: in that
case they may have to take but a few days' journey before finding the
stretches of sheltered, long-grass land that they seek. For instance,
when I wished to move my own Elkhorn steer brand on to a new
ranch I had to spend barely a week in travelling north among the
Little Missouri Bad Lands before finding what was then untrodden
ground far outside the range of any of my neighbors' cattle. But if a
large outfit is going to shift its quarters it must go much farther; and
both the necessity and the chance for long wanderings were especially
great when the final overthrow of the northern Horse Indians opened
the whole upper Missouri basin at one sweep to the stockmen. Then
the advance-guards or explorers, each on one horse and leading
another with food and bedding, were often absent months at a time,
threading their way through the trackless wastes of plain, plateau, and
river-bottom. If possible they would choose a country that would be
good for winter and summer alike; but often this could not be done,
and then they would try to find a well-watered tract on which the

cattle could be summered, and from which they could be driven in fall to their sheltered winter range—for the cattle in winter eat snow, and an entirely waterless region, if broken, and with good pasturage, is often the best possible winter ground, as it is sure not to have been eaten off at all during the summer; while in the bottoms the grass is always cropped down soonest. Many outfits regularly shift their herds every spring and fall; but with us in the Bad Lands all we do, when cold weather sets in, is to drive our beasts off the scantily grassed river-bottom back ten miles or more among the broken buttes and plateaus of the uplands to where the brown hay, cured on the stalk, stands thick in the winding coulées.

These lookouts or forerunners having returned, the herds are set in motion as early in the spring as may be, so as to get on the ground in time to let the travel-worn beasts rest and gain flesh before winter sets in. Each herd is accompanied by a dozen, or a score, or a couple of score, of cowboys, according to its size, and beside it rumble and jolt the heavy four-horse wagons that hold the food and bedding of the men and the few implements they will need at the end of their journey. As long as possible they follow the trails made by the herds that have already travelled in the same direction, and when these end they strike out for themselves. In the upper Missouri basin, the pioneer herds soon had to scatter out and each find its own way among the great dreary solitudes, creeping carefully along so that the cattle should not be overdriven and should have water at the halting-places. An outfit might thus be months on its lonely journey, slowly making its way over melancholy, pathless plains, or down the valleys of the lonely rivers. It was tedious, harassing work, as the weary cattle had to be driven carefully and quietly during the day and strictly guarded at night, with a perpetual watch kept for Indians or white horse-thieves. Often they would skirt the edges of the streams for days at a time, seeking for a ford or a good swimming crossing, and if the water was up and the quicksand deep the danger to the riders was serious and the risk of loss among the cattle very great.

At last, after days of excitement and danger and after months of weary, monotonous toil, the chosen ground is reached and the final camp pitched. The footsore animals are turned loose to shift for themselves, outlying camps of two or three men each being established to hem them in. Meanwhile the primitive ranch-house, outbuildings, and corrals are built, the unhewn cottonwood logs being chinked with moss and mud, while the roofs are of branches covered with dirt, spades and axes being the only tools needed for the work. Bunks, chairs, and tables are all homemade, and as rough as the houses they are in. The supplies of coarse, rude food are carried perhaps two or three hundred miles from the nearest town, either in the ranch-wagons or else by some regular freighting outfit, the huge canvas-topped prairie-schooners of which are each drawn by several yoke of oxen, or perhaps by six or eight mules. To guard against the numerous mishaps of prairie travel, two or three of these prairie-schooners usually go together, the brawny teamsters, known either as "bull-whackers" or as "mule-skinners," stalking beside their slow-moving teams.

The small outlying camps are often tents, or mere dugouts in the ground. But at the main ranch there will be a cluster of log buildings, including a separate cabin for the foreman or ranchman; often another in which to cook and eat; a long house for the men to sleep in; stables, sheds, a blacksmith's shop, etc.—the whole group forming quite a little settlement, with the corrals, the stacks of natural hay, and the patches of fenced land for gardens or horse pastures. This little settlement may be situated right out in the treeless, nearly level open, but much more often is placed in the partly wooded bottom of a creek or river, sheltered by the usual background of sombre brown hills.

When the northern plains began to be settled, such a ranch would at first be absolutely alone in the wilderness, but others of the same sort were sure soon to be established within twenty or thirty miles on one side or the other. The lives of the men in such places were strangely cut off from the outside world, and, indeed, the same is true to a hardly less extent at the present day. Sometimes the wagons are sent for provisions, and the beef steers are at stated times driven off for shipment. Parties of hunters and trappers call now and then. More rarely small bands of emigrants go by in search of new homes, impelled by the restless, aimless craving for change so deeply grafted in the breast of the American borderer: the white-topped wagons are loaded with domestic goods, with sallow, dispirited-looking women, and with tow-headed children; while the gaunt, moody frontiersmen slouch alongside, rifle on shoulder, lank, homely, uncouth, and yet with a curious suggestion of grim strength underlying it all. Or cowboys from neighboring ranches will ride over, looking for lost horses or seeing if their cattle have strayed off the range. But this is all. Civilization seems as remote as if we were living in an age long past. The whole existence is patriarchal in character: it is the life of men who live in the open, who tend their herds on horseback, who go armed and ready to guard their lives by their own prowess, whose wants are very simple, and who call no man master. Ranching is an occupation like those of vigorous, primitive pastoral peoples, having little in common with the humdrum, workaday business world of the nineteenth century; and the free ranchman in his manner of life shows more kinship to an Arab sheik than to a sleek city merchant or tradesman.

By degrees the country becomes what in a stock-raising region passes for well settled. In addition to the great ranches smaller ones are established, with a few hundred, or even a few score, head of cattle apiece; and now and then miserable farmers straggle in to fight a losing and desperate battle with drought, cold, and grasshoppers. The wheels of the heavy wagons, driven always over the same course from one ranch to another, or to the remote frontier towns from which they get their goods, wear ruts in the soil, and roads are soon formed, perhaps originally following the deep trails made by the vanished buffalo. These roads lead down the river-bottoms or along the crests of the divides or else strike out fairly across the prairie, and a man may sometimes journey a hundred miles along one without coming to a house or a camp of any sort. If they lead to a shipping-point whence the beeves are sent to market, the cattle, travelling in single file, will have worn many and deep paths on each side of the wheel-marks; and the roads between important places which are regularly used either by the United States Government, by stage-coach lines, or by freight teams become deeply worn landmarks—as, for instance, near us, the Deadwood and the old Fort Keogh trails.

Cattle-ranching can only be carried on in its present form while the population is scanty; and so in stock-raising regions, pure and simple, there are usually few towns, and these are almost always at the shipping-points for cattle. But, on the other hand, wealthy cattlemen, like miners who have done well, always spend their money freely; and accordingly towns like Denver, Cheyenne, and Helena, where these two classes are the most influential in the community, are far pleasanter places of residence than cities of five times their population in the exclusively agricultural States to the eastward.

A true "cow town" is worth seeing—such a one as Miles City, for instance, especially at the time of the annual meeting of the great Montana Stock Raisers' Association. Then the whole place is full to overflowing, the importance of the meeting and the fun of the attendant frolics, especially the horse-races, drawing from the surrounding ranch country many hundreds of men of every degree, from the rich stock-owner worth his millions to the ordinary cowboy who works for forty dollars a month. It would be impossible to imagine a more typically American assemblage, for although there are always a certain number of foreigners, usually English, Irish, or German, yet they have become completely Americanized; and on the whole it would be difficult to gather a finer body of men, in spite of their numerous shortcomings. The ranch-owners differ more from each other than do the cowboys; and the former certainly compare very favorably with similar classes of capitalists in the East. Anything more foolish than the demagogic outcry against "cattle kings" it would be difficult to imagine. Indeed, there are very few businesses so absolutely legitimate as stock-raising and so beneficial to the nation at large; and a successful stock-grower must not only be shrewd, thrifty, patient, and enterprising, but he must also possess qualities of personal bravery, hardihood, and self-reliance to a degree not demanded in the least by any mercantile occupation in a community long settled. Stockmen are in the West the pioneers of civilization, and their daring and adventurousness make the after-settlement of the region possible. The whole country owes them a great debt.

The most successful ranchmen are those, usually Southwesterners, who have been bred to the business and have grown up with it; but many Eastern men, including not a few college graduates, have also done excellently by devoting their whole time and energy to their work—although Easterners who invest their money in cattle without knowing anything of the business or who trust all to their subordinates, are, naturally enough, likely to incur heavy losses. Stockmen are learning more and more to act together; and certainly the meetings of their associations are conducted with a dignity and good sense that would do credit to any parliamentary body.

But the cowboys resemble one another much more and outsiders much less than is the case even with their employers, the ranchmen. A town in the cattle country, when for some cause it is thronged with men from the neighborhood, always presents a picturesque sight. On the wooden sidewalks of the broad, dusty streets the men who ply the various industries known only to frontier existence jostle one another as they saunter to and fro or lounge lazily in front of the straggling, cheap-looking board houses. Hunters come in from the plains and the mountains, clad in buckskin shirts and fur caps, greasy and unkempt, but with resolute faces and sullen, watchful eyes, that are ever on the alert. The teamsters, surly and self-contained, wear slouch-hats and great cowhide boots; while the stage-drivers, their faces seamed by the hardship and exposure of their long drives with every kind of team, through every kind of country, and in every kind of weather, proud of their really wonderful skill as reinsmen and conscious of their high standing in any frontier community, look down on and sneer at the "skin-hunters" and the plodding drivers of the white-topped prairie-schooners. Besides these there are trappers, and wolfers whose business is to poison wolves, with shaggy, knock-kneed ponies to carry their small bales and bundles of furs—beaver, wolf, fox, and occasionally otter; and silent sheep-herders, with cast-down faces, never able to forget the absolute solitude and monotony of their dreary lives, nor to rid their minds of the thought of the woolly idiots they pass all their days in tending. Such are the men who have come to town, either on business or else to frequent the flaunting saloons and gaudy hells of all kinds in search of the coarse, vicious excitement that in the minds of many of them does duty as pleasure—the only form of pleasure they have ever had a chance to know. Indians too, wrapped in blankets, with stolid, emotionless faces, stalk silently round among the whites, or join in the gambling and horse-racing. If the town is on the borders of the mountain country, there will also be sinewy lumbermen, rough-looking miners, and packers whose business it is to guide the long mule and pony trains that go where wagons cannot and whose work in packing needs special and peculiar skill; and mingled with and drawn from all these classes are desperadoes of every grade, from the gambler up through the horse-thief to the murderous professional bully, or, as he is locally called, "bad man"—now, however, a much less conspicuous object than formerly.

But everywhere among these plainsmen and mountain men, and more important than any are the cowboys—the men who follow the calling that has brought such towns into being. Singly, or in twos or threes, they gallop their wiry little horses down the street, their lithe, supple figures erect or swaying slightly as they sit loosely in the saddle; while their stirrups are so long that their knees are hardly bent, the bridles not taut enough to keep the chains from clanking. They are smaller and less muscular than the wielders of axe and pick; but they are as hardy and self-reliant as any men who ever breathed—with bronzed, set faces, and keen eyes that look all the world straight in the face without flinching as they flash out from under the broad-brimmed hats. Peril and hardship, and years of long toil broken by weeks of brutal dissipation, draw haggard lines across their eager faces, but never dim their reckless eyes nor break their bearing of defiant self-confidence. They do not walk well, partly because they so rarely do any work out of the saddle, partly because their *chaparejos* or leather overalls hamper them when on the ground; but their appearance is striking for all that, and picturesque too, with their jingling spurs, the big revolvers stuck in their belts, and bright silk handkerchiefs knotted loosely round their necks over the open collars of the flannel shirts. When drunk on the villainous whiskey of the frontier towns, they cut mad antics, riding their horses into the saloons, firing their pistols right and left, from boisterous light-heartedness rather than from any viciousness, and indulging too often in deadly shooting affrays, brought on either by the accidental contact of the moment or on account of some long-standing grudge, or perhaps because of bad blood between two ranches or localities; but except while on such sprees they are quiet, rather self-contained men, perfectly frank and simple, and on their own ground treat a stranger with the most whole-souled hospitality, doing all in their power for him and scorning to take any reward in return. Although prompt to resent an injury, they are not at all apt to be rude to outsiders, treating them with what can almost be called a grave courtesy. They are much better fellows and pleasanter companions than small farmers or agricultural laborers; nor are the mechanics and workmen of a great city to be mentioned in the same breath.

The bulk of the cowboys themselves are Southwesterners; but there are also many from the Eastern and the Northern States, who, if they begin young, do quite as well as the Southerners. The best hands are fairly bred to the work and follow it from their youth up. Nothing can be more foolish than for an Easterner to think he can become a cowboy in a few months' time. Many a young fellow comes out hot with enthusiasm for life on the plains, only to learn that his clumsiness is greater than he could have believed possible; that the cowboy business is like any other and has to be learned by serving a painful apprenticeship; and that this apprenticeship implies the endurance of rough fare, hard living, dirt, exposure of every kind, no little toil, and month after month of the dullest monotony. For cowboy work there is need of special traits and special training, and young Easterners should be sure of themselves before trying it: the struggle for existence is very keen in the far West, and it is no place for men who lack the ruder, coarser virtues and physical qualities, no matter how intellectual or how refined and delicate their sensibilities. Such are more likely to fail there than in older communities. Probably during the past few years more than half of the young Easterners who have come West with a little money to learn the cattle business have failed signally and lost what they had in the beginning. The West, especially the far West, needs men who have been bred on the farm or in the workshop far more than it does clerks or college graduates.

Some of the cowboys are Mexicans, who generally do the actual work well enough, but are not trustworthy; moreover, they are always regarded with extreme disfavor by the Texans in an outfit, among whom the intolerant caste spirit is very strong. Southern-born whites will never work under them, and look down upon all colored or half-caste races. One spring I had with my wagon a Pueblo Indian, an excellent rider and roper, but a drunken, worthless, lazy devil; and in the summer of 1886 there were with us a Sioux half-breed, a quiet, hard-working, faithful fellow, and a mulatto, who was one of the best cow-hands in the whole round-up.

Cowboys, like most Westerners, occasionally show remarkable versatility in their tastes and pursuits. One whom I know has abandoned his regular occupation for the past nine months, during which time he has been in succession a bartender, a school-teacher, and a probate judge! Another, whom I once employed for a short while, had passed through even more varied experiences, including those of a barber, a sailor, an apothecary, and a buffalo-hunter.

As a rule the cowboys are known to each other only by their first names, with, perhaps, as a prefix, the title of the brand for which they are working. Thus I remember once overhearing a casual remark to the effect that "Bar Y Harry" had married "the Seven Open A girl," the latter being the daughter of a neighboring ranchman. Often they receive nicknames, as, for instance, Dutch Wannigan, Windy Jack, and Kid Williams, all of whom are on the list of my personal acquaintances.

No man travelling through or living in the country need fear molestation from the cowboys unless he himself accompanies them on their drinking-bouts, or in other ways plays the fool, for they are, with us at any rate, very good fellows, and the most determined and effective foes of real law-breakers, such as horse and cattle thieves, murderers, etc. Few of the outrages quoted in Eastern papers as their handiwork are such in reality, the average Easterner apparently considering every individual who wears a broad hat and carries a six-shooter a cowboy. These outrages are, as a rule, the work of the roughs and criminals who always gather on the outskirts of civilization, and who infest every frontier town until the decent citizens become sufficiently numerous and determined to take the law into their own hands and drive them out. The old buffalo-hunters, who formed a distinct class, became powerful forces for evil once they had destroyed the vast herds of mighty beasts the pursuit of which had been their means of livelihood. They were absolutely shiftless and improvident; they had no settled habits; they were inured to peril and hardship, but entirely unaccustomed to steady work; and so they afforded just the materials from which to make the bolder and more desperate kinds of criminals. When the game was gone they hung round the settlements for some little time, and then many of them naturally took to horse-stealing, cattle-killing, and highway robbery, although others, of course, went into honest pursuits. They were men who died off rapidly, however; for it is curious to see how many of these plainsmen, in spite of their iron nerves and thews, have their constitutions completely undermined, as much by the terrible hardships they have endured as by the fits of prolonged and bestial revelry with which they have varied them.

The "bad men," or professional fighters and man-killers, are of a different stamp, quite a number of them being, according to their light, perfectly honest. These are the men who do most of the killing in frontier communities; yet it is a noteworthy fact that the men who are killed generally deserve their fate. These men are, of course, used to brawling, and are not only sure shots, but, what is equally important, able to "draw" their weapons with marvellous quickness. They think nothing whatever of murder, and are the dread and terror of their associates; yet they are very chary of taking the life of a man of good standing, and will often weaken and back down at once if confronted fearlessly. With many of them their courage arises from confidence in their own powers and knowledge of the fear in which they are held; and men of this type often show the white feather when they get in a tight place. Others, however, will face any odds without flinching; and I have known of these men fighting, when mortally wounded, with a cool, ferocious despair that was terrible. As elsewhere, so here, very quiet men are often those who in an emergency show themselves best able to hold their own. These desperadoes always try to "get the drop" on a foe—that is, to take him at a disadvantage before he can use his own weapon. I have known more men killed in this way, when the affair was wholly one-sided, than I have known to be shot in fair fight; and I have known fully as many who were shot by accident. It is wonderful, in the event of a street fight, how few bullets seem to hit the men they are aimed at.

During the last two or three years the stockmen have united to put down all these dangerous characters, often by the most summary exercise of lynch-law. Notorious bullies and murderers have been taken out and hung, while the bands of horse and cattle thieves have been regularly hunted down and destroyed in pitched fights by parties of armed cowboys; and as a consequence most of our territory is now perfectly law-abiding. One such fight occurred north of me early last spring. The horse-thieves were overtaken on the banks of the Missouri; two of their number were slain, and the others were driven on the ice, which broke, and two more were drowned. A few months previously another gang, whose headquarters were near the Canadian line, were surprised in their hut; two or three were shot down by the cowboys as they tried to come out, while the rest barricaded themselves in and fought until the great log hut was set on fire, when they broke forth in a body, and nearly all were killed at once, only one or two making their escape. A little over two years ago one committee of vigilantes in eastern Montana shot or hung nearly sixty—not, however, with the best judgment in all cases.

QUESTIONS

1. Before the cattleman's West was opened by ranchers like Roose-velt, it was known as "The Great American Desert." How does Roosevelt's description justify or explain this designation?

2. How does this essay indicate that the West was changing even as Roosevelt was writing? Explain.

3. Discuss the attitude toward non-whites and non-Americans re-vealed in this essay (written before the beginning of the twentieth century). In his day, Roosevelt was considered a liberal. How have attitudes changed during the last eighty years?

4. Compare Roosevelt's description of the activities and personalities of cowboys with that given in Emerson Hough's "A Day at the Ranch," which appears later in this section.

5. Choose one of the stories in the "Fiction" section of this book and compare its characters with the Westerners described in Roosevelt's essay.

DOUGLAS BRANCH

THE LONG DRIVE NORTH

The history of the cattle-trail yet to be written will be a story of severe vicissitudes financially, and of a gradual retreat west as homesteaders appropriated its domain and northern cattlemen built enclosures and invoked injunctions to keep back the Texas drives that meant cheaper prices and possibly carried infection to their own cattle.

The northern drives became established as an institution in 1867, when Abilene, on the Kansas Pacific Railroad (then making desultory progress westward) achieved a "cowtown consciousness," and despatched "press-agents" south to urge the advantages of taking herds to Abilene. This year marked the beginning of organized and extensive trail-driving, with the isolated drives in 1866 of Goodnight and Loving, Jim Daugherty, George Duffield, and earlier pioneer drives, fading for the most part into a vague tradition.

When by 1885 Nebraska, Colorado, and Kansas had enacted laws prohibiting the transportation across their borders of Southern cattle, there came the end of the great drives—an end foreshadowed in 1880 by the closure of the Chisholm trail, the customary route from the Red River station on the Texas border into Kansas, by "fool hoe-men," who had preempted practically its whole length, and were tearing its hoof-trampled surface into rows of clods. In 1884 another enemy of the trail, the railroad, successfully invaded the Southwest, and brought thirty thousand cows northward in this first year. But the trail lingered after a fashion until 1895. Ten million cattle and one million horses had been driven its length from Texas to waiting markets; its end was the end of a splendid chapter in the history of the cattle industry, the end of an economic system and the end of the cowboy as a craftsman and gentleman. Thereafter he was merely an employee of "a corporation operating for profit."

Life on the cattle-trails contained much that was wearisome, hard, most unsentimentally tedious. In taking the herds for drives of seventy days or of four months, there were swollen streams to swim, wild runs of cattle that had to be checked by a few men on tired mounts galloping over unknown land, perhaps bandits or Indians to face—the first drives after the Civil War met both—and hardships that lacked even the virtue of the spectacular—drives all day in rain and mud, snatches of sleep on wet ground, sore and useless horses, bad cooking or none at all if brush and chips were wet. Yet men went up the trail year after year, finding work ready for them on the northern ranges at a better wage than Texas cattlemen paid, choosing to go back to Texas and come north with another herd in the next year. Much of the reason lay in an indefinable pride of profession. "A cowboy is not a graduate in his art until he has been up the trail. His education has been sadly neglected if he has never taken a course in this, the highest, branch of the bovine curriculum"—this was the dictum of the trail.

When young Jim Cook asked his boss to make him a trail-hand, the old cattleman replied, "They tell me that you can catch a cow and shoot a rabbit's eye out every pop. Now if you can ride for the next four months without a whole night's sleep, and will turn your gun loose on any damned Indian that tries to steal our horses, why, git ready." And Jim Cook, of course, got ready.

A trail-herd might be directed by the owner himself, or by his straw-boss, the trail-foreman—perhaps by a middleman that might be a "native" known to the cattlemen personally or by reputation, or an outsider whose only recommendation was his money. The elastic code of the Texans of the early days provided differently for each contingency. A buyer of southwest Texas might purchase from his neighbors a herd of 8,000 or 10,000 steers, with no payment at the time of the purchase. The stock-owners knew that the buyer needed all the money at his disposal to meet the expenses of the drive; they would not take a note for the purchase price, for honest men dealing with each other needed no notes. The only evidence of debt was the tally of the cattle, giving the numbers in each class, including the mark and the brand they bore. With the other kind of middleman—one instance, cited by Edgar Bronson, will be sufficient: "There was one notorious bit of mixed humor and thrift, when 1200 cattle were converted into 2400, in making the running tally or count, by selecting an isolated hill as the place of their delivery to the monocled, crop-carrying, straight-spurred British buyer, and the simple expedient of running the herd *round* the hill for recount until their actual number was doubled."

The "outfit" that drove the cattle up the trail varied in its numbers with the wealth and wisdom of the owner. There is record of a herd of twenty-five hundred "old mossy-horn steers" driven up the trail in 1876 by twenty-five riders with six head of horses to the man—quite a pageant in view of the outfit of ten men who drove five thousand steers, mostly three-year-olds, a few years later. By 1880 custom suggested that a small herd of eight hundred be taken up the trail by five riders, a herd of fifteen hundred by eight men, and larger herds commensurately.

The first work for the cowboy who had signed to go "up trail" was road-branding. Since a herd might include cattle of several brands, from different owners or from different ranches of the same owner, a common brand—a road-brand—was needed. The work of driving the cattle through a chute and pressing the road-brand on each cow as it was forced through was hard; but anticipations of the drive hurrying the work, the branding went ahead at a lively rate, the mark not burned as deeply as the original brand had been burned. Those cowboys that had been up the trail before subtly boasted of it as they worked by singing some trail ballad, or perhaps a topical adaptation of a familiar song, as:

> How dear to my heart are the scenes of my trailhood,
> When fond recollections present them to view—
> The water barrel, the old chuck-wagon,
> And the cook who called me to chew.

Once the road-branding was done the herd of perhaps three thousand cattle, with its outfit of sixteen or eighteen cowboys, a cook and his wagon, and a horse-wrangler with the *remuda*, was started northward; if the branding were continued until late in the afternoon, the cattle were allowed to rest until the next dawn. Then, once the cook's call of "Grub pile!" had been answered and the men had saddled their mounts, the drive began. The herd was "drifted" with very little pushing, grazing as it went. By nine o'clock or a little later the men urged the cattle closer together; two riders at each side "pointed" the lead steers at a smart pace, and "swing riders" behind them pushed in the flanks of the herd. Just behind the cattle rode the "tail riders" to keep in the lame and the recalcitrant. "Riding tail" was the least desirable position; these trail-men rode in clouds of dust tossed up by the moving herd, and bore the full brunt of the heat and the smell. The cattle just before them were lame or stupid; those "on the point" had taken the lead of the herd apparently as a recognition of their own importance, and were the least timid and the best physically of the herd.

With the approach of noon, the attention of the cattle turned again to the grass about them, and the swing-riders had to keep in a constant gallop to hold the cows from turning out to graze on the margin of the trail. The cook and the boss went ahead to locate the noon camp, some spot about half a mile from the trail so that the cattle should have fresh grass for the hour's grazing; and by the time the herd came up to the camp, the flap-board on the chuck-wagon had been let down, and a cold lunch was ready for the trail-drivers.

The men smoked and exchanged comments on those cows whose appearance or behavior had made them conspicuous. The cowboy's quick eyes noted and catalogued the individualities of cattle, simply as a mental habit. This keen, almost subconscious detailing of the life about them was a characteristic of frontiersmen. The contribution of the cowboys was an idiom rich with brevities of description, and in these moments when the herd was grazing they spoke with a vivid terseness of cattle and horses and men. Once a few of the cows began to lie down to chew their cuds, the boss knew that they had grazed enough, and gave the signal to resume the drive.

A system of signals came early into use on the trail. The signals were largely borrowed from the plains Indians; they were made principally with the hat, held in the left hand, while the right held the reins. The movement to break camp and move up the trail was simply a wave of the hat in the direction to be taken, made first by the boss, then passed by the line-riders to the point-men. The signal to graze the cattle was again a wave of the hat, toward the side of the trail on which the herd was to be rested.

The morning's drive of six to ten miles might be bettered in the afternoon. The length of this drive was closely related to the distance to water. If the afternoon wore on and there was no sign of water, the cattle would become restless and ill-tempered; but with the first smell of water the lead-cattle, always the most acute, began to bellow, and quickened their pace. "Their necks were stretched and mouths open with continual bawling. It looks like a walking-race; they shuffle along with the most busy determination, careless of aught but the getting over the ground." At last, when the river-bank was reached, the lead steers rushed in till water was halfway up their flanks, and began to drink. The rest followed, spreading out at the bank, going in to drink, and wallow, and stand in placid satiation.

"I have met but few men who knew how to water cattle properly," writes an old cattleman. There was danger that the body of the herd might pour in a mass upon the front cattle, forming a close-trampling pack forcing down the river bottom, sending some frightened cows out to drown in the current, crushing others into the mud; danger of running the cattle into a bank of quicksand; and danger of permitting them to stand still in the water until some became bogged and had to be pulled out by ropes in a slow and often ineffectual process, or be deserted.

Crossing a herd over a flooded stream, muddy and running with a swift current, was a situation escaped only by the trail-drivers of the late summer. The lead-cattle instinctively feared such water, and the point-riders had hard work in urging them on. Sometimes these riders would force their own horses out into the stream to convince the cattle that there was no danger. Once the cattle were out to their swimming depth, they usually went on to the opposite bank with the rest of the herd following. But if a piece of driftwood struck against a steer, or if the leaders became alarmed at the swiftness of the current, the cattle might "mill" in a panic-stricken circle, becoming a confused, struggling mass as other cattle followed. Then came crucial labors for the trail-men; the cattle on the bank had to be checked, and a point-rider had to force his mount into the midst of the frightened mass, break the mill, and force some of the cattle to lead off in swimming for the shore.

Charles Siringo writes of finding the "Salt Fork," near the Kansas line, "bank full and still rising. It was at least half a mile to the opposite side and drift wood was coming down at a terrible rate, which made it dangerous to cross." But the attempt was made; "the old lead steers went right into the foaming water without a bit of trouble and of course the balance followed." The horse of one of the point-riders sank, frightening the lead cattle, and the whole herd turned back in terrible confusion. "Suffice it to say, we remained there seven days without anything to eat except fresh meat without salt. It rained during the whole time nearly, so that we didn't get much sleep on account of having to stay with the cattle night and day."

The classic item in the story of stream-crossing is the entry for June 23, 1866, in the journal of George Duffield: "worked all day in the River trying to make the Beeves swim and did not get one over. Had to go back to Prairie Sick and discouraged. Have *not* got the *Blues* but am in *Hel of a fix.*"

The cattle, once again on the trail, were paced until about sunset, "bedding" time. The boss slowly waved his hat about his head in a circle, and the herd was moved off the trail to its bed ground. The first of the four watches of the night took its place; and the other men gathered about the cook's campfire, to eat generously of a hot supper.

As each of the night-herders rode his arc of the circle of the resting herd, the slow, deep-sounded notes of old songs—"My Bonnie Lies Over the Ocean," "When You and I Were Young, Maggie," and various cloyingly sweet songs that permitted a soothing prolongation of each note—or of the cowboy ballads ("Sam Bass," "The Cowboy's Dream," "The Dying Cowboy," were probably the most popular) quieted the cattle and helped the herder to stay awake. A rider did not dare let drowsiness overtake him; the vagaries of cattle were beyond anticipation, and sleeping on herd duty was unpardonable, meriting instant dismissal. "There was a limit to the endurance of even a rough rider," wrote Jim Cook. "I have been so close to that limit that on one or two occasions I would get a little piece of chewing tobacco from one of the men and, mixing it with saliva, would rub it on my eyelids. This is great treatment when the thoughts seem to be bent on having a nap."

For the cattle did not always lie quietly, getting on their feet only at midnight, for a few moments' exchange of lowing before they lay down again; but startled by some trifle, the sound of a breaking bunch of dry weeds, the cough of a horse, the restiveness of some cow in the herd, perhaps with no cause that the cowboys ever discovered, the whole herd might rise in an uncontrollable torrent. Once frightened, the herd seemed to rise as a unit, rushing away in a frantic mass, perhaps with little bluish flames, from the friction of their bodies, playing at the tips of their horns.

With the first sounds of the stampede each cowboy awoke, mounted the horse he had staked near him, and rode out to help the night-herders in the attempt to break the flight. "It is beef against horseflesh, with the odds on the beef for the first hundred yards." Here was dangerous work for the trail-men. The situation called for a dashing, swearing daredevil, with a horse unafraid to gallop in the dark over unknown country, as eager to end the stampede as his rider.

"The thing to be done is to outrun the herd, neck or nothing." Once up with the leaders of the cattle, the attempt was made to swing them about, by pressing against a leader and using the quirt, or by firing his revolver to the front and on one side of the leaders, a lively pony perhaps aiding by nipping at the hides of the cattle. The cowboys continued to force the swerve until the cattle were milling about in a great circle, round and round in a compact mass. To stop the ineffectual churning and to guard against another wild rush by the cattle trembling but still alert, the cowboys would sing in unison some familiar ballad, or sound that old call of the Texans, which began with "Whoop!" and continued with variations that might have been adapted from a Comanche war-yell. A tenderfoot would have wondered to see cowboys riding about cutting back cattle that were trying to escape from the mill, and to hear them celebrating in chorus the exploits of some train-robber who seemed idiotically irrelevant:

> Sam used to deal in race-stock, once called the Denton mare,
> He matched her in scrub races, and took her to the Fair.
> Sam used to coin the money and spent it just as free.
> He always drank good whisky wherever he might be.

After the stampede came a hasty inventory. The stumble of a horse, a sudden swerve of the stampeding cattle, might crush to death a cowboy and his horse; cattle might rush over a bluff or off a steep river-bank, killing some and crippling others of their number in the "pile-up." A stumbling steer would be trampled on by those behind him; some might be gored by the long horns of those they brushed against; legs might be broken and hoofs crushed in the turmoil. If the riders failed to check the herd and hold it in a mass it might become widely scattered, demanding a delay of days while the remnants were gathered. Duffield had worked to the limit of endurance, and uselessly, when he wrote, "Hard run & Wind Big stampede and here we are among the Indians with 150 head of cattle gone—hunted all day & the Rain pouring down with but poor success Dark days are these to me Nothing but Bread and Coffee Hands all Growling & Swearing—everything wet & cold Beeves gone. . . ."

The cause of a stampede was often subtle and unpredictable. One herd that had come from the old King ranch, in south Texas, and had become accustomed to a Mexican cook on the drive to Dodge City, left with a new outfit for a Dakota Indian agency. Once this herd "got wind" of the new cook, a negro, it "made a jump off the bed ground" and attempted to stampede.

A "loony" steer in a herd might keep the rest incessantly nervous. One of John Chisum's herds that seemed to have the habit of stampeding was met on the road by its owner; he ordered the cattle bedded for the night, and rode through the herd for a few minutes, when he pointed out the cause of the stampedes—a one-eyed steer, with wide and crooked horns. The steer was cut out, driven away, and shot; there were no more stampedes on that trip.

Again, a cowboy's carelessness might be the cause. Young Jim Cook, riding about a bedded herd, noticed an old black cow apart from the others; each time as he came around he tried to see how near to that cow he could ride, and after several times around he touched the cow with his foot. With a bound and a snort the cow rose and plunged away—and the stampede was on. Once Robert Wright, riding with an ox-team drive, hung his red and yellow coat over a gentle steer in the "cavayado" of oxen—the rest of the cattle took flight in one of the most devastating stampedes of the sixties. Wright suggested that a wolf had frightened the cattle, and the boss believed him; but some twenty wagons had been completely wrecked, one man's leg and another's arm had been broken, and most of the men were badly bruised.

A storm was almost certain to cause a stampede. Cattle drifted before a strong rain or a wind; all the men could do was to stay with them and sing to them. When lightning and thunder began it was almost impossible to hold all the cattle; with luck most of the herd might be held in a drifting mass. George Scott remembers a night when thirteen steers were killed by lightning and the rest of the herd stampeded in all directions, through creeks and over fences.

Danger of Indian attacks on the trail-herds passed after the first few years of the great drives; the Indian bugaboo died more slowly. In 1878 the Northern Cherokees attempted an outbreak, the last defiant gesture of the Indians on the Territory; but thirteen years later the grangers still feared that parties of marauding Indian bucks might descend on their homesteads in all the glories of war. In this year Captain Bill McDonald of the Texas Rangers traced an Indian scare that gained wide credence to a granger who had heard the revels of a group of cowboys that killed a beef and as they were roasting it capered about the fire and shot their revolvers as a prodigal diversion.

An old Kansas newspaper man has suggested that the cattlemen annually manufactured an Indian scare, if a legitimate one was not forthcoming, to discourage the immigration of "nesters" who were closing the open range of the great herds. Surely it was not the cowboy of the late seventies and the eighties who feared the Indian. "The noble red man never loses anything by neglecting to ask for it," was a range aphorism. The cowboy knew "Lo" as "a lazy, dirty, thieving beggar, who has no business at all on the face of the earth." In the time when Indians in the Territory—those on the Cherokee strip were the worst—might stampede a herd and cause great loss of beef, they could be appeased by the gift of a few aged, footsore steers, or a stray yearling or two. One trail-driver relates with gusto how an Indian chief, old Yellow-Bear, came to his camp and demanded bread. The driver told the cook not to give him any, and the red man in his wrath stamped his foot down in a pan of dough the cook was working, and stalked away.

The work of the buffalo-hunters, that ended in the early seventies, had made the northern Indians pitiable when the cowboys came to know them. In 1877 a trail-herd ran afoul of the whole Cheyenne tribe, close to the border of the Territory. "They were half starved, all the buffalo having drifted south, and their ponies were too poor and weak to follow them up. We traded them out of lots of blankets, trinkets, etc. For a pint of flour or coffee they would give their whole soul—and body thrown in for good measure. We soon ran out of chuck too, having swapped it all off to the hungry devils."

For the first few years after the Civil War Indian murders and thefts were a tragic menace to trail-driving. The story of the killing of the pioneer cattleman, Oliver Loving, in 1867, when he was surrounded by Comanches as he rode up the Pecos, is one that for the honest, unwhimpering courage of Loving and the cool fidelity of his companion, Bill Wilson, found two days later and nursed back to health, deserves to live in the straightforward narrative of Frederick Bechdolt. In those days vigilance night and day, with good fortune, was the price of crossing intact a herd through the Indian Territory.

Writes an old trail-driver, "The Indians would sometimes come into camp and beg from us, demanding fat beeves, but we always managed to pacify them. But the grangers displayed a degree of animosity toward the trail-drivers that was almost unbearable."

The gradual change from the old system of open ranges to a system of surveys, deeds, and fences, caught the trail, twisted it, flung it westward, and finally swallowed it. A trail-boss complained in 1884, "Now there is so much land taken up and fenced in that the trail for most of the way is little better than a crooked lane, and we have hard lines trying to find enough range to feed on. These fellows from Ohio, Indiana, and other northern and western states—the 'bone and sinew,' as politicians call them—have made farms, enclosed pastures, and fenced in water-holes till you can't rest; and I say, damn such bone and sinew!" But the cause of a free range and an open drive northward was already lost. When in 1874 the trail-drivers first found watering-places fenced in with barbed wire, they forced the herds through, furious at such malevolent devices. There would have been more "bloody chapters" in cattle-range history if the "fool hoe-men" had dared to open fire on these notoriously accurate gunmen, the cowboys. Many a homesteader's dog "sicked" on the cattle was shot into fragments by the trail-drivers. Kansas jayhawkers who attempted to charge toll on herds crossing their ranges found themselves outdone in sharp practices by the trail-drivers, who issued worthless checks or used open force; but the grangers won the long struggle by sheer force of numbers—by the irrevocable march of civilization, as the platitude runs.

The cattle-drives now, to the nearest railroad siding or from one ranch to another as owners change, are feebly reminiscent of the great drives from as far south as Cameron County, Texas, on the Rio Grande, into Kansas, and perhaps on into the northwest country to stock new ranges. And with the ardors and the importance of the trail no longer present to affect cowboy character, it is easier to understand why the cowboy of to-day prefers phonograph records made in New Jersey to the old songs of the cattle-trail.

QUESTIONS

1. This essay is typical of almost all journalistic and historical writing about the early days of the cattle industry. It is wistful and nostalgic in describing the end of the long cattle drives from Texas to northern railheads and ranges. What, for instance, does Branch mean when he says that the end of the long drives "marked the end of the cowboy as a craftsman and gentleman"?

2. Does Branch's knowledge of cattle drives and their practices come from personal observation or from the accounts of other men? What evidence do you find in the essay to support your conclusion?

3. This essay describes the work done by old-time cowboys during trail drives. Why is so little of this work described in fiction or shown in motion pictures?

4. Write a brief paper describing a typical trail crew and the functions of its members.

5. Explain how the growth of homesteading on the Kansas, Nebraska, and Colorado plains made trail driving difficult or impossible. How did the extension of railroads help to make trail drives unnecessary?

EMERSON HOUGH
A DAY AT THE RANCH

During days, or perhaps weeks, of the busy season, when most of the men are absent on the round-ups, the door of the home ranch may be closed. It may be closed, but it is not locked, for on the frontier locks and bars are unknown. The necessities of a country make its customs, and in the remote parts of the plains and mountains hospitality is practically a necessity. The traveller is perhaps far from home, and is hungry or athirst when he falls upon the cabin of some man to whom he is a stranger. When that occurs the stranger goes into the unlocked house, helps himself to the bacon and flour, cooks his meal, and departs as he came. In time he may repay the courtesy himself at his own cabin and perhaps in the same way. There was a touch of feudal largeness and liberality in some of the customs of the earlier cattle days, and the fact that they were necessary rendered them none the less beautiful. Perhaps the state of the social relations among the cattle men of the early range was approached most closely by the life of the great Southern plantations in *ante bellum* days, from which, indeed, it may in part have had its origin. The ways of the South always flavoured the life of the cattle country, whether in Texas or Wyoming, far more than the ways of the North and East. Perhaps the zest which many Eastern men found in ranch life was the zest of novelty, and this a novelty to be measured by degrees of latitude and not of longitude. We must credit the South with the origin and establishment of the cattle trade, and with many of its most interesting, its broadest, and most beautiful features. The more exact methods, the better system, the perfection of detail, and utilization of things once neglected came from the North, and came, alas! with a shock fatal to some of the customs of the good old days. In the past the lock of the ranch door was nothing but a rude wooden latch, as easily opened from without as from within. To-day there may be iron padlocks upon some of the doors of the houses on the range.

There is no lock upon the door of our ranch house, whether it be empty or occupied. Such as it is, it constitutes the only home the cowboy has. Hither he returns from the more active duties of the round-up or the drive, and takes up the less exacting routine of everyday ranch life. Of work proper, as a farm labourer would consider it, the cowboy has little real conception. He is a horseman and nothing more, and has little inclination for any work that can not be done in the saddle. Thus, if he feels obliged to go out for wood, he goes out on horseback, and his idea of the correct way to get a log of wood to camp is to drag it at the end of his lariat. If a wagon is mired down in the quicksands of a soft crossing, the cowboy who comes to the aid of the driver does not dismount and get himself muddy in the labour of getting the wagon out, but makes fast his rope to some holding place on the wagon and trusts to his saddle girths for the rest, knowing that his plucky little pony will in this way pull a considerable load, though it would break its neck in rebellion if hitched up to the wagon. The cowboy has a mild contempt for all walking and driving men. In his own line of work he can be a miracle of tireless energy. Out of that line he is a prodigy of more or less good-natured laziness.

We may suppose, then, that a day of ordinary ranch life is not one of great activity or haste. The chores which the cowpuncher considers within his province are very few and simple. If in the winter some horses are kept up under feed in the ranch stables, he may feed his own horse, but no other man's. In the later days of ranch life the cowboy has come to be more of a hewer of wood and a drawer of water, more interested in the haying operations and other portions of the ranch economy, but primarily and properly the genuine cowpuncher had to do, as he understood it, only with cows, which were to be handled by himself only while he was in the saddle. It was the chief concern of the rancher in the early days to see that his cattle had a fair show in the struggle with Nature. Efforts toward ameliorating the conditions of the animals were very crude and little considered. Food and shelter were things which the cattle were supposed to find for themselves. The ranch proper has none of the grinding detail of the farm, and the cowboy proper is as different from the farm labourer as a wild hawk from a domestic fowl.

The day at the ranch begins early, for by daybreak the men have slept enough. There is little to induce them to sit up late at night. Sometimes a trapper or wolfer stops at the ranch, and there may be spirited games inaugurated over the well-worn and greasy pack of cards, the currency being what money the cowpunchers may have, together with due bills against their coming pay day, these perhaps staked against strings of coyote feet and wolf scalps which are good for so much bounty at the county seat. Of reading the cowpuncher does but little, and his facilities for obtaining literature are very limited. The periodicals reaching the cow camp are apt to be of the sensational, pink-tinted sort, with crude pictures and lurid letter-text. His books are too often of much the same type, though at some of the ranches there may be some few works of fiction of a better sort. Whatever the books at the ranch may be, from society novel to farrier's guide, the cowpuncher reads them all over and over again until he is tired of seeing them. Not having much more to do of an evening, he goes to bed. It is supposed by some misguided souls that when the so-called wild cowboys of a ranch have met at night after the close of their exciting duties the scene at the ranch house is one of rude hilarity and confusion. Really quite the opposite of this is true. The interior of a ranch house of an evening offers rather a quiet and orderly appearance. Liquor is something rarely seen there, because it comes very rarely, and does not last long when it comes. As a rule, the cowpuncher is rather a silent man, though not so silent as the melancholy sheep herder, who rarely endures the terrible monotony of his calling for more than seven years without becoming insane. A cowboy who is very "mouthy" is not usually in high repute at a cow camp, and one disposed to personal brilliance or sarcastic comment on the peculiarities of his fellow-men is apt to meet with swift and effectual discouragement. Rude and unlettered though he be, and treating his companions with a rough and ready familiarity, the cowpuncher yet accords to his neighbour the right to live the life and go the gait which seems most pleasing to himself. One does not intrude upon the rights of others in the cow country, and he looks to it very promptly that no one shall intrude upon his. In the cow towns or at the cow camps one never hears the abusiveness or rude speech common in the older settlements. On the range, especially in the earlier days, if a man applied to another an epithet which in the States would be taken as something to be endured or returned in kind, the result would have been the essential and immediate preparations for a funeral.

In all countries where the home is unknown and the society is made up of males altogether, the men grow very morose and surly, and all the natural ugliness of their dispositions comes out. They are more apt to magnify small slights and slips, and more apt to get into trouble over small matters of personal honour. Upon the other hand, the best possible correction for this tendency is the acknowledged fact that it is not personally safe to go into a quarrel. It was never safe to quarrel on the cow range.

The cook, of course, is the first one up about the camp, and he "makes the breakfast" in his own room. The toilet of the cowpuncher is simple, and, after he has kicked off his blankets, it is but a few moments before he is at the table eating his plateful of beef or bacon and beans. The meal does not last long, and those which follow it later in the day are much the same. The city club man is fond of wild game as an adjunct to a good dinner. The "granger" sets oysters and ice cream as the highest possible luxuries of life. The cowboy thinks of fresh green vegetables in his epicurean dreams, and he longs for the indigestible pie of civilization. Any pure cowpuncher would sell his birthright for half a dozen pies. The cow cook can not make actual pies, only leathery imitations encasing stewed dried apples. One remembers very well a certain Christmas dinner in a little far-away Western plains town which cost two men twenty-five dollars, and which consisted of some badly cooked beef, one can of oysters, a frosted cake, and five green onions, the latter obtained from somewhere by a hothouse miracle. This dinner was voted a very extraordinary and successful affair. The men at the ranch house are not averse to an occasional change in their diet, and fresh game is appreciated. Deer, antelope, wild turkey, and sometimes smaller game often appeared on the *menu* of the ranch in the old days, but big game is scarce now over most of the range, and small game has rarely had much attention from the cowboys, who, as a rule, do not at best do a great deal of hunting.

After breakfast, if this be in the winter season and in a cold Northern country, the first work is attending to the riding horses kept in the stables, which are in such a country a necessity. Behind each horse in the stable is a long wooden peg, upon which hang the bridle and saddle. Each man has his own place reserved, and resents any intrusion upon his rights as to saddle, bridle, and rope. One man may use freely the tobacco or whisky of a fellow-cowpuncher, but he may not touch his rope, quirt, or other parts of his riding outfit. Of course, one man will not want to use another's saddle. "I wouldn't ride a mile in that thing o' yourn fer the best heifer that runs the range," says the cowpuncher, referring contemptuously to the prized saddle of another. "I'd plum have a misery if I had to ride yourn," is the reply.

Part or all of the horse herd will not be kept up at the ranch house, but will be watched, so that their whereabouts will be known. A man may be sent out in the morning to bring in the horse herd, and then ensues one of the most picturesque events of the day. The bunch of horses comes up on a gallop, urged by the cowpuncher behind them. All sorts of horses are in the collection, all of them rough of coat and hard of form, and not one of them has a pleasant expression of countenance as he turns into the ranch corral, with his ears drooping and his eye rolling about in search of trouble. Inside the corral each horse runs about and dodges behind his fellows when he fancies himself wanted, doing his best to escape till he actually feels the circle of the rope, when he falls into meek but mutinous quiet. The cowpuncher leads him out, and throws on his back the heavy saddle, the pony meanwhile standing the picture of forlornness and despair, apparently upon his very last legs and quite unfit for travel. To his airs and attitudes the cowpuncher gives no attention, but proceeds to cinch up the saddle. As he begins this the pony heaves a deep, long breath, which converts him temporarily into something of the figure of a balloon. The cowpuncher knows what this means, and, putting his foot against the side of the pony, he gives a quick, strong pull on the girth, which causes the pony to grunt in a grieved way and to lessen his size abruptly. The hind cinch is not drawn tight, for in regard to that a cow horse feels that it has certain rights to breathing room which even a cowpuncher is bound to respect. In any case, the pony may pitch a little when the cowboy swings into the saddle, especially if it has not been ridden for some time. It may do this because it is happy or because it is not happy, but the cowpuncher does not pay much attention to it unless it be very violent, in which case he may join the yells of his companions as the pony goes thumping stiff-legged over a dozen yards or so before it settles down.

The conventional picture of a cowboy shows him going at a sweeping gallop over the plains, his hair flying wildly and his horse *ventre à terre*, its eyes bulging out in the exultation of speed. Sometimes the cowboy rides hard on the round-up or when he comes to town, but when he sets out across the range on his day's work at the ranch he does not spur and gallop his horse. He goes at a steady, ceaseless, choppy little trot, which it tires the life out of a tenderfoot to follow all day. This short trot is a natural gait for the cow pony, and it will maintain it for a long time if not crowded too hard. These little horses make very enduring driving horses when broken to that work, and a team of them has been known to pull a light wagon eighty miles in a day's drive—a feat which would be impossible upon Eastern roads and in the Eastern atmosphere.

As Jim, our cowpuncher, rides along on his day's work, quite alone, of course, he sees many things which the tenderfoot would not notice. He notes where a deer has crossed the ranch road, where the wolves have been playing in the sand, where the "bob cat" has walked along the muddy bank. He sees the track of the horse which crossed, and can tell whether or not it is a fresh track. Perhaps it is part of his day's work to look up some of the ranch horses which have strayed away. Perhaps his ranch is under fence, and if so he must ride the line to see that the fence is not down at any point. In the early days no man needed to worry about fences, but of later times the faithful cowboy who works on a fenced ranch is sometimes called contemptuously a "pliers man" by the rustlers, who have no fences of their own, this name coming from the tools which the cowboy carries in order to mend a break if he finds one in the wire fence. The cowpuncher's eye, from force of habit, is keen to note any unbranded animal that may be running on his range. If the law or his conscience in regard to Mavericks permit it—and as to Mavericks the conscience of all good cowpunchers is wide—our solitary rider may forthwith set about correcting the deficiency in the unbranded calf running with or without the company of the cow. It is not unknown that a cowpuncher has built a fire, heated his iron, taken his place again in the saddle, roped and thrown his calf, and then dragged it up to him as he sat in the saddle, finishing the branding without dismounting. This, however, is the act of a stylist in cowpunching.

The range in summer time is a breezy and not unpleasant place to be, in spite of the brilliant sun. The cowpuncher has the equanimity of good digestion and well-oxygenated blood as he goes on his morning ride across the country. Always his eye roams over the expanse ahead. He can tell farther than the tenderfoot can see what is going on out on the horizon. He knows what is this distant horseman crossing the flat ahead. If it is a cowboy, he knows him because he rides straight up in his stirrups, with no crooking-back of the leg. If it is an Indian, he will be sitting hunched up, with his stirrups very short and his leg bent back under the horse's belly, riding with the calf of his leg rather than with the thigh or knee, and, moreover, kicking his horse all the time. If Jim, the cowboy, does not think this horseman should be there at this part of the range, he may stop and unsling the big field glasses which he sometimes carries with him as an aid in his work. With these glasses he swings his gaze across the whole sweep of country steadily, seeing a strange panorama, not all of which would be visible if he waited to ride up close enough to see with the unaided eye. He sees a little bunch of young cows running up out of a draw, and suspects that the gray wolves may have pulled down a calf there. He sees the coyotes, reddish in the warm sun, sneaking off across the plain. He notes the low swoop of a big eagle, and he watches a long time the actions of a bunch of antelope. A little cloud of dust arising steadily from one spot attracts his attention, and, looking for a long time at this, he sees it is caused by two big bulls which are waging one of the stubborn and exciting combats of the cattle plains. Interested in this, he closes the glasses and rides over to "see the fun"; for a fight of any kind is not foreign to his preferences. He draws up by the side of the intent fighters, not close enough to disturb them, and, taking a chew of tobacco, throws his leg over the horn of his saddle as he sits, offering mental wagers on the winner. The two great animals charge and charge again, their solid foreheads meeting with dull thumps, their backs bowing up strongly, their muscles cording out in relief as they thrust and shove, each trying to get at the side of the other, their hind legs going fairly up on their toes as they clash in the encounter. The herd stands near by, watching the contest with eager interest, the heads of the cows thrown high, occasionally an animal running away a bit in fright, only to return to the fascination of the spectacle. The eyes of the fighting bulls glare, and foam hangs from their mouths. They pant and grumble, their sides momentarily growing more densely covered with the white dust. Thus they fight till at length one tires and can no longer withstand the steady shove of his antagonist. He weakens, turns swiftly to one side, swerving cunningly clear of the rapid thrust at his side which follows, and runs off discomfited, the other retiring pawing, shaking his head, and bellowing. This will give the cowpuncher something to talk about tonight.

As he rides on over the range, the cowpuncher keeps out an eye along the watering places to note any animal that may have become mired down. When he sees a big steer thus entrapped, and with life enough left in it to warrant an attempt at its rescue, Jim rides up to the edge of the boggy place and sets about pulling out the animal. He does not like to get his rope muddy for the sake of a Texas steer, but still he may do so upon occasion. With a sweep of the wrist he lands the rope about the horns of the creature, the latter meantime snorting and shaking its head in resentment, and having no understanding of the intention of it all. Heading the pony up the bank, Jim sets in the spurs, and the sturdy little horse, which takes as much delight as its master in showing its superiority over all horned things, stiffens its muscles and strains at the rope. If the steer's neck holds together, it comes out of the mud. Then, if it has not been bogged down for very long, and still has most of its quota of original sin, the steer is extremely apt to reward its rescuers with a sudden and determined charge as quickly as it gets on its feet, for it knows nothing about the service that has been rendered, and feels only that its dignity has been injured by these creatures which it hates. But the charge is not rapid enough to catch the swift-footed little pony.

Perhaps Jim notes in his rounds a steer that is standing apart by itself, with its head down, dull and stupid. Or perhaps it will so stand for a time, and then run about frantic and crazy, as though intoxicated. Jim knows what is the cause of this. The animal has been eating the "loco weed," against which instinct gives it apparently no protection. The effect of this herb is to stupefy or render crazed the animal eating of it. From the Spanish word *loco*—"mad, crazy"—comes the expression common on the range, "locoed." To say that a man is "locoed" means that he is foolish, absurd, crazy. If Jim sees too much loco weed about, he may drive the cattle away from that part of the range.

Jim does not love a rattlesnake, nor does his pony, and the latter can smell one a long way, turning its head to where it lies curled up under the shade of the Spanish bayonet. Jim takes a shot or so at the snake with his six-shooter, not heeding the objections of the pony to the gun. A cow horse has to get used to a great many strange things that go on upon its back. Or Jim may dismount and kill the snake with his quirt, rather a short-range weapon for such a case, though this does not seem to trouble him. He may skin the snake if it be a very large one, turning the skin back from the neck, and pulling it free as he holds the head down with his foot. Snake fat is good for softening leather, and so is the fat of the prairie dog, at which Jim occasionally tries a shot, just to "keep his hand in."

Thus on the cowpuncher rides in the course of his day's work, across wide flats and around high, red buttes, over rough gullies and *coulees* (*"arroyos"* these would be called in the Southwest), and all the time he is observant of all that transpires about him, near at hand or at a distance. Perhaps he takes a straight course across country, on his way out to one of the "line camps" of the ranch, to see how matters are progressing there. He may take out a letter to one of the boys at that camp, a letter which has perhaps lain at the nearest post office for a month before the ranch wagon went to town, and which has been at the ranch a couple of weeks, or more in addition, but which none the less seems fresh to the cowboy receiving it. It may be from his "girl," as he calls it (his *"dulce,"* it would be in the South), and if so Jim will not take the answer back with him, even though he stay overnight at the line camp, for the composition of the cowpuncher's reply is perhaps a portentous thing, to be accomplished only after long and studious effort.

As Jim turns back in his course, and rides toward the home ranch again, if it be among his plans to return to the ranch the same day, he may be a trifle hungry, but he does not mind that. It may perhaps rain, and make the going bad over the soft flats, but he does not mind that either. It is a part of his daily training to be calm and philosophical. If he be thirsty, he dismounts at the first water hole and drinks, fearless of the alkali which would nearly kill a tenderfoot, but which does not trouble him any more than it does the hardiest steer. He is fitted to survive in these hard surroundings. He belongs in this landscape of butte and plain and scarp and valley, this rugged, hard-faced man who so confidently holds on his way, from his narrowed eyes seeing all the wide sweep of the earth and air about him.

Perhaps it is night by the time he gets back to the ranch house, coming in a wide circle in a direction opposite to that in which he went out. Perhaps he does not get back to camp at all that night, even though he wishes to do so, for even the cowpuncher can go astray in the labyrinth of the wilderness. One occasion comes to mind in which an able cowboy lost his way in a big Texas "pasture," all of which was under fence. He had, almost unbelievable thing, gone out on foot into the *chaparral* to get his horse, which led him a chase into the heart of the dense thicket, where the blended cover stood higher than his head, matted and almost impenetrable. In spite of the fact that he knew the country perfectly, he got lost and wandered directly away from the ranch house, and spent three days in the *chaparral*, all the time, it seems, getting farther and farther away from home. He had water but once in that time, and was in a desperate plight. At last he met a bunch of horses, and noticed that one had a bit of rope about its neck, and which he therefore thought might prove gentle. His belief was correct, and he was able to go up to this horse and catch it. Mounting it bareback, he urged it on and gave it its head, and soon the horse took him to a road, which later led him to a town at the edge of the "pasture," thirty miles from the ranch house.

Perhaps on some of his daily rides about the range Jim spies one or more cows with calves which have escaped the round-up, and to which the attention of the branding iron should be given. If he does not have any branding iron with him, which is very likely the case, and if the calves are anywhere near the home ranch, he rounds them up and drives them in ahead of him, perhaps having four or five in his herd by the time he gets to the house. These he turns into the big ranch corral, and soon a miniature branding bee is going on. The fire is built near the mouth of the corral, and Jim rides into the corral to get the calves. He knows far too much to go in on foot, for a range cow will often charge a footman, not recognising man in that segregated form, and taking him to be some enemy less redoubtable. The cows and calves run around the limit of the corral, Jim leisurely following, his rope trailing out in the dust behind him. Jim has just eaten his dinner, and is in no hurry. Between his teeth still rests the toothpick which he has whittled for himself from the tough yellow wood of the *Palo a Maria*, and on this Jim chews meditatively as he lazily follows after the little calf which is with the big dun cow. Jim slowly takes up the slack of the trailing rope, coiling it in his left hand, and then he lets drop the great noose, bending back a few inches of the noose upon the rope, and grasping both together a little way from the eye of the rope. He then rides on a trifle faster, and with a swift whirl the rope now begins to move about his head, the wrist turning smoothly with it, and the noose of the rope waving in its line like the back of a snake, undulating up and down as well as circling about. The cow pony knows all about this, and Jim pays little attention to the horse. The pony takes him to just the right distance from the right calf, and Jim launches the rope with a swirling swoop which rarely fails in its aim. Enjoying this very much, the little cow horse sets back on its hind legs, and the poor calf comes over, to be dragged to the iron and treated as it would have been on the spring round-up if it had not in some way slipped through the lines. And as it staggers away free of the corral, the heartless cowpunchers say blithely, "Did you hear the ten dollars drop in the box?"

Some day, as the cowpuncher is riding his rounds about the range, his quick eye may note out on the horizon a faint cloud which has not the appearance of a dust trail. This he regards intently, stopping his pony and looking steadfastly toward the spot. The little cloud does not pass away or grow less, but widens and rises, and all at once fans out on the wind, taking on the unmistakable blue of smoke. There is fire! One might think there would be no harm in a simple little fire, but not so impressed seems the usually unperturbed cowpuncher. There is something in the sight of this little crawling fire which causes him to turn his horse and ride as hard as he can for the ranch house. He knows that the whole range may burn, that the stock may be utterly robbed of their only food, that the ranch is to be ruined and the cattle are to starve unless that little creeping line of blue can be quickly met and conquered. He does not pause to ask how it was started—perhaps by accident of some camp fire left uncovered, perhaps by the deliberate act of some malicious rustler, who would be shot like a dog if found in the act of firing the grass. There is no time to think of anything but the remedy, if any still be possible. On parts of the range, especially that where the ground is high and dry and the grass chiefly the short and scattered buffalo grass or gramma grass, the fire will not spread so rapidly, and can be more easily handled, though even there the food of the range can be entirely destroyed by the flames which eat slowly on. If the grass be full and high, as it is on some parts of the cattle country, more especially along the streams and valleys, and if the wind be strong and in the right direction, the prairie fire will soon be a terrible thing. A swift sea of flame will roll across the range, driving forward or destroying everything in its path. Fences and buildings, if there are any, corrals and stables, everything is in danger. If there has been a little hay put up for winter feed, even the ploughed fire guard may prove insufficient to protect the stacks. There is danger that the entire profit of the season will be destroyed, and all the possibilities for the ensuing season jeopardized. The cowpuncher swears sternly as he rides, and every man who rolls out of the house and into saddle swears also as he rides for the flames. There is excitement, but there is no confusion, for each exigency of the calling is known by these men, and they are ready with the proper expedient to meet it. Some of the men look to the buildings carefully, back-burning a broad strip about them, so that the full sweep of the fire will not need to be met there. This is done by lighting fires, a little at a time, farther and farther back against the wind, not enough grass being allowed to burn at once to make a serious blaze, and the fire being under the control of the men, who stand ready to whip it out with wet blankets, green rawhides, or anything which comes handiest.

If the haystacks and the houses be considered safe, all the men unite in fighting the main fire, which is a more serious and difficult matter, a dangerous one if the grass be heavy and the wind high. Riding along the edge of the line of the flame, two cowpunchers drag at the ends of their ropes a wet, green hide, a pile of wet blankets, anything which will serve to drag down and beat out the flame which is eating on. The men "straddle the fire," one riding on each side the line of fire, so that the hide drags along the burning grass, the two riding along the edge of the burning in this way, back and forth, until they have dragged out and smothered down the flames, or found their attempt a hopeless one. Sometimes this work may go on for hours, and it may be either in the day or the night, as the case may happen. Though they be hot and tired and thirsty from the long hours of work in the withering heat, they do not pause, but keep on until the fire is checked or until it has burst away from them, beyond all human control, and so rolled on across the range in its course of desolation. It must be a bad fire if the cowboys do not check it, for they rush into the work with all that personal carelessness of fatigue or danger which marks them in all their work, and so labour as long as they can sit their saddles, sometimes coming out of the smoke with eyebrows singed off, hands blistered, and faces black and grimed, their eyes small and red from the glare and heat of the battle with this enemy of the range. When they are through the fight they sleep, eat, and vow revenge. Ill fares it with the man who fires the range if his offence be ever traced to him. This disastrous disturbance, which imperils the welfare of so many and so much, which sends the cattle in a frightened mass hurrying across the range, mingled with the antelope and deer and wolves, which must also move before the flames—this is something too serious for even the cowman to face with unconcern. He dreads nothing more than a fire. But his diligence and skill in fighting the fire usually confine it in such way that it will burn itself out without a general destruction of the range. If there is little wind, the fire may be caught and stopped at a roadway, or at a dry creek bed, or on high, hard ground, where the rocks and bare earth give the fighters a better chance to wipe out the flames. Behind the ultimate edge of the fire's progress, back to the point where the cowpuncher first saw the tiny line of smoke, there may lie a dozen miles of blackened, smoking prairie, where in the spring the wild plovers will whistle and the big curlews with bent bills will stalk about and utter their wild and shrilly mellow calls.

Such may be some of the incidents of a day on the ranch in one part or another of the cattle country, local conditions, of course, affecting the daily routine and the general features of the work. It may be seen that the cowboy is rather a watchman than a labourer, a guard rather than a workman. His life at the ranch is rather one of alertness than of exertion. Yet his is no easy or idle task, as any one may find who, not bred to the work, undertakes to do it for the first time. What seems so easy is really difficult. It would take years of practice to rival the cowboy in some of the simplest features of his daily occupation. He is in a way a skilled labourer, competent only after long and hard years of apprenticeship. To measure the force of this assertion, let us suppose that the affairs of a single ranch district were left for a season in the hands of other than skilled cowboys, the place of the latter being taken by men who could not sit a "mean" horse, who could not rope and throw a steer, and who had had no experience in reading range brands. Would not a round-up conducted by such gentlemen be a pleasing affair? Would not a drive left to such hands be a reminiscence to dwell upon in after years? How would the season's profits come out if many ranch owners had cowboys about as skilful, let us say, as they themselves in the practical profession of the cowpuncher? No one ever heard of a cowboy's union or of a strike of cowpunchers; yet, if ever a department of labour had capital at its mercy, these riders of the range could have if they chose. Suppose that there was a general walk-out of the cowboys on a round-up just as the herd was formed for the cutting out, it being further added that each cowpuncher had a gun and a playful way of using it! There is a theme for some writer of short stories on Western life, and sufficiently inaccurate to be inviting. Such a scene could never occur in actual life, because the cowpuncher does not hold himself as a servant, but as his own master. He has no delegates, and belongs to no society save that of the plains, which has time out of mind been a society of the individual, embraced under no classification and subject to no control beyond that of personal honour.

Our friend Jim—and proud may you be if he calls you friend!—is a man able to read brands and ride horses, to follow signs and mark calves, to ride all day and all night, to go hungry and thirsty, to go without shelter or home or guidance, always having in mind the thing he started out to do, the duty that is to be performed. This duty he will do without overseeing. He is his own overseer. He needs no instruction nor advice. No higher type of employee ever existed, nor one more dependable. The rudest of the rude in some ways, he is the very soul of honour in all the ways of his calling. The very blue of the sky, bending evenly above all men alike, has reflected into his heart the instinct of justice—that justice which is at the core of all this wild trade of the range. It is not the ranchman, the man who puts the money into the business, who is the centre of the occupation. It is not he who has made the cattle business. It is the cowpuncher, whom you may be glad to have call you friend.

The actual life in the saddle of an active cowboy is not a long one upon the average, for the hardships of it are too steady, the accidents too common. Any injury received in the pursuit of his calling he bears stoically, after the fashion of the plains, whose precedents were established where there was "lack of woman's nursing, there was dearth of woman's tears." Under all the ills of life the cowboy " 'quits himself like a man." That is his standard. There are some who ask for the gallop of the cowboy, and not the quiet trot, some who think his crudeness and his wildness should be made his distinguishing features. Rather let us say that his chief traits are his faithfulness and manliness. There is his standard—to be a "square man." If you called him a hero, he would not know what you meant.

QUESTIONS

1. Roosevelt, Branch, and Hough all agree that the cattle business was pioneered by men from one part of America. What part was that? The North? The South? The Midwest? Explain.

2. If one of the few books in the ranch house was a farrier's guide, what kind of information did that book contain? At the beginning of this century, thousands of men worked as farriers; now few do. Now thousands of men work in filling stations and tire shops. What is the relationship between the two occupations?

3. Why should "the terrible monotony" of a sheepherder's life make him more melancholy than a cowboy?

4. Hough describes the minute observations routinely made by a cowboy doing his day's work. Compare them to the observations that must be made by a doctor or detective.

5. How does the attitude of a cowboy toward his rope and saddle resemble that of a professional baseball player toward his glove and bats? Explain.

6. Write a brief paper in which you compare a day in a cowboy's life with a day in the life of a farmer, a city bus driver, or a high-school teacher.

JACK SCHAEFER

MEANWHILE, BACK AT
THE RANCH

He still wears a big hat and high-heeled boots, and there is a holster at his hip. He still sits a stock saddle with easy assurance. Jogging along a ridge top against the western sky, he still has the old-time look. But the holster carries no gun, only a small, ingenious tattooing outfit. He spends more time in a truck or jeep than in the saddle. He has a pencil in hand much more often than a rope. In fact, pencil and clip board and scales are his major tools.

He probably has a degree from an agricultural college and now and again takes in a refresher field day at a college experiment station. Of an evening, while his college-graduate wife keeps the kids quiet in front of their favorite "western" television serial, he retires to another room in his neat, up-to-date house to read serious articles with such formidable titles as: *The Application of Modern Engineering Principles to Beef Production,* or *The Influence of Moisture, Flavor and Color on Acceptability and Intake of a Ration for Beef Cattle.*

Only at branding time (if the boss does not insist on the chute method) does he ride free and swing a loop as in the old days. He may claim that roping and throwing the critters for the iron is still the faster, more humane method—and as long as he retains the old skill, he may be right. But there is another reason for using it: "Well," he may admit, "we still have to have *some* fun."

He is the modern cowboy.

No. The label no longer fits. The foreman of the great King Ranch in Texas states bluntly: "We don't use the word cowboy." Call him the modern cowman, that is, by dictionary definition, "a man who raises and tends cattle." The raising and the tending are ever more removed from those of the cowboy's time.

He is the modern cowman, forerunner of a new breed, a trained professional in quite a new sense, keeping pace with a positive revolution in his field.

Cattle raising is becoming a beef-manufacturing industry, tied to automation and scientific research, relying for help on the slide rule and the data processing electronic computer.

Of course, horses will always be used in rough, undeveloped country to which the cow may be forced as demands upon our fertile valleys and level lands increase. Here, the old ways, modernized and mechanized some but still distinctive, will persist. But the number of old-style cattle operations steadily diminishes. They face increasing pressures from an ever more highly developed economy.

"I admonished these men to scrutinize, coldly and without sentiment, each of their different enterprises; and not to cling to a losing venture simply because father or grandfather prospered from it—look to the future and not to the past."

That is Dr. M. E. Ensminger (his doctorate is itself significant) telling in his regular syndicated magazine column of the advice he recently gave the owners of a large ranch.

It is good advice: sound, practical, in tune with the times, however harsh it seems to those of us who look back nostalgically (and, alas, sentimentally) to the old days.

Paradoxically, perhaps, what is happening to cattle raising is a penalty of success. Beef is the most popular meat, out in front of all other meats in annual per capita consumption in the United States. It's the prime display attraction at meat counters in most retail food stores. The demand, pushing back from the retail outlets, for better beef and for standardized carcasses that can be prepackaged into uniform cuts for self-service displays builds up increasing competitive pressures.

The population explosion and ever-rising land values add their impetus. Land-use acquires an ever higher premium. We are moving into an era in which, for the cowman, every acre must produce the most beef possible of the best grade at the least cost for the highest return.

And all that, of course, means a constant effort to improve stock, that is, to increase the efficiency of the stock as beef-manufacturing units.

It is an interesting fact that beef breeding research has trailed behind that in other fields—poultry, swine, even sheep. But lost time is being made up fast with intensive work under way at experiment stations and on progressive ranches in key areas. (The two major developments, aside from the amazing advance of the grain sorghums as feeds, are beef breeding research and artificial insemination.) Let me, an amateur observer who has knocked a bit about several of these ranches, talk about it in my own bumbling way.

There are four main factors involved in achieving a profitable animal—that is, an efficient beef-producing unit:

(1) weight at birth;
(2) rate of gain during effective life;

(3) efficiency of gain, of feed conversion;
(4) carcass quality.

Obviously, an animal that has good weight at birth, that gains rapidly while on its mother and continues to gain as a stocker on pasture and again as a feeder being prepared for market, that does this efficiently for a high ratio of feed into flesh, that then dresses out with plenty of lean, well-marbled meat, tender and of good flavor, and no excess of fat or enlarged bone, is the cowman's ideal.

All these characteristics, in varying degree, are inheritable, transmittable. But will they be? The way to find out is to find out. The old method of "eyeball testing," of judging an animal by its appearance, still of necessity much in use at stock shows, is no longer adequate.

Performance-tested is a familiar phrase in the industry. A performance-tested bull, for example, is one whose own performance (for the first three factors above) from birth to maturity has been carefully checked; the records are available. The new phrase is *progeny-tested.* That is, comparable records are also available of his actual get. The canny cowman who once bought only performance-tested bulls now insists on those progeny-tested, too. But the reason is not necessarily to buy them. That is no longer necessary—though it may be an excellent business proposition.

Here enters artificial insemination, the A.I. of the industry. The use of the technique is still limited in rough range cow country, to be sure. Not only is it relatively new in beef cattle, but there are problems of rounding up loose-ranging animals. Still it's getting more and more attention, because the economic differences stemming from artificial breeding are downright startling.

To begin with, it puts the services of high-quality bulls within the reach and means of the average cowman. By breeding the cows artificially, he can cut his breeding cost per calf far below what it would be if he had to raise or buy and maintain such bulls himself. With natural breeding under ranch conditions, one of them would sire 25 to 30 calves per year; with artificial methods the number may be as many as 5,000.

An interesting sidelight here is that there seems to be a reluctance on the part of the beef breed associations to accept artificial breeding with any special enthusiasm. I am looking at a table of regulations they have adopted. Out of the 13 associations only two accept artificial methods for registry purposes with no restrictions, one other with only one mild restriction. Another was in process of revising rules at the time the table was prepared. The remaining nine all are definite that a calf can be registered only if the owner of the mother is also owner or co-owner of the sire and if the calf is conceived before the death of the sire. A few add further restrictions to maintain a semblance of order in lineage, in breeding, etc., records which do protect a range cowman from mating his cows with bloodlines too like their own. Restrictions also seem aimed at keeping conditions surrounding the use of the technique as close to natural as possible.

So here is a modern cowman, a trained professional, pencil in one hand, tally sheet clipped to board in the other, jotting down what the scales say about a plump calf whose mother (a tattooed number on the calf's ear) is half a mile away with other cows, and whose sire (a tattooed letter on the ear) is 1,000 miles away at an experiment station.

Take a good look at the man: He represents an industry in transition. He is straight out of the past, in his big hat and worn levis and high-heeled boots, straight out of a Remington drawing, with the lanky, lean-hipped figure of the true horseman. At the same time, he is very much of the present—and a symbol of the future, of the emerging future of the cattle business.

His name is Bruce Oxley. Like so many of the cowmen of the early days, he was born in the east and spent some of his boyhood there. Then, still in the tradition, his family went west, all the way to California. At a school there, at which horsemanship and camping trips into a nearby national forest were major activities, he absorbed the same urges that made cowboys in the old days: a deep interest in horses, in outdoor work, and in the great open spaces. What profession could still offer a fair chance at a living relationship with these things? Right. Ranching, the cattle business.

But this is the second half of the 20th century. A youngster can no longer just attach himself to some cow outfit and really learn the business by watching and imitating and doing; not if he is to keep pace with it.

Bruce went to the agricultural branch of the University of California at Davis, meeting the future there in two ways: in the form of such studies as animal husbandry and range management, and in the person of a fellow-student named Carol who would soon be his wife. A stretch working at a California feedlot (where cattle are finished for market) for practical experience; another in the Army, completing the ROTC service done in college; and then, ready for it, to his present position.

So here, a few years later, is Bruce Oxley, modern cowman, 27 years old, father of two children, foreman of a 2,200-acre ranch in central California which normally runs 300 head of cows. The ranch is not typical of the industry as a whole, because it has both a purebred breeding herd and a "commercial" cow herd. Most ranchers specialize either in raising punched calves for sale to other ranchers for replacement purposes, or in raising calves destined only for slaughter. But the ranch operations show some important, promising techniques. It is a significant comment on modern methods and modern stock (and on Bruce himself) that most of the time he can handle the entire operation of the ranch with the aid of only one regular assistant. The owner, too, is sometimes on hand to help with the work, but Bruce has the year-round responsibility.

The major aim of this ranch is to develop a herd of high-quality brood cows which will produce ever better herd replacements. The ranch, like cattle raising itself, is in transition. That is, while emphasis is on developing the purebred herd, it still runs many merely "commercial" cows. The two activities, in a sense, complement each other, but the two operations, purebred and commercial, are kept carefully separate. The California climate, with its year-round clemency helps on that—breeding and thus calving for the two divisions are so arranged that they come at different times.

There are a thousand and one things that always need to be done around a ranch, even a modern ranch. Just take for granted that Bruce does them, or sees to it that they are done, and let's concentrate on the major chores through the swing of the seasons.

During January, February and March, he is busy breeding the purebred stock, driving out in the early morning in a truck to one section of the ranch (a breeding "pasture" may run to 400 acres of hilly, rolling range), shifting to horseback (there is still no substitute for a good horse in this) to cut out cows and drive them into the breeding corrals. From one section of the ranch to another in the morning, then a second round in the afternoon—and a rebreeding of these same cows in the evening for greater certainty before letting them out of the corrals. A full, long day—day after day.

April—and there are echoes out of the past. Branding time.

This is for the commercial calves. Branding, vaccinating, dehorning, mothering-up or matching calf to cow so the right number can be tattooed on the ear (the purebred calves are carefully marked at birth). All this work is done by the old method of roping and "stretching 'em out."

The neighbors gather from other ranches, and stout Quarter-Horses strut their stuff, and ropes fly, and the bawling of calves mingles with the joshing of men, and the tangy smell of burnt hair and hide floats on the air, and the work moves swiftly and efficiently, and the talk is good, and the following barbecue is better than Delmonico's best.

And meanwhile, through April and on into May, last year's commercial calves, young steers now, along with the heifers not to be kept as herd replacements, are being cut out and sent to the feeders or packers. Bruce goes there, too, to record such things as the grades given by the government grader, carcass weights, rib eye areas, thickness of fat coverings, etc.

June and July are the weaning months—all calves being weaned, weighed and started on their rate-of-gain tests.

August, September and October. This is catch-up time, the no-immediate-pressure time to *try* to catch up on all projects and general work that must be done at one time or another and might as well be done right now.

November and December, and the purebreds are doing their duty: calving. Bruce is riding out regularly, holster at his hip, watching the mothers, helping them when necessary, recording exact birth dates, sexes, tattooing the newborn ears with the right numbers and letters. The end of the year is in sight. The end of the work? Shucks, with the new calendar it will all start all over again—with the experiences and data of the old year to be applied to plannings for the new.

Data? No end to it. Bruce has been assembling it all through those months. He has been keeping careful records on every animal on the ranch. Performance-testing and progeny-testing are part of the ranch routine. A look at a brood cow's record sheets . . . such symbols as *A.D.G.* (Average Daily Gain, for any specific period, No. 2 of those inheritable traits), *TDN* Conv. (Total Digestible Nutrients Conversion, the number of pounds of feed required to produce a pound of gain, No. 3 of those traits), and *I.P.R. Ind.* (International Performance Registry Index, rating from the organization which sets up standards for breeders). Paper work . . . paper work.

One sheet, front and back, for the cow's immunization record through the years against all the bovine diseases that might beset her, and for data on her various breedings, and ample space for "general information" and "remarks" about her. Another sheet fairly bristling with symbols: On one side her ancestry, name, brand, tattoo number, birth date, registry number, etc.—and her "individual performance record" as calf and as yearling and as brood cow. On the other side the really vital statistics: her "production record," calf by calf, through the circling of the seasons. Ten columns for ten calves (the data will show up again on each calf's own sheet) and each column runs the full gamut from birth to destiny: birth data, weaning data, stocker data, feeder data, over-all growth data, carcass data.

And always (here the scientific approach shows in most distinct form), on every sheet for every animal and for every data division, there is space for an index figure—a calculation designed to take into account variations in exact ages and changes in conditions and environment from year to year and from one batch of cattle to another, so that at any time, accurate comparisons of one animal with another can be made.

The modern cowman has to have a good head for figures. And beyond that, for the breeding and culling and marketing decisions always coming up, he has to have a thorough knowledge of genetics and to keep pace with the new knowledge which is constantly being reported in the journals he reads.

In California, feed costs are more important than in the Midwest, the very home of grain surpluses. Midwest steers are apt to lead somewhat longer lives, be permitted to go on manufacturing beef for a few more months. (Thus, at last, visiting in California, I found out why the beef there seemed more like veal than that back home in New Mexico, which gets most of its meat from the Midwest. I remembered an old saying of the Old West, that the only meat truly fit for a man is seven-year-old bull. But that, of course, is out of an untutored, unscientific age. "Maybe we've grown softer and need softer food," remarked another young California cowman quite in tune with these times but reminiscent of older times in his zest for his work. "Anyway, young beef is what housewives are used to nowadays, what they like, what they'll pick any time against darker, older meat.")

And where is the current revolution heading? Pick a paragraph out of that article on applying engineering principles to beef production, which the modern cowman was reading at the start of this piece. It was written by Dr. W. J. Graff, dean of instruction at Texas A&M University.

"Producers today can fit the environment to the most productive livestock breeds and fit the breeds to the environment. . . . More animals—particularly swine and poultry—are raised indoors in birth-to-market confinement under crowded conditions. . . . All the essentials of the feed program will be brought right to the animal. . . ."

Swine and poultry—cattle next. Imagine the "ranch" of the future, already here in many respects. Raising cattle, bred precisely to such environment, perhaps not indoors, but in birth-to-market confinement under crowded conditions, somewhat like chickens in their tiny wire compartments reduced to brief lifetimes of eating and laying eggs until they reach the feed-conversion point of diminishing returns.

Steers will stand with scant leg room, munching on hormone-prompted rations brought to them from an automatic mixer by a conveyor system which will be pushing them ever more rapidly towards the time at which they will be drugged with tranquilizers and then shipped off to market.

And the cowman, after a day of brain-taxing work and pencil-finger exercise, will shed his coveralls and put on a gray flannel suit to drive his wife in their sleek new car to a rodeo to see the old skills in action.

But once in a while, during time off, he will pull on his boots and pick his big hat off a hook (they will still be around in some closet) and saddle his horse and jog off for a ride into whatever back country remains. Jogging along, seeing beside him the unmistakable outline of his shadow on the ground, he will remember, with no loss of pride in his present profession, the man he once was, the rootin', tootin', hard-working, hard-playing American cowboy.

QUESTIONS

1. "Cattle raising is becoming a beef-manufacturing industry, tied to automation and scientific research, relying for help on the slide rule and the data processing electronic computer." Why is this sentence particularly significant in an article that appeared in *Think,* a magazine published by the IBM Corporation?

2. "Jogging along, . . . he will remember . . . the man he once was, the rootin', tootin', hard-working, hard-playing American cowboy." Do you think people in other vocations—medical specialists in large cities, pilots of modern commercial jet planes, and captains of automated, computerized ocean freighters and tankers—also regret the passing of more romantic days when medicine was a humane art, when pilots flew by the seat of their pants, and when seamanship was a mystery as well as a science?

3. The insistence upon scientific beef production, says Schaefer, is "sound, practical, in tune with the times, however harsh it seems to those of us who look back nostalgically (and, alas, sentimentally) to the old days." Why are most authors of Western stories nostalgic and sentimental? ·

4. Does Schaefer's picture of the future cattle ranch, where steers are penned together and fed by conveyer belt, repel you? Will industrial efficiency eventually destroy the joy and romance of almost all vocations? Comment.

5. It has been claimed that most Western stories have little or nothing to do with the cattle business—that they deal with conflict between men on a raw, unsettled frontier. Comment.

DONALD JACKSON

MEMORIES OF
BIG COUNTRY

The American cowboy has been declared extinct so often, as well as more damning things like romantic, hackneyed and, worst of all, *irrelevant*, that he is about convinced it's true. What he represents has always tickled the public fancy more than what he is—the sad destiny of heroes. He represents—oh, freedom, of course, individualism, man alone, natural man, self-sufficiency, personal liberty as a life-style. Maybe he was some or all of those things and sometimes still is. But he is also lonely and confused. Lonely because he is old and obsolete and it is his bleak privilege to look around and see nobody who's much like him, and nobody who much cares, except those who care too much. Confused because he doesn't quite know or understand what happened to him. Once it was all so simple and natural and now it's all so—changed, so complicated, so busy and fast and cold, and a man can't really put his finger on where it went sour.

The remnants are scattered in bunkhouses and trailers and line shacks at the ends of dirt roads in Arizona and Nevada and Montana, old men with photograph albums and memories and advice that is sometimes tolerated, sometimes not. Cumulatively they are a kind of lost generation, united by character and pride, by their own kind of knowledge and their own kind of ignorance, by a belief in ideals blurred now by time and circumstance. Like all old men they hanker for veneration. They are united most in the things they dislike: college boys, especially "snotty-nosed" college boys; fences; nesters; most forms of government; most kinds of machinery; welfare; in with it: Easterners moving into ranching, soft men looking for tax dodges; the pace of life, automobiles and television and friendly Western towns turning chill; neighbors getting too busy to help each other; too many people, too little space, too much rush, too much government.

"In most instances you realize your reward is in what effort you spent," says 79-year-old Casey Barthelmess of Montana. "What I want to say is that appreciation comes to you according to the effort you spend in acquiring it. I think we've lost our sense of appreciation. It's getting cultivated out of us. I can't tell you how hard it is to lose your old friends. My wife and I went to a funeral the other day and we were the only ones that went on to the cemetery, the only ones.

We've grown out of our way of life, my way of life. We enjoyed individualism. Each of us was an essential part—how can I say it?—everyone was concerned with your welfare. You were essential to me and I was essential to you and there was a feeling of security and the thing was, your *essentialness* was recognized. You knew damn well you couldn't get along without your neighbor and he couldn't get along without you and it was recognized. I don't know whether the present-day setup considers this something we've lost or not, but we do, I do."

Somehow people aren't the same. "Everybody knew how to handle cattle back then," says 72-year-old Lee Panky of Nevada. "Nobody was helpless. And the cowboys and ranchers got along better, everybody did. You'd round up your neighbor's cow with yours and send him a check. Nobody does that no more. A man's word was his bond. If a fella said he'd do something he'd come damn near doing it. These fellas nowadays will tell you anything and do nothing.

"Everything was loose. It was loose, y'know." The words trail off, dissolving and blending with the eternal fulminations of old men.

"We had this gangling old boy working as a horse wrangler on the L O Ranch out of Miles City," Barthelmess remembers. "His name was A.D.J. Hooper. He could only count to 14. One day he was out wrangling the horses and Old Bones, the wagon boss, came up and asked him how many mounts he had. Well, A.D.J. Hooper puzzled it a while and finally said, 'I got five 14s, two 11s and a nine.' "

Most cowboys had little tolerance for school, but like A.D.J. they made do with what they knew. They never spend much time thinking about themselves or what other people think of them. Many are natural storytellers, with a gift for savory language and tales that arrive at their conclusion frazzled but undaunted. They lean heavily on exaggeration, the credulity of a listening dude, or both.

"I remember hearing about the old trail drive up from Texas," says 67-year-old Curly Witzel of Wyoming. "Seems one time they got the herd to the Red River, and it was high, they couldn't cross. But they found a big old cottonwood tree, hollowed out, a-laying across the river. They rode across to test it out and then brought all the cattle across on the tree. When they got to the other side and counted 'em, they found they was 177 short. They went back and found those 177 had turned off at one of the limbs."

Lee Panky remembers a night when he was in a New Mexico line camp, a log cabin with just a canvas windbreak for a door. Line camps are solitary outposts on the perimeters of large ranches where cowboys often spend the winter months watching over the herds. "I was sleeping when I heard something moving in the cabin, then it jumps on my bed and lies down and starts purring. Turns out it was a cougar. I had my pistol handy just in case the gentleman wanted to get under my tarp. But he presently got up and walked out, I put a door up the next day."

Fred Martin sat in his linoleum-floored living room and took a long pull on the pint bottle at his elbow. He smacked his lips. "If I could ever get out of debt," he said, "I'd probably be two or three times a millionaire." Martin is 85, owner of a large ranch on the San Augustín Plain of New Mexico, two or three times an outlaw and some kind of storyteller. Belief is not particularly necessary to appreciate his stories, nor particularly expected.

"In 1910," he began, "I won the bronc-riding at the Cheyenne rodeo. Got $500. Afore long the whores had a hand in each pocket, and I was about broke inside of ten days. I was ashamed to go back to the ranch where I was working, so I went into this bar. Soon a fella looked like a cowpuncher come in, and I asked if I could buy him a drink.

"He said he was with a government pack train, with 64 mules and 14 packers. Told me a boy had just quit the day before, so I took a job as a packer at $50 a month. Cowpunchers were only getting $35 or $40.

"Well, we loaded these mules on a train at Cheyenne. Nobody knew where we was going. We had whisky and cards, though, so I didn't care. Went to Fort Sam Houston in Texas. Goddam roses were blooming there, and it was January. I felt right silly in my coonskin cap and fur coat. Then about March we got orders to go to Eagle Pass on the Mexican border. I got in a row there with this Dutchman who was selling beer. Kicked over his tub of ice. This big fat ugly old captain called me and another boy in and told us we was fired. I had about $35 and no horse.

"This other boy, he was from Gillette, Wyo. He said he kinda liked the country down there and asked me to take off cross-country with him. But I was lacking a horse. He took off, and I felt just flatass lonesome and bad. I talk pretty good Mexican so I thought I'd go across the border to Piedras Negras. D'reckly I got there here comes the Mexican captain riding a beautiful bay horse. Son of a bitch got off and whopped his reins two or three times around a hitching rack and went to get a *cerveza* or something. I thought, 'Fred, here's where you get mounted.' I took that horse. Cut off the sword—I didn't need no sword, wasn't gonna fight no combats like that—and swum across the Rio Grande.

"Well, I caught up with this boy on his way to El Paso. We got a job breaking horses in the Glass Mountains, made about $100. It was starting to get kinda hot so this old boy said he wanted to go back to Wyoming. I said I didn't want no more snow and blizzards. We went to El Paso and he got on a train.

"I went into the Vargas Hotel. I was kinda looking for a

compadre, y'know? Saw this fella drinking alone and I stepped up. After a while he says, 'Friend, I need help, can you do anything?' I told him I could ride any man's horse and do a lotta goddam things. Said he was working for a Mexican cattleman who'd branded about a hundred thousand calves that spring, biggest cattleman in the world. The revolution had come along, and he was trying to get his cattle into Texas before old Pancho Villa grabbed 'em. So I hired out to him, and here I go back to Mexico.

"I was riding point on the cattle herd one day, and I was always the biggest coward there was. We had to be afraid of both the *federales* and Villa. D'reckly I saw a little dust and all of a sudden a troop of *federales* came a-kicking up. There were 12 of us and a hunnert of them. They killed a couple of our men, pinned the rest of us down in mesquite. We tied a shirt on a mesquite stick and surrendered.

"They put us in jail in this little town, and we stayed there all summer. Took my boots and everything. Finally we were sentenced— 11 a.m. against the adobe wall. I was thinking that I had a lot of life to live—it just worries me to think about dying, does yet. I was nervous. But next thing I knew I heard a hell of a lot of shooting, and I was thinking, 'Well, this'll be the last of Fred.' But all of a sudden here comes Villa and he captures the whole outfit. There were 200 of us in jail, and Villa let us all go, long as we joined his army. I didn't know what he was fighting for and didn't care. I made my mind up right quick."

Martin drained the last of the bottle. "And that," he said, "is how I became a lieutenant in Villa's army." Directly he fell asleep.

There are actually two distinct varieties of cowboy in the American West, and one isn't a cowboy at all but a buckaroo. The sources were Texas and Mexico. The Texans spread west and north with the great herds, west to New Mexico and Arizona, north up the old trails to Colorado, Wyoming and Montana. Even today most cowboys past 60 in those states have a Texas background, or else their fathers did. The Mexican influence arrived by way of California and spread through Nevada, Oregon and Idaho. There cowboys are known as buckaroos, an Americanization of the Spanish word *vaquero.*

The two have different styles and mutual suspicions. Cowboys tie their ropes to their saddle horns; buckaroos keep them loose, which is known as "dallying." Cowboys use hemp ropes, buckaroos rawhide ropes or *reatas.* Arizonans double-cinch their saddles, Nevadans use a single cinch. Northern men complain about the lack of water in the South; Southerners shudder when they think of Montana winters. The line between the two is generally taken as the Colorado River: the Great Basin, north and west of the river, is buckaroo country. One

Arizona cowboy who spent a season in Oregon reported back that life there was "an ice-breaking, hay-making, light-bread-eating, tea-drinking son of a bitch."

What they have in common is their code, the 19th Century principles of honor and pride and loyalty that determine how they face life, work and other people. Dimly they may perceive its galloping irrelevance. Die for the herd? Nowadays? When the herd is owned by some corporation from Delaware?—but it's too late to change.

Pride encompasses everything from roping skill to self-sufficiency in a line camp, from the "waterfall" in a cowboy's hat ("You can tell a lot from that waterfall—whether a guy is half a cowboy or a whole cowboy or no cowboy at all") to the way he wears his Levi's ("They just hang differently on a cowboy").

The long drives and roundups were the central facts of ranch life. Cattle would be rounded up and branded in spring, rounded up again and shipped in fall. The roundup outfit included a cook and his wagon, a *remuda* with seven or eight horses per man, and anywhere from 10 to 40 cowboys. Life was hard but agreeable. The hard parts were the hours (up at 4 in the morning, work till dusk, then two hours' night guard) and the weather. The agreeable parts were the camaraderie and the horses. "What kept you there was the horses," says one buckaroo. "You tried to make your horse better than the other guy's. That was the fun of it."

Cattle are still driven to their shipping points at a few large ranches, but most cattlemen ship them in vans that load at the home ranch. Spring is still branding time, but the cowboys on roundup nowadays are fed hot food brought out in a pickup truck, and most stay out only a few days at a time. Most ranchers use branding chutes, which clamp a calf in place while it is branded, rather than the old head-and-heels roping method. Quicker. Easier. More efficient.

"It used to be if you wanted a cowboy to quit, you'd just have to tell him to dig a posthole. Give him a shovel and he'd break the handle. He was insulted." The cowboy's work was on horseback, and *only* on horseback. Not any longer. The modern cowpuncher, whatever his vintage, has to be pump repairman, hay loader, truck driver, ice breaker, posthole digger, wood chopper and a dozen other things which don't require a horse's support. There is still riding and roping to be done in the spring and fall but not much, not enough to teach a boy how to cowboy.

Pain and hardship have never been considerations. The code doesn't permit it. Seventy-year-old Raymond Holt, who winters alone in a line camp in Arizona, broke his neck when a bronco bucked him. Eighty-five-year-old Johnny Mullins of Arizona has broken his hip twice and his pelvis once in the last three years but still rides and pulls his load. "It never hurt a cowpuncher to get skinned up," says Lee Panky. "He calls it 'skinned up,' " says his wife. "He broke his wrist, his foot, his shoulder and a kneecap." "Kneecap didn't 'mount to nothing," he replies. "Two guys sewed it up with a sacking needle good as new." They concede little, if anything, to age. At 72, Panky is "figuring on getting a little place of my own soon." At 67, Curly Witzel is the father of a two-year-old son.

Raymond Holt's line camp is about 50 miles northeast of Flagstaff, Ariz. He lives alone from Dec. 1 to March 1 every year in a two-room cement house—no plumbing, no electricity. He has no neighbors—the closest are Navajos on a reservation 15 miles away, across the Little Colorado River. He crosses the days off on a wall calendar, not because the time passes slowly but because it's the only way he can keep track of the date. He subscribes to a daily newspaper and several magazines, but since he only goes into Flagstaff for the mail once a week they have a tendency to pile up.

"I found I'll be troubled by the census this year," he said as he sliced the breakfast bacon. "Gonna send me a damn form." He stirred the sourdough pancake batter, poured it on the skillet and put it on his wood stove.

Holt broke his neck on the day Pearl Harbor was bombed, and his tongue hasn't felt right since. He believes that he has to keep it moving more or less constantly or it will stiffen up. As a result he talks all the time, to himself. "I read the paper out loud, try to keep my mouth straight." Most of the time he mutters. He's not used to company.

On a nail next to his door hung his rain slicker. His name was penciled on it like a brand—the right side of the H serving as the left side of the O.

"This job is okay for a dumb old stumblebum," he said as he dished out the pancakes, "but anybody that follers me is plain ignorant. The cowpunching life is silly nowadays. There's no roping or running, no excitement. The cattle are all gentle now." He subsided into mutters.

After breakfast he got in his pickup and drove to the reservation, stopping on the way to look at some Indian "hydrolifics" on a rock. "The Indians have the idea," he said. "They know there's something, whether it's God or what. The white man's church is only a gag and a grab and a steal and everything else. I like the Navajo Eagle clan. They say that when your soul leaves your body it soars like an eagle, and you can see everything."

A hawk sat motionless on a ledge above the rutted road. The dust settled back into the stillness behind the truck. Even the sky was quiet.

Holt drove up to a small cluster of Navajo hogans, igloo-shaped huts made of adobe. An old man and woman were butchering a goat. Their son sat on a rail.

"Just came by to look around," Holt said self-consciously. The Indians smiled and nodded.

"How much you want for one of them goat hides?" he asked. He turned and whispered, "I'll offer 'em a buck. Make a good rug. They'll ask three, but they'll come down."

The Indians conferred. Finally the younger man held up three fingers. Holt held up one. Nobody compromised. Holt got back into his pickup. "They'll steal the bridle reins offa your bridle if you let 'em," he said. He began muttering again. "They 'sposed to have some millions' worth of uranium rights here, but the white man'll cheat 'em out of it, you can bet. Bookkeepers and lawyers."

He drove back, across the dry river bottom, past a herd of Indian sheep and goats. "I used to steal from 'em long time ago," he said. "I took some unbranded cattle, did some moonshining, but I'm not a good criminal or I woulda kept it up and made money."

Back at his camp he fed his three Morgan horses and set about preparing lunch. He took out an album full of old pictures of himself riding, standing uncomfortably with other cowboys, lecherously ogling a girl. "I never married, hell no. Seemed plumb silly. You don't know when they gonna get tired or have to go to the doctor or what the hell." He leafed quickly through a stack of pictures. "Well, it was cold and disagreeable all right," he said, "but it didn't hurt you none."

He walked bowlegged to the stove, still muttering. "On t'other hand," he said, "construction work mighta been a damn sight better."

What is disappearing is the song of the land. The cowboy—like wild horses, longhorn cattle, grizzly bears, like so many wild places and animals and people—is a casualty of the shrinking landscape. Breaking up the open range destroyed his theater. Technology rendered his skills, and his pride, obsolete. He can ignore it or grumble about it, turn back in nostalgia or turn aside and shrug. It doesn't matter.

There are a few exceptions, and there probably always will be—younger men who manage to become cowboys and live by the cowboy code despite the odds, despite everything. You can still round some Western corners and get a sudden whiff of timelessness, but it's rare, too rare. Mostly the land wears the badges of this century, and mostly the men do too.

Not all the cowboys whose memories include a different time are sentimental about it. "Some of them old days weren't so damned good," says one. "I'd hate to drop back to the old team and wagon. And some of them oldtime hands weren't worth so much either. Hell's probably overloaded with a lot of 'em."

The cold-eyed epitaph is that the cowboy was right for his time and place, and that time and place have changed. History as evolution—we don't lose, we just change.

But of course we are losing something, regardless of what we may gain. We are losing a kind of man—the damn-the-risk, bring-on-the-grizzlies kind of man, and his personal view of America, the idea that land equals liberty, that open space gives a man the freedom to be what he wants, to work out his own destiny, and demands that he have the strength equal to that freedom. A few men like this remain in the West, not many. They and the idea are all that survive.

> It's now I'm on the scaffold,
> My moments are not long;
> You may forget the singer
> But don't forget the song.

QUESTIONS

1. Compare the cowboys described by Jackson with those described by Roosevelt, Branch, and Hough. How are they similar? How are they different?

2. Jackson says that the cowboys he describes reveal "the sad destiny of heroes." How are these cowboys like old professional athletes or aging actors or actresses? How are they different? Explain.

3. Jackson says that for cowboys, "Pain and hardship have never been considerations." How does their attitude compare with that of football players, boxers, policemen, firemen, or motion picture stuntmen?

4. According to one cowboy, what is lacking in modern life is a feeling of each individual's essentialness. What does he mean? Do you think he is right?

5. Many uneducated men lived successful lives as cowboys; some, indeed, could not read or write. Why would such men find living in America much more difficult today?

PART TWO

FICTION

No brief anthology can do full justice to Western stories. Many of the best of them are novels, with well known titles like *The Virginian* or *Riders of the Purple Sage* or *Destry Rides Again* or *Shane*—books whose conflicts and characters need space for full development. But a collection of short fiction does have special advantages: it offers a range of experience and a variety of styles that a few novels could never provide. So this collection is intended as an introduction—an encouragement to further reading.

The stories reprinted here have been chosen either because they are the work of some of the best known of Western writers or because they illustrate themes and tendencies most characteristic of popular Western literature. They are presented in rough chronological order of publication, so that they illustrate the slow development of literary conventions and attitudes toward the West.

The first two stories, indeed, are not "Westerns" at all, if the term is narrowly defined. They are about miners, not cowboys, and their action takes place in California rather than in the traditional cattleman's West. But Bret Harte and Jack London did much to establish a tradition for frontier literature, and all subsequent writers have owed something to their example. Harte popularized a sentimental portrayal of rude pioneers and an unambivalent attitude toward rough justice and lynch law. London used both a keen eye for Western landscape and a feeling for larger-than-life heroes to establish many of the conventions of almost all subsequent adventure and Western stories.

With Owen Wister's *The Virginian* (1902), the modern Western story was born. Although this novel has a structural integrity of its own, much of it is nonetheless a pastiche of short stories published during the previous decade. One of those stories was "Balaam and Pedro," which is reprinted here. In this story the character of the Virginian, the archetypal Western hero, is demonstrated in his punishment of Balaam, a cruel rancher who abuses horses.

Wister's short story, with its comparatively uncomplicated action and characters, created a small sensation when it was first published. The explicit description of Balaam's maiming of a horse revolted some readers; and Theodore Roosevelt, a friend, wrote to ask Wister to revise the story, to change or obscure the nature of the action. But the character of the Virginian, a simple, heroic avenger, charmed readers then, just as it has millions of others during the three-quarters of a century since.

"Balaam and Pedro" should be compared with "The Bride Comes to Yellow Sky," a short story published at about the same time. Here, too, are some of the archetypal ingredients of the popular Western story—the little town, with its dusty street; the saloon, with an imperturbable bartender and a terrified traveling salesman; the menace, who carries two six-guns and terrorizes the town; and the heroic marshal, who ordinarily acts directly to keep the peace. But the action of the story is turned and stopped by novel circumstances, by a complication new and strange and almost incomprehensible to both of the chief characters. Consequently *The Bride Comes to Yellow Sky* is a unique and puzzling story, an ironic anti-Western, the creation of an artist who wrote about the West before the Western story had become a predictable product and a recognizable embodiment of formula and tradition.

Clarence Mulford and Zane Grey are two of the most famous names in the history of the Western story. Both of these authors published much of their best work before the Second World War, and their writing is now dated by careful observance of genteel proprieties, popular taboos, and modes of expression no longer in fashion. But they perfected the popular Western story; Mulford created Hopalong Cassidy, one of the best-known Western heroes, and Grey wrote some of the all-time best sellers of popular literature.

A short story by Vardis Fisher comes as a startling change in a collection of otherwise conventional Western stories, for Fisher wrote outside the tradition of the popular Western story. Although he lived in the West and wrote about the land he knew, he never used the stock characters and situations developed by Mulford, Grey, and the hosts of writers who filled the pulp magazines of the third and fourth decades of the twentieth century. His stories were not commercial entertainment, and his fiction never commanded the large audiences achieved by popular writers. But he brought fresh vision and highly personal insight to descriptions of life in the West.

It is no derogation, however, to say that all but one of the other authors of the fiction reprinted here have been popular entertainers, ordinarily writing for mass circulation magazines like *Colliers* and the *Saturday Evening Post*. The magazines are now dead, having lost much of their audience and most of their advertisers to television. But it was these magazines and the authors they published that created "adult Westerns"; the writers continued to use the scenes, the situations, and the conflicts of traditional horse opera, but they complicated and made much more credible the characterization of the people in the stories. The same kind of complication and verisimilitude are now to be found in the best contemporary Western films and television programs.

This selection of fiction ends with a story by Walter Van Tilburg Clark, an author who has both used and rejected traditional situations and stereotypes. His well known novel *The Ox-Bow Incident* looks superficially conventional but proves to be an indictment of many of the values and assumptions of most Western stories. Another of his books, *The Trail of the Cat*, is laid in the West, but it owes more to Joseph Conrad than to Owen Wister. His short story reprinted here is seemingly conventional, and it is in some ways similar to Jack London's "All Gold Canyon," with which it may profitably be compared. But it is also highly individual in its close observation of nature and in its characterization and plot development. As an excellent example of fiction in any genre, it is an excellent last example of fiction of the West.

BRET HARTE
TENNESSEE'S PARTNER

I do not think that we ever knew his real name. Our ignorance of it certainly never gave us any social inconvenience, for at Sandy Bar in 1854 most men were christened anew. Sometimes these appellatives were derived from some distinctiveness of dress, as in the case of "Dungaree Jack"; or from some peculiarity of habit, as shown in "Saleratus Bill," so called from an undue proportion of that chemical in his daily bread; or from some unlucky slip, as exhibited in "The Iron Pirate," a mild, inoffensive man, who earned that baleful title by his unfortunate mispronunciation of the term "iron pyrites." Perhaps this may have been the beginning of a rude heraldry; but I am constrained to think that it was because a man's real name in that day rested solely upon his own unsupported statement. "Call yourself Clifford, do you?" said Boston, addressing a timid newcomer with infinite scorn; "hell is full of such Cliffords!" He then introduced the unfortunate man, whose name happened to be really Clifford, as "Jaybird Charley,"—an unhallowed inspiration of the moment that clung to him ever after.

But to return to Tennessee's Partner, whom we never knew by any other than this relative title. That he had ever existed as a separate and distinct individuality we only learned later. It seems that in 1853 he left Poker Flat to go to San Francisco, ostensibly to procure a wife. He never got any farther than Stockton. At that place he was attracted by a young person who waited upon the table at the hotel where he took his meals. One morning he said something to her which caused her to smile not unkindly, to somewhat coquettishly break a plate of toast over his upturned, serious, simple face, and to retreat to the kitchen. He followed her, and emerged a few moments later, covered with more toast and victory. That day week they were married by a justice of the peace, and returned to Poker Flat. I am aware that something more might be made of this episode, but I prefer to tell it as it was current at Sandy Bar,—in the gulches and bar-rooms,—where all sentiment was modified by a strong sense of humor.

Of their married felicity but little is known, perhaps for the reason that Tennessee, then living with his partner, one day took occasion to say something to the bride on his own account, at which, it is said, she smiled not unkindly and chastely retreated,—this time as far as Marysville, where Tennessee followed her, and where they went to housekeeping without the aid of a justice of the peace. Tennessee's Partner took the loss of his wife simply and seriously, as was his fashion. But to everybody's surprise, when Tennessee one day returned from Marysville, without his partner's wife,—she having smiled and retreated with somebody else,—Tennessee's Partner was the first man to shake his hand and greet him with affection. The boys who had gathered in the cañon to see the shooting were naturally indignant. Their indignation might have found vent in sarcasm but for a certain look in Tennessee's Partner's eyes that indicated a lack of humorous appreciation. In fact, he was a grave man, with a steady application to practical detail which was unpleasant in a difficulty.

Meanwhile a popular feeling against Tennessee had grown up on the Bar. He was known to be a gambler; he was suspected to be a thief. In these suspicions Tennessee's Partner was equally compromised; his continued intimacy with Tennessee after the affair above quoted could only be accounted for on the hypothesis of a copartnership of crime. At last Tennessee's guilt became flagrant. One day he overtook a stranger on his way to Red Dog. The stranger afterward related that Tennessee beguiled the time with interesting anecdote and reminiscence, but illogically concluded the interview in the following words: "And now, young man, I'll trouble you for your knife, your pistols, and your money. You see your weppings might get you into trouble at Red Dog, and your money's a temptation to the evilly disposed. I think you said your address was San Francisco. I shall endeavor to call." It may be stated here that Tennessee had a fine flow of humor, which no business preoccupation could wholly subdue.

This exploit was his last. Red Dog and Sandy Bar made common cause against the highwayman. Tennessee was hunted in very much the same fashion as his prototype, the grizzly. As the toils closed around him, he made a desperate dash through the Bar, emptying his revolver at the crowd before the Arcade Saloon, and so on up Grizzly Cañon; but at its farther extremity he was stopped by a small man on a gray horse. The two men looked at each other a moment in silence. Both were fearless, both self-possessed and independent, and both types of a civilization that in the seventeenth century would have been called heroic, but in the nineteenth simply "reckless."

"What have you got there?—I call," said Tennessee quietly.

"Two bowers and an ace," said the stranger as quietly, showing two revolvers and a bowie-knife.

"That takes me," returned Tennessee; and, with this gambler's epigram, he threw away his useless pistol and rode back with his captor.

It was a warm night. The cool breeze which usually sprang up with the going down of the sun behind the chaparral-crested mountain was that evening withheld from Sandy Bar. The little cañon was stifling with heated resinous odors, and the decaying driftwood on the Bar sent forth faint sickening exhalations. The feverishness of day and its fierce passions still filled the camp. Lights moved restlessly along the bank of the river, striking no answering reflection from its tawny current. Against the blackness of the pines the windows of the old loft above the express-office stood out staringly bright; and through their curtainless panes the loungers below could see the forms of those who were even then deciding the fate of Tennessee. And above all this, etched on the dark firmament, rose the Sierra, remote and passionless, crowned with remoter passionless stars.

The trial of Tennessee was conducted as fairly as was consistent with a judge and jury who felt themselves to some extent obliged to justify, in their verdict, the previous irregularities of arrest and indictment. The law of Sandy Bar was implacable, but not vengeful. The excitement and personal feeling of the chase were over; with Tennessee safe in their hands, they were ready to listen patiently to any defense, which they were already satisfied was insufficient. There being no doubt in their own minds, they were willing to give the prisoner the benefit of any that might exist. Secure in the hypothesis that he ought to be hanged on general principles, they indulged him with more latitude of defense than his reckless hardihood seemed to ask. The Judge appeared to be more anxious than the prisoner, who, otherwise unconcerned, evidently took a grim pleasure in the responsibility he had created. "I don't take any hand in this yer game," had been his invariable but good-humored reply to all questions. The Judge—who was also his captor—for a moment vaguely regretted that he had not shot him "on sight" that morning, but presently dismissed this human weakness as unworthy of the judicial mind. Nevertheless, when there was a tap at the door, and it was said that Tennessee's Partner was there on behalf of the prisoner, he was admitted at once without question. Perhaps the younger members of the jury, to whom the proceedings were becoming irksomely thoughtful, hailed him as a relief.

For he was not, certainly, an imposing figure. Short and stout, with a square face, sunburned into a preternatural redness, clad in a loose duck "jumper" and trousers streaked and splashed with red soil, his aspect under any circumstances would have been quaint, and was now even ridiculous. As he stooped to deposit at his feet a heavy carpetbag he was carrying, it became obvious, from partially developed legends and inscriptions, that the material with which his trousers had been patched had been originally intended for a less ambitious covering. Yet he advanced with great gravity, and after shaking the hand of each person in the room with labored cordiality, he wiped his serious perplexed face on a red bandana handkerchief, a shade lighter than his complexion, laid his powerful hand upon the table to steady himself, and thus addressed the Judge:—

"I was passin' by," he began, by way of apology, "and I thought I'd just step in and see how things was gittin' on with Tennessee thar,—my pardner. It's a hot night. I disremember any sich weather before on the Bar."

He paused a moment, but nobody volunteering any other meteorological recollection, he again had recourse to his pocket-handkerchief, and for some moments mopped his face diligently.

"Have you anything to say on behalf of the prisoner?" said the Judge finally.

"Thet's it," said Tennessee's Partner, in a tone of relief. "I come yar as Tennessee's pardner,—knowing him nigh on four year, off and on, wet and dry, in luck and out o' luck. His ways ain't aller my ways, but thar ain't any p'ints in that young man, thar ain't any liveliness as he's been up to, as I don't know. And you sez to me, sez you,—confidential-like, and between man and man,—sez you, 'Do you know anything in his behalf.' and I sez to you, sez I,—confidential-like, as between man and man,—'What should a man know of his pardner?' "

"Is this all you have to say?" asked the Judge impatiently, feeling, perhaps, that a dangerous sympathy of humor was beginning to humanize the court.

"Thet's so," continued Tennessee's Partner. "It ain't for me to say anything agin' him. And now, what's the case? Here's Tennessee wants money, wants it bad, and doesn't like to ask it of his old pardner. Well, what does Tennessee do? He lays for a stranger, and he fetches that stranger; and you lays for *him*, and you fetches *him*; and the honors is easy. And I put it to you, bein' a fa'r-minded man, and to you, gentlemen all, as fa'r-minded men, ef this isn't so."

"Prisoner," said the Judge, interrupting, "have you any questions to ask this man?"

"No! no!" continued Tennessee's Partner hastily. "I play this yer hand alone. To come down to the bed-rock, it's just this: Tennessee, thar, has played it pretty rough and expensive-like on a stranger, and on this yer camp. And now, what's the fair thing? Some would say more, some would say less. Here's seventeen hundred dollars in coarse gold and a watch,—it's about all my pile,—and call it square!" And before a hand could be raised to prevent him, he had emptied the contents of the carpetbag upon the table.

For a moment his life was in jeopardy. One or two men sprang to their feet, several hands groped for hidden weapons, and a suggestion to "throw him from the window" was only overridden by a gesture from the Judge. Tennessee laughed. And apparently oblivious to the excitement, Tennessee's Partner improved the opportunity to mop his face again with his handkerchief.

When order was restored, and the man was made to understand, by the use of forcible figures and rhetoric, that Tennessee's offense could not be condoned by money, his face took a more serious and sanguinary hue, and those who were nearest to him noticed that his rough hand trembled slightly on the table. He hesitated a moment as he slowly returned the gold to the carpetbag, as if he had not yet entirely caught the elevated sense of justice which swayed the tribunal, and was perplexed with the belief that he had not offered enough. Then he turned to the Judge, and saying, "This yer is a lone hand, played alone, and without my pardner," he bowed to the jury and was about to withdraw, when the Judge called him back:—

"If you have anything to say to Tennessee, you had better say it now."

For the first time that evening the eyes of the prisoner and his strange advocate met. Tennessee smiled, showed his white teeth, and saying, "Euchred, old man!" held out his hand. Tennessee's Partner took it in his own, and saying, "I just dropped in as I was passin' to see how things was gettin' on," let the hand passively fall, and adding that "it was a warm night," again mopped his face with his handkerchief, and without another word withdrew.

The two men never again met each other alive. For the unparalleled insult of a bribe offered to Judge Lynch—who, whether bigoted, weak, or narrow, was at least incorruptible—firmly fixed in the mind of that mythical personage any wavering determination of Tennessee's fate; and at the break of day he was marched, closely guarded, to meet it at the top of Marley's Hill.

How he met it, how cool he was, how he refused to say anything, how perfect were the arrangements of the committee, were all duly reported, with the addition of a warning moral and example to all future evil-doers, in the "Red Dog Clarion," by its editor, who was present, and to whose vigorous English I cheerfully refer the reader. But the beauty of that midsummer morning, the blessed amity of earth and air and sky, the awakened life of the free woods and hills, the joyous renewal and promise of Nature, and above all, the infinite serenity that thrilled through each, was not reported, as not being a part of the social lesson. And yet, when the weak and foolish deed was done, and a life, with its possibilities and responsibilities, had passed out of the misshapen thing that dangled between earth and sky, the birds sang, the flowers bloomed, the sun shone, as cheerily as before; and possibly the "Red Dog Clarion" was right.

Tennessee's Partner was not in the group that surrounded the ominous tree. But as they turned to disperse, attention was drawn to the singular appearance of a motionless donkey-cart halted at the side of the road. As they approached, they at once recognized the venerable "Jenny" and the two-wheeled cart as the property of Tennessee's Partner, used by him in carrying dirt from his claim; and a few paces distant the owner of the equipage himself, sitting under a buckeye-tree, wiping the perspiration from his glowing face. In answer to an inquiry, he said he had come for the body of the "diseased," "if it was all the same to the committee." He didn't wish to "hurry anything"; he could "wait." He was not working that day; and when the gentlemen were done with the "diseased," he would take him. "Ef thar is any present," he added, in his simple, serious way, "as would care to jine in the fun'l, they kin come." Perhaps it was from a sense of humor, which I have already intimated was a feature of Sandy Bar,—perhaps it was from something even better than that, but two thirds of the loungers accepted the invitation at once.

It was noon when the body of Tennessee was delivered into the hands of his partner. As the cart drew up to the fatal tree, we noticed that it contained a rough oblong box,—apparently made from a section of sluicing,—and half filled with bark and the tassels of pine. The cart was further decorated with slips of willow and made fragrant with buckeye-blossoms. When the body was deposited in the box, Tennessee's Partner drew over it a piece of tarred canvas, and gravely mounting the narrow seat in front, with his feet upon the shafts, urged the little donkey forward. The equipage moved slowly on, at that decorous pace which was habitual with Jenny even under less solemn circumstances. The men—half curiously, half jestingly, but all good-humoredly—strolled along beside the cart, some in advance, some a little in the rear of the homely catafalque. But whether from the narrowing of the road or some present sense of decorum, as the cart passed on, the company fell to the rear in couples, keeping step, and otherwise assuming the external show of a formal procession. Jack Folinsbee, who had at the outset played a funeral march in dumb show upon an imaginary trombone, desisted from a lack of sympathy and appreciation,—not having, perhaps, your true humorist's capacity to be content with the enjoyment of his own fun.

The way led through Grizzly Cañon, by this time clothed in funereal drapery and shadows. The redwoods, burying their mocca-sined feet in the red soil, stood in Indian file along the track, trailing an uncouth benediction from their bending boughs upon the passing bier. A hare, surprised into helpless inactivity, sat upright and pulsating in the ferns by the roadside as the cortège went by. Squirrels hastened to gain a secure outlook from higher boughs; and the blue-jays, spreading their wings, fluttered before them like outriders, until the outskirts of Sandy Bar were reached, and the solitary cabin of Tennessee's Partner.

Viewed under more favorable circumstances, it would not have been a cheerful place. The unpicturesque site, the rude and unlovely outlines, the unsavory details, which distinguish the nest-building of the California miner, were all here with the dreariness of decay superadded. A few paces from the cabin there was a rough inclosure, which, in the brief days of Tennessee's Partner's matrimonial felicity, had been used as a garden, but was now overgrown with fern. As we approached it, we were surprised to find that what we had taken for a recent attempt at cultivation was the broken soil about an open grave.

The cart was halted before the inclosure, and rejecting the offers of assistance with the same air of simple self-reliance he had displayed throughout, Tennessee's Partner lifted the rough coffin on his back, and deposited it unaided within the shallow grave. He then nailed down the board which served as a lid, and mounting the little mound of earth beside it, took off his hat and slowly mopped his face with his handkerchief. This the crowd felt was a preliminary to speech, and they disposed themselves variously on stumps and boulders, and sat expectant.

"When a man," began Tennessee's Partner slowly, "has been running free all day, what's the natural thing for him to do? Why, to come home. And if he ain't in a condition to go home, what can his best friend do? Why, bring him home. And here's Tennessee has been running free, and we brings him home from his wandering." He paused and picked up a fragment of quartz, rubbed it thoughtfully on his sleeve, and went on: "It ain't the first time that I've packed him on my back, as you see'd me now. It ain't the first time that I brought him to this yer cabin when he couldn't help himself; it ain't the first time that I and Jinny have waited for him on yon hill, and picked him up and fetched him home, when he couldn't speak and didn't know me. And now that it's the last time, why"—he paused and rubbed the quartz gently on his sleeve—"you see it's sort of rough on his pardner. And now, gentlemen," he added abruptly, picking up his long-handled shovel, "the fun'l's over; and my thanks, and Tennessee's thanks, to you for your trouble."

Resisting any proffers of assistance, he began to fill in the grave, turning his back upon the crowd, that after a few moments' hesitation, gradually withdrew. As they crossed the little ridge that hid Sandy Bar from view, some, looking back, thought they could see Tennessee's Partner, his work done, sitting upon the grave, his shovel between his knees, and his face buried in his red bandana handkerchief. But it was argued by others that you couldn't tell his face from his handkerchief at that distance, and this point remained undecided.

In the reaction that followed the feverish excitement of that day, Tennessee's Partner was not forgotten. A secret investigation had cleared him of any complicity in Tennessee's guilt, and left only a suspicion of his general sanity. Sandy Bar made a point of calling on him, and proffering various uncouth but well-meant kindnesses. But from that day his rude health and great strength seemed visibly to decline; and when the rainy season fairly set in, and the tiny grass-blades were beginning to peep from the rocky mound above Tennessee's grave, he took to his bed.

One night, when the pines beside the cabin were swaying in the storm and trailing their slender fingers over the roof, and the roar and rush of the swollen river were heard below, Tennessee's Partner lifted his head from the pillow, saying, "It is time to go for Tennessee; I must put Jinny in the cart"; and would have risen from his bed but for the restraint of his attendant. Struggling, he still pursued his singular fancy: "There, now, steady, Jinny,—steady, old girl. How dark it is! Look out for the ruts,—and look out for him, too, old gal. Sometimes, you know, when he's blind drunk, he drops down right in the trail. Keep on straight up to the pine on the top of the hill. Thar! I told you so!—thar he is,—coming this way, too,—all by himself, sober, and his face a-shining. Tennessee! Pardner!"

And so they met.

QUESTIONS

1. Compare the reaction of Tennessee's Partner to the desertion of his wife to his reaction to the death of his partner. Is this story an example of the essentially anti-woman orientation of frontier and Western stories?

2. Tennessee's Partner has no name of his own. The Virginian and the Lone Ranger are similarly without names. Why, do you think, are many Western story heroes essentially nameless? Is each a kind of Everyman, symbolic of a type, a class, or of almost all humanity?

3. Why is Tennessee's captor and judge called Judge Lynch? Why do almost all frontier or Western stories seem to approve, or at least to extenuate, lynch law?

4. During the nineteenth century, many characters in fiction died of "broken hearts." In contemporary fiction, such deaths are almost never found. How do you account for the change?

5. Bret Harte's stories were among the first and most popular representations of the California gold rush days. His characters

were oversimplified, sentimentalized, and frequently faintly ridiculous. How does the humorous tone of "Tennessee's Partner" compare with the tone of the modern Western? Compare "Tennessee's Partner" with "Stage to Lordsburg" (p. 188).

JACK LONDON

ALL GOLD CANYON

It was the green heart of the canyon, where the walls swerved back from the rigid plan and relieved their harshness of line by making a little sheltered nook and filling it to the brim with sweetness and roundness and softness. Here all things rested. Even the narrow stream ceased its turbulent down-rush long enough to form a quiet pool. Knee-deep in the water, with drooping head and half-shut eyes, drowsed a red-coated, many-antlered buck.

On one side, beginning at the very lip of the pool, was a tiny meadow, a cool, resilient surface of green that extended to the base of the frowning wall. Beyond the pool a gentle slope of earth ran up and up to meet the opposing wall. Fine grass covered the slope—grass that was spangled with flowers, with here and there patches of color, orange and purple and golden. Below, the canyon was shut in. There was no view. The walls leaned together abruptly and the canyon ended in a chaos of rocks, moss-covered and hidden by a green screen of vines and creepers and boughs of trees. Up the canyon rose far hills and peaks, the big foothills, pine-covered and remote. And far beyond, like clouds upon the border of the sky, towered minarets of white, where the Sierra's eternal snows flashed austerely the blazes of the sun.

There was no dust in the canyon. The leaves and flowers were clean and virginal. The grass was young velvet. Over the pool three cottonwoods sent their snowy fluffs fluttering down the quiet air. On the slope the blossoms of the wine-wooded manzanita filled the air with springtime odors, while the leaves, wise with experience, were already beginning their vertical twist against the coming aridity of summer. In the open spaces on the slope, beyond the farthest shadow-reach of the manzanita, poised the mariposa lilies, like so many flights of jewelled moths suddenly arrested and on the verge of trembling into flight again. Here and there that woods harlequin, the madrone, permitting itself to be caught in the act of changing its pea-green trunk to madder-red, breathed its fragrance into the air from great clusters of waxen bells. Creamy white were these bells, shaped like lilies-of-the-valley, with the sweetness of perfume that is of the springtime.

There was not a sigh of wind. The air was drowsy with its weight of perfume. It was a sweetness that would have been cloying had the air been heavy and humid. But the air was sharp and thin. It was as starlight transmuted into atmosphere, shot through and warmed by sunshine, and flower-drenched with sweetness.

An occasional butterfly drifted in and out through the patches of light and shade. And from all about rose the low and sleepy hum of mountain bees—feasting Sybarites that jostled one another good-naturedly at the board, nor found time for rough discourtesy. So quietly did the little stream drip and ripple its way through the canyon that it spoke only in faint and occasional gurgles. The voice of the stream was a drowsy whisper, ever interrupted by dozings and silences, ever lifted again in the awakenings.

The motion of all things was a drifting in the heart of the canyon. Sunshine and butterflies drifted in and out among the trees. The hum of the bees and the whisper of the stream were a drifting of sound. And the drifting sound and drifting color seemed to weave together in the making of a delicate and intangible fabric which was the spirit of the place. It was a spirit of peace that was not of death, but of smooth-pulsing life, of quietude that was not silence, of movement that was not action, of repose that was quick with existence without being violent with struggle and travail. The spirit of the place was the spirit of the peace of the living, somnolent with the easement and content of prosperity, and undisturbed by rumors of far wars.

The red-coated, many-antlered buck acknowledged the lordship of the spirit of the place and dozed knee-deep in the cool, shaded pool. There seemed no flies to vex him and he was languid with rest. Sometimes his ears moved when the stream awoke and whispered; but they moved lazily, with foreknowledge that it was merely the stream grown garrulous at discovery that it had slept.

But there came a time when the buck's ears lifted and tensed with swift eagerness for sound. His head was turned down the canyon. His sensitive, quivering nostrils scented the air. His eyes could not pierce the green screen through which the stream rippled away, but to his ears came the voice of a man. It was a steady, monotonous, singsong voice. Once the buck heard the harsh clash of metal upon rock. At the sound he snorted with a sudden start that jerked him through the air from water to meadow, and his feet sank into the young velvet, while he pricked his ears and again scented the air. Then he stole across the tiny meadow, pausing once and again to listen, and faded away out of the canyon like a wraith, soft-footed and without sound.

The clash of steel-shod soles against the rocks began to be heard, and the man's voice grew louder. It was raised in a sort of chant and became distinct with nearness, so that the words could be heard:

> "Tu'n around an' tu'n yo' face
> Untoe them sweet hills of grace
>   (D' pow'rs of sin yo' am scornin'!).
> Look about an' look aroun'
> Fling yo' sin-pack on d' groun'
>   (Yo' will meet wid d' Lord in d' mornin'!)."

A sound of scrambling accompanied the song, and the spirit of the place fled away on the heels of the red-coated buck. The green screen was burst asunder, and a man peered out at the meadow and the pool and the sloping side-hill. He was a deliberate sort of man. He took in the scene with one embracing glance, then ran his eyes over the details to verify the general impression. Then, and not until then, did he open his mouth in vivid and solemn approval:

"Smoke of life an' snakes of purgatory! Will you just look at that! Wood an' water an' grass an' a side-hill! A pocket-hunter's delight an' a cayuse's paradise! Cool green for tired eyes! Pink pills for pale people ain't in it. A secret pasture for prospectors and a resting-place for tired burros. It's just booful!"

He was a sandy-complexioned man in whose face geniality and humor seemed the salient characteristics. It was a mobile face, quick-changing to inward mood and thought. Thinking was in him a visible process. Ideas chased across his face like wind-flaws across the surface of a lake. His hair, sparse and unkempt of growth, was as indeterminate and colorless as his complexion. It would seem that all the color of his frame had gone into his eyes, for they were startlingly blue. Also, they were laughing and merry eyes, within them much of the naiveté and wonder of the child; and yet, in an unassertive way, they contained much of calm self-reliance and strength of purpose founded upon self-experience and experience of the world.

From out the screen of vines and creepers he flung ahead of him a miner's pick and shovel and gold-pan. Then he crawled out himself into the open. He was clad in faded overalls and black cotton shirt, with hobnailed brogans on his feet, and on his head a hat whose shapelessness and stains advertised the rough usage of wind and rain and sun and camp-smoke. He stood erect, seeing wide-eyed the secrecy of the scene and sensuously inhaling the warm, sweet breath of the canyon-garden through nostrils that dilated and quivered with delight. His eyes narrowed to laughing slits of blue, his face wreathed itself in joy, and his mouth curled in a smile as he cried aloud:

"Jumping dandelions and happy hollyhocks, but that smells good to me! Talk about your attar o' roses an' cologne factories! They ain't in it!"

He had the habit of soliloquy. His quick-changing facial expressions might tell every thought and mood, but the tongue, perforce, ran hard after, repeating, like a second Boswell.

The man lay down on the lip of the pool and drank long and deep of its water. "Tastes good to me," he murmured, lifting his head and gazing across the pool at the side-hill, while he wiped his mouth with the back of his hand. The side-hill attracted his attention. Still lying on his stomach, he studied the hill formation long and carefully. It was a practised eye that traveled up the slope to the crumbling canyon-wall and back and down again to the edge of the pool. He scrambled to his feet and favored the side-hill with a second survey.

"Looks good to me," he concluded, picking up his pick and shovel and gold-pan.

He crossed the stream below the pool, stepping agilely from stone to stone. Where the side-hill touched the water he dug up a shovelful of dirt and put it into the gold-pan. He squatted down, holding the pan in his two hands, and partly immersing it in the stream. Then he imparted to the pan a deft circular motion that sent the water sluicing in and out through the dirt and gravel. The larger and the lighter particles worked to the surface, and these, by a skilful dipping movement of the pan, he spilled out and over the edge. Occasionally, to expedite matters, he rested the pan and with his fingers raked out the large pebbles and pieces of rock.

The contents of the pan diminished rapidly until only fine dirt and the smallest bits of gravel remained. At this stage he began to work very deliberately and carefully. It was fine washing, and he washed fine and finer, with a keen scrutiny and delicate and fastidious touch. At last the pan seemed empty of everything but water; but with a quick semi-circular flirt that sent the water flying over the shallow rim into the stream, he disclosed a layer of black sand on the bottom of the pan. So thin was this layer that it was like a streak of paint. He examined it closely. In the midst of it was a tiny golden speck. He dribbled a little water in over the depressed edge of the pan. With a quick flirt he sent the water sluicing across the bottom, turning the grains of black sand over and over. A second tiny golden speck rewarded his effort.

The washing had now become very fine—fine beyond all need of ordinary placer mining. He worked the black sand, a small portion at a time, up the shallow rim of the pan. Each small portion he examined sharply, so that his eyes saw every grain of it before he allowed it to slide over the edge and away. Jealously, bit by bit, he let the black sand slip away. A golden speck, no larger than a pin-point, appeared on the rim, and by his manipulation of the water it returned to the bottom of the pan. And in such fashion another speck was disclosed, and another. Great was his care of them. Like a shepherd he herded his flock of golden specks so that not one should be lost. At last, of the pan of dirt nothing remained but his golden herd. He counted it, and then, after all his labor, sent it flying out of the pan with one final swirl of water.

But his blue eyes were shining with desire as he rose to his feet. "Seven," he muttered aloud, asserting the sum of the specks for which he had toiled so hard and which he had so wantonly thrown away. "Seven," he repeated, with the emphasis of one trying to impress a number on his memory.

He stood still a long while, surveying the hillside. In his eyes was a curiosity, new-aroused and burning. There was an exultance about his bearing and a keenness like that of a hunting animal catching the fresh scent of game.

He moved down the stream a few steps and took a second panful of dirt.

Again came the careful washing, the jealous herding of the golden specks, and the wantonness with which he sent them flying into the stream. His golden herd diminished. "Four, five," he muttered, and repeated, "five."

He could not forbear another survey of the hill before filling the pan farther down the stream. His golden herds diminished. "Four, three, two, two, one," were his memory tabulations as he moved down the stream. When but one speck of gold rewarded his washing, he stopped and built a fire of dry twigs. Into this he thrust the gold-pan and burned it till it was blue-black. He held up the pan and examined it critically. Then he nodded approbation. Against such a color-background he could defy the tiniest yellow speck to elude him.

Still moving down the stream, he panned again. A single speck was his reward. A third pan contained no gold at all. Not satisfied with this, he panned three times again, taking his shovels of dirt within a foot of one another. Each pan proved empty of gold, and the fact, instead of discouraging him, seemed to give him satisfaction. His elation increased with each barren washing, until he arose, exclaiming jubilantly:

"If it ain't the real thing, may God knock off my head with sour apples!"

Returning to where he had started operations, he began to pan up the stream. At first his golden herds increased—increased prodigiously. "Fourteen, eighteen, twenty-one, twenty-six," ran his memory tabulations. Just above the pool he struck his richest pan—thirty-five colors.

"Almost enough to save," he remarked regretfully as he allowed the water to sweep them away.

The sun climbed to the top of the sky. The man worked on. Pan by pan, he went up the stream, the tally of results steadily decreasing.

"It's just booful, the way it peters out," he exulted when a shovelful of dirt contained no more than a single speck of gold.

And when no specks at all were found in several pans, he straightened up and favored the hillside with a confident glance.

"Ah, ha! Mr. Pocket!" he cried out, as though to an auditor hidden somewhere above him beneath the surface of the slope. "Ah, ha! Mr. Pocket! I'm a-comin', I'm a-comin', an' I'm shorely gwine to get yer! You heah me, Mr. Pocket? I'm gwine to get yer as shore as punkins ain't cauliflowers!"

He turned and flung a measuring glance at the sun poised above him in the azure of the cloudless sky. Then he went down the canyon, following the line of shovel-holes he had made in filling the pans. He crossed the stream below the pool and disappeared through the green screen. There was little opportunity for the spirit of the place to return with its quietude and repose, for the man's voice, raised in ragtime song, still dominated the canyon with possession.

After a time, with a greater clashing of steel-shod feet on rock, he returned. The green screen was tremendously agitated. It surged back and forth in the throes of a struggle. There was a loud grating and clanging of metal. The man's voice leaped to a higher pitch and was sharp with imperativeness. A large body plunged and panted. There was a snapping and ripping and rending, and amid a shower of falling leaves a horse burst through the screen. On its back was a pack, and from this trailed broken vines and torn creepers. The animal gazed with astonished eyes at the scene into which it had been precipitated, then dropped its head to the grass and began contentedly to graze. A second horse scrambled into view, slipping once on the mossy rocks and regaining equilibrium when its hoofs sank into the yielding surface of the meadow. It was riderless, though on its back was a high-horned Mexican saddle, scarred and discolored by long usage.

The man brought up the rear. He threw off pack and saddle, with an eye to camp location, and gave the animals their freedom to graze. He unpacked his food and got out frying-pan and coffee-pot. He gathered an armful of dry wood, and with a few stones made a place for his fire.

"My!" he said, "but I've got an appetite. I could scoff iron-filings an' horseshoe nails an' thank you kindly, ma'am, for a second helpin'."

He straightened up, and, while he reached for matches in the pocket of his overalls, his eyes traveled across the pool to the side-hill. His fingers had clutched the match-box, but they relaxed their hold and the hand came out empty. The man wavered perceptibly. He looked at his preparations for cooking and he looked at the hill.

"Guess I'll take another whack at her," he concluded, starting to cross the stream.

"They ain't no sense in it, I know," he mumbled apologetically. "But keepin' grub back an hour ain't goin' to hurt none, I reckon."

A few feet back from his first of test-pans he started a second line.

The sun dropped down the western sky, the shadows lengthened, but the man worked on. He began a third line of test-pans. He was cross-cutting the hillside, line by line, as he ascended. The center of each line produced the richest pans, while the ends came where no colors showed in the pan. And as he ascended the hillside the lines grew perceptibly shorter. The regularity with which their length diminished served to indicate that somewhere up the slope the last line would be so short as to have scarcely length at all, and that beyond could come only a point. The design was growing into an inverted "V." The converging sides of this "V" marked the boundaries of the gold-bearing dirt.

The apex of the "V" was evidently the man's goal. Often he ran his eye along the converging sides and on up the hill, trying to divine the apex, the point where the gold-bearing dirt must cease. Here resided "Mr. Pocket"—for so the man familiarly addressed the imaginary point above him on the slope, crying out:

"Come down out o' that, Mr. Pocket! Be right smart an' agreeable, an' come down!"

"All right," he would add later, in a voice resigned to determination. "All right, Mr. Pocket. It's plain to me I got to come right up an' snatch you out bald-headed. An' I'll do it! I'll do it!" he would threaten still later.

Each pan he carried down to the water to wash, and as he went higher up the hill the pans grew richer, until he began to save the gold in an empty baking powder can which he carried carelessly in his hip-pocket. So engrossed was he in his toil that he did not notice the long twilight of oncoming night. It was not until he tried vainly to see the gold colors in the bottom of the pan that he realized the passage of time. He straightened up abruptly. An expression of whimsical wonderment and awe overspread his face as he drawled:

"Gosh darn my buttons! if I didn't plumb forget dinner!"

He stumbled across the stream in the darkness and lighted his long-delayed fire. Flapjacks and bacon and warmed-over beans constituted his supper. Then he smoked a pipe by the smouldering coals, listening to the night noises and watching the moonlight stream through the canyon. After that he unrolled his bed, took off his heavy shoes, and pulled the blankets up to his chin. His face showed white in the moonlight, like the face of a corpse. But it was a corpse that knew its resurrection, for the man rose suddenly on one elbow and gazed across at his hillside.

"Good night, Mr. Pocket," he called sleepily. "Good night."

He slept through the early gray of morning until the direct rays of the sun smote his closed eyelids, when he awoke with a start and looked about him until he had established the continuity of his existence and identified his present self with the days previously lived.

To dress, he had merely to buckle on his shoes. He glanced at his fireplace and at his hillside, wavered, but fought down the temptation and started the fire.

"Keep yer shirt on, Bill; keep yer shirt on," he admonished himself. "What's the good of rushin'? No use in gettin' all het up an' sweaty. Mr. Pocket 'll wait for you. He ain't a-runnin' away before you can get your breakfast. Now, what you want, Bill, is something fresh in yer bill o' fare. So it's up to you to go an' get it."

He cut a short pole at the water's edge and drew from one of his pockets a bit of line and a draggled fly that had once been a royal coachman.

"Mebbe they'll bite in the early morning," he muttered, as he made his first cast into the pool. And a moment later he was gleefully crying: "What 'd I tell you, eh? What 'd I tell you?"

He had no reel, nor any inclination to waste time, and by main strength, and swiftly, he drew out of the water a flashing ten-inch trout. Three more, caught in rapid succession, furnished his breakfast. When he came to the stepping-stones on his way to his hillside, he was struck by a sudden thought, and paused.

"I'd just better take a hike down-stream a ways," he said. "There's no tellin' who may be snoopin' around."

But he crossed over on the stones, and with a "I really oughter take that hike," the need of the precaution passed out of his mind and he fell to work.

At nightfall he straightened up. The small of his back was stiff from stooping toil, and as he put his hand behind him to soothe the protesting muscles, he said:

"Now what d'ye think of that? I clean forgot my dinner again! If I don't watch out, I'll sure be degeneratin' into a two-meal-a-day crank.

"Pockets is the hangedest things I ever see for makin' a man absent-minded," he communed that night, as he crawled into his blankets. Nor did he forget to call up the hillside, "Good night, Mr. Pocket! Good night!"

Rising with the sun, and snatching a hasty breakfast, he was early at work. A fever seemed to be growing in him, nor did the increasing richness of the test-pans allay this fever. There was a flush in his cheek other than that made by the heat of the sun, and he was oblivious to fatigue and the passage of time. When he filled a pan with dirt, he ran down the hill to wash it; nor could he forbear running up the hill again, panting and stumbling profanely, to refill the pan.

He was now a hundred yards from the water, and the inverted "V" was assuming definite proportions. The width of the paydirt steadily decreased, and the man extended in his mind's eye the sides of the "V" to their meeting place far up the hill. This was his goal, the apex of the "V," and he panned many times to locate it.

"Just about two yards above that manzanita bush an' a yard to the right," he finally concluded.

Then the temptation seized him. "As plain as the nose on your face," he said, as he abandoned his laborious cross-cutting and climbed to the indicated apex. He filled a pan and carried it down the hill to wash. It contained no trace of gold. He dug deep, and he dug shallow, filling and washing a dozen pans, and was unrewarded even by the tiniest golden speck. He was enraged at having yielded to the temptation, and berated himself blasphemously and pridelessly. Then he went down the hill and took up the cross-cutting.

"Slow an' certain, Bill; slow an' certain," he crooned. "Shortcuts to fortune ain't in your line, an' it's about time you know it. Get wise, Bill; get wise. Slow an' certain's the only hand you can play; so get to it, an' keep to it, too."

As the cross-cuts decreased, showing that the sides of the "V" were converging, the depth of the "V" increased. The gold-trace was dipping into the hill. It was only at thirty inches beneath the surface that he could get colors in his pan. The dirt he found at twenty-five inches from the surface, and at thirty-five inches yielded barren pans. At the base of the "V," by the water's edge, he had found the gold colors at the grass roots. The higher he went up the hill, the deeper the gold dipped. To dig a hole three feet deep in order to get one test-pan was a task of no mean magnitude; while between the man and the apex intervened an untold number of such holes to be dug. "An' there's no tellin' how much deeper it'll pitch," he sighed, in a moment's pause, while his fingers soothed his aching back.

Feverish with desire, with aching back and stiffening muscles, with pick and shovel gouging and mauling the soft brown earth, the man toiled up the hill. Before him was the smooth slope, spangled with flowers and made sweet with their breath. Behind him was devastation. It looked like some terrible eruption breaking out on the smooth skin of the hill. His slow progress was like that of a slug, befouling beauty with a monstrous trail.

Though the dipping gold-trace increased the man's work, he found consolation in the increasing richness of the pans. Twenty cents, thirty cents, fifty cents, sixty cents, were the values of the gold found in the pans, and at nightfall he washed his banner pan, which gave him a dollar's worth of gold-dust from a shovelful of dirt.

"I'll just bet it's my luck to have some inquisitive one come buttin' in here on my pasture," he mumbled sleepily that night as he pulled the blankets up to his chin.

Suddenly he sat upright. "Bill!" he called sharply. "Now, listen to me, Bill; d'ye hear! It's up to you, to-morrow mornin', to mosey round

an' see what you can see. Understand? To-morrow morning, an' don't
you forget it!"

He yawned and glanced across at his side-hill. "Good night, Mr.
Pocket," he called.

In the morning he stole a march on the sun, for he had finished
breakfast when its first rays caught him, and he was climbing the wall
of the canyon where it crumbled away and gave footing. From the
outlook at the top he found himself in the midst of loneliness. As far
as he could see, chain after chain of mountains heaved themselves
into his vision. To the east his eyes, leaping the miles between range
and range and between many ranges, brought up at least against the
white-peaked Sierras—the main crest, where the backbone of the
Western world reared itself against the sky. To the north and south he
could see more distinctly the cross-systems that broke through the
main trend of the sea of mountains. To the west the ranges fell away,
one behind the other, diminishing and fading into the gentle foothills
that, in turn, descended into the great valley which he could not see.

And in all that mighty sweep of earth he saw no sign of man nor
of the handiwork of man—save only the torn bosom of the hillside at
his feet. The man looked long and carefully. Once, far down his own
canyon, he thought he saw in the air a faint hint of smoke. He looked
again and decided that it was the purple haze of the hills made dark
by a convolution of the canyon wall at its back.

"Hey, you, Mr. Pocket!" he called down into the canyon. "Stand
out from under! I'm a-comin', Mr. Pocket! I'm a-comin'!"

The heavy brogans on the man's feet made him appear clumsy-
footed, but he swung down from the giddy height as lightly and airily
as a mountain goat. A rock, turning under his foot on the edge of the
precipice, did not disconcert him. He seemed to know the precise
time required for the turn to culminate in disaster, and in the
meantime he utilized the false footing itself for the momentary
earth-contact necessary to carry him on into safety. Where the earth
sloped so steeply that it was impossible to stand for a second upright,
the man did not hesitate. His foot pressed the impossible surface for
but a fraction of the fatal second and gave him the bound that carried
him onward. Again, where even the fraction of a second's footing was
out of the question, he would swing his body past by a moment's
hand-grip on a jutting knob of rock, a crevice, or a precariously rooted
shrub. At last, with a wild leap and yell, he exchanged the face of the
wall for an earthslide and finished the descent in the midst of several
tons of sliding earth and gravel.

His first pan of the morning washed out over two dollars in coarse
gold. It was from the centre of the "V." To either side the diminution
in the values of the pans was swift. His lines of cross-cutting holes were
growing very short. The converging sides of the inverted "V" were

only a few yards apart. Their meeting-point was only a few yards
above him. But the pay-streak was dipping deeper and deeper into the
earth. By early afternoon he was sinking the test-holes five feet before
the pans could show the gold-trace.

For that matter, the gold-trace had become something more than
a trace; it was a placer mine in itself, and the man resolved to come
back after he had found the pocket and work over the ground. But the
increasing richness of the pans began to worry him. By late afternoon
the worth of the pans had grown to three and four dollars. The man
scratched his head perplexedly and looked a few feet up the hill at the
manzanita bush that marked approximately the apex of the "V." He
nodded his head and said oracularly:

"It's one o' two things, Bill: one o' two things. Either Mr.
Pocket's spilled himself all out an' down the hill, or else Mr. Pocket's
so rich you maybe won't be able to carry him all away with you. And
that 'd be an awful shame, wouldn't it, now?" He chuckled at
contemplation of so pleasant a dilemma.

Nightfall found him by the edge of the stream, his eyes wrestling
with the gathering darkness over the washing of a five-dollar pan.

"Wisht I had an electric light to go on working," he said.

He found sleep difficult that night. Many times he composed
himself and closed his eyes for slumber to overtake him; but his blood
pounded with too strong desire, and as many times his eyes opened
and he murmured wearily, "Wisht it was sun-up."

Sleep came to him in the end, but his eyes were open with the
first paling of the stars, and the gray of dawn caught him with
breakfast finished and climbing the hillside in the direction of the
secret abiding-place of Mr. Pocket.

The first cross-cut the man made, there was space for only three
holes, so narrow had become the pay-streak and so close was he to the
fountainhead of the golden stream he had been following for four
days.

"Be ca'm, Bill; be ca'm," he admonished himself, as he broke
ground for the final hole where the sides of the "V" had at last come
together in a point.

"I've got the almighty cinch on you, Mr. Pocket, an' you can't
lose me," he said many times as he sank the hole deeper and deeper.

Four feet, five feet, six feet, he dug his way down into the earth.
The digging grew harder. His pick grated on broken rock. He
examined the rock. "Rotten quartz," was his conclusion as, with the
shovel, he cleared the bottom of the hole of loose dirt. He attacked
the crumbling quartz with the pick, bursting the disintegrating rock
asunder with every stroke.

He thrust his shovel into the loose mass. His eye caught a gleam
of yellow. He dropped the shovel and squatted suddenly on his heels.

As a farmer rubs the clinging earth from fresh-dug potatoes, so the man, a piece of rotten quartz held in both hands, rubbed the dirt away.

"Sufferin' Sardanopolis!" he cried. "Lumps an' chunks of it! Lumps an' chunks of it!"

It was only half rock he held in his hand. The other half was virgin gold. He dropped it into his pan and examined another piece. Little yellow was to be seen, but with his strong fingers he crumbled the quartz away till both hands were filled with glowing yellow. He rubbed the dirt away from fragment after fragment, tossing them into the gold-pan. It was a treasure-hole. So much had the quartz rotted away that there was less of it than there was of gold. Now and again he found a piece to which no rock clung—a piece that was all gold. A chunk, where the pick had laid open the heart of the gold, glittered like a handful of yellow jewels, and he cocked his head at it and slowly turned it around and over to observe the rich play of the light upon it.

"Talk about yer Too Much Gold diggin's!" the man snorted contemptuously. "Why, this diggin' 'd make it look like thirty cents. This diggin' is All Gold. An' right here an' now I name this yere canyon 'All Gold Canyon,' b' gosh!"

Still squatting on his heels, he continued examining the fragments and tossing them into the pan. Suddenly there came to him a premonition of danger. It seemed a shadow had fallen upon him. But there was no shadow. His heart had given a great jump up into his throat and was choking him. Then his blood slowly chilled and he felt the sweat of his shirt cold against his flesh.

He did not spring up nor look around. He did not move. He was considering the nature of the premonition he had received, trying to locate the source of the mysterious force that had warned him, striving to sense the imperative presence of the unseen thing that threatened him. There is an aura of things hostile, made manifest by messengers too refined for the senses to know; and this aura he felt, but knew not how he felt it. His was the feeling as when a cloud passes over the sun. It seemed that between him and life had passed something dark and smothering and menacing; a gloom, as it were, that swallowed up life and made for death—his death.

Every force of his being impelled him to spring up and confront the unseen danger, but his soul dominated the panic, and he remained squatting on his heels, in his hands a chunk of gold. He did not dare to look around, but he knew by now that there was something behind him and above him. He made believe to be interested in the gold in his hand. He examined it critically, turned it over and over, and rubbed the dirt from it. And all the time he knew that something behind him was looking at the gold over his shoulder.

Still feigning interest in the chunk of gold in his hand, he listened intently and he heard the breathing of the thing behind him. His eyes searched the ground in front of him for a weapon, but they saw only the uprooted gold, worthless to him now in his extremity. There was his pick, a handy weapon on occasion; but this was not such an occasion. The man realized his predicament. He was in a narrow hole that was seven feet deep. His head did not come to the surface of the ground. He was in a trap.

He remained squatting on his heels. He was quite cool and collected; but his mind, considering every factor, showed him only his helplessness. He continued rubbing the dirt from the quartz fragments and throwing the gold into the pan. There was nothing else for him to do. Yet he knew that he would have to rise up, sooner or later, and face the danger that breathed at his back. The minutes passed, and with the passage of each minute he knew that by so much he was nearer the time when he must stand up, or else—and his wet shirt went cold against his flesh again at the thought—or else he might receive death as he stooped there over his treasure.

Still he squatted on his heels, rubbing dirt from gold and debating in just what manner he should rise up. He might rise up with a rush and claw his way out of the hole to meet whatever threatened on the even footing above ground. Or he might rise up slowly and carelessly, and feign casually to discover the thing that breathed at his back. His instinct and every fighting fibre of his body favored the mad, clawing rush to the surface. His intellect, and the craft thereof, favored the slow and cautious meeting with the thing that menaced and which he could not see. And while he debated, a loud, crashing noise burst on his ear. At the same instant he received a stunning blow on the left side of his back, and from the point of impact felt a rush of flame through his flesh. He sprang up in the air, but halfway to his feet collapsed. His body crumpled in like a leaf withered in sudden heat, and he came down, his chest across his pan of gold, his face in the dirt and rock, his legs tangled and twisted because of the restricted space at the bottom of the hole. His legs twitched convulsively several times. His body was shaken with a mighty ague. There was a slow expansion of the lungs, accompanied by a deep sigh. Then the air was slowly, very slowly, exhaled, and his body as slowly flattened itself down into inertness.

Above, revolver in hand, a man was peering down over the edge of the hole. He peered for a long time at the prone and motionless body beneath him. After a while the stranger sat down on the edge of the hole so that he could see into it, and rested the revolver on his knee. Reaching his hand into a pocket, he drew out a wisp of brown paper. Into this he dropped a few crumbs of tobacco. The combination became a cigarette, brown and squat, with the ends turned in. Not once did he take his eyes from the body at the bottom of the hole. He lighted the cigarette and drew its smoke into his lungs with a caressing intake of the breath. He smoked slowly. Once the cigarette went out and he relighted it. And all the while he studied the body beneath him.

In the end he tossed the cigarette stub away and rose to his feet. He moved to the edge of the hole. Spanning it, a hand resting on each edge, and with the revolver still in the right hand, he muscled his body down into the hole. While his feet were yet a yard from the bottom he released his hands and dropped down.

At the instant his feet struck bottom he saw the pocket-miner's arm leap out, and his own legs knew a swift, jerking grip that overthrew him. In the nature of the jump his revolver-hand was above his head. Swiftly as the grip had flashed about his legs, just as swiftly he brought the revolver down. He was still in the air, his fall in process of completion, when he pulled the trigger. The explosion was deafening in the confined space. The smoke filled the hole so that he could see nothing. He struck the bottom on his back, and like a cat's the pocket-miner's body was on top of him. Even as the miner's body passed on top, the stranger crooked in his right arm to fire; and even in that instant the miner, with a quick thrust of elbow, struck his wrist. The muzzle was thrown up and the bullet thudded into the dirt of the side of the hole.

The next instant the stranger felt the miner's hand grip his wrist. The struggle was now for the revolver. Each man strove to turn it against the other's body. The smoke in the hole was clearing. The stranger, lying on his back, was beginning to see dimly. But suddenly he was blinded by a handful of dirt deliberately flung into his eyes by his antagonist. In that moment of shock his grip on the revolver was broken. In the next moment he felt a smashing darkness descend upon his brain, and in the midst of the darkness even the darkness ceased.

But the pocket-miner fired again and again, until the revolver was empty. Then he tossed it from him and, breathing heavily, sat down on the dead man's legs.

The miner was sobbing and struggling for breath. "Measly skunk!" he panted; "a-campin' on my trail an' lettin' me do the work, an' then shootin' me in the back!"

He was half crying from anger and exhaustion. He peered at the face of the dead man. It was sprinkled with loose dirt and gravel, and it was difficult to distinguish the features.

"Never laid eyes on him before," the miner concluded his scrutiny. "Just a common an' ordinary thief, hang him! An' he shot me in the back! He shot me in the back!"

He opened his shirt and felt himself, front and back, on his left side.

"Went clean through, and no harm done!" he cried jubilantly. "I'll bet he aimed all right all right; but he drew the gun over when he pulled the trigger—the cur! But I fixed 'm! Oh, I fixed 'm!"

His fingers were investigating the bullet-hole in his side, and a shade of regret passed over his face. "It's goin' to be stiffer'n hell," he said. "An' it's up to me to get mended an' get out o' here."

He crawled out of the hole and went down the hill to his camp. Half an hour later he returned, leading his pack-horse. His open shirt disclosed the rude bandages with which he had dressed his wound. He was slow and awkward with his left-hand movements, but that did not prevent his using the arm.

The bight of the pack-rope under the dead man's shoulders enabled him to heave the body out of the hole. Then he set to work gathering up his gold. He worked steadily for several hours, pausing often to rest his stiffening shoulder and to exclaim:

"He shot me in the back, the measly skunk! He shot me in the back!"

When his treasure was quite cleaned up and wrapped securely into a number of blanket-covered parcels, he made an estimate of its value.

"Four hundred pounds, or I'm a Hottentot," he concluded. "Say two hundred in quartz an' dirt—that leaves two hundred pounds of gold. Bill! Wake up! Two hundred pounds of gold! Forty thousand dollars! An' it's yourn—all yourn!"

He scratched his head delightedly and his fingers blundered into an unfamiliar groove. They quested along it for several inches. It was a crease through his scalp where the second bullet had ploughed.

He walked angrily over to the dead man.

"You would, would you?" he bullied. "You would, eh? Well, I fixed you good an' plenty, an' I'll give you a decent burial, too. That's more'n you'd have done for me."

He dragged the body to the edge of the hole and toppled it in. It struck the bottom with a dull crash, on its side, the face twisted up to the light. The miner peered down at it.

"An' you shot me in the back!" he said accusingly.

With pick and shovel he filled the hole. Then he loaded the gold on his horse. It was too great a load for the animal, and when he had gained his camp he transferred part of it to his saddle-horse. Even so, he was compelled to abandon a portion of his outfit—pick and shovel and gold-pan, extra food and cooking utensils, and divers odds and ends.

The sun was at the zenith when the man forced the horses at the screen of vines and creepers. To climb the huge boulders the animals were compelled to uprear and struggle blindly through the tangled mass of vegetation. Once the saddle-horse fell heavily and the man removed the pack to get the animal on its feet. After it started on its way again the man thrust his head out from among the leaves and peered up at the hillside.

"The measly skunk!" he said, and disappeared.

There was a ripping and tearing of vines and boughs. The trees surged back and forth, marking the passage of the animals through the midst of them. There was a clashing of steel-shod hoofs on stone, and now and again a sharp cry of command. Then the voice of the man was raised in song:—

> "Tu'n around an' tu'n yo' face
> Untoe them sweet hills of grace
> (D' pow'rs of sin yo' am scornin'!).
> Look about an' look aroun'
> Fling yo' sin-pack on d' groun'
> (Yo' will meet wid d' Lord in d' mornin'!)."

The song grew faint and fainter, and through the silence crept back the spirit of the place. The stream once more drowsed and whispered; the hum of the mountain bees rose sleepily. Down through the perfume-weighted air fluttered the snowy fluffs of the cottonwoods. The butterflies drifted in and out among the trees, and over all blazed the quiet sunshine. Only remained the hoof-marks in the meadow and the torn hillside to mark the boisterous trail of the life that had broken the peace of the place and passed on.

QUESTIONS

1. How does London succeed in making a solitary man an attractive and sympathetic character? How is the miner's character revealed in speech and action?

2. Why do lone prospectors have "the habit of soliloquy"? Could this habit have any relation to the fact that some of the best-known works of English literature have been written in prisons?

3. Good writers of popular fiction frequently have an article-writer's skill in describing and dramatizing scientific or technical operations. Does London succeed in making clear the exact procedure the miner followed in locating and excavating "Mr. Pocket"? What visual image does he use repeatedly?

4. Compare the beginning of "All Gold Canyon" with that of "The Indian Well" (p. 290). How do the attitudes toward nature and the descriptions of it differ in the two stories?

5. Using the same two stories, compare the miner's attitude toward his horses ("All Gold Canyon") with Suttler's attitude toward his burro ("The Indian Well"). Compare both with Owen Wister's comments in "Balaam and Pedro" (the story that follows this) on Western treatment of animals.

OWEN WISTER

BALAAM AND PEDRO

His horses were led to the water, and would not drink. Therefore Balaam was lashing them heavily. He looked across Butte Creek, and was aware of a tall man watering his horse on the opposite bank. Strangers to each other, the two exchanged a slight nod, and each was continuing his business, when Balaam saw a second traveller, a young fellow whom he knew.

"Hello, Shorty!" said Balaam. ·

"Morning."

Shorty turned out of the trail on the further side of Butte Creek and came to the bank.

"That's Mr. Balaam your letter's for," he informed the tall man, who got on his horse, and drawing an envelope from his battered overalls, crossed the creek.

The note was from the owner of two horses Balaam had borrowed many weeks before, in the early spring, promising to return them at once. The message was civil; it hoped "this dunning reminder" might be excused. It had not come straight, but deviously, in the pockets of three successive cow-punchers. It was ten days old, and looked a hundred years. As Balaam read it he wished he had sent the horses back before. Their owner was a judge, and a great man in the Territory.

"Well," the ranchman said, musing aloud in his annoyance, "he wants them by the 30th. Well, this is the 24th, and time enough yet."

"This is the 27th," said the messenger.

And Shorty, from the further bank, echoed: "Yes. It's sure the 27th." He and his pony stood under a cottonwood, and idly looked across at the talkers.

It was Balaam's mistake. He had drifted three sunrises behind the progress of the month. Days look alike, and often lose their names a hundred miles from a railroad. Balaam realized that it would not be so easy now to return the horses at the time requested, and his vexation increased. Suddenly, perceiving the date of the Judge's letter, he held it out to the messenger and struck the paper.

"What's your idea in bringing me that two weeks late?" he said, instantly convinced that all his own delay since the early spring was this messenger's fault.

The man explained that the note had been given him only on the preceding night, and he had hurried away from the round-up at once.

"Last night! Why didn't you chuck the thing away, my friend, instead of packing it over here the 27th of the month? You'd have been just as useful, and saved yourself an extra ride." And Balaam laughed with a grating snarl.

The cow-puncher levelled a lazy eye on Balaam, and after pondering a moment, decided to smile at "such talk from a mis'able little runt like that," as he explained later to Shorty in a gentle voice. He was a Virginian, and there was much sunny leisure in his speech and way.

"Are you going back to the round-up?" asked Balaam.

"No, seh. Not if the hawses is round hyeh yet."

"Round here yet? And supposing they're not?"

"Why, if you have them sent along back the Judge will be right sorry for youh trouble. He sent awdehs with this hyeh letteh *directin'* I was to shu'ly fetch two hawses if they was hyeh. The Judge has friends goin' to arrive from New Yawk for a trip to Montana."

Balaam grunted with displeasure, and thought of the sixty or seventy days since he had told the Judge he would return the horses at once. He looked across at Shorty seated in the shade, and through his uneasy thoughts his instinct irrelevantly noted what a good pony the youth rode. It was the same animal he had seen once or twice before. But something must be done. The Judge's horses were far out on the big range, and must be found and driven in, which would take certainly the rest of this day, possibly part of the next.

Balaam called to one of his men and gave some sharp orders, emphasizing details, repeating directions, and enjoining haste, while the large and patient Virginian leaned slightly against his horse, with one arm over the saddle, hearing and understanding; for out of Balaam's situation he derived an amusement that his face did not in the least reveal. The man departed to saddle up for his search on the big range, and Balaam resumed the unhitching of his team.

"Cow-punching?" he inquired of Shorty. He ignored the Virginian.

"Got better employment," said Shorty, haughtily.

Then Balaam knew at once that Shorty had no employment whatever, and had probably been turned off the round-up for going to sleep while night-herding.

"Good pony of yours," he said to Shorty, striking his own horse in the jaw, because he held back, and did not come down to the water and drink as the other was doing.

"Your trace ain't undone," commented the Virginian, pointing.

Balaam loosed the strap he had forgotten, and cut the horse again for consistency's sake as the animal now came down, bewildered, with his head in the air, stopping short and snuffing.

The on-lookers were not much surprised at any of this, for Wyoming horses do not, as a rule, have a good time. Balaam's temper was his own, but his notions of how to treat animals were altogether those of his community. Perhaps it is inevitable that people who in the ordinary scope of their business year after year must slice off the ears of so many floundering half-throttled calves, and smell so continually the odor of live veal under the branding-irons, should in time blunt their sensibilities, and exterminate whatever of humanity for dumb beasts may once have existed within them. There was a time, not so very long ago, when most enlightened potentates extracted secrets and obedience by slowly cracking the bones or twisting off the thumbs of those who had the misfortune to differ from them in matters politic and religious. This is not thought well of to-day; and there are signs that cruelty to anything, even to a horse, will come to be generally discountenanced. But not quite yet.

"Quit the round-up?" inquired Balaam.

"That's what I done," said Shorty. "Yesterday morning."

"How far have they got?"

"Workin' Little Muddy to-day and to-morrow. They'll finish up this week."

"You must have slept at the Sand Hill outfit coming down."

Shorty nodded. "What's Carew doin' havin' a man like Sorgy Trampas work fer him, anyway?" said he.

The observing Balaam now drew another inference—that Shorty had played cards in the evening at the Sand Hill, Carew's ranch, and that in the morning his pocket was empty and Trampas's pocket was full. Balaam looked at this very young man, and knew he was in trouble; and he determined to own the very young man's horse that day.

"Carew's an Englishman, and hires Trampas because he don't know enough not to," said Balaam.

Here the Virginian made a reflection. "Most astonishin' thing in natural history," said he, not addressing any one in particular, "is the number of useful facts them English ain't aware of."

"Carew 'll be sure sorry he hired Trampas some day," said Shorty, vindictively. "And the sooner he is, the better for his chances of ownin' his own calves."

This was more slander than was creditable for one cow-puncher to speak of another.

"Oh yes!" thought Balaam, scrutinizing the dusty youth with some contempt. "Trampas put up a deck on him, and took his money. That's as plain as you please. Hello, Shorty!" he called out, for Shorty was departing, "don't you like dinner any more? Grub's ready about now."

Shorty forded the creek and slung his saddle off, and on invitation turned Pedro, his buckskin pony, into Balaam's pasture. This was green, the rest of the wide world being yellow except only where Butte Creek, with its bordering cottonwoods, coiled away into the desert distance like a green snake without end. The Virginian also turned his horse into the pasture. He must stay at the ranch till the Judge's horses should be found.

"Mrs. Balaam's East yet," said her lord, leading the way to his dining-room.

He wanted Shorty to dine with him, and could not exclude the Virginian, much as he should have enjoyed this. Balaam hated a man he could not bully.

"See any Indians?" he inquired, as they ate.

"Na-a-!" said Shorty, in disdain of recent rumors.

"They ain't a-travellin' over hyeh," said the Virginian. "Bow-Laig Range is whar they was repawted."

"What business have they got off the reservation, I'd like to know," said the ranchman—"Bow-Leg or anywhere?"

"Oh, it's just a hunt, and kind of visitin' their friends on the South Reservation," Shorty explained. "Squaws along and all."

"Well, if the folks at Washington don't keep squaws and all where they belong," said Balaam, in a rage, "the folks in Wyoming Territory 'll do a little job that way themselves."

"There's a petition out," said Shorty. "Paper's goin' East with a lot of names to it. But they ain't no harm, them Indians ain't."

"No harm?" rasped out Balaam. "You don't seem to learn anything in this country, Jim Gill, except what you know about the Drybone hog ranch. Why don't you get hired there for assistant bartender, and quit punching cows, which is too much physical exercise for you? No harm? Was it white men druv off the O. C. yearlings?"

Balaam's Eastern grammar was sometimes at the mercy of his Western feelings. The thought of the perennial stultification of Indian affairs at Washington, whether by politician or philanthropist, was always sure to arouse him. He walked impatiently about while he spoke, and halted at the window. Out in the world the unclouded day was shining, and Balaam's eye travelled across the plains to where a blue line, faint and pale, lay along the end of the vast yellow distance. That was the beginning of the Bow-Leg Mountains. Somewhere over there were the red men, ranging in unfrequented depths of rock and pine—their forbidden ground.

Dinner was ready, and they sat down.

"And I suppose," Balaam continued, still hot on the subject, "you'd claim Indians object to killing a white man when they run onto him good and far from human help? These peaceable Indians are just the worst in the business."

"That's so," assented the easy-opinioned Shorty, exactly as if he had always maintained this view. "Chap started for Sunk Creek three weeks ago. Trapper, he was; old like, with a red shirt. One of his horses come into the round-up Toosday. Man 'ain't been heard from." He ate in silence for a while, evidently brooding in his childlike mind. Then he said, querulously, "I'd sooner trust one of them Indians than I would Sorgy Trampas."

Balaam slanted his fat bullet-head far to one side, and laying his spoon down (he had opened some canned grapes), laughed steadily at his guest with a harsh relish of irony.

The guest ate a grape, and perceiving he was seen through, smiled back rather miserably.

"Say, Shorty," said Balaam, his head still slanted over, "what's the figures of your bank balance just now?"

"I ain't usin' banks," murmured the youth.

Balaam chuckled. "I wouldn't," he said. "It's liable to puff a man up, and make him feel he's better than his neighbors."

"Which it ain't American to feel," observed the Virginian, "even when you're inside a bank."

Balaam put some more grapes on Shorty's plate, and sliding a cigar from his waistcoat, sent it rolling to his guest.

"Matches are behind you," he added. He gave a cigar to the Virginian as an after-thought, but, to his disgust, the man put it in his pocket and lighted a pipe.

"A bank account's awful comfortable all the same," said Shorty; "I've had one twiced. Laramie First National, and Buffalo, when I was ridin' on Powder River. And onced I sent some money back home—November, seventy-nine. I wisht I'd a-kep' it. There's a bill I got to renoo first day of—" Shorty stopped amazed; his hair could not rise up on end, being always so, but his voice stuck in his throat. Balaam had turned round from a cupboard holding a very nice-looking bottle.

"It's Old Peachbottom," he whispered, lovingly, though why he should whisper is not clear.

"Most folks claim—" Shorty began, but the lad mustered wisdom enough to check the remainder of his observation, which was going to be, "this ranch is total abstinence."

"What do they claim, Shorty?" cackled Balaam, gloating wickedly over his deep-filled glass. "I guess you'd claim that's pretty good. Fill her up, man!" (for the diffident cow-puncher had poured himself a slight quantity)—"fill up! You'll get nothing like that in Drybone, not though you were a stockholder in the hog ranch."

Indeed, Shorty could, in his present plight, get nothing at all at that establishment, unless for love, and the proprietor was not one who held love to be a good consideration. The Virginian helped himself to the liquor when Balaam pushed it to him, and the host with his guests smoked and drank without further talk.

"Well, I guess I'll be pulling out for town," said Shorty, after a proper portion of Old Peachbottom. He put on his hat and stood in the open door. "Can I take your mail fer yu'?" he inquired, "or do anything in Drybone?"

Balaam was locking up the bottle.

"And thank yu' fer a sure good dinner, Mr. Balaam," added the guest, with a certain shyness.

It was exceptional to make such an acknowledgment at all, or, at any rate, so directly. But the hospitality had been exceptional, and Shorty could not know that Balaam was thinking about Pedro, the buckskin pony. They walked to the pasture and lifted down the bars.

"Got a rope?" Balaam asked.

"Don't need to rope him. I can walk right up to Pedro. You stay back."

Hiding his bridle behind him, Shorty walked to the river-bank, where the pony was switching his long tail in the shade, and speaking persuasively to him, came nearer till he laid his hand on Pedro's dusky mane, which was many shades darker than his hide. He turned expectantly, and his master came up to his expectations with a piece of bread.

"Eats that, does he?" said Balaam, over the bars.

"Likes the salt," said Shorty. "Now, n-n-ow, here! Yu' don't guess yu'll be bridled, don't yu'? Open your teeth! Yu'd like to play yu' was nobody's horse and live private? Or maybe yu'd prefer ownin' a saloon?"

Pedro evidently enjoyed this talk and the dodging he made about the bit. Once fairly in his mouth, he accepted the inevitable, and followed Shorty to the bars, who there turned and extended his hand.

"Shake!" he said to his pony, who lifted his fore foot quietly and put it in his master's hand. Then the master tickled his nose, and he wrinkled it and flattened his ears, pretending to bite. His face wore an expression of knowing relish over this performance. "Now the other hoof," said Shorty, and horse and master shook hands with their left. "I learned him that," said the cowboy, with pride and affection. "Say, Pede," he continued, in Pedro's ear, "ain't yu' the best little horse in the country? What? Here, now! Keep out of that, you dead-beat! There ain't no more bread." He pinched the pony's nose, one quarter of which was wedged into his pocket.

"Quite a lady's little pet!" said Balaam, with the rasp in his voice. "That kind of tomfoolery makes me sick. Pity this isn't New York, now, where there's a big market for harmless horses. Gee-gees, the children call them."

"He ain't no gee-gee," said Shorty, offended. "He'll beat any cow-pony workin' you've got. Yu' can turn him on a half-dollar. Don't need to touch the reins. Hang 'em on one finger and swing yer body, and he'll turn."

Balaam knew this, and he knew the pony was only a four-year-old. "Well," he said, "Drybone's had no circus this season. Maybe they'd buy tickets to see Pedro. He's good for that, anyway."

Shorty became gloomy, and a smile crossed the face of the Virginian, smoking his pipe to himself, for he perceived what Balaam was getting at.

"Try a circus," persisted that worthy. "Alter your plans for spending cash in town, and make a little money instead."

Shorty, having no plans to alter and no cash to spend, grew still more gloomy.

"What'll you take for that pony?" said Balaam.

Shorty spoke up instantly. "A hundred dollars couldn't buy that piece of stale mud off his back," he asserted, looking off into the sky grandiosely.

But Balaam looked at Shorty. "You keep the mud," he said, "and I'll give you thirty dollars for the horse."

Shorty did a little professional laughing, and began to walk towards his saddle.

"Give you thirty dollars," repeated Balaam, picking a stone up and slinging it into the river.

"How far do yu' call it to Drybone?" Shorty remarked, stooping to investigate the bucking-strap on his saddle—a superfluous performance, for Pedro never bucked.

"You won't have to walk," said Balaam. "Stay all night, and I'll send you over comfortably in the morning when the wagon goes for the mail."

"Walk!" Shorty retorted. "Drybone's twenty-five miles. Pedro 'll put me there in three hours and not know he done it." He lifted the saddle on the horse's back. "Come, Pedro," said he.

"Come, Pedro!" mocked Balaam.

There followed a little silence.

"No, sir," mumbled Shorty, with his head under Pedro's belly, busily cinching. "A hundred dollars is bottom figures."

Balaam, in his turn, now duly performed some professional laughing, which was noted by Shorty under the horse's belly. He stood up and squared round on Balaam. "Well, then," he said, "what 'll yu' give fer him?"

"Thirty dollars," said Balaam, looking far off into the sky, as Shorty had looked.

"Oh, come, now," expostulated Shorty.

It was he who now did the feeling for an offer, and this was what Balaam liked to see. "Why, yes," he said, "thirty," and looked surprised that he should have to mention the sum so often.

"I thought yu'd quit them first figures," said the cow-puncher, "fer yu' can see I ain't goin' to look at 'em."

Balaam climbed up on the fence and sat there. "I'm not crying for your Pedro," he observed, dispassionately. "Only it struck me you were dead-broke, and wanted to raise cash to renew a note and keep yourself going till you hunted up a job and could buy him back." He hooked his right thumb inside his waistcoat pocket. "But I'm not crying for him," he repeated. "He'd stay right here, of course. I wouldn't part with him. Why does he stand that way? Hello!" Balaam suddenly straightened himself, like a man who has made a discovery.

"Hello what?" said Shorty, on the defensive.

Balaam was staring at Pedro with a judicial frown. Then he stuck out a finger at the horse, keeping the thumb hooked in his pocket. So meagre a gesture was felt by the ruffled Shorty to be no just way to point at Pedro. "What's the matter with that fore leg there?" said Balaam.

"Which? Nothin's the matter with it!" snapped Shorty.

Balaam climbed down from his fence and came over with elaborate deliberation. He passed his hand up and down the off fore leg. Then he spit slenderly. "Mm!" he said, thoughtfully; and added, with a shade of sadness; "that's always to be expected when they're worked too young."

Shorty slid his hand slowly over the disputed leg. "What's to be expected?" he inquired—"that they'll eat hearty? Well, he does."

At this retort the Virginian permitted himself to laugh in audible sympathy. He hoped Balaam was not going to work Pedro out of Shorty.

"Sprung," continued Balaam, with a sigh. "Whirling round short when his bones were soft did that. Yes."

"Sprung!" Shorty said, with a bark of indignation. "Come on, Pede; you and me 'll spring for town."

He caught the horn of his saddle, and as he swung into place the horse rushed away with him. "O-ee! yoi-yup, yup, yup!" sang Shorty, in the shrill cow dialect. He made Pedro play an exhibition game of speed, bringing him round close to Balaam in a wide circle, and then he vanished in dust down the left-bank trail.

Balaam looked after him and laughed harshly. He had seen trout dash about like that when the hook in their jaw first surprised them. He knew Shorty would show the pony off, and he knew Shorty's love for Pedro was not equal to his need of money. He called to one of his men, asked something about the dam at the mouth of the cañon, where the main irrigation ditch began, made a remark about the prolonged drought, and then walked to his dining-room door, where, as he expected, Shorty met him.

"Say," said the youth, "do you consider that's any kind of a way to talk about a good horse?"

"Any dude could see the leg's sprung," said Balaam. But he looked at Pedro's shoulder, which was well laid back; and he admired his points, dark in contrast with the buckskin, and also the width between the eyes.

"Now you know," whined Shorty, "that it ain't sprung any more than your leg's cork. If you mean the right leg ain't just plumb straight, I can tell you he was born so, for I branded him and seen it then. That don't make no difference, for it ain't weak. Try him onced. Just as sound and strong as iron. Never stumbles. And he don't never go to jumpin' with yu'. He's kind and he's smart." And the master petted his pony, who lifted a hoof for another hand-shake.

Of course Balaam had never thought the leg was sprung, and he now took on an unprejudiced air of wanting to believe Shorty's statements if he only could.

"Maybe there's two years' work left in that leg," he remarked.

"Maybe there's two dollars comin' to Shorty for a mighty good hawse," observed the Virginian to himself. "Better give him away, Shorty," he said aloud, sardonically. "His laig's busted and he's no good. Mr. Balaam says so."

He foresaw what sort of a bargain his feather-headed friend was going to make under the stress of poverty. But he could not interfere. He would not have said even the little that he had save for his dislike of Balaam—a feeling he had conceived at first sight. In bets, card games, horse deals, and other matters of business a man must take care of himself, and wise on-lookers must hold their peace.

That evening Shorty again had a cigar and some more Old Peachbottom. He had parted with Pedro for forty dollars, a striped Mexican blanket, and a pair of spurs. Undressing over in the bunkhouse, he said to the Virginian, "I'll sure buy Pedro back off him just as soon as ever I rustle some cash." The Virginian grunted. He was thinking he should have to travel hard to get the horses to the Judge by the 30th.

In the early dawn Shorty sat up among his blankets on the floor of the bunkhouse, and saw the various sleepers coiled or sprawled in their beds; and their breathing had not yet grown restless at the nearing of day. He stepped to the door carefully, and saw the crowding blackbirds begin their walk and chatter in the mud of the littered and trodden corrals. From beyond, among the cottonwoods, came continually the smooth unemphatic sound of the doves answering each other invisibly; and against the empty ridge of the river-bluff lay the moon, no longer shining, for there was established a new light through the sky. Pedro stood in the pasture close to the bars. The cowboy slowly closed the door behind him, and sitting down on the step, drew his money out and idly handled it, taking no comfort just then from its possession. Then he put it back, and after dragging on his boots, crossed to the pasture and held a last talk with his pony, brushing the cakes of mud from his hide where he had rolled, and passing a lingering hand over his mane. As the sounds of the morning came increasingly from tree and plain, Shorty glanced back to see that no one was yet out of the cabin, and then put his arms round the horse's neck, laying his head against him. For a moment the cowboy's insignificant face was exalted by the emotion he would never have let others see. He hugged tight this animal, who was dearer to his heart than anybody in the world.

"Good-by, Pedro," he said—"good-by."

Pedro looked for bread.

"No," said the master, sorrowfully, "not any more. Yu' knew well I'd give it yu' if I had it. You and me didn't figure on this, did we, Pedro? Good-by."

He hugged his pony again, and returned to the ranch. After breakfast he and his belongings departed to Drybone, and Pedro from his field calmly watched his departure; for horses recognize even less than men the momentous corners that their destinies turn. The pony stopped feeding to look at the mail-wagon pass by; but the master sitting in the wagon forebore to turn his head.

It was a grievous day for that master that his pony must pass into other hands. Shorty was scarcely an admirable character; even more shiftless than his kind, and under ill luck less stoic. His mother's sense of responsibility for him was entirely relieved by his birth, and he grew up accidentally, receiving, as he matured towards manhood, no other instruction than the appropriate dissipations for each advancing period imparted by competent friends. Yet in him lived a native tenderness for animals, which, like charity, covers a multitude of sins. Therefore was Shorty's sorrow keen, though he might soon forget it. Pedro the unknowing felt no sorrow. But this parting was nevertheless a grievous evil day for him also. Men are in the hands of fate alone; horses are in the hands of men. Balaam, though well brought up once, in New Jersey, a man who could read books and believed in matrimony and monogamy, and often washed, knew no kindness for animals, as has been seen. He was the rule, Shorty the exception. Yet Balaam was at least half civilized.

Resigned to wait for the Judge's horses, Balaam went into his office this dry bright morning and read nine accumulated newspapers;

for he was behindhand. Then he rode out on the ditches, and met his man returning with the troublesome animals at last. He hastened home and sent for the Virginian. He had made a decision.

"See here," he said; "those horses are coming. What trail would you take over to the Judge's?"

"Sho'tes' trail's right through the Bow-Laig Mountains," said the man, in his gentle voice.

"Guess you're right. It's dinner-time. We'll start right afterwards. We'll make Little Muddy Crossing by sundown, and Sunk Creek to-morrow, and the next day'll see us through. Can a wagon get through Sunk Creek Cañon?"

The Virginian smiled. "I reckon it can't, seh, and stay resembling a wagon."

Balaam told them to saddle Pedro and one pack-horse, and drive the bunch of horses into a corral, roping the Judge's two, who proved extremely wild. He had decided to take this journey himself on remembering certain politics soon to be rife in Cheyenne. For Judge Henny was indeed a greater man than Balaam.

This personally conducted return of the horses would temper its tardiness, and, moreover, the sight of some New York visitors would be a good thing after seven months of no warmer touch with that metropolis than the Sunday *Herald*, always eight days old when it reached the N- lazy Y.

They forded Butte Creek, and crossing the well-travelled trail which follows down to Drybone, turned their faces towards the uninhabited country that began immediately, as the ocean begins off a sandy shore. And as a single mast on which no sail is shining stands at the horizon and seems to add a loneliness to the surrounding sea, so the long gray line of fence, almost a mile away, that ended Balaam's land on this side the creek, stretched along the waste ground and added desolation to the plain. No solitary watercourse with margin of cottonwoods or willow thickets flowed here to stripe the dingy yellow world with interrupting color, nor were cattle to be seen dotting the distance, nor moving objects at all, nor any bird in the soundless air. The last gate was shut by the Virginian, who looked back at the pleasant trees of the ranch, and then followed on in single file across the sagebrush desert of No Man's Land.

There were five horses. Balaam led on Pedro, his squat figure stiff in the saddle, but solid as a rock, and tilted a little forward, as his habit was. One of the Judge's horses came next, a sorrel, dragging back continually on the rope by which he was led. After him ambled Balaam's wise pack-animal, carrying the light burden of two days' food and lodging. She was an old mare who could still go when she chose, but had been schooled by the years, and kept the trail, giving no trouble to the long cow-puncher who came behind her. He also sat solid as a rock, yet subtly bending to the struggles of the wild horse he led, as a steel spring bends and balances and resumes its poise.

Thus they made but slow time, and when they topped the last dull rise of ground and looked down on the long slant of ragged caked earth to the crossing of Little Muddy, with its single tree and few mean bushes, the final distance where eyesight ends had deepened to violet from the thin steady blue they had stared at for so many hours, and all heat was gone from the universal dryness. The horses drank a long time from the sluggish yellow water, and its alkaline taste and warmth were equally welcome to the men. They built a little fire, and when supper was ended, smoked but a short while and in silence before they got in the blankets that were spread in a smooth place beside the water.

They had picketed the two horses of the Judge in the best grass they could find, letting the rest go free to find pasture where they could. When the first light came, the Virginian attended to breakfast, while Balaam rode away on the sorrel to bring in the loose horses. They had gone far out of sight, and when he returned with them, after some two hours, he was on Pedro. Pedro was soaking with sweat, and red froth creamed from his mouth. The Virginian saw the horses must have been hard to drive in, especially after Balaam brought them the wild sorrel as a leader.

"If you'd kep' ridin' him, 'stead of changin' off on your hawse, they'd have behaved quieter," said the cow-puncher.

"That's good seasonable advice," said Balaam, sarcastically. "I could have told you that now."

"I could have told you when you started," said the Virginian, heating the coffee for Balaam.

Balaam was eloquent on the outrageous conduct of the horses. He had come up with them evidently striking back for Butte Creek, with the old mare in the lead.

"But I soon showed her the road she was to go," he said, as he drove them now to the water.

The Virginian noticed the slight limp of the mare, and how her pastern was cut as if with a stone or the sharp heel of a boot.

"I guess she'll not be in a hurry to travel except when she's wanted to," continued Balaam. He sat down, and sullenly poured himself some coffee. "We'll be in luck if we make any Sunk Creek this night."

He went on with his breakfast, thinking aloud for the benefit of his companion, who made no comments, preferring silence to the discomfort of talking with a man whose vindictive humor was so thoroughly uppermost. He did not even listen very attentively, but continued his preparations for departure, washing the dishes, rolling the blankets, and moving about in his usual way of easy and visible good-nature.

"Six o'clock already," said Balaam, saddling the horses. "And we'll not get started for ten minutes more." Then he came to Pedro. "So you haven't quit fooling yet, haven't you?" he exclaimed, for the pony shrank as he lifted the bridle. "Take that for your sore mouth!" and he rammed the bit in, at which Pedro flung back and reared.

"Well, I never saw Pedro act that way, yet," said the Virginian. "On the round-up he's the gentles' hawse in the outfit."

"Ah, rubbish!" said Balaam. "They're all the same. Not a bastard one but's laying for his chance to do for you. Some 'll buck you off, and some 'll roll with you, and some 'll fight you with their fore feet. They may play good for a year, but the Western pony's man's enemy, and when he judges he's got his chance, he's going to do his best. And if you come out alive it won't be his fault." Balaam paused for a while, packing. "You've got to keep them afraid of you," he said next; "that's what you've got to do if you don't want trouble. That Pedro horse there has been fed, hand-fed, and fooled with like a d—— pet, and what's that policy done? Why, he goes ugly when he thinks it's time, and decides he'll not drive any horses into camp this morning. He knows better now."

The Virginian said nothing. These dogmas concerning the disposition of the Western pony and the way he should be disciplined were familiar to him, but he still believed that, except in the case of certain vicious brutes, confidence and not fear was the relation to establish between horse and rider in Wyoming as well as in Virginia. And he wondered how Balaam, with these views and his temper ever ready to enforce them on far less than average provocation, ever managed to keep a sound horse on his ranch.

He had heard cow-punchers say to refractory ponies, "You keep still, or I'll Balaam you!" and he now understood the aptness of the expression.

Meanwhile Balaam began to lead Pedro to the creek for a last drink before starting across the torrid drought. The horse held back on the rein a little, and Balaam turned and cut the whip across his forehead. A delay of forcing and backing followed, while the Virginian, already in the saddle, waited. The minutes passed, and no immediate prospect, apparently, of getting nearer Sunk Creek.

"He ain' goin' to follow you while you're beatin' his haid," the cow-puncher at length remarked.

"Do you think you can teach me anything about horses?" retorted Balaam.

"Well, it don't look like I could," said the Virginian, lazily.

"Then don't try it, so long as it's not your horse, my friend."

Again the cow-puncher levelled his eye on Balaam. "All right," he said, in the same gentle voice. "And don't you call me your friend. You've made that mistake twiced."

The road was shadeless, as it had been from the start, and they could not travel fast. During the first few hours all coolness was driven out of the glassy morning, and another day of illimitable sun invested the world with its blaze. The pale Bow-Leg range was coming nearer, but its hard hot slants and rifts suggested no sort of freshness, and even the pines that spread for wide miles along near the summit counted for nothing in the distance and the glare, but seemed mere patches of dull dry discoloration. No talk was exchanged between the two travellers, for the cow-puncher had nothing to say and Balaam was sulky, so they moved along in silent endurance of each other's company and the tedium of the journey.

But the slow succession of rise and fall in the plain changed and shortened. The earth's surface became lumpy, rising into mounds and knotted systems of steep small hills cut apart by staring gashes of sand, where water poured in the spring from the melting snow. After a time they ascended through the foot-hills till the plain below was for a while concealed, but came again into view in its entirety, distant and a thing of the past, while some magpies sailed down to meet them from the new country they were entering. They passed up through a small transparent forest of dead trees standing stark and white, and a little higher came on a line of narrow moisture that crossed the way and formed a stale pool among some willow thickets. They turned aside to water their horses, and found near the pool a circular spot of ashes and some poles lying, and beside these a cagelike edifice of willow wands built in the ground.

"Indian camp," observed the Virginian.

There were the tracks of five or six horses on the farther side of the pool, and they did not come into the trail, but led off among the rocks on some system of their own.

"They're about a week old," said Balaam. "It's part of that outfit that's been hunting."

"They've gone on to visit their friends," added the cow-puncher.

"Yes, on the Southern Reservation. How far do you call Sunk Creek now?"

"Well," said the Virginian, calculating, "it's mighty nigh fo'ty miles from Muddy Crossin', an' I reckon we've come eighteen."

"Just about. It's noon." Balaam snapped his watch shut. "We'll rest here till 12.30."

When it was time to go, the cow-puncher looked musingly at the mountains. "We'll need to travel right smart to get through the cañon to-night," he said.

"Tell you what," said Balaam; "we'll rope the Judge's horses together and drive 'em in front of us. That'll make speed."

"Mightn't they get away on us?" objected the Virginian.
"They're pow'ful wild."

"They can't get away from me, I guess," said Balaam, and the
arrangement was adopted. "We're the first this season over this piece
of the trail," he observed presently.

His companion had noticed the ground already, and assented.
There were no tracks anywhere to be seen over which winter had not
come and gone since they had been made. Presently the trail wound
into a sultry gulch that hemmed in the heat and seemed to draw down
the sun's rays more vertically. The sorrel horse chose this place to
make a try for liberty. He suddenly whirled from the trail, dragging
with him his less inventive fellow. Leaving the Virginian with the old
mare, Balaam headed them off, for Pedro was quick, and they came
jumping down the bank together, but swiftly crossed up on the other
side, getting much higher before they could be reached. It was no
place for this sort of game, as the sides of the ravine were ploughed
with steep channels, broken with jutting knobs of rock, and impeded
by short twisted pines that swung out from their roots horizontally
over the pitch of the hill. The Virginian helped, but used his horse
with more judgment, keeping as much on the level as possible, and
endeavoring to anticipate the next turn of the runaways before they
made it, while Balaam attempted to follow them close, wheeling short
when they doubled, heavily beating up the face of the slope, veering
again to come down to the point he had left, and whenever he felt
Pedro begin to flag, driving his spurs into the horse and forcing him to
keep up the pace. He had set out to overtake and capture on the side
of a mountain these two animals who had been running wild for many
weeks, and now carried no weight but themselves, and the futility of
such work could not penetrate his obstinate and rising temper. He
had made up his mind not to give in. The Virginian soon decided to
move slowly along for the present, preventing the wild horses from
passing down the gulch again, but otherwise saving his own animal
from useless fatigue. He saw that Pedro was reeking wet, with mouth
open, and constantly stumbling, though he galloped on. The cowpuncher kept the group in sight, driving the pack-horse in front of
him, and watching the tactics of the sorrel, who had now undoubtedly
become the leader of the expedition, and was at the top of the gulch,
in vain trying to find an outlet through its rocky rim to the levels
above. He soon judged this to be no thoroughfare, and changing his
plan, trotted down to the bottom and up the other side, gaining more
and more, for in this new descent Pedro had fallen twice. Then the
sorrel showed the cleverness of a genuinely vicious horse. The
Virginian saw him stop and fall to kicking his companion with all the
energy a short rope would permit. The rope slipped, and both,

unencumbered, reached the top and disappeared. Leaving the pack-horse for Balaam, the Virginian started after them, and came into a high table-land, beyond which the mountains began in earnest. The runaways were moving across toward these at an easy rate. He followed for a moment, then looking back, and seeing no sign of Balaam, waited, for the horses were sure not to go fast when they reached good pasture or water.

He got out of the saddle and sat on the ground watching, till the mare came up slowly into sight, and Balaam behind her. When they were near, Balaam dismounted and struck Pedro fearfully, until the stick broke, and he raised the splintered half to continue.

Seeing the pony's condition, the Virginian spoke, and said, "I'd let that hawse alone."

Balaam turned to him, but, wholly possessed by passion, did not seem to hear, and the cow-puncher noticed how white and like that of a maniac his face was. The stick slid to the ground.

"He played he was tired," said Balaam, looking at the Virginian with glazed eyes. The violence of his rage affected him physically, like some stroke of illness. "He played out on me on purpose." The man's voice was dry and light. "He's perfectly fresh now," he continued, and turned again to the coughing, swaying horse, whose eyes were closed. Not having a stick, he seized the animal's unresisting head and shook it. The Virginian watched him a moment, and rose to stop such a spectacle. Then, as if conscious he was doing no real hurt, Balaam ceased, and turning again in a slow fashion, looked across the level, where the runaways were still visible.

"I'll have to take your horse," he said; "mine's played out on me."

"You ain' goin' to touch my hawse."

Again the words seemed not entirely to reach Balaam's under-standing, so dulled by rage were his senses. He made no answer, but mounted Pedro, and the failing pony walked mechanically forward, while the Virginian, puzzled, stood looking after him. Balaam seemed without purpose of going anywhere, and stopped in a moment. The cow-puncher was about to advise him to get off, when he saw him lean over Pedro's neck and reach a hand down between his ears. The ranchman's arm and shoulder worked fiercely and twisted, when suddenly Pedro sank motionless, and his head rolled flat on the earth. Balaam, flung sharply on the ground, was jammed beneath him, and the cow-puncher ran, and taking the saddle-horn, shifted the horse's dead weight a little from the prisoner's body.

"Are you hurt?" he said, as Balaam raised himself and stood up slowly, looking sullenly at the fallen Pedro.

"No. But I got an eye out on him."

The cowboy heard these words without at first realizing their import; but the horse lifted his head and turned it piteously round, and he saw the ruined eye that Balaam's fingers had blinded.

Then Balaam was rolled to the ground again by the towering Virginian, in whose brawn and sinew the might of justice was at work; and, half stunned, the ranchman felt for his pistol, keeping one arm over his face till the weapon came out, and, together with his hand, was instantly stamped into the dust.

"Don't try that," said the Virginian, and lifted him, not able to struggle. He slung him so that he lay as though his skull were cracked, his crushed hand bleeding where it hung fallen across Pedro's saddle.

Vengeance had come and gone, and the Virginian looked down at the horse and the man prone in the middle of the open table-land. No anxiety and no special thought or plan stirred in his mind as he stood, until he found himself stooping over Balaam and saying aloud, "No, he ain't dead." Then came the first definite idea—a curious businesslike reflection that, after all, Pedro was Balaam's property and not his. This criticism he immediately answered, and that set his brain working as usual.

"He ain't hurt bad," he asserted, again aloud; and as he put the man in an easier position, the sunlight flashed on the six-shooter where it lay, and he secured it.

"She ain't so pretty as she was," he remarked, examining the weapon, "but she'll go right handy yet."

Strength was in a measure returning to Pedro. He was a young horse, and the exhaustion of neither pain nor over-riding was enough to affect him long or seriously. He got himself on his feet and walked waveringly over to the old mare, and stood by her for comfort. The cow-puncher came up to him; and Pedro, after starting back slightly, seemed to comprehend that he was in friendly hands. It was plain that he would soon be able to travel slowly if no weight was on him, and that he would be a very good horse again. Whether they abandoned the runaways or not, there was no staying here for night to overtake them without wood or water. The day was still high, and what its next few hours had in store the Virginian could not say, and he left them to take care of themselves, determining meanwhile that he would take command of the minutes, and maintain the position he had assumed both as to Balaam and Pedro. He took Pedro's saddle off, threw the mare's pack to the ground, put Balaam's saddle on her, and on that stowed or tied her original pack, which he could do, since it was so light. Then he went to Balaam, who was sitting up.

"I reckon you can travel," said the Virginian. "And youh hawse can. If you're comin' with me, you'll ride your mare. I'm goin' to trail them hawses. If you're not comin' with me, youh hawse comes with me, and you'll take fifty dollahs for him."

Balaam was indifferent to this good bargain. He did not look at the other or speak, but rose and searched about him on the ground. The Virginian was also indifferent as to whether Balaam chose to answer or not. He had spoken words that required no answer save action, and he did not care whether Balaam decided to come with him or go his own way. Seeing Balaam searching the ground, he finished what he had to say.

"I have your six-shooter, and you'll have it when I'm ready for you to. Now I'm goin'," he concluded.

Balaam's intellect was clear enough now, and he saw that though the rest of this journey would be nearly intolerable, more of the truth would inevitably become known through the Territory if he returned to his ranch than if he should go on. Paying his visit to the Judge might possibly conceal the most humiliating part of the story; whereas if his men saw him return prematurely and without Pedro, it was plain that they would have their curiosity satisfied by the Virginian at the first opportunity. The position was at best a bitter one. He looked at the impassive cow-puncher getting ready to go, and tying a rope on Pedro's neck to lead him; then he looked at the mountains where the runaways had vanished, and it did not seem credible to him that he had come into such straits. He climbed stiffly on the mare, and the three horses in single file took up their journey once more and came slowly among the mountains. The perpetual desert was ended, and they crossed a small brook, where they missed the trail. The Virginian dismounted to find where the horses had turned off, and discovered they had gone straight up the ridge by this watercourse.

"There's been a man camped in here inside a month," he said, kicking up a rag of red flannel. "White man and two horses. Ours have went up his old tracks."

It was not easy for Balaam to speak yet, and he kept his silence. But he remembered that Shorty had spoken of a trapper who had started for Sunk Creek.

For three hours they followed the runaways' course over softer ground, and steadily ascending, passed one or two springs at length, where the mud was not yet settled in the hoof-prints. Then they came through a corner of pine forest and down a sudden bank among quaking-asps to a green park, where the runaways beside a stream were grazing at ease, but saw them coming and started on again, following down the stream. For the present all to be done was to keep them in sight. This creek received tributaries and widened, making a valley for itself. Above the bottom, lining the first terrace of the ridge, began the pines, and stretched back unbroken over intervening summit and basin, to cease at last where the higher peaks presided.

"This hyeh's the middle fork of Sunk Creek," said the Virginian. "We'll get on to our right road again where they join."

Soon a game trail marked itself along the stream. If this would only continue, the runaways would be nearly sure to follow it down into the cañon. Then there would be no way for them but to go on and come out into their own country, where they would make for the Judge's ranch of their own accord. The great point was to reach the cañon before dark. They passed into permanent shadow; for though the other side of the creek shone in full day, the sun had departed behind the ridges immediately above them. Coolness filled the air, and the silence, which in this deep valley of invading shadow seemed too silent, was relieved by the birds. Not birds of song, but a freakish band of gray talkative observers, who came calling and croaking along through the pines, and inspected the cavalcade, keeping it company for a while, and then flying up into the woods again. The travellers came round a corner on a little spread of marsh, and from somewhere in the middle of it rose a buzzard and sailed on its black pinions into the air above them, wheeling and wheeling, but did not grow distant. As it swept over the trail something fell from its claw, a rag of red flannel, and each man in turn looked at it as his horse went by.

"I wonder if there's plenty elk and deer hyeh?" said the Virginian.

"I guess there is," Balaam replied, speaking at last. The travellers had become strangely reconciled.

"There's game 'most all over these mountains," the Virginian continued; "country not been settled long enough to scah them out." So they fell into casual conversation, and for the first time were glad of each other's company.

The sound of a new bird came from the pines above—the hoot of an owl—and was answered from some other part of the wood. This they did not particularly notice at first, but soon they heard the same note, unexpectedly distant, like an echo. The game trail, now quite a defined path beside the river, showed no sign of changing its course or fading out into blank ground, as these uncertain guides do so often. It led consistently in the desired direction, and the two men were relieved to see it continue. Not only were the runaways easier to keep track of, but better speed was made along this valley. The pervading imminence of night more and more dispelled the lingering afternoon, though there was yet no twilight in the open, and the high peaks opposite shone yellow in the invisible sun. But now the owls hooted again. Their music had something in it that caused both the Virginian and Balaam to look up at the pines and wish this valley would end. Perhaps it was early for night-birds to begin; or perhaps it was that the sound never seemed to fall behind, but moved abreast of them among the trees above as they rode on without pause; but some influence made the faces of the travellers grave. The spell of evil which the sight of the wheeling buzzard had begun deepened as evening grew, while ever and again along the creek the singular call and answer of the owls wandered among the darkness of the trees not far away.

The sun was gone from the peaks when at length the other side of the stream opened into a long wide meadow. The trail they followed, after crossing a flat willow thicket by the water, ran into dense pines, that here for the first time reached all the way down to the water's edge. The two men came out of the willows, and saw ahead the capricious runaways leave the bottom and go up the hill and enter the wood.

"We must hinder that," said the Virginian, and dropped Pedro's rope. "There's your six-shooter. You keep the trail, and camp down there"—he pointed to where the trees came to the water—"till I head them hawses off. I may not get back right away." He galloped up the open hill and went into the pine, choosing a place above where the vagrants had disappeared.

Balaam dismounted, and picking up his six-shooter, took the rope off Pedro's neck and drove him slowly down towards where the woods began. Its interior was already dim, and Balaam saw that here must be their stopping-place to-night, since there was no telling how wide this pine strip might extend along the trail before they could come out of it and reach another suitable camping-ground. Pedro had recovered his strength, and he now showed signs of restlessness. He shied where there was not even a stone in the trail, and finally turned sharply round. Balaam expected he was going to rush back on the way they had come; but the horse stood still, breathing excitedly, and he was urged forward again, though he turned more than once. But when they were a few paces from the wood, and Balaam had got off preparatory to camping, the horse snorted and dashed into the water, and stood still there. The astonished Balaam followed to turn him; but Pedro seemed to lose control of himself, and plunged to the middle of the river, and was evidently intending to cross. Fearing he would escape to the opposite meadow and add to their difficulties, Balaam, with the idea of turning him round, drew his six-shooter and fired in front of the horse, divining, even as the flash cut the dusk, the secret of all this—the Indians—but too late. His bruised hand had stiffened, marring his aim, and he saw Pedro fall over in the water, then rise and struggle up the bank on the further shore, where he now hurried also, to find he had broken the pony's leg.

He needed no interpreter for the voices of the seeming owls that had haunted the latter hour of their journey, and he knew that his beast's keener instinct had perceived the destruction that lurked in the interior of the wood. The history of the trapper whose horse had returned without him might have been—might still be—his own; and he thought of the rag that had fallen from the buzzard's talons when he had been disturbed at his meal in the marsh. "Peaceable" Indians were still in these mountains, and some few of them had for the past hour been skirting his journey unseen, and now waited in the wood they expected him to enter. They had been too wary to use their rifles or show themselves, lest these travellers should be only part of a larger company following, who would hear the noise of a shot, and catch them in the act of murder. So, safe under the cover of the pines, they had planned to sling their silent noose, and drag the white man from his horse as he passed through the trees.

Balaam looked over the river at the omnious wood, and then he looked at Pedro, the horse he had first crippled and now ruined, to whom he probably owed his life. He was lying on the ground quietly, looking over the green meadow, where dusk was gathering. Perhaps he was not suffering from his wound yet, as he rested on the ground; and into his animal intelligence there probably came no knowledge of this final stroke of his fate. At any rate, no sound of pain came from Pedro, whose friendly and gentle face remained turned towards the meadow. Once more Balaam fired his pistol, and this time the aim was true, and the horse rolled over, with the ball through his brain. It was the best reward that remained for him.

Then Balaam remounted the old mare, and turned from the middle fork of Sunk Creek. He dashed across the wide field, and went over a ridge, and found his way along in the night till he came to the old trail—the road they would never have left but for him and his obstinacy. He unsaddled the weary horse by Sunk Creek, where the cañon begins, letting her drag a rope and find pasture and water, while he, lighting no fire to betray him, crouched close under a tree till the light came. He thought of the Virginian in the wood. But what could either have done for the other had he stayed to look for him among the pines? If the cow-puncher came back to the corner, he would follow Balaam's tracks or not. They would meet, at any rate, where the creeks join.

Balaam reached the Judge's ranch late in the next afternoon, and after telling how he came to arrive alone, he went to bed with stiff joints and a blinding pain in his head.

A search party immediately started out. The Virginian was a man much valued by the Judge, much loved by his fellow-cowboys, and the search party hunted for him with a will in the valley where he had disappeared into the woods; but they hunted vainly. His last word to Balaam, that he might not "get back right away," haunted the ranchman during the three days he lay sick. Balaam was not always incapable of feeling, and now he could think of his tall travelling companion without hatred, and with a man's respect for a better man than himself. He returned to his ranch while the search party was still away in the Bow-Leg Mountains.

One day in November, when the water in Butte Creek ran low after the long dry season, and a floor of ice spread out from either bank to where the current was too swift to freeze yet, Balaam stood by the ford at his ranch. The cottonwoods were naked of leaves, and pale like ghosts in the stillness of the cold sunshine.

A traveller rode along on the other side of the stream, and stopping, said, "Morning, Mr. Balaam."

"Hello, Shorty!"

Shorty dismounted, and threw earth on the ice, so his horse should not fall; and Balaam, on his side, threw some also. Shorty crossed over. He was cheerful because of a humble momentary prosperity of purse.

"And so I come back, yu' see," he said. "Fer I always figured on gettin' Pedro back as soon as I could. And I'll give yu' more'n yu' gave me fer him, Mr. Balaam."

"Why, where have you been living, anyway,' Shorty?" said Balaam, with a laugh, adopting the offensive. "You're clean behind the times."

Shorty looked blank.

"Didn't you hear," Balaam continued, "how the Indians got after me on the Bow-Leg trail?"

Shorty had not heard. "I've been ridin' in Coloraydo," he explained.

"Well, they got after me and that Virginia man. But they didn't get *me.*" Balaam wagged his head to imply this escape was due to his own superior intelligence. The Virginian had been stupid, and so the Indians had got him. "And they shot your horse," Balaam continued.

He satisfied Shorty's curiosity with a story that could never be contradicted, though there was left in the cowboy's brain a misty sense of something unaccounted for.

"Stop and get some dinner with the boys," concluded Balaam. He did not invite Shorty to his own table this time, but he felt that he owed the youth a meal for the lies he had just been telling him.

Having eaten, Shorty rode away in low spirits along the bleak trail, for he had made so certain of once more owning Pedro, his friend whom he had taught to shake hands.

QUESTIONS

1. Why does the Virginian feel that he cannot interfere when Balaam is trying to buy Shorty's horse? How does his silence show his observance of an important part of "the Code of the West"?

2. Shorty has only one good quality—his love of animals. What are his weaknesses?

3. Balaam was a man "well brought up once, in New Jersey, a man who could read books and believed in matrimony and monogamy, and often washed." Yet he is the villain of the story. Why are Easterners so often the villains of Western stories?

4. When this story was written, Wister had already projected the writing of a novel of which it would be a part. How does the end of the story indicate that there are still "loose ends" to be tied up?

5. Balaam's bargaining with Shorty is compared to the playing of a trout. How are the two activities similar?

6. This story was written more than seventy-five years ago. What techniques of style or narration help to date it?

STEPHEN CRANE

THE BRIDE COMES TO YELLOW SKY

The great Pullman was whirling onward with such dignity of motion
that a glance from the window seemed simply to prove that the plains
of Texas were pouring eastward. Vast flats of green grass, dull-hued
spaces of mesquit and cactus, little groups of frame houses, woods of
light and tender trees, all were sweeping into the east, sweeping over
the horizon, a precipice.

A newly married pair had boarded this coach at San Antonio.
The man's face was reddened from many days in the wind and sun,
and a direct result of his new black clothes was that his brick-colored
hands were constantly performing in a most conscious fashion. From
time to time he looked down respectfully at his attire. He sat with a
hand on each knee, like a man waiting in a barber's shop. The glances
he devoted to other passengers were furtive and shy.

The bride was not pretty, nor was she very young. She wore a
dress of blue cashmere, with small reservations of velvet here and
there, and with steel buttons abounding. She continually twisted her
head to regard her puff sleeves, very stiff, straight, and high. They
embarrassed her. It was quite apparent that she had cooked, and that
she expected to cook, dutifully. The blushes caused by the careless
scrutiny of some passengers as she had entered the car were strange to
see upon this plain, under-class countenance, which was drawn in
placid, almost emotionless lines.

They were evidently very happy. "Ever been in a parlor-car
before?" he asked, smiling with delight.

"No," she answered, "I never was. It's fine, ain't it?"

"Great! And then after a while we'll go forward to the diner, and
get a big lay-out. Finest meal in the world. Charge a dollar."

"Oh, do they?" cried the bride. "Charge a dollar? Why, that's too
much—for us—ain't it, Jack?"

"Not this trip, anyhow," he answered bravely. "We're going to go
the whole thing."

Later he explained to her about the trains. "You see, it's a
thousand miles from one end of Texas to the other; and this train runs
right across it, and never stops but four times." He had the pride of an
owner. He pointed out to her the dazzling fittings of the coach; and in
truth her eyes opened wider as she contemplated the sea-green figured

velvet, the shining brass, silver, and glass, the wood that gleamed as darkly brilliant as the surface of a pool of oil. At one end a bronze figure sturdily held a support for a separated chamber, and at convenient places on the ceiling were frescos in olive and silver.

To the minds of the pair, their surroundings reflected the glory of their marriage that morning in San Antonio; this was the environment of their new estate; and the man's face in particular beamed with an elation that made him appear ridiculous to the negro porter. This individual at times surveyed them from afar with an amused and superior grin. On other occasions he bullied them with skill in ways that did not make it exactly plain to them that they were being bullied. He subtly used all the manners of the most unconquerable kind of snobbery. He oppressed them; but of this oppression they had small knowledge, and they speedily forgot that infrequently a number of travelers covered them with stares of derisive enjoyment. Historically there was supposed to be something infinitely humorous in their situation.

"We are due in Yellow Sky at 3:42," he said, looking tenderly into her eyes.

"Oh, are we?" she said, as if she had not been aware of it. To evince surprise at her husband's statement was part of her wifely amiability. She took from a pocket a little silver watch; and as she held it before her, and stared at it with a frown of attention, the new husband's face shone.

"I bought it in San Anton' from a friend of mine," he told her gleefully.

"It's seventeen minutes past twelve," she said, looking up at him with a kind of shy and clumsy coquetry. A passenger, noting this play, grew excessively sardonic, and winked at himself in one of the numerous mirrors.

At last they went to the dining-car. Two rows of negro waiters, in glowing white suits, surveyed their entrance with the interest, and also the equanimity, of men who had been forewarned. The pair fell to the lot of a waiter who happened to feel pleasure in steering them through their meal. He viewed them with the manner of a fatherly pilot, his countenance radiant with benevolence. The patronage, entwined with the ordinary deference, was not plain to them. And yet, as they returned to their coach, they showed in their faces a sense of escape.

To the left, miles down a long purple slope, was a little ribbon of mist where moved the keening Rio Grande. The train was approaching it at an angle, and the apex was Yellow Sky. Presently it was apparent that, as the distance from Yellow Sky grew shorter, the husband became commensurately restless. His brick-red hands were more insistent in their prominence. Occasionally he was even rather absent-minded and far-away when the bride leaned forward and addressed him.

As a matter of truth, Jack Potter was beginning to find the shadow of a deed weigh upon him like a leaden slab. He, the town marshal of Yellow Sky, a man known, liked, and feared in his corner, a prominent person, had gone to San Antonio to meet a girl he believed he loved, and there, after the usual prayers, had actually induced her to marry him, without consulting Yellow Sky for any part of the transaction. He was now bringing his bride before an innocent and unsuspecting community.

Of course people in Yellow Sky married as it pleased them, in accordance with a general custom; but such was Potter's thought of his duty to his friends, or of their idea of his duty, or of an unspoken form which does not control men in these matters, that he felt he was heinous. He had committed an extraordinary crime. Face to face with this girl in San Antonio, and spurred by his sharp impulse, he had gone headlong over all the social hedges. At San Antonio he was like a man hidden in the dark. A knife to sever any friendly duty, any form, was easy to his hand in that remote city. But the hour of Yellow Sky—the hour of daylight—was approaching.

He knew full well that his marriage was an important thing to his town. It could only be exceeded by the burning of the new hotel. His friends could not forgive him. Frequently he had reflected on the advisability of telling them by telegraph, but a new cowardice had been upon him. He feared to do it. And now the train was hurrying him toward a scene of amazement, glee, and reproach. He glanced out of the window at the line of haze swinging slowly in toward the train.

Yellow Sky had a kind of brass band, which played painfully, to the delight of the populace. He laughed without heart as he thought of it. If the citizens could dream of his prospective arrival with his bride, they would parade the band at the station and escort them, amid cheers and laughing congratulations, to his adobe home.

He resolved that he would use all the devices of speed and plains-craft in making the journey from the station to his house. Once within that safe citadel, he could issue some sort of a vocal bulletin, and then not go among the citizens until they had time to wear off a little of their enthusiasm.

The bride looked anxiously at him. "What's worrying you, Jack?"

He laughed again. "I'm not worrying, girl; I'm only thinking of Yellow Sky."

She flushed in comprehension.

A sense of mutual guilt invaded their minds and developed a finer tenderness. They looked at each other with eyes softly aglow.

But Potter often laughed the same nervous laugh; the flush upon the bride's face seemed quite permanent.

The traitor to the feelings of Yellow Sky narrowly watched the speeding landscape. "We're nearly there," he said.

Presently the porter came and announced the proximity of Potter's home. He held a brush in his hand, and, with all his airy superiority gone, he brushed Potter's new clothes as the latter slowly turned this way and that way. Potter fumbled out a coin and gave it to the porter, as he had seen others do. It was a heavy and muscle-bound business, as that of a man shoeing his first horse.

The porter took their bag, and as the train began to slow they moved forward to the hooded platform of the car. Presently the two engines and their long string of coaches rushed into the station of Yellow Sky.

"They have to take water here," said Potter, from a constricted throat and in mournful cadence, as one announcing death. Before the train stopped his eye had swept the length of the platform, and he was glad and astonished to see there was none upon it but the station-agent, who, with a slightly hurried and anxious air, was walking toward the water-tanks. When the train had halted, the porter alighted first, and placed in position a little temporary step.

"Come on, girl," said Potter, hoarsely. As he helped her down they each laughed on a false note. He took the bag from the negro, and bade his wife cling to his arm. As they slunk rapidly away, his hang-dog glance perceived that they were unloading the two trunks, and also that the station-agent, far ahead near the baggage-car, had turned and was running toward him, making gestures. He laughed, and groaned as he laughed, when he noted the first effect of his marital bliss upon Yellow Sky. He gripped his wife's arm firmly to his side, and they fled. Behind them the porter stood, chuckling fatuously.

The California express on the Southern Railway was due at Yellow Sky in twenty-one minutes. There were six men at the bar of the Weary Gentleman Saloon. One was a drummer, who talked a great deal and rapidly; three were Texans, who did not care to talk at that time; and two were Mexican sheepherders, who did not talk as a general practice in the Weary Gentleman Saloon. The barkeeper's dog lay on the board walk that crossed in front of the door. His head was on his paws, and he glanced drowsily here and there with the constant vigilance of a dog that is kicked on occasion. Across the sandy street were some vivid green grass-plots, so wonderful in appearance, amid the sands that burned near them in a blazing sun, that they caused a doubt in the mind. They exactly resembled the grass mats used to represent lawns on the stage. At the cooler end of the railway station, a man without a coat sat in a tilted chair and smoked his pipe. The fresh-cut bank of the Rio Grande circled near the town, and there could be seen beyond it a great plum-colored plain of mesquit.

Save for the busy drummer and his companions in the saloon, Yellow Sky was dozing. The new-comer leaned gracefully upon the bar, and recited many tales with the confidence of a bard who has come upon a new field.

"—and at the moment that the old man fell down-stairs with the bureau in his arms, the old woman was coming up with two scuttles of coal, and of course—"

The drummer's tale was interrupted by a young man who suddenly appeared in the open door. He cried: "Scratchy Wilson's drunk, and has turned loose with both hands." The two Mexicans at once set down their glasses and faded out of the rear entrance of the saloon.

The drummer, innocent and jocular, answered: "All right, old man. S'pose he has? Come in and have a drink, anyhow."

But the information had made such an obvious cleft in every skull in the room that the drummer was obliged to see its importance. All had become instantly solemn. "Say," said he, mystified, "what is this?" His three companions made the introductory gesture of eloquent speech; but the young man at the door forestalled them.

"It means, my friend," he answered, as he came into the saloon, "that for the next two hours this town won't be a health resort."

The barkeeper went to the door, and locked and barred it; reaching out of the window, he pulled in heavy wooden shutters, and barred them. Immediately a solemn, chapel-like gloom was upon the place. The drummer was looking from one to another.

"But say," he cried, "what is this, anyhow? You don't mean there is going to be a gun-fight?"

"Don't know whether there'll be a fight or not," answered one man, grimly; "but there'll be some shootin'—some good shootin'."

The young man who had warned them waved his hand. "Oh, there'll be a fight fast enough, if any one wants it. Anybody can get a fight out there in the street. There's a fight just waiting."

The drummer seemed to be swayed between the interest of a foreigner and a perception of personal danger.

"What did you say his name was?" he asked.

"Scratchy Wilson," they answered in chorus.

"And will he kill anybody? What are you going to do? Does this happen often? Does he rampage around like this once a week or so? Can he break in that door?"

"No; he can't break down that door," replied the barkeeper. "He's tried it three times. But when he comes you'd better lay down on the floor, stranger. He's dead sure to shoot at it, and a bullet may come through."

Thereafter the drummer kept a strict eye upon the door. The time had not yet been called for him to hug the floor, but, as a minor precaution, he sidled near to the wall. "Will he kill anybody?" he said again.

The man laughed low and scornfully at the question.

"He's out to shoot, and he's out for trouble. Don't see any good in experimentin' with him."

"But what do you do in a case like this? What do you do?"

A man responded: "Why, he and Jack Potter—"

"But," in chorus the other men interrupted, "Jack Potter's in San Anton'."

"Well, who is he? What's he got to do with it?"

"Oh, he's the town marshal. He goes out and fights Scratchy when he gets on one of these tears."

"Wow!" said the drummer, mopping his brow. "Nice job he's got."

The voices had toned away to mere whisperings. The drummer wished to ask further questions, which were born of an increasing anxiety and bewilderment; but when he attempted them, the men merely looked at him in irritation and motioned him to remain silent. A tense waiting hush was upon them. In the deep shadows of the room their eyes shone as they listened for sounds from the street. One man made three gestures at the barkeeper; and the latter, moving like a ghost, handed him a glass and a bottle. The man poured a full glass of whisky, and set down the bottle noiselessly. He gulped the whisky in a swallow, and turned again toward the door in immovable silence. The drummer saw that the barkeeper, without a sound, had taken a Winchester from beneath the bar. Later he saw this individual beckoning to him, so he tiptoed across the room.

"You better come with me back of the bar."

"No, thanks," said the drummer, perspiring; "I'd rather be where I can make a break for the back door."

Whereupon the man of bottles made a kindly but peremptory gesture. The drummer obeyed it, and, finding himself seated on a box with his head below the level of the bar, balm was laid upon his soul at sight of various zinc and copper fittings that bore a resemblance to armor-plate. The barkeeper took a seat comfortably upon an adjacent box.

"You see," he whispered, "this here Scratchy Wilson is a wonder with a gun—a perfect wonder; and when he goes on the war-trail, we hunt our holes—naturally. He's about the last one of the old gang that used to hang out along the river here. He's a terror when he's drunk. When he's sober he's all right—kind of simple—wouldn't hurt a fly—nicest fellow in town. But when he's drunk—whoo!"

There were periods of stillness. "I wish Jack Potter was back from San Anton'," said the barkeeper. "He shot Wilson up once,—in the leg,—and he would sail in and pull out the kinks in this thing."

Presently they heard from a distance the sound of a shot, followed by three wild yowls. It instantly removed a bond from the men in the darkened saloon. There was a shuffling of feet. They looked at each other. "Here he comes," they said.

A man in a maroon-colored flannel shirt, which had been purchased for purposes of decoration, and made principally by some Jewish women on the East Side of New York, rounded a corner and walked into the middle of the main street of Yellow Sky. In either hand the man held a long, heavy, blue-black revolver. Often he yelled, and these cries rang through a semblance of a deserted village, shrilly flying over the roofs in a volume that seemed to have no relation to the ordinary vocal strength of a man. It was as if the surrounding stillness formed the arch of a tomb over him. These cries of ferocious challenge rang against walls of silence. And his boots had red tops with gilded imprints, of the kind beloved in winter by little sledding boys on the hillsides of New England.

The man's face flamed in a rage begot of whisky. His eyes, rolling, and yet keen for ambush, hunted the still doorways and windows. He walked with the creeping movement of the midnight cat. As it occurred to him, he roared menacing information. The long revolvers in his hands were as easy as straws; they were moved with an electric swiftness. The little fingers of each hand played sometimes in a musician's way. Plain from the low collar of the shirt, the cords of his neck straightened and sank, straightened and sank, as passion moved him. The only sounds were his terrible invitations. The calm adobes preserved their demeanor at the passing of this small thing in the middle of the street.

There was no offer of fight—no offer of fight. The man called to the sky. There were no attractions. He bellowed and fumed and swayed his revolvers here and everywhere.

The dog of the barkeeper of the Weary Gentleman Saloon had not appreciated the advance of events. He yet lay dozing in front of his master's door. At sight of the dog, the man paused and raised his revolver humorously. At sight of the man, the dog sprang up and walked diagonally away, with a sullen head, and growling. The man yelled, and the dog broke into a gallop. As it was about to enter an alley, there was a loud noise, a whistling, and something spat the ground directly before it. The dog screamed, and, wheeling in terror, galloped headlong in a new direction. Again there was a noise, a whistling, and sand was kicked viciously before it. Fear-stricken, the dog turned and flurried like an animal in a pen. The man stood laughing, his weapons at his hips.

Ultimately the man was attracted by the closed door of the Weary Gentleman Saloon. He went to it, and, hammering with a revolver, demanded drink.

The door remaining imperturbable, he picked a bit of paper from the walk, and nailed it to the framework with a knife. He then turned his back contemptuously upon this popular resort, and, walking to the opposite side of the street, and spinning there on his heel quickly and lithely, fired at the bit of paper. He missed it by a half-inch. He swore at himself, and went away. Later he comfortably fusilladed the windows of his most intimate friend. The man was playing with this town; it was a toy for him.

But still there was no offer of fight. The name of Jack Potter, his ancient antagonist, entered his mind, and he concluded that it would be a glad thing if he should go to Potter's house, and by bombardment induce him to come out and fight. He moved in the direction of his desire, chanting Apache scalp-music.

When he arrived at it, Potter's house presented the same still front as had the other adobes. Taking up a strategic position, the man howled a challenge. But this house regarded him as might a great stone god. It gave no sign. After a decent wait, the man howled further challenges, mingling with them wonderful epithets.

Presently there came the spectacle of a man churning himself into deepest rage over the immobility of a house. He fumed at it as the winter wind attacks a prairie cabin in the North. To the distance there should have gone the sound of a tumult like the fighting of two hundred Mexicans. As necessity bade him, he paused for breath or to reload his revolvers.

Potter and his bride walked sheepishly and with speed. Sometimes they laughed together shamefacedly and low.

"Next corner, dear," he said finally.

They both put forth the efforts of a pair walking bowed against a strong wind. Potter was about to raise a finger to point the first appearance of the new home when, as they circled the corner, they came face to face with a man in a maroon-colored shirt, who was feverishly pushing cartridges into a large revolver. Upon the instant the man dropped his revolver to the ground, and, like lightning, whipped another from its holster. The second weapon was aimed at the bridegroom's chest.

There was a silence. Potter's mouth seemed to be merely a grave for his tongue. He exhibited an instinct to at once loosen his arm from the woman's grip, and he dropped the bag to the sand. As for the bride, her face had gone as yellow as old cloth. She was a slave to hideous rites, gazing at the apparitional snake.

The two men faced each other at a distance of three paces. He of the revolver smiled and with a new and quiet ferocity.

"Tried to sneak up on me," he said. "Tried to sneak up on me!" His eyes grew more baleful. As Potter made a slight movement, the man thrust his revolver venomously forward. "No; don't you do it, Jack Potter. Don't you move a finger toward a gun just yet. Don't you move an eyelash. The time has come for me to settle with you, and I'm goin' to do it my own way, and loaf along with no interferin'. So if you don't want a gun bent on you, just mind what I tell you."

Potter looked at his enemy. "I ain't got a gun on me, Scratchy," he said. "Honest, I ain't." He was stiffening and steadying, but yet somewhere at the back of his mind a vision of the Pullman floated: the sea-green figured velvet, the shining brass, silver, and glass, the wood that gleamed as darkly brilliant as the surface of a pool of oil—all the glory of the marriage, the environment of the new estate. "You know I fight when it comes to fighting, Scratchy Wilson; but I ain't got a gun on me. You'll have to do all the shootin' yourself."

His enemy's face went livid. He stepped forward, and lashed his weapon to and fro before Potter's chest. "Don't you tell me you ain't got no gun on you, you whelp. Don't tell me no lie like that. There ain't a man in Texas ever seen you without no gun. Don't take me for no kid." His eyes blazed with light, and his throat worked like a pump.

"I ain't takin' you for no kid," answered Potter. His heels had not moved an inch backward. "I'm takin' you for a —— fool. I tell you I ain't got a gun, and I ain't. If you're goin' to shoot me up, you better begin now; you'll never get a chance like this again."

So much enforced reasoning had told on Wilson's rage; he was calmer. "If you ain't got a gun, why ain't you got a gun?" he sneered. "Been to Sunday-school?"

"I ain't got a gun because I've just come from San Anton' with my wife. I'm married," said Potter. "And if I'd thought there was going to be any galoots like you prowling around when I brought my wife home, I'd had a gun, and don't you forget it."

"Married!" said Scratchy, not at all comprehending.

"Yes, married. I'm married," said Potter, distinctly.

"Married?" said Scratchy. Seemingly for the first time, he saw the drooping, drowning woman at the other man's side. "No!" he said. He was like a creature allowed a glimpse of another world. He moved a pace backward, and his arm, with the revolver, dropped to his side. "Is this the lady?" he asked.

"Yes; this is the lady," answered Potter.

There was another period of silence.

"Well," said Wilson at last, slowly, "I s'pose it's all off now."

"It's all off if you say so, Scratchy. You know I didn't make the trouble." Potter lifted his valise.

"Well, I 'low it's off, Jack," said Wilson. He was looking at the ground. "Married!" He was not a student of chivalry; it was merely that in the presence of this foreign condition he was a simple child of the earlier plains. He picked up his starboard revolver, and, placing both weapons in their holsters, he went away. His feet made funnel-shaped tracks in the heavy sand.

QUESTIONS

1. Notice that the scene shifts, or the narrator changes his perspective, a number of times in this story. How many shifts are there, and where do they occur? What effect do these shifts have on the development of the story? How might such shifts be indicated in a motion picture treatment of the story?

2. At the beginning of the story, Jack Potter is shown as uncomfortable in new clothes, apprehensive about Yellow Sky's reaction to his marriage. How do these feelings of Potter's relate to Scratchy Wilson's discomfort at the end of the story?

3. How would the story be different if it were told entirely from the point of view of Jack Potter? Or of Scratchy Wilson? Or of Potter's bride?

4. Although the drummer has no part in the development of the conflict or in the confrontation of the two major characters, he has an important part in the structure and presentation of the story. What is his function?

5. What kind of walk would cause "funnel-shaped tracks"? What effect does Crane achieve by ending his story with this sentence: "His feet made funnel-shaped tracks in the heavy sand"?

6. Stephen Crane always made effective use of color in descriptions. How does color help to characterize Jack Potter? His wife? The town of Yellow Sky?

7. This story takes place in the West, but is it "a Western"? How is it like the other stories in this collection? How is it different?

CLARENCE MULFORD

HOPALONG SITS IN

Hopalong Cassidy dismounted in front of the rough-boarded hotel, regarding it with a curious detachment which was the result of a lifetime's experience with such hybrid affairs. He knew what it would be even before he left the saddle: saloon, gambling house and hotel, to mention its characteristics in the order of their real importance.

Hopalong entered the main room and found that it ran the full length of the building. A bar paralleled one wall, card tables filled the open space; and in the inside corner near the door was a pine desk on which was a bottle of muddy ink, a corroded pen, a paper-covered notebook of the kind used in schools for compositions, and a grimy showcase holding cigars and tobaccos. Behind the desk on the wall was a short piece of board with nails driven in it, and on the nails hung a few keys.

A shiftless person with tobacco-stained lips arose from a near-by table, looking inquiringly at the newcomer.

"Got a room?" asked Hopalong.

"Yeah. Two dollars, in advance," replied the clerk.

"By the week," suggested Hopalong.

"Twelve dollars—we don't count Sundays," said the clerk with a foolish grin.

"Eat on the premises?" asked the newcomer, sliding a gold coin across the desk.

The clerk tossed the coin into the air, listened to the ring as it struck the board, tossed it into a drawer, made change and hooked a thumb over his shoulder.

"Right in yonder," he said, indicating the other half of the building. "Doors open six to eight; twelve to one; six to seven. Pay when you eat an' take what you get. Come with me an' I'll show you the room."

Hopalong obeyed, climbing the steep and economical stairs with just the faintest suggestion of a limp. As they passed down the central hall, he could see into the rooms on each side. They were all alike, even to the arrangement of the furniture. The beds all stood with their heads against the hall wall, in the same relative positions.

"Reckon this will do," he grunted, looking past the clerk into the room indicated. "Stable out back?"

"Yeah. Take yore hoss around an' talk to the stableman," said the clerk, facing around. "Dinner in about an hour."

Hopalong nodded and fell in behind his guide, found the stairs worse in descent than in ascent, and arranged for the care of his horse. When he returned to the room he dropped his blanket roll on the foot of the bed, and then looked searchingly and slowly at the canvas walls. There was nothing to be seen, and shaking his head gently, he went out and down again to wander about the town until time to enter the dining room.

After dinner he saddled his horse and rode down the wide cattle trail, going southward in hope of meeting the SV herd. This was the day it was due; but he was too old a hand to worry about a trail herd being behind time. Johnny Nelson would reach the town when he got there, and there was no reason to waste any thought about the matter. Still, he had nothing else to do, and he pushed on at an easy lope.

He, himself, had been over at Dodge City, where he had learned that Johnny Nelson had a herd on the trail and was bound north. It was a small herd of selected cattle driven by a small outfit. He had not seen Johnny for over a year, and it was too good an opportunity to let pass. For the pleasure of meeting his old friend he had written a letter to him addressed to an important mail station on the new trail, where all outfits called for mail. Some days later he had left Dodge and ridden west, and now he was on hand to welcome the SV owner.

Hopalong passed two herds as he rode, and paused to exchange words with the trail bosses. One of the herds was bound for Wyoming, and the other for Dakota. Trailing had not been very brisk so far this season, but from what the two bosses had heard it was due to pick up shortly. About mid-afternoon Hopalong turned and started back toward town, reaching the hotel soon after the dining-room doors opened.

After supper the town came to life, and as darkness fell, the street was pretty well filled with men. The greater part of the town's population was floating: punchers, gamblers and others whose occupations were not so well known.

The main room of the hotel came to life swiftly, the long bar was well lined and the small tables began to fill. The noise increased in volume and it was not long before the place was in full swing. From time to time brawls broke out in the street and made themselves heard; and once pistol shots caused heads to raise and partly stilled the room.

Hopalong sat lazily in a chair between two windows, his back to the wall, placidly engaged in watching the activities about him. More and more his eyes turned to one particular table, where a game of poker was under way, and where the rounds of drinks came in a steady procession. His curiosity was aroused, and he wondered if the situation was the old one.

To find out, he watched to see which player drank the least liquor, and he found that instead of one man doing that, there were two. To a man of Hopalong's experience along the old frontier, that suggested a very pertinent thought; and he watched more keenly now to see if he could justify it. So far as he was concerned, it was purely an impersonal matter; he knew none of the players and cared nothing who lost in the game. As hand followed hand, and the liquor began to work, the cheating became apparent to him and threatened to become apparent to others; and he found his gorge slowly rising.

Finally one of the players, having lost his last chip and being unable to buy more, pushed back his chair and left the table, reeling toward the street door. Just then, elbowing his way from the crowd at the bar, came one of the trail bosses with whom Hopalong had talked that afternoon. The newcomer stopped behind the vacant chair and gestured toward it inquiringly.

"Shore. Set down," said one of the sober players. The others nodded their acquiescence, soberly or drunkenly as the case might be, and more drinks were ordered. The two sober men had drunk round for round with the others, and yet showed no effects from it. Hopalong flashed a glance at the bar, and nodded wisely. Very likely they were being served tea.

Hopalong pulled his chair out from the wall, tipped it back and settled down, his big hat slanting well before his eyes. He had ridden all day and was tired, and he found himself drowsing. After an interval, the length of which he did not know, he was aroused to alertness by a shouted curse; but before he could get to his feet or roll off the chair, a shot roared out, almost deafening him. There was a quick flurry at the table, a struggle, and he saw the trail boss, disarmed, being dragged and pushed toward the door. Hopalong removed his sombrero and looked at the hole near the edge of the brim. He was inserting the tip of his little finger into it when one of the players, in a hurried glance around the room, saw the action.

"Close, huh?" inquired the gambler with momentary interest, and then looked around the room again. Several men had pushed out from the crowd and stood waiting in a little group, closely watching the room. As he glimpsed these men, the gambler's face lost its trace of anxiety and he smiled coldly.

Hopalong's eyes flicked from the gambler to the watchful guards and back again, and then he turned slowly to look at the wall behind him, just back of his right ear. The bullet hole was there.

"Yeah, it was close," he said slowly, grinning grimly. "At first I reckoned mebby it might be an old one; but that hole in the wall says it ain't. Who stepped on that fool's pet corn?"

"Nobody; just too much liquor," answered the gambler. "Sometimes it makes a man ugly. Now he's busted up the game, for I shore don't care for a four-hander. Mebby you'd like to take his place?"

"I might," admitted Hopalong with no especial interest. "What you playin', an' how steep?"

"Draw, with jackpots after a full house or better," replied the gambler, looking swiftly but appraisingly at the two drunken players. They had leaned over the table again, and were not to be counted upon to make denials of any statement. "Two bits, an' two dollars; just a friendly game, to pass away the time."

"All right," replied Hopalong, thinking that friendship came rather high in Trailville, if that was the measure of a friendly game.

The gambler waved a hand, and four men stepped to the table. After a moment's argument they took the helpless players from their chairs and started them toward the front door.

Hopalong smiled, thinking that now the game was less than four-handed. He said nothing, however, but stepped forward and dropped into one of the vacant chairs.

"We can get a couple more to take their places," Hopalong said, and nodded gently as his prophecy was fulfilled. He smiled a welcome to the two men and waited until the gambler had taken his own chair. Then Hopalong leaned forward. "You can call me Riordan," he said.

"Kitty out a white chip every game for the house," said the gambler, reaching for the cards. "We play straights between threes and flushes; no fancy combinations. A faced card on the draw can't be taken."

"You playin' for the house?" asked Hopalong needlessly. He was drawing a hand from a pocket as he spoke, and at the gambler's answering nod, he opened the hand and pushed the coins toward the other. "You got chips enough to sell me some," he said.

The game got under way, and the liquor began to arrive. Hopalong was smiling inwardly: he was well fortified to meet the conditions of this game. In the first place, he could stand an amazing amount of whisky; but he did not intend to crowd his capacity by drinking every round. In the second, poker was to him a fine art; and the more dishonest the game, the finer his art—thanks to Tex Ewalt. He always met crookedness with crookedness rather than to cause trouble, but he let the others set the pace.

He looked like a common frontier citizen, with perhaps a month's wages in his pockets, and he believed that was the reason for the moderate limit set by the gambler, who was a tinhorn, and satisfied with small pickings if he could not do better; but as a matter of fact, Hopalong was a full partner in a very prosperous northern ranch, and he could write a check for six figures and have it honored. Last, and fully as important, he was able to take care of himself in any frontier situation from cutting cards to shooting lead. He believed that he was going to thoroughly enjoy his stay in Trailville.

"On the trail?" carelessly asked the gambler as the cards were cut for the first deal.

"No," answered Hopalong, picking up the deck by diagonal corners in case the cards had been shaved. "I'm just driftin' toward home."

As the game went on it appeared that he had a bad poker weakness: every time he had a poor hand and bluffed strongly, his mouth twitched. It took some time for this to register with the others, but when it did, he found that he was very promptly called; and his displeasure in his adversaries' second sight was plain to all who watched.

Along about the middle of the game his mouth must have twitched by accident, for he raked in a pot that had been well built up and leveled up nearly all his loss. The game seesawed until midnight, when it broke up; and Hopalong found that he cashed in twenty dollars less chips than he had bought; twenty dollars' worth of seeds, from which a crop might grow. He knew that he would be a welcomed addition to any poker game in this hotel, that his weaknesses were known, and his consistent and set playing was now no secret.

He went to his room, closed the door and lighted the lamp, intending to go to bed; but the room was too hot for comfort. There was not a breath of air stirring, and as yet the coolness of the night had not overcome the heat stored up by the walls and roof during the day. He stood for a moment in indecision and then, knowing that another hour would make an appreciable difference in the temperature of the room, he turned and left it, going down to the street.

The night was dark, but star-bright, and he stood for a moment looking about him. The saloons and gambling shacks were going full blast, but they had no appeal for him. He walked toward the corner of the hotel and looked back toward the stables; and then he remembered that he had seen a box against the side wall of the barroom. That was just what he wanted, and he moved slowly along the wall, feeling his way in the deeper shadow, found it, and seated himself with a sigh of relief, leaning back against the wall and relaxing.

Men passed up and down the street, and human voices rose and fell in the buildings along it. Time passed with no attempt on Hopalong's part to keep track of it, but by the deepening chill which comes at that altitude, he believed that the room would now be bearable. About to get up and make a start for the street, he heard and saw two men lazily approach the corner of the building and lean against it, and glance swiftly about them. From the faint light of the front window he thought that he knew who one of them was; and as soon as the man spoke, he was certain of the identity.

"You know what to do," said the speaker. "I looked 'em over good. There's about two hundred head of fine, selected cattle, four-year-olds. It'll be easy to run off most of 'em, or mebby all of 'em. Take 'em round about into Wolf Hollow, an' then scatter 'em to hell an' gone. We'll round 'em up later. Don't bungle it *this* time. Get goin'."

The two men separated, one moving swiftly to where a horse was standing across the street. He mounted quickly and rode away. The other moved out of sight around the corner and disappeared, apparently into the hotel. Three men came past the corner and paused to argue drunkenly; and by the time they had moved on again Hopalong knew that he had lost touch with the man who held his interest.

The coast being clear, Hopalong moved slowly toward the street, went into the bar-room and glanced about as he made his way to the stairs. Reaching his room, he closed the door behind him and listened for a few moments. During lulls in the general noise downstairs he could hear a man snoring.

Undressing, he stretched out and gave himself over to a period of quiet but intensive thought. He had nothing positive to go upon; the horseman had ridden off so quickly that he was gone before Hopalong could come to any decision about following him; he realized that by the time he could have saddled up the man would have been out of reach. He did not know for sure that the two men had referred to the SV herd, nor where to find it if he did know. All he could do was to wait, and to keep his ears open and his wits about him. It would be better to conceal his interest in Johnny Nelson and Johnny's cattle. As a matter of fact he had nothing but unfounded suspicions for the whole structure he was building up.

Back in Dodge City he had been well informed about Trailville and the conditions obtaining there, since a large per cent of the unholy population of Dodge had packed up and gone to the new town. The big herds no longer crossed the Arkansas near the famous old cattle town, to amble up the divide leading to the Sawlog. The present marshal of Dodge was a good friend of Hopalong's, and had been thorough in his pointers and remarks.

Hopalong had learned from him, for one thing, that a good trail herd with a small outfit would be likely to lose cattle and have a deal of trouble before it passed the new town; especially if the trail crew was further reduced in numbers by some of the men receiving time off to enjoy an evening in the town. Further than that the marshal had mentioned one man by name, Bradley, and stressed it emphatically; and only tonight Hopalong had heard that man's name called out while the poker game was under way, and had looked with assumed carelessness across the table at the player who had answered to it.

Hopalong had taken pains during the remainder of the evening to be affable to this gentleman, and to study him; he had been so affable and friendly that he even had forborne giving a hint that he knew the gentleman cheated when occasion seemed to warrant it. And this man Bradley was the man he had overheard speak just a few minutes before at the corner of the building.

Perhaps, after all, he would ride down the trail in the morning, if he knew that he was not observed doing it, and try to get in touch with Johnny, even though he did not know how far away the SV herd might be. He knew that the herd numbered about two hundred head of the best cattle to be found on four ranches; and he knew that the outfit would be small. He feared . . . Ah, hell! What was the use of letting unfounded suspicions make a fool of him, and keep him awake? He turned over on his side and went to sleep like a child.

He was the second man through the dining-room door the next morning, and soon thereafter he left town, bound down the trail, hoping that the SV herd was within a day's ride, and that he could meet it unobserved. He had not covered a dozen miles before he saw a horseman coming toward him up the trail, and something about the man seemed to be familiar. It was not long before he knew the rider to be Bradley.

The two horsemen nodded casually and pulled up, stopping almost leg to leg.

"Leavin' us, Riordan?" asked the upbound man.

"No," answered Hopalong. "The town's dead durin' daylight, an' I figgered to look over the country an' kill some time."

"There ain't nothin' down this way to see," replied the other. "Nor up the other way, neither," he added.

"Ride with you, then, as far as town," said Hopalong, deciding not to show even a single card of his hand.

They went on up the trail at a slow and easy gait, talking idly of this and that, and then Hopalong turned sidewise and asked a question with elaborate casualness.

"Who's town marshal, Bradley?" he asked.

"Slick Cunningham. Why?" asked Bradley, flashing a quick glance at his companion.

Hopalong was silent for a moment, turning the name over in his mind; and then his expression faintly suggested relief.

"Never heard of him," he admitted, and laughed gently, his careless good nature once more restored. "Reckon, accordin' to that, he never heard of me, neither."

"Oh, Slick's all right; he minds his own business purty well," said Bradley, and grinned broadly. "Anyhow, he's out of town right now."

Continuing a purely idle conversation, they soon saw the town off on one side of the trail, and Bradley raised a hand.

"There she is," he said, pulling up. "I've got a couple of errands to do that wouldn't interest you none; so I'll quit you here, an' see you in town tonight."

"Keno," grunted Hopalong, and headed for the collection of shacks that was Trailville. He was halfway to town when he purposely lost his hat. Wheeling, he swung down to scoop it up, and took advantage of the movement to glance swiftly backward; and he was just in time to see Bradley dipping down into a hollow west of the trail. The remainder of the short ride was covered at a walk, and was a thoughtful one.

The day dragged past, suppertime came and went, and again the big room slowly filled with men. Hopalong sat in the same chair, tipped back against the wall, the bullet hole close to his head. Bradley soon came in, stopping at the bar for a few moments, and then led the same group of card players to the same table. Looking around for Hopalong, they espied him, called him by his new name of Riordan and gestured toward the table. In a few moments the game was under way.

The crowd shifted constantly, men coming and going from and to the street. There was a group bunched at the bar, close to the front door. Two men came in from the street, pushing along the far side of the group, eager to quench their thirst. One of them was Slick Cunningham, town marshal, just back from a special assignment. His name was not even as old as Trailville. He glanced through a small opening in the group to see who was in the room, and as his gaze settled on the men playing cards with Bradley, he stiffened and stepped quickly backward, covered by the group.

"Outside, George," he whispered to his companion. "Pronto! Stand just outside the door an' wait for me!"

George was mildly surprised, but he turned and sauntered to the street, stopping when he reached it.

The marshal was nowhere in sight, but he soon appeared around the corner of the building, and beckoned his friend to his side.

"I just had a good look through the window," he said hurriedly. "I knowed it was him; an' it shore is! When Bradley said he was figgerin' on takin' his pick of that SV herd I told him, an' all of you, too, that he was gettin' ready to pull a grizzly's tail. An' he is! Nelson was one of the old Bar 20 gang. . . . An' who the hell do you reckon is sittin' between Bradley an' Winters, playin' poker with 'em? Hopalong Cassidy! Hopalong Cassidy, damn his soul!"

"Thought you said he was up in Montanny?" replied George, with only casual interest.

"He was! But, great Gawd! he don't have to stay there, does he?

You get word to Bradley, quick as you can. Settin' elbow to elbow
with Cassidy! If that don't stink, then I don't know what does!
Cassidy here in Trailville, an' Nelson's cattle comin' up the trail! I'm
tellin' you that somethin's wrong!"

"You reckon he knows anything?" asked George, to whom the
name of Hopalong Cassidy did not mean nearly so much as it did to
his companion.

"Listen!" retorted the marshal earnestly. "Nobody on Gawd's
gray earth knows how much that feller knows! I've never run up ag'in
him yet when he didn't know a damn sight more than I wanted him
to; an' what he don't know, he damn soon finds out. You get word to
Bradley. I'm pullin' out of town, an' I'm stayin' out till this mess is all
cleaned up. If Cassidy sees me, he'll know that I know him; an' if he
knows that I know him, he'll know that I'll pass on the word to my
friends. I'll give a hundred dollars to see him buried."

"You mean that?" asked George, with sudden interest.

Slick peered into his eyes through the gloom, and then snorted
with disgust.

"Don't you be a damn fool!" he snapped. "I didn't say that I
wanted to see *you* buried, did I?"

"Hell with that!" retorted George. "I'm askin' you if you really
mean that as an offer; if you'll pay a hundred dollars to the man that
kills him?"

"Well, I didn't reckon nobody would be fool enough to take me
up," said Slick, but he suddenly leaned forward again, as a new phase
of the matter struck him. "Yes, you damn fool! Yes, I will!" He pulled
his hat down firmly and nodded. "My share of that herd money will
come to a lot more than a hundred dollars; but if that pizen pup stays
alive around here we won't steal a head, an' I won't get a cent. Yes,
the offer goes; but you better get help, an' split it three ways. There's
only one man in town who would have any kind of a chance, an' his
name ain't George."

"I'll take care of that end of it," replied George; "an' now I'm
goin' in to get word to Bradley. So long."

"So long," said Slick, and forthwith disappeared around the
corner on his way to the little corral behind the marshal's office. There
was a good horse in that corral, and a horse was just what he wanted at
the moment.

George pushed through the group, signaled to the bartender,
ordered a drink, and whispered across the counter. Placing his glass on
the bar, George moved carelessly down the room, nodding to right
and to left. He stopped beside the busy poker table, grunted a
greeting to the men he knew, and dragged up a chair near Bradley's
right elbow, where he could look at the cards in his friend's hand, and

by merely raising his eyes, looked over their tops at the player on the left.

Hopalong had dropped out for that deal, and was leaning back in his chair, his eyes shaded by the brim of his hat. His placid gaze was fixed on the window opposite and he was wondering whose face it was that he had glimpsed in the little patch of light outside. The face had been well back, and the beams of light from the lamps had not revealed it well; but it was something to think about, and, having nothing else to do at the moment, he let his mind dwell on it. He did not like faces furtively peering in through lighted windows.

Bradley chuckled, pulled in the pot and tossed his cards unshown into the discard.

"Hello, George," he said, turning to smile at the man on his right.

"Hello, Bill. Won't nobody call yore hand tonight?"

"They don't call me at the right time," laughed Bradley, in rare good humor. "This seems to be my night." He looked up at the man who now stepped into his circle of vision. "What is it, Tom?"

"Bartender wants to see you, Bill. Says it's important, an' won't take more'n a minute."

"Deal me out this hand," said Bradley, pushing back his chair and following the messenger.

Hopalong let the cards lay as they fell, and when the fifth had dropped in front of him his fingers pushed them into a neat, smooth-sided book, and he watched the faces of the other players as the hands were picked up. The house gambler was in direct line with that part of the bar where Bradley had stopped, and Hopalong's gaze, lifting from the face of the player, for a moment picked out Bradley and the bartender. The latter was looking straight at him and the expression on the man's face was grim and hostile. Hopalong looked at the next player, lifted his own cards and riffled the corners to let the pips flash before his eyes.

"She's open," said the man on the dealer's left, tossing a chip into the center of the table.

"Stay," grunted Hopalong, doing likewise in his turn. A furtive face at the window, a message for Bradley, and a suddenly hostile bartender—and Johnny's herd was small, selected, and had a small outfit with it. Suspicions, suspicions, always suspicions! He bent his head, and then raised it quickly and looked at George before that person had time to iron out his countenance. From that instant Hopalong did not like George, and determined to keep an eye on him.

Bradley returned, slapped George on the shoulder and drew up to the table, watching the play. Not once did he look at Hopalong.

When the play came around to Hopalong it had been raised

twice, and that person, studying his cards intently, suddenly looked over their tops and tossed them away. Bradley's expression changed a flash too late.

"They ain't runnin' for me," growled Hopalong, glancing from Bradley to George. "Game's gettin' tiresome, but I'll try a few more hands."

"Hell!" growled Bradley, affable and smiling again. "That ain't the trouble—the game's too small to hold a feller's interest."

"Right!" quickly said the house gambler, nodding emphatically as he sensed a kill. "Too tee-totally damn small! Let's play a round of jackpots to finish this up; an' then them that don't want to play for real money can't say they was throwed out cold."

"I'll set out the round of jacks an' come in on the new game," said Hopalong, risking quick glances around the room. No one seemed to be paying any particular attention to him.

"Me, too. No, I'll give you fellers a chance," said Bradley.

"Don't need to give me no chance," said a player across from him. "I'm ready for the big game."

Hopalong saw a young man push through the crowd near the door and head straight for the table. As he made his way down the room he was the cynosure of all eyes, and a ripple of whispered comment followed him. Hopalong did not know it, but the newcomer was a killer famous for his deeds around Trailville—a man who would kill for money, who had always "got" his man, and who was a close friend of Bradley's.

"Hello, Bill," the newcomer addressed Bradley, and then dropped into the chair which George surrendered to him as if he was expected to do so; and thereupon George moved toward the bar and was lost to sight.

Bradley nodded, smiled and faced the table again, gesturing with both hands.

"Riordan, meet Jim Hawes. Jim, Riordan's a stranger here."

The two men exchanged nods, sizing each other up. Hawes saw a typical cowpuncher, past middle age; but a man whose deeds rang from one edge of the cattle country to the other; a man whose reputation would greatly enhance that of anybody who managed to kill him with a gun in an even break. His mantle of fame would rest automatically upon the shoulders of his master.

Hopalong saw a vicious-faced killer, cold, unemotional, and of almost tender years. There was a swagger in his every movement and one could easily see that he was an important individual. The young man's eyes were rather close together, and his chin receded. To Hopalong, both of these characteristics were danger marks. He had found, in his own experience, that the prognathous jaw is greatly overrated. Hawes reminded him of a weasel.

"Haven't had a game for a long time," said Hawes, speaking with almost pugnacious assurance. "Reckon I'll set in an' give her a whirl."

"She's goin' to be a real one, Jim," said the house dealer uneasily. His profession, to his way of thinking, called for a little trickery with the cards upon occasion; but with Jim Hawes in the game only an adept would dare attempt it; not so much that Hawes was capable of detecting fine work, but because he would shoot with as little compunction as a rattler strikes.

"I like 'em big; the bigger the better," boasted Hawes, his cold eyes on Hopalong. "What you say, Riordan?" he asked, and the way he said the words made them a challenge. It appeared that his humor was not a pleasant one tonight.

"I'd rather have 'em growed up," replied Hopalong, looking him in the eyes, "*Well* growed up," amended Hopalong, his gaze unswerving.

Somewhere in the room a snicker sounded, quickly hushed as Hawes glanced toward the sound. The room had grown considerably quieter, ears functioning instead of tongues, and this, in itself, was a hint to an observing man. Hawes' gaze was back again like a flash, and he kept it set on the stranger's face while he slowly, with his left hand, drew his chair closer to the table, in the space provided for him by Bradley. He, too, sensed the quiet of the room, and a tight, knowing smile wreathed his thin lips.

"We'll make it growed up enough for you, Mister Riordan," he said, his left hand now drawing a roll of bills from a pocket. "How's five, an' twenty?" he challenged.

"Cents or dollars," curiously asked Hopalong, his face expressionless.

Hawes flushed, but checked the fighting words before they reached his teeth.

"What makes *you* reckon it might be cents?" he demanded, triumphantly.

"Just had a feelin' that it might be," calmly answered Hopalong. "Either one is a waste of time."

Bradley raised his eyebrows, regarding the speaker intently.

"Yeah?" he softly inquired. "How do you grade a growed-up game?"

"It all depends who I'm playin' with," answered Hopalong, his eyes on Hawes' tense face.

"Five an' fifty—*dollars!*" snapped the youth, showing his teeth.

"She's improvin' with every word," chuckled the house player.

"Damn near of age, anyhow," said Hopalong, nodding. "Straight draw poker? Threes, straights, flushes, an' so forth? No fancy hands?"

"The same game we have been playin'," said the house player. "Jackpots after full houses, or better. That suit everybody?"

Silence gave consent, the chips were redeemed at the old figure, deftly stacked and counted by the house player, and resold at the new prices. Hopalong drew out a roll of dirty bills, peeled off two of them, and with them bought a thousand dollars' worth of chips. He placed the remainder of the roll on the table near the chips, and nodded at it.

"When that's gone, I'm busted," he said, and looked at Hawes.

"Oh, don't worry! There's mine," sneered the youth, and bought the same amount of counters. Inwardly he thrilled; in so steep a game, cheating would be a great temptation to anyone inclined that way; and a crooked play would be justification for what followed it, and would suit him as well as any other excuse.

The player who had announced that he was ready for the bigger game now raised both hands toward heaven, pushed back his chair, and motioned grandiloquently toward the table; but no one in the room cared to take his place: the game was far too steep for them, and they sensed a deadly atmosphere.

"Quittin' us, Frank?" asked Bradley, with a knowing grin.

"Cold an' positive! My money comes harder than your'n, Bradley; an' I ain't got near as much of it. No, sir! I'll get all the excitement I'll need, just settin' back an' watchin' the play."

He had been sitting on Hopalong's left, and when he withdrew from the game, he pulled his chair back from the table, and now he drew it farther out of the way. Hopalong shifted in that direction, to even up the spacing; but as he stopped, he sensed Bradley's nearness, and saw that the latter had moved after him, but too far. Bradley's impetus had carried him even closer to Hopalong than he had been before. Bradley smiled apologetically and moved back, but only for a few inches. The fleeting expression on Hawes' face revealed satisfaction, and dressed the blundering shift with intent. What intent? In Hopalong's mind there could be only one; and that one, deadly.

The game got under way, and it was different from the more or less innocent affair which had preceded it. It was different in more ways than one. In the first place there was now present a thinly veiled hostility, an atmosphere of danger. In the second, a man could bluff with more assurance; a player would think twice before he would toss in fifty dollars to call a hand when he, himself, held little. In the third, a clever card manipulator would be tempted to make use of his best mastered tricks of sleight of hand; and should any man call for a new deck, or palm the old one for a moment, it would be well to give thought to the possible substitution of a cold deck. Here was the kind of a game Hopalong could enjoy; he had cut his teeth on them, and had been given excellent instruction by a past master of the game. Tex Ewalt had pronounced him proficient.

The first few hands were more in the nature of skirmishes, for with the change in the stakes had come a change in the style of play.

Hopalong's fingers were calloused, but the backs of his fingers were not; and he now bunched his cards in his left hand, face to the palm, and let the backs of the fingers of his right hand brush gently down the involved patterns, searching for pin pricks. As the cards were dealt to him, Hopalong idly pushed them about on the table, to get a different slant of lamplight on each one. If the polish had been removed by abrasives or acids the reflected light would show it.

At last came a jackpot, and it was passed three times, growing greatly in the process. The house player picked up the cards to deal, shuffling them swiftly, and ruffled them together with both hands hiding them. He pushed the deck toward Hopalong for the cut, in such a manner that if the latter chose the easier and more natural movement, he would cut with his nearest, or left, hand. If he did this, his fingers would naturally grasp the sides of the deck, and not the ends; and if the cards were trimmed, such a cut might well be costly.

As the dealer took his hand off the deck, Hopalong let his left hand reach for his cigarette; and it being thus occupied, and quite innocently so, he reached across his body with the idle right and quite naturally picked up the upper part of the deck by the ends. The dealer showed just the slightest indication of annoyance at this loss of time, and, finding Hopalong's bland gaze on the cards, forewent switching the cut, and dealt them as they lay.

Hawes opened for ten dollars. Bradley saw and raised it only five. Hopalong qualified. The dealer saw, and Hawes saw Bradley's raise, and boosted the limit. The others dropped out. Hawes showed his openers and took the pot. As the play went on, Hopalong observed a strange coincidence. The ante was five dollars; the limit, fifty. Every time that Hawes opened for ten dollars, and Bradley raised it five, or Bradley opened for ten, and Hawes raised it five, the opener thereupon boosted the limit when his time came, and very often dropped out on the next round to let the other win. Here was team work: Hawes and Bradley vs. all.

Hopalong glanced inquiringly at the house player, and caught an almost imperceptible wink directed at himself. There was no need for these two men to go into conference where teamwork was concerned; they knew how to join forces without previous agreements. And now, teamwork was called for as a matter of self-preservation.

The play went on without much action, and Hawes picked up the cards, bunching them for the deal. He was not an expert, and a dozen men in the room saw the clumsy switch, and held their breaths; but nothing violent happened. Apparently the other three players had not seen anything of interest. Bradley opened for ten dollars. Hopalong, looking at his cards, saw three kings and a pair of tens. He passed, and smiled inwardly at the dealer's poorly concealed look of amazement. The house player saw, but when both Hawes and Bradley had raised the limit in turn, he threw his hand in the discard and watched Bradley take the pot by default.

Hopalong, toying idly with his cards, now looked at them again, and swore loudly and bitterly.

"Damn fool! I thought it was two pairs . . . Will you *look* at that?"

Hopalong's outspread cards revealed their true worth, and the house player chuckled deep in his throat, his eyes beaming with congratulations.

"Pat king full," he said. "Well, Riordan, it can be beat."

"It can," admitted Hopalong, trying to smile. For an instant the two men looked understandingly into each other's eyes.

There was now no question about the status of this game. Both Hopalong and the house player had seen the clumsy switch; and it had been followed by a pat king full. The bars were now down and the rules were up. It was just a case of outcheating cheaters, and the devil take the less adept.

On Bradley's deal Hawes took another small pot by default, and Hopalong picked up the cards. His big hands moved swiftly, his fingers flicking almost in a blur of speed. The house player watched him, and then, curiously, against his habit, picked up each card as it fell in front of him. Seven, five, eight, and six of hearts. The fifth card seemed to intrigue him greatly: with it he would get the measure of a dexterous player's real mentality; and he hoped desperately that he would not have to play a pat hand. He sighed, picked up the card, and saw the jack of clubs. For a moment he regarded the dealer thoughtfully, and almost affectionately, and then he swiftly made up his mind. He would risk one play for the sake of knowledge. He opened for a white chip.

Hawes saw, and raised a red. Bradley stayed. Hopalong dropped out. The house player saw, and raised a blue, a true mark of confidence in a stranger's dealing ability; and almost before the chips had struck the table, Hawes saw and raised the limit. Bradley stayed, and the house player, rubbing his chin thoughtfully, evened it up, and asked for one card. He looked at it and turned it over, face up on the table. It was the four of hearts.

"Thanks," he said, nodding to Hopalong. "I needed that. It costs fifty dollars to play with me," he said to the others.

Hawes thought swiftly. As a heart, the card would fill a flush; as a four spot, it would build up three of a kind, a straight, a full house or four of a kind. Had it been a jack he would have hesitated; but now he tried to hide his elation, and tossed in a hundred dollars to see and to raise. Bradley sighed and dropped out.

"You took two cards," murmured the house player thoughtfully. "Mebby—mebby you got another; but I doubt it. She's up ag'in."

"Once more," said Hawes, his eyes glinting.

"Well, it's my business to know a bluff when I see one," said the house player, studying his adversary. "It's my best judgment that you . . . Well, anyhow, I'll back it, Hawes, an' boost her once more."

"*Gracias!*" laughed Hawes, a little tensely. "When I went to school a four spot was a right small card. See you, an' raise ag'in."

"An' once more."

"Ag'in."

"Once more."

"Ag'in."

"An' once more," said the house player. "I allus like to play a hand like this clean to the end. They're right scarce."

Suddenly Hawes had a disturbing suspicion. Could it be that his opponent had held four of a kind pat? He, himself, had thrown away an ace and a queen. That left two possible high fours: kings or jacks. He looked at his own cards, and decided that he had pressed them for all they were worth.

"Then show it to me!" he growled, calling.

"It's the gambler's prayer," said the house player, laying down his cards slowly and one by one. The five of hearts joined the face-up four; then the six, and then the seven. He looked calmly over the top of the last card, holding it close to his face; and then, sighing, placed it where it belonged, and dropped both hands under the edge of the table.

"Straight flush," he said calmly.

Hawes flushed and then went pale. Both of his hands were on the table, while the house player's were out of sight. He swore in his throat and started to toss his cards into the discard, but the house player checked him.

"It's a showdown, Hawes. I paid as much to see your hand as you paid to see mine. Turn 'em over."

Hawes obeyed, slamming the cards viciously, and four pleasant ten-spots lay in orderly array.

"Hard luck for a man to git a hand like that at the wrong time," said the winner.

He drew in the chips and picked up the cards. A thought passed through his mind: when playing with keen, smart men, a foolish play will often win. In such a case, two successive bluffs often pay dividends. The house player chuckled in his throat.

"Jacks to open this one," the house player—it was his deal—announced as Hopalong cut. It pleased him to see the way in which Hopalong followed the natural way to cut the deck, and lifted it by the sides; but it only showed confidence, because the dealer wanted no cut at all, and switched it perfectly as he took it up again. In what he was about to do, he would accomplish two things: he would return a favor, and also help Hawes into the situation the latter had been looking for. To make plain his own innocence in the matter, he talked while he dealt.

"The art of cuttin' cards is a fine one," he said. "You hear a lot about slick dealin', but hardly a word about slick cuttin'. That's because it's mighty rare. Why, once I knowed a feller that could cut . . . Oh, well. I'll tell that story after the hand is played."

But it so happened that the house player never told that lie.

Hawes passed. Bradley opened for ten. Hopalong stayed, and the dealer dropped out. Hawes raised it five, and Bradley tossed in a blue and a white chip, seeing, and raising the limit. Hopalong leveled up and added another blue. Hawes dropped out. Bradley studied his hand and saw. He drew two cards and Hopalong took one. The latter would have been very much surprised if he had been disappointed, for he had detected the switched cut. Bradley pushed out a blue chip, and Hopalong saw and raised another. Bradley pushed in two, and Hopalong two more. Back and forth it went, time after time.

Hawes leaned over and looked at Bradley's hand. He studied Hopalong a moment, and gave thought to the straight flush he had just had the misfortune to call. Straight flushes do not come two in a row—at least, that was so in his experience. He leaned forward, his left hand resting on his piled chips.

"Side bet, Riordan?" he inquired sneeringly.

"How much?" asked Hopalong, a little nervously.

"How much you got?" snapped Hawes.

"Plenty."

"Huh! Dollars, or *cents?*" sneered Hawes, quoting an unpleasant phrase.

"Dollars. Lemme see. Five, ten, fifteen, twenty, twenty-five, thirty, thirty-five, forty, forty-one, two, three, four, five, six—forty-six hundred, leavin' me ham an' aig money. You scared?"

"Scared hell!" snapped Hawes. He counted his own resources, found them greatly short, and looked inquiringly at Bradley. "Lend me the difference?" he asked.

Bradley nodded, and beckoned to the head bartender.

"Give Hawes what he needs, an' put a memo in the safe," he ordered.

In a few moments the game went on, the side bets lying apart from the pot. Then Bradley, grinning triumphantly, raised the limit again, certain that Riordan did not have money enough left to meet it. It was a sucker trick, but sometimes it worked.

Hopalong looked at him curiously, hesitated, went through his pockets, and then turned a worried face to his adversary.

"Anybody in the room lend me fifty dollars?" he asked, loudly; and not a voice replied. Hawes' malignant gaze had swept the crowd and held it silent. Not a man dared to comply with the request.

"Is that the way you win yore pots, Bradley?" asked Hopalong coldly.

"I've raised you. Call or quit."

Hopalong's right hand dug down into a pocket, and he laughed nastily as he dropped a fifty-dollar bill on top of the chips in the center of the table.

"What you got, tin-horn?" he asked.

"I got the gambler's second prayer," chuckled Bradley, exposing four aces, and reaching for the pot.

"But I got the first," grunted Hopalong. "Same little run of hearts that we saw before."

For a moment there was an utter silence, and then came a blur of speed from Hawes, but just the instant before it came, Bradley fell off his chair to the left, his own left arm falling across Hopalong's right forearm, blocking a draw; but other men had discovered, when too late, that Hopalong's left hand was the better of the two. The double roar seemed to bend the walls, and sent the lamp flames leaping, to flicker almost to extinction. One went out, the other two recovered. The smoke thinned to show Hawes sliding from his chair, and Bradley on the floor where he had fallen by his own choice, with both hands straining at the Mexican spur which spiked his cheek.

The two leveled Colts held the crowd frozen in curious postures. Hands were raised high, or held out well away from belts. Hopalong backed to the wall, his left-hand gun still smoking. He felt the wall press against him, and then he nodded swiftly to the house player.

"You had a hell of a lot to say about the cut, after you switched it! Now, let's see what you know about a *draw!*" As Hopalong spoke, he shoved both guns into their sheaths, and slowly crossed his arms.

The gambler made no move, scarcely daring to breathe. He still doubted his senses.

"All right, then. Get out, an' stay out!" ordered Hopalong, and as the house player passed through the door, another man came in; a man unsteady on his feet, and covered with sweat and dust and blood.

The newcomer leaned against the bar for a moment, his gaze searching the room; and as he saw his old friend, Hopalong Cassidy, his old friend recognized him. It was Johnny Nelson.

"Hoppy!" he called, joyously.

"Johnny! What's up?"

"They rushed us in the dark, an' shot all of us up. Not seriously, but we're out of action. They got every head—near two hundred!"

Johnny Nelson's gaze wavered, rested for an instant on the open window to one side of his friend, and across the room from him; and, vague and unsteady as he was, he yielded to the gunman's instinct. His right hand dropped, and twisted up like a flash to the top of the holster, and the crash of his shot became a scream in the night outside the open window. George had lost his hundred-dollar fee—and with it, his life.

"Pullin' down on you, from the dark, Hoppy; but I got the skunk," muttered Johnny. He leaned against the bar again and took the whisky which an ingratiating bartender placed under his nose. "They got 'em all. Hoppy—near two hundred head."

Hopalong had his back to the wall again, both guns out and raised for action.

"Good kid!" he called. "I just made a trade with the fellers that stole your cattle. They can keep the steers, and we'll keep the poker winnin's I made by outcheating them two cheaters. Two hundred head at near thirty dollars apiece, kid—which gives you a bigger profit, an' saves you twelve hundred miles of trailin'. Watch the room, kid." He raised his hand. "Bartender, cash in them chips at five, ten an' fifty. *Pronto!*"

It did not take long to turn the counters into money, and Hopalong, backing past the table and toward his capable friend, picked up his winnings, jammed them into a pocket, and slowly reached the stair door.

"It's a tight corner, kid," said Hopalong crisply. "But yo're in no shape to ride. Up them stairs, in front of me." He stepped aside for his friend to pass, and then he stepped back again, his foot feeling for the first tread. His gaze flicked about the room, and he smiled thinly.

"My name's Cassidy," he said, and the smile now twisted his hard face. "My friends call me Hopalong. When I go to bed, I go to sleep. Any objections?"

The spellbound silence was broken by murmurs of surprise. Several faces showed quick friendliness, and a man in a far corner slowly got to his feet.

"An old friend of your'n is a right good friend of mine, Cassidy," he said, glancing slowly and significantly around the room. "Anybody that can't wait for daylight will taste my lead. Good night, you old hoss-thief!"

"Good night, friend," said Hopalong. The door slowly closed, and the crowd listened to the accented footsteps of a slightly lame, red-haired gentleman who made his unhurried way upward.

The man in the corner licked his lips and looked slowly around again.

"An' I meant what I said," he announced, and sat down to find his glass refilled.

QUESTIONS

1. It has been said that most Western stories are conflicts between good guys and bad guys. Hoppy smokes, drinks, cheats, and kills. Is he a "good guy"? Why, or why not?

2. In almost all Western stories—from *The Virginian* to the television series "Maverick"—the hero is a superior poker player. What qualities of mind and personality does this superiority require?

3. What is Johnny Nelson's function in this story? How would the character of Hopalong Cassidy suffer if Nelson were not a part of the story?

4. Much popular literature succeeds because of the technical knowledge or local color it contains. What special knowledge is given in this story?

5. Compare the character and accomplishments of Hopalong Cassidy with those of James Bond, Ian Fleming's popular fictional secret agent. How are they alike? How are they dissimilar?

ZANE GREY

CANYON WALLS

I

"Wal, heah's another forkin' of the trail," said Monty, as he sat cross-legged on his saddle and surveyed the prospect. "Thet Mormon shepherd gave me a good steer. But doggone it, I hate to impose on anyone, even Mormons."

The scene was Utah, north of the great canyon, with the wild ruggedness and magnificence of that region visible on all sides. Monty could see clear to the Pink Cliffs that walled the ranches and ranges northward from this country of breaks. He had come up out of the abyss, across the desert between Mt. Trumbull and Hurricane Ledge, and he did not look back. Kanab must be thirty or forty miles, as a crow flies, across this valley dotted with sage. But Monty did not know Utah, or anything of this north rim country.

He rolled his last cigarette. He was hungry and worn out, and his horse was the same. Should he ride on to Kanab and throw in with one of the big cattle companies north of there, or should he take to one of the lonely canyons and hunt for a homesteader in need of a rider? The choice seemed hard to make, because Monty was tired of gun fights, of two-bit rustling, of gambling, and the other dubious means by which he had managed to live in Arizona. Not that Monty entertained any idea that he had ever reverted to real dishonesty! He had the free-range cowboy's elasticity of judgment. He could find excuses even for his latest escapade. But one or two more stunts like the one at Longhill would be bound to make him an outlaw. He reflected that if he were blamed for the Green Valley affair, also, which was not improbable, he might find himself already an outlaw, whether he personally agreed or not.

If he rode on to the north ranches, sooner or later someone from Arizona would come along; on the other hand, if he went down into the breaks of the canyon he might find a job and a hiding place where he would be safe until the whole thing blew over and was forgotten. Then he would take good care not to fall into another mess. Bad company and too free use of the bottle had brought Monty to this pass, which he really believed was completely undeserved.

Monty dropped his leg back and slipped his boot into the stirrup. He took the trail to the left and felt relief that the choice was made. It meant that he was avoiding towns and ranches, outfits of curious cowboys, and others who might have undue interest in wandering riders.

In about an hour, as the shepherd had directed, the trail showed up. It appeared to run along the rim of a canyon. Monty gazed down with approving eyes. The walls were steep and very deep, so deep that he could scarcely see the green squares of alfalfa, the orchards and pastures, the groves of cottonwoods, and a gray log cabin down below. He saw cattle and horses toward the upper end. At length the trail started down, and for a while thereafter Monty lost his perspective, and dismounting, he walked down the zigzag path leading his horse.

He saw, at length, that the canyon was boxed in by a wild notch of cliff and thicket and jumbled wall, from under which a fine stream of water flowed. There were still many acres that might have been under cultivation. Monty followed the trail along the brook, crossed it above where the floor of the canyon widened and the alfalfa fields lay richly green, and so on down a couple of miles to the cottonwoods. When he emerged from the fringe of trees, he was close to the cabin, and he could see where the canyon opened wide, with sheer red-gold walls, right out on the desert. It was sure enough a lonely retreat, far off the road, out of the grass country, a niche in the endless colored canyon walls.

The cottonwoods were shedding their fuzzy seeds that covered the ground like snow. An irrigation ditch ran musically through the yard. Chickens, turkeys, calves had the run of the place. The dry odor of the canyon here appeared to take on the fragrance of wood smoke and fresh baked bread.

Monty limped on, up to the cabin porch, which was spacious and comfortable, where no doubt the people who lived here spent many hours during fine weather. He saw a girl through the open door. She wore gray linsey, ragged and patched. His second glance made note of her superb build, her bare feet, her brown arms, and eyes that did not need half their piercing quality to see through Monty.

"Howdy, miss," hazarded Monty, though this was Mormon country.

"Howdy, stranger," she replied, very pleasantly, so that Monty decided to forget that he was looking for a fictitious dog.

"Could a thirsty rider get a drink around heah?"

"There's the brook. Best water in Utah."

"An' how about a bite to eat?"

"Tie up your horse and go around to the back porch."

Monty did as he was bidden, not without a few more glances at the girl, who he observed made no movement. But as he turned the corner of the house he heard her call, "Ma, there's a tramp gentile cowpoke coming back for a bite to eat."

When Monty reached the rear porch, another huge enclosure under the cottonwoods, he was quite prepared to encounter a large woman, of commanding presence, but of most genial and kindly face.

"Good afternoon, ma'am," began Monty, lifting his sombrero. "Shore you're the mother to thet gurl out in front—you look alike an' you're both orful handsome—but I won't be took fer no tramp gentile cowpuncher."

The woman greeted him with a pleasant laugh. "So, young man, you're a Mormon?"

"No, I ain't no Mormon, either. But particular, I ain't no tramp cowpoke," replied Monty with spirit, and just then the young person who had roused it appeared in the back doorway, with a slow, curious smile on her face. "I'm just lost an' tuckered out an' hungry."

For reply she motioned to a pan and bucket of water on a nearby bench, and a clean towel hanging on the rail. Monty was quick to take the hint, but performed his ablutions most deliberately. When he was ready at last, his face shining and refreshed, the woman was setting a table for him, and she bade him take a seat.

"Ma'am, I only asked fer a bite," he said.

"It's no matter. We've plenty."

And presently Monty sat down to a meal that surpassed any feast he had ever attended. It was his first experience at a Mormon table, the fame of which was known on every range. He had to admit that distance and exaggeration had not lent enchantment here. Without shame he ate until he could hold no more, and when he arose he made the Mormon mother a gallant bow.

"Lady, I never had sech a good dinner in all my life," he said fervently. "An' I reckon it won't make no difference if I never get another. Jest rememberin' this one will be enough."

"Blarney. You gentiles shore have the gift of gab. Set down and rest a little."

Monty was glad to comply, and leisurely disposed his long, lithe, dusty self in a comfortable chair. He laid his sombrero on the floor, and hitched his gun around, and looked up, genially aware that he was being taken in by two pairs of eyes.

"I met a shepherd lad on top an' he directed me to Andrew Boller's ranch. Is this heah the place?"

"No. Boller's is a few miles further on. It's the first big ranch over the Arizona line."

"Shore I missed it. Wal, it was lucky fer me. Are you near the Arizona line heah?"

"We're just over it."

"Oh, I see. Not in Utah atall," said Monty thoughtfully. "Any men about?"

"No. I'm the Widow Keetch, and this is my daughter Rebecca."

Monty guardedly acknowledged the introduction, without mentioning his own name, an omission the shrewd, kindly woman evidently noted. Monty was quick to feel that she must have had vast experience with menfolk. The girl, however, wore an indifferent, almost scornful air.

"This heah's a good-sized ranch. Must be a hundred acres jist in alfalfa," continued Monty. "You don't mean to tell me you two womenfolks run this ranch alone?"

"We do, mostly. We hire the plowing, and we have firewood hauled. And we always have a boy around. But year in and out we do most of the work ourselves."

"Wal, I'll be dogged!" exclaimed Monty. "Excuse me—but it shore is somethin' to heah. The ranch ain't so bad run down at thet. If you'll allow me to say so, Mrs. Keetch, it could be made a first-rate ranch. There's acres of uncleared land."

"My husband used to think so," replied the widow sighing. "But since he's gone we have just about managed to live."

"Wal, wal! Now I wonder what made me ride down the wrong trail. . . . Mrs. Keetch, I reckon you could use a fine, young, sober, honest, hard-workin' cowhand who knows all there is about ranchin'."

Monty addressed the woman in cool easy speech, quite deferentially, and then he shifted his gaze to the dubious face of the daughter. He was discovering that it had a compelling charm. She laughed outright, as if to say that she knew what a liar he was! That not only discomfited Monty, but roused his ire. The sassy Mormon filly!

"I guess I could use such a young man," returned Mrs. Keetch shortly, with her penetrating eyes on him.

"Wal, you're lookin' at him right now," said Monty fervently. "An' he's seein' nothin' less than the hand of Providence heah."

The woman stood up decisively. "Fetch your horse around," she said, and walked off the porch to wait for him. Monty made haste, his mind in a whirl. What was going to happen now? That girl! He ought to ride right on out of this canyon; and he was making up his mind to do it when he came back round the house to see that the girl had come to the porch rail. Her great eyes were looking at his horse. The stranger did not need to be told that she had a passion for horses. It would help some. But she did not appear to see Monty at all.

"You've a fine horse," said Mrs. Keetch. "Poor fellow! He's lame and tuckered out. We'll turn him loose in the pasture."

Monty followed her down a shady lane of cottonwoods, where the water ran noisily on each side, and he trembled inwardly at the content of the woman's last words. He had heard of the Good Samaritan ways of the Mormons. And in that short walk Monty did a deal of thinking. They reached an old barn beyond which lay a green pasture with an orchard running down one side. Peach trees were in bloom, lending a delicate border of pink to the fresh spring foliage.

"What wages would you work for?" asked the Mormon woman earnestly.

"Wal, come to think of thet, for my board an' keep. . . . Anyhow till we get the ranch payin'," replied Monty.

"Very well, stranger, that's a fair deal. Unsaddle your horse and stay," said the woman.

"Wait a minnit, ma'am," drawled Monty. "I got to substitute somethin' fer thet recommend I gave you. . . . Shore I know cattle an' ranchin' backward. But I reckon I should have said I'm a no-good, gun-throwin' cowpuncher who got run out of Arizona."

"What for?" demanded Mrs. Keetch.

"Wal, a lot of it was bad company an' bad licker. But at thet I wasn't so drunk I didn't know I was rustlin' cattle."

"Why do you tell me this?" she demanded.

"Wal, it is kinda funny. But I jist couldn't fool a kind woman like you. Thet's all."

"You don't look like a hard-drinking man."

"Aw, I'm not. I never said so, ma'am. Fact is, I ain't much of a drinkin' cowboy, atall."

"You came across the canyon?" she asked.

"Shore, an' by golly, thet was the orfullest ride, an' slide, an' swim, an' climb I ever had. I really deserve a heaven like this, ma'am."

"Any danger of a sheriff trailing you?"

"Wal, I've thought about thet. I reckon one chance in a thousand."

"He'd be the first one I ever heard of from across the canyon, at any rate. This is a lonesome, out-of-the-way place—and if you stayed away from the Mormon ranches and towns—"

"See heah, ma'am," interrupted Monty sharply. "You shore ain't goin' to take me on?"

"I am. You might be a welcome change. Lord knows I've hired every kind of a man. But not one of them ever lasted. You might."

"What was wrong with them hombres?"

"I don't know. I never saw much wrong except they neglected their work to moon around after Rebecca. But she could not get along with them, and she always drove them away."

"Aw, I see," exclaimed Monty, who did not see at all. "But I'm not one of the moonin' kind, ma'am, an' I'll stick."

"All right. It's only fair, though, to tell you there's a risk. The young fellow doesn't live who can seem to let Rebecca alone. If he could he'd be a godsend to a distracted old woman."

Monty wagged his bare head thoughtfully and slid the brim of his sombrero through his fingers. "Wal, I reckon I've been most everythin' but a gawdsend, an' I'd shore like to try thet."

"What's your name?" she asked with those searching gray eyes on him.

"Monty Bellew, Smoke fer short, an' it's shore shameful well known in some parts of Arizona."

"Any folks living?"

"Yes, back in Iowa. Father an' mother gettin' along in years now. An' a kid sister growed up."

"You send them money every month, of course?"

Monty hung his head. "Wal, fact is, not so reg'lar as I used to. . . . Late years times have been hard fer me."

"Hard nothing! You've drifted into hard ways. Shiftless, drinking, gambling, shooting cowhand—now, haven't you been just that?"

"I'm sorry, ma'am—I—I reckon I have."

"You ought to be ashamed. I know boys. I raised nine. It's time you were turning over a new leaf. Suppose we begin by burying that name Monty Bellew."

"I'm shore willin' an' grateful, ma'am."

"Then it's settled. Tend to your horse. You can have the little cabin there under the big cottonwood. We've kept that for our hired help, but it hasn't been occupied much lately."

She left Monty then and returned to the ranch house. And he stood a moment irresolute. What a balance was struck there! Presently he slipped saddle and bridle off the horse, and turned him into the pasture. "Baldy, look at thet alfalfa," he said. Weary as Baldy was he lay down and rolled and rolled.

Monty carried his equipment to the tiny porch of the cabin under the huge cottonwood. He removed his saddlebags, which contained the meager sum of his possessions. Then he flopped down on a bench.

"Doggone it!" he muttered. His senses seemed to be playing with him. The leaves rustled above and the white cottonseeds floated down; the bees were murmuring; water tinkled softly beyond the porch; somewhere a bell on a sheep or calf broke the stillness. Monty had never felt such peace and tranquillity, and his soul took on a burden of gratitude.

Suddenly a clear, resonant voice called out from the house. "Ma, what's the name of our new hand?"

"Ask him, Rebecca. I forgot to," replied the mother.

"If that isn't like you!"

Monty was on his way to the house and soon hove in sight of the young woman on the porch. His heart thrilled as he saw her. And he made himself some deep, wild promises.

"Hey, cowboy. What's your name?" she called.

"Sam," he called back.

"Sam what?"

"Sam Hill."

"For the land's sake! . . . That's not your name."

"Call me Land's Sake, if you like it better."

"*I* like it?" She nodded her curly head sagely, and she regarded Monty with a certainty that made him vow to upset her calculations or die in the attempt. She handed him down a bucket. "Can you milk a cow?"

"I never saw my equal as a milker," asserted Monty.

"In that case I won't have to help," she replied. "But I'll go with you to drive in the cows."

II

From that hour dated Monty's apparent subjection. He accepted himself at Rebecca's valuation—that of a very small hired boy. Monty believed he had a way with girls, but evidently that way had never been tried upon this imperious young Mormon miss.

Monty made good his boast about being a master hand at the milking of cows. He surprised Rebecca, though she did not guess that he was aware of it. For the rest, Monty never looked at her when she was looking, never addressed her, never gave her the slightest hint that he was even conscious of her sex.

Now he knew perfectly well that his appearance did not tally with this domesticated kind of a cowboy. She realized it and was puzzled, but evidently he was a novelty to her. At first Monty sensed the usual slight antagonism of the Mormon against the gentile, but in the case of Mrs. Keetch he never noticed this at all, and less and less from the girl.

The feeling of being in some sort of trance persisted with Monty, and he could not account for it, unless it was the charm of this lonely Canyon Walls Ranch, combined with the singular attraction of its young mistress. Monty had not been there three days before he realized that sooner or later he would fall, and great would be the fall thereof. But his sincere and ever-growing admiration for the Widow Keetch held him true to his promise. It would not hurt him to have a terrible case over Rebecca, and he resigned himself to his fate. Nothing could come of it, except perhaps to chasten him. Certainly he would never let her dream of such a thing. All the same, she just gradually and imperceptibly grew on Monty. There was nothing strange in this. Wherever Monty had ridden there had always been some girl who had done something to his heart. She might be a fright—a lanky, slab-sided, red-headed country girl—but that had made no difference. His comrades had called him Smoke Bellew, because of his propensity for raising so much smoke where there was not even any fire.

Sunday brought a change at the Keetch household. Rebecca appeared in a white dress and Monty caught his breath. He worshiped from a safe distance through the leaves. Presently a two-seated buckboard drove up to the ranch house, and Rebecca lost no time climbing in with the young people. They drove off, probably to church at the village of White Sage, some half dozen miles across the line. Monty thought it odd that Mrs. Keetch did not go.

There had been many a time in Monty's life when the loneliness and solitude of these dreaming canyon walls might have been maddening. But Monty found strange ease and solace here. He had entered upon a new era in his life. He hated to think that it might not last. But it would last if the shadow of the past did not fall on Canyon Walls.

At one o'clock Rebecca returned with her friends in the buckboard. And presently Monty was summoned to dinner, by no less than Mrs. Keetch's trenchant call. He had not anticipated this, but he brushed and brightened himself up a bit, and proceeded to the house. Mrs. Keetch met him as he mounted the porch steps. "Folks," she announced, "this is our new man, Sam Hill. . . . Sam, meet Lucy Card and her brother Joe, and Hal Stacey."

Monty bowed, and took the seat assigned to him by Mrs. Keetch. She was beaming, and the dinner table fairly groaned with the load of good things to eat. Monty defeated an overwhelming desire to look at Rebecca. In a moment he saw that the embarrassment under which he was laboring was silly. These Mormon young people were quiet, friendly, and far from curious. His presence at Widow Keetch's table was more natural to them than it seemed to him. Presently he was at ease and dared to glance across the table. Rebecca was radiant. How had it come that he had not observed her beauty before? She appeared like a gorgeous opening rose. Monty did not risk a second glance and he thought that he ought to go far up the canyon and crawl into a hole. Nevertheless, he enjoyed the dinner and did ample justice to it.

After dinner more company arrived, mostly on horseback. Sunday was evidently the Keetches' day at home. Monty made several unobtrusive attempts to escape, once being stopped in his tracks by a single glance from Rebecca, and the other times failing through the widow's watchfulness. He felt that he was very dense not to have noticed sooner how they wished him to feel at home with them. At length, toward evening, Monty left Rebecca to several of her admirers, who outstayed the other visitors, and went off for a sunset stroll under the canyon walls.

Monty did not consider himself exactly a dunce, but he would not interpret clearly the experience of the afternoon. There were, however, some points that he could be sure of. The Widow Keetch had evidently seen better days. She did not cross the Arizona line into Utah. Rebecca was waited upon by a host of Mormons, to whom she appeared imperiously indifferent one moment and alluringly coy the next. She was a spoiled girl, Monty decided. He had not been able to discover the slightest curiosity or antagonism toward him in these visitors, and as they were all Mormons and he was a gentile, it changed some preconceived ideas of his.

Next morning the new hand plunged into the endless work that needed to be done about the ranch. He doubled the amount of water in the irrigation ditches, to Widow Keetch's delight. And that day passed as if by magic. It did not end, however, without Rebecca crossing Monty's trail, and it earned for him a very pleasant compliment from her, anent the fact that he might develop into a real good milkman.

The days flew by and another Sunday came, very like the first one, and that brought the month of June around. Thereafter the weeks were as short as days. Monty was amazed to see what a diversity of tasks he could put an efficient hand to. But, then, he had seen quite a good deal of ranch service in his time, aside from driving cattle. And it so happened that here was an ideal farm awaiting development, and he put his heart and soul into the task. The summer was hot, especially in the afternoon under the reflected heat from the canyon walls. He had cut alfalfa several times. And the harvest of fruit and grain was at hand. There were pumpkins so large that Monty could scarcely roll one over; bunches of grapes longer than his arm; great luscious peaches that shone like gold in the sunlight, and other farm products of proportionate size.

The womenfolk spent days putting up preserves, pickles, fruit. Monty used to go out of his way to smell the fragrant wood fire in the back yard under the cottonwoods, where the big brass kettle steamed with peach butter. "I'll shore eat myself to death when winter comes," he said.

Among the young men who paid court to Rebecca were two brothers, Wade and Eben Tyler, lean-faced, still-eyed young Mormons who were wild-horse hunters. The whole southern end of Utah was overrun by droves of wild horses, and according to some of the pioneers they were becoming a menace to the range. The Tylers took such a liking to Monty, the Keetches' new hand, that they asked Mrs. Keetch to let him go with them on a hunt in October, over in what they called the Siwash. The widow was prevailed upon to give her consent, stipulating that Monty should fetch back a supply of venison. And Rebecca said she would allow him to go if he brought her one of the wild mustangs with a long mane and a tail that touched the ground.

So when October rolled around, Monty rode off with the brothers, and three days' riding brought them to the edge of a wooded region called the Buckskin Forest. It took a whole day to ride through the magnificent spruces and pines to reach the rim of the canyon. Here Monty found the wildest and most wonderful country he had ever seen. The Siwash was a rough section where the breaks in the rim afforded retreat for the thousands of deer and wild horses, as well as the cougars that preyed upon them. Monty had the hunt of his life, and by the time these fleeting weeks were over, he and the Tylers were fast friends.

Monty returned to Canyon Walls Ranch, pleased to find that he had been sorely needed and missed by the Keetches, and he was keen to have a go at his work again. Gradually he thought less and less of that Arizona escapade which had made him a fugitive. A little time spent in that wild country had a tendency to make past things appear dim and faraway. He ceased to start whenever he saw strange riders coming up the canyon gateway. Mormon sheepmen and cattlemen, when in the vicinity of Canyon Walls, always paid the Keetches a visit. Still Monty never ceased to pack a gun, a fact that Mrs. Keetch often mentioned. Monty said it was just a habit that he hadn't gotten over from his cattle-driving days.

He went to work clearing the upper end of the canyon. The cottonwood, scrub oak, and brush were as thick as a jungle. But day by day the tangle was mowed down under the sweep of Monty's ax. In his boyhood on the Iowa farm he had been a rail splitter. How many useful things were coming back to him! Every day Rebecca or Mrs. Keetch or the boy, Randy, who helped at chores, drove up in the big go-devil and hauled firewood. And when the winter's wood, with plenty to spare, had been stored away, Mrs. Keetch pointed with satisfaction to a considerable saving of money.

The leaves did not change color until late in November, and then they dropped reluctantly, as if not sure that winter could actually come to Canyon Walls this year. Monty even began to doubt that it would. But frosty mornings did come, and soon thin skims of ice formed on the still pools. Sometimes when he rode out of the canyon gateway on the desert, he could see the white line reaching down from the Buckskin, and Mt. Trumbull was wearing its crown of snow. But no real winter came to the canyon. The gleaming walls seemed to have absorbed enough of the summer sun to carry over. Every hour of daylight found Monty outdoors at one of the tasks which multiplied under his eye. After supper he would sit before the little stone fireplace he had built in his cabin, and watch the flames, and wonder about himself and how long this interlude could last. He began to wonder why it could not last always; and he went so far in his calculation as to say that a debt paid fully canceled even the acquiring of a few cattle not his own, in that past which receded ever farther over time's horizon. After all, he had been just a wild, irresponsible cowboy, urged on by drink and a need of money. At first he had asked only that it be forgotten and buried; but now he began to think he wanted to square that debt.

The winter passed, and Monty's labors had opened up almost as many new acres as had been cleared originally. Canyon Walls Ranch now took the eye of Andrew Boller, who made Widow Keetch a substantial offer for it. Mrs. Keetch laughed her refusal, and the remark she made to Boller mystified Monty for many a day. It was something about Canyon Walls someday being as great a ranch as that one of which the church had deprived her!

Monty asked Wade Tyler what the widow had meant, and Wade replied that he had once heard how John Keetch had owed the bishop a sum of money, and that the great ranch, after Keetch's death, had been confiscated. But that was one of the few questions Monty never asked Mrs. Keetch. The complexity and mystery of the Mormon Church did not interest him. It had been a shock, however, to find that two of Mrs. Keetch's Sunday callers, openly courting Rebecca's hand, already had wives. "By golly, I ought to marry her myself," declared Monty with heat, as he thought beside his fire, and then he laughed at his conceit. He was only Rebecca's hired help.

How good it was to see the green burst out again upon the cottonwoods, and the pink on the peach trees! Monty had now been at Canyon Walls a full year. It seemed incredible to him. It was the longest spell he had ever remained in one spot. He could see a vast change in the ranch. And what greater transformation had that labor wrought in him!

"Sam, we're going to need help this spring," said Mrs. Keetch one morning. "We'll want a couple of men and a teamster—a new wagon."

"Wal, we shore need aplenty," drawled Monty, "an' I reckon we'd better think hard."

"This ranch is overflowing with milk and honey. Sam, you've made it blossom. We must make some kind of a deal. I've wanted to speak to you before, but you always put me off. We ought to be partners."

"There ain't any hurry, ma'am," replied Monty. "I'm happy heah, an' powerful set on makin' the ranch a goin' concern. Funny no farmer heahabouts ever saw its possibilities afore. Wal, thet's our good luck."

"Boller wants my whole alfalfa cut this year," continued Mrs. Keetch. "Saunders, a big cattleman, no Mormon by the way, is ranging south. And Boller wants to gobble all the feed. How much alfalfa will we be able to cut this year?"

"Countin' the new acreage, upward of two hundred tons."

"Sam Hill!" she cried incredulously.

"Wal, you needn't Sam Hill me. I get enough of thet from Rebecca. But you can gamble on the ranch from now on. We have the soil an' the sunshine—twice as much an' twice as hot as them farmers out in the open. An' we have water. Lady, we're goin' to grow things on the Canyon Wall."

"It's a dispensation of the Lord," she exclaimed fervently.

"Wal, I don't know about thet, but I can guarantee results. We start some new angles this spring. There's a side canyon up heah thet I cleared. Jist the place fer hogs. You know what a waste of fruit there was last fall. We'll not waste anythin' from now on. We can raise feed enough to pack this canyon solid with turkeys, chickens, an' hogs."

"Sam, you're a wizard, and the Lord surely guided me that day I took you on," replied Mrs. Keetch. "We're independent now and I see prosperity ahead. When Andrew Boller offered to buy this ranch I saw the handwriting on the wall."

"You bet. An' the ranch is worth twice what he offered."

"Sam, I've been an outcast too, in a way, but this will sweeten my cup."

"Wal, ma'am, you never made me no confidences, but I always took you fer the happiest woman I ever seen," declared Monty stoutly.

At this juncture Rebecca Keetch, who had been listening thoughtfully to the talk, as was her habit, spoke feelingly: "Ma, I want a lot of new dresses. I haven't a decent rag to my back. And look there!" She stuck out a shapely foot, bursting from an old shoe. "I want to go to Salt Lake City and buy some things. And if we're not poor any more—"

"My dear daughter, I cannot go to Salt Lake," interrupted the mother, a tone of sadness in her voice.

"But I can. Sue Tyler is going with her mother," burst out Rebecca eagerly. "Why can't I go with them?"

"Of course, daughter, you must have clothes to wear. And I have long thought of that. But to go to Salt Lake! . . . I don't know. It worries me. . . . Sam, what do you think of Rebecca's idea?"

"Which one?" asked Monty.

"About going to Salt Lake to buy clothes."

"Perfickly redic'lous," replied Monty blandly.

"*Why?*" flashed Rebecca, turning upon him with her great eyes aflame.

"Wal, you don't need no clothes in the fust place—"

"Don't I?" demanded Rebecca hotly. "You bet I don't need any clothes for *you*. You never even look at me. I could go around here positively stark naked and you'd never even see me."

"An' in the second place," continued Monty, with a wholly assumed imperturbability, "you're too young an' too crazy about boys to go on sech a long journey alone."

"Daughter, I—I think Sam is right," said Rebecca's mother.

"I'm eighteen years old," cried Rebecca. "And I wouldn't be going alone."

"Sam means you should have a man with you."

Rebecca stood for a moment in speechless rage, then she broke down. "Why doesn't the damn fool—offer to take me—then?"

"*Rebecca!*" cried Mrs. Keetch, horrified.

Monty meanwhile had been undergoing a remarkable transformation.

"Lady, if I was her dad—"

"But you're—not," sobbed Rebecca.

"Shore it's lucky fer you I'm not. For I'd spank some sense into you. . . . But I was goin' to say I'd drive you back from Kanab. You could go that far with the Tylers."

"There, daughter. . . . And maybe next year you *could* go to Salt Lake," added Mrs. Keetch consolingly.

Rebecca accepted the miserable compromise, but it was an acceptance she did not care for, as was made plain to Monty by the dark look she gave him as she flounced away.

"Oh, dear," sighed Mrs. Keetch. "Rebecca is a good girl. But nowadays she often flares up like that. And lately she has been acting queer. If she'd only set her heart on some man!"

III

Monty had his doubts about the venture to which he had committed himself. But he undertook it willingly enough, because Mrs. Keetch was obviously so pleased and relieved. She evidently feared for this high-spirited girl. And so it turned out that Rebecca rode as far as Kanab with the Tylers, with the understanding that she would return in Monty's wagon.

The drive took Monty all day and there was a good deal of upgrade in the road. He did not believe he could make the thirty miles back in daylight hours, unless he got a very early start. And he just about knew he never could get Rebecca Keetch to leave Kanab before dawn. Still the whole prospect was one that offered adventure, and much of Monty's old devil-may-care spirit seemed roused to meet it.

He camped on the edge of town, and next morning drove in and left the old wagon at a blacksmith shop for needed repairs. The four horses were turned into pasture. Then Monty went about executing Mrs. Keetch's instructions, which had to do with engaging helpers and making numerous purchases. That evening saw a big, brand-new shiny wagon at the blacksmith shop, packed full of flour, grain, hardware, supplies, harness, and whatnot. The genial storekeeper who waited upon Monty averred that Mrs. Keetch must have had her inheritance returned to her. All the Mormons had taken a kindly interest in Monty and his work at Canyon Walls, which had become the talk all over the range. They were likable men, except for a few gray-whiskered old patriarchs who belonged to another day. Monty did not miss seeing several pretty Mormon girls; and their notice of him pleased him immensely, especially when Rebecca happened to be around to see.

Monty seemed to run into her every time he entered a store. She spent all the money she had saved up, and all her mother had given her, and she even borrowed the last few dollars he had in his pockets.

"Shore, you're welcome," said Monty in reply to her thanks. "But ain't you losin' your haid a little?"

"Well, so long's I don't lose it over *you*, what do you care?" she retorted, saucily, with another of those dark glances which had mystified him before.

Monty replied that her mother had expressly forbidden her to go into debt for anything.

"Don't you try to boss me, Sam Hill," she warned, but she was still too happy to be really angry.

"Rebecca, I don't care two bits what you do," said Monty shortly.

"Oh, don't you?— Thanks! You're always flattering me," she returned mockingly.

It struck Monty then that she knew something about him or about herself which he did not share.

"We'll be leavin' before sunup," he added briefly. "You'd better let me have all your bundles so I can take them out to the wagon an' pack them tonight."

Rebecca demurred, but would not give a reason, which could only have been because she wanted to gloat over her purchases. Monty finally prevailed upon her; and it took two trips for him and a boy he had hired to carry the stuff out to the blacksmith's shop.

"Lord, if it should rain!" said Monty, remembering that he had no extra tarpaulin. So he went back to the store and got one, and hid it, with the idea of having fun with Rebecca in case a storm threatened on the way back to the ranch.

After supper Rebecca drove out to Monty's camp with some friends.

"I don't care for your camping out like this. You should have gone to the inn," she said loftily.

"Wal, I'm used to campin'," he drawled.

"Sam, they're giving a dance for me tonight," announced Rebecca.

"Fine. Then you needn't go to bed atall, an' we can get an early start."

The young people with Rebecca shouted with laughter, and she looked dubious.

"Can't we stay over another day?"

"I should smile we cain't," retorted Monty with unusual force. "An' if we don't get an early start we'll never reach home tomorrow. So you jist come along heah, young lady, about four o'clock."

"In the morning?"

"In the mawnin'. I'll have some breakfast fer you."

It was noticeable that Rebecca made no rash promises. Monty rather wanted to give in to her—she was so happy and gay—but he remembered his obligations to Mrs. Keetch, and remained firm.

As they drove off Monty's sharp ears caught Rebecca complaining—"and I can't do a solitary thing with that stubborn Arizona cowpuncher."

This rather pleased Monty, as it gave him distinction, and was proof that he had not yet betrayed himself to Rebecca. He would proceed on these lines.

That night he did a remarkable thing, for him. He found out where the dance was being held, and peered through a window to see Rebecca in all her glory. He did not miss, however, the fact that she did not appear to outshine several other young women there. Monty stifled a yearning that had not bothered him for a long time. "Doggone it! I ain't no old gaffer. I could dance the socks off some of them Mormons." He became aware presently that between dances some of the young Mormon men came outdoors and indulged in desultory fist fights. He could not see any real reason for these encounters, and it amused him. "Gosh, I wonder if thet is jist a habit with these hombres. Fact is, though, there's shore not enough girls to go round. . . . Holy mackerel, how I'd like to have my old dancin' pards heah! Wouldn't we wade through thet corral! . . . I wonder what's become of Slim an' Cuppy, an' if they ever think of me. Doggone!"

Monty sighed and returned to camp. He was up before daylight, but did not appear to be in any rush. He had a premonition what to expect. Day broke and the sun tipped the low desert in the east, while Monty leisurely got breakfast. He kept an eye on the lookout for Rebecca. The new boy, Jake, arrived with shiny face, and later one of the men engaged by Mrs. Keetch came. Monty had the two teams fetched in from pasture, and hitched up. It was just as well that he had to wait for Rebecca, because the new harness did not fit and required skilled adjustment, but he was not going to tell her that. The longer she made him wait the longer would be the scolding she would get.

About nine o'clock she arrived in a very much overloaded buckboard. She was gay of attire and face, and so happy that Monty, had he been sincere with himself, could never have reproved her. But he did it, very sharply, and made her look like a chidden child before her friends. This reacted upon Monty so pleasurably that he began afresh. But this was a mistake.

"Yah! Yah! Yah!" she cried. And her friends let out a roar of merriment.

"Becky, you shore have a tiptop chaperon," remarked one frank-faced Mormon boy. And other remarks were not wanting to convey the hint that at least one young rider in the world had not succumbed to Rebecca's charms.

"Where am I going to ride?" she asked curtly.

Monty indicated the high driver's seat. "Unless you'd rather ride with them two new hands in the old wagon."

Rebecca scorned to argue with Monty, but climbed quickly to the lofty perch.

"Girls, it's nearer heaven than I've ever been yet," she called gayly.

"Just what do you mean, Becky?" replied a pretty girl with roguish eyes. "So high up—or because—"

"Go along with you," interrupted Rebecca with a blush. "You think of nothing but men. I wish you had . . . but good-by—good-by. I've had a lovely time."

Monty clambered to the driver's seat, and followed the other wagon out of town, down into the desert. Rebecca appeared to want to talk.

"Oh, it was a wonderful change! I had a grand time. But I'm glad you wouldn't let me go to Salt Lake. It'd have ruined me, Sam."

Monty felt subtly flattered, but he chose to remain aloof and disapproving.

"Nope. Hardly that. You was ruined long ago, Miss Rebecca," he drawled.

"Don't call me miss," she flashed. "And see here, Sam Hill—do you hate us Mormons?"

"I shore don't. I like all the Mormons I've met. They're jist fine. An' your ma is the best woman I ever knew."

"Then I'm the only Mormon you've no use for," she retorted with bitterness. "Don't deny it. I'd rather you didn't add falsehood to your—your other faults. It's a pity, though, that we can't get along. Mother depends on you now. You've certainly pulled us out of a hole. And I—I'd like you—if you'd let me. But you always make me out a wicked, spoiled girl. Which I'm not. . . . Why couldn't you come to the dance last night? They wanted you. Those girls were eager to meet you."

"I wasn't asked—not thet I'd of come anyhow," stammered Monty.

"You know perfectly well that in a Mormon town or home you are always welcome," she said. "What did you want? Would you have had me stick my finger in the top hole of your vest and look up at you like a dying duck and say, 'Sam, please come'?"

"My Gawd, no. I never dreamed of wantin' you to do anythin'," replied Monty hurriedly. He was getting beyond his depth here, and began to doubt his ability to say the right things.

"*Why* not? Am I so hideous? Aren't I a human being? A *girl?*" she asked with resentful fire.

Monty deliberated a moment, as much to recover his scattered wits as to make an adequate reply.

"Wal, you shore are a live human critter. An' as handsome as any gurl I ever seen. But you're spoiled somethin' turrible. You're the most orful flirt I ever watched, an' the way you treat these fine Mormon boys is shore scandalous. You don't know what you want more'n one minnit straight runnin'. An' when you get what you want you're sick of it right away."

"Oh, is that *all?*" she burst out, and then followed with a peal of riotous laughter. But she did not look at him or speak to him again for several long hours.

Monty liked the silence better. He still had the thrill of her presence, without her disturbing chatter. A nucleus of a thought tried to wedge its way into his consciousness—that this girl was not completely indifferent to him. But he squelched it.

At noon they halted in a rocky depression, where water filled the holes, and Rebecca got down to sit in the shade of a cedar.

"I want something to eat," she declared imperiously.

"Sorry, but there ain't nothin'," replied Monty imperturbably, as he mounted to the seat again. The other wagon rolled on, crushing the rocks with its wide tires.

"Are you going to starve me into submission?"

Monty laughed at her. "Wal, I reckon if someone took a willow switch to your bare legs an'—wal, he might get a little submission out of you."

"You're worse than a Mormon," she cried in disgust, as if that was the very depth of depravity.

"Come along, youngster," said Monty with pretended weariness. "If we don't keep steppin' along lively we'll never get home to-night."

"Good! I'll delay you as much as I can. . . . Sam, I'm scared to death to face Mother." And she giggled.

"What about?"

"I went terribly in debt. But I didn't lose my 'haid' as you say. I thought it all out. I won't be going again for ages. And I'll work. It was the change in our fortunes that tempted me."

"Wal, I reckon we can get around tellin' your ma," said Monty lamely.

"You wouldn't give me away, Sam?" she asked in surprise, with strange intent eyes. And she got up to come over to the wagon.

"No, I wouldn't. Course not. What's more I can lend you the money—presently."

"Thanks, Sam. But I'll tell Mother."

She scrambled up and rode beside him again for miles without speaking. It seemed nothing to Monty to ride in that country and keep silent. The desert was not conducive to conversation. It was so beautiful that talking seemed out of place. Mile after mile of rock and sage, of black ridge and red swale, and always the great landmarks looming as if unattainable. Behind them the Pink Cliffs rose higher the farther they traveled; to their left the long black fringe of the Buckskin gradually sank into obscurity; in front rolled away the colorful desert, an ever-widening bowl that led the gaze to the purple chaos in the distance—that wild region of the riven earth called the canyon country.

Monty did not tell Rebecca that they could not get even half way home that day, and that they would have to make camp for the night. But eventually, as a snow squall formed over Buckskin, he told her it likely would catch up with them and turn to rain.

"Oh, Sam!" she wailed. "If my things get wet!"

He did not give her any assurance or comfort, and about mid-afternoon, when the road climbed toward a low divide, he saw that they would not miss the storm. But he would make camp at the pines where they could easily weather it.

Before sunset they reached the highest point along the road, from which the spectacle down toward the west made Monty acknowledge that he was gazing at the grandest panorama his enraptured eyes had ever viewed.

Rebecca watched with him, and he could feel her absorption.

Finally she sighed and said, as if to herself, "One reason I'll marry a Mormon—if I have to—is that I never want to leave Utah."

They halted in the pines, low down on the far side of the divide, where a brook brawled merrily, and here the storm, half snow and half rain, caught them. Rebecca was frantic. She did not know where her treasures were packed.

"Oh, Sam, I'll never forgive you!"

"*Me?* What have I got to do about it?" he asked, in pretended astonishment.

"Oh, you *knew* all the time that it would rain," she wailed. "And if you'd been half a man—if you didn't *hate* me so, you—you could have saved my things."

"Wal, if thet's how you feel about it I'll see what I can do," he drawled.

And in a twinkling he jerked out the tarpaulin and spread it over the new wagon where he had carefully packed her cherished belongings. And in the same twinkling her woebegone face changed to joy. Monty thought for a moment that she was going to kiss him and he was scared stiff.

"Ma was right, Sam. You are the wonderfullest man," she said. "But—why didn't you *tell* me?"

"I forgot, I reckon. Now this rain ain't goin' to amount to much. After dark it'll turn off cold. I put some hay in the bottom of the wagon, heah, an' a blanket. So you can sleep comfortable."

"*Sleep!* . . . Sam, you're not going to stop here?"

"Shore am. This new wagon is stiff, an' the other one's heavy loaded. We're blamed lucky to reach this good campin' spot."

"But, Sam, we can't stay here. We must drive on. It doesn't make any difference how *long* we are, so that we keep moving."

"An' kill our horses, an' then not get in. Sorry, Rebecca. If you hadn't delayed us five hours we might have done it, allowin' fer faster travel in the cool of the mawnin'."

"Sam, do you want to see my reputation ruined?" she asked, her great accusing eyes on him.

"Wal! . . . Rebecca Keetch, if you don't beat me! I'll tell you what, miss. Where I come from a man can entertain honest desire to spank a crazy gurl without havin' evil intentions charged agin him!"

"You can spank me to your heart's content—but—Sam—take me home first."

"Nope. I can fix it with your ma, an' I cain't see thet it amounts to a darn otherwise."

"Any Mormon girl who stayed out on the desert—all night with a gentile—would be ruined!" she declared.

"But we're not alone," yelled Monty, red in the face. "We've got two men and a boy with us."

"No Mormon will ever—believe it," sobbed Rebecca.

"Wal, then, to hell with the Mormons who won't," exclaimed Monty, exasperated beyond endurance.

"Mother will make you marry me," ended Rebecca, with such tragedy of eye and voice that Monty could not but believe such a fate would be worse than death for her.

"Aw, don't distress yourself Miss Keetch," responded Monty with profound dignity. "I couldn't be druv to marry you—not to save your blasted Mormon Church—nor the whole damn world of gentiles from—from conflaggeration!"

IV

Next day Monty drove through White Sage at noon, and reached Canyon Walls about mid-afternoon, completing a journey he would not want to undertake again, under like circumstances. He made haste to unburden himself to his beaming employer.

"Wal, Mrs. Keetch, I done about everythin' as you wanted," he said. "But I couldn't get an early start yestiddy mawnin' an' so we had to camp at the pines."

"Why couldn't you?" she demanded, as if seriously concerned.

"Wal, fer several reasons, particular thet the new harness wouldn't fit."

"You shouldn't have kept Rebecca out all night," said the widow severely.

"I don't know how it could have been avoided," replied Monty mildly. "You wouldn't have had me kill four good horses."

"Did you meet anyone?" she asked.

"Not even a sheepherder."

"Did you stop at White Sage?"

"Only to water, an' we didn't see no one."

"Maybe we can keep the Mormons from finding out," returned Mrs. Keetch with relief. "I'll talk to these new hands. Mormons are close-mouthed when it's to their interest."

"Wal, ma'am, heah's the receipts, an' my notes an' expenditures," added Monty, handing them over. "My pore haid shore buzzed over all them figgers. But I got the prices you wanted. I found out you gotta stick to a Mormon. But he won't let you buy from no other storekeeper, if he can help it."

"Indeed he won't. . . . Well, daughter, what have you to say for yourself? I expected to see you with the happiest of faces. But you look the way you used to when you stole jam. I hope it wasn't your fault Sam had to keep you all night on the desert."

"Yes, Ma, it was," admitted Rebecca, and though she spoke frankly she plainly feared her mother's displeasure.

"So. And Sam wouldn't tell on you, eh?"

"No, I don't know why he wouldn't! Not out of any feelings for me. . . . Come in, Ma, and let me confess the rest—while I've still got the courage."

Mrs. Keetch looked worried. Monty saw that her anger would be a terrible thing if aroused.

"Ma'am, don't be hard on the gurl," he said, with his easy drawl and smile. "Jist think! She hadn't been to Kanab fer two years. Two years! An' she a growin' gurl. Kanab is some shucks of a town. I was surprised. An' she was jist a kid let loose."

"Sam Hill! So you have fallen into the ranks at last," exclaimed Mrs. Keetch, while Rebecca telegraphed him a grateful glance.

"Lady, I don't savvy about the ranks," replied Monty stiffly. "But I've been falling from grace all my life. Thet's why I'm—"

"No matter," interrupted the widow hastily, and it struck Monty that she did not care to have him confess his shortcomings before Rebecca. "Unpack the wagons and put the things on the porch, except what should go to the barn."

Monty helped the two new employees unpack the old wagon first, and then directed them to the barn. Then he removed Rebecca's many purchases and piled them on the porch. All the time his ears burned over the heated argument going on within the house. Rebecca seemed to have relapsed into tears while her mother still continued to upbraid her. Monty drove out to the barn considerably disturbed by the sound of the girl's uncontrolled sobbing.

"Doggone! The old lady's hell when she's riled," he thought. "Now I wonder which it was. Rebecca spendin' all her money an' mine, an' this runnin' up bills—or because she made us stay a night out . . . or mebbe it's somethin' I don't know a blamed thing about. . . . Whew, but she laid it onto thet pore kid. Doggone the old Mormon! She'd better not pitch into me."

Supper was late that night and the table was set in the dusk. Mrs. Keetch had regained her composure, but Rebecca's face was woebegone and pallid from weeping. Monty's embarrassment seemed augmented by the fact that she squeezed his hand under the table. But it was a silent meal, soon finished; and while Rebecca reset the table for the new employees, Mrs. Keetch drew Monty aside on the porch. It suited him just as well that dusk was deepening into night.

"I am pleased with the way you carried out my instructions," said Mrs. Keetch. "I could not have done so well. My husband John was never any good in business. You are shrewd, clever, and reliable. If this year's harvest shows anything near what you claim, I can do no less than make you my partner. There is nothing to prevent us from developing another canyon ranch. John had a lien on one west of here. It's bigger than this and uncleared. We could acquire that, if you thought it wise. In fact we could go far. Not that I am money mad, like many Mormons are. But I would like to show them. . . . What do you think about it, Sam?"

"Wal, I agree, 'cept makin' me full pardner seems more'n I deserve. But if the crops turn out big this fall—an' you can gamble on it—I'll make a deal with you fer five years or ten or life."

"Thank you. That is well. It insures comfort in my old age as well as something substantial for my daughter. . . . Sam, do you understand Rebecca?"

"Good Lord, no," exploded Monty.

"I reckoned you didn't. Do you realize that where she is concerned you are wholly unreliable?"

"What do you mean, ma'am?" he asked, thunderstruck.

"She can wind you round her little finger."

"Huh! . . . She jist cain't do anythin' of the sort," declared Monty, trying to appear angry. The old lady might ask a question presently that would be exceedingly hard to answer.

"Perhaps you do not know it. That'd be natural. At first I thought you a pretty deep, clever cowboy, one of the devil-with-the-girls kind, and that you would give Rebecca the lesson she deserves. But now I think you a soft-hearted, easy-going, *good* young man, actually stupid when it comes to a girl."

"Aw, thanks, ma'am," replied Monty, most uncomfortable, and then his natural spirit rebelled. "I never was accounted stupid about gentile gurls."

"Rebecca is no different from any girl. I should think you'd have seen that the Mormon style of courtship makes her sick. It is too simple, too courteous, too respectful, and too much bordering on the religious to stir her heart. No Mormon will ever get Rebecca, unless I force her to marry him. Which I have been pressed to do and which I hope I shall never do."

"Wal, I respect you fer thet, ma'am," replied Monty feelingly. "But why all this talk about Rebecca? I'm shore mighty sympathetic, but how does it concern me?"

"Sam, I have not a friend in all this land, unless it's you."

"Wal, you can shore gamble on me. If you want I—I'll marry you an' be a dad to this gurl who worries you so."

"Bless your heart! . . . No, I'm too old for that, and I would not see you sacrifice yourself. But, oh, wouldn't that be fun—and revenge?"

"Wal, it'd be heaps of fun," laughed Monty. "But I don't reckon where the revenge would come in."

"Sam, you've given me an idea," spoke up the widow, in a quick whisper. "I'll threaten Rebecca with this. That I could marry you and make you her father. If that doesn't chasten her—then the Lord have mercy upon us."

"She'd laugh at you."

"Yes. But she'll be scared to death. I'll never forget her face one day when she confessed that you claimed she should be switched— well, it must have been sort of shocking, if you said it."

"I shore did, ma'am," he admitted.

"Well, we begin all over again from today," concluded the widow thoughtfully. "To build anew! Go back to your work and plans. I have the utmost confidence in you. My troubles are easing. But I have not one more word of advice about Rebecca."

"I cain't say as you gave me any advice at all. But mebbe thet's because I'm stupid. Thanks, Mrs. Keetch an' good night."

The painful hour of confused thinking which Monty put in that night, walking in the moonlight shadows under the canyon walls, resulted only in increasing his bewilderment. He ended it by admitting he was now in love with Rebecca, ten thousand times worse than he had ever loved any girl before, and that she could wind him around her little finger all she wanted to. If she knew! But he swore he would never let her find it out.

Next day seemed to bring the inauguration of a new regime at Canyon Walls. The ranch had received an impetus, like that given by water run over rich dry ground. Monty's hours were doubly full. Always there was Rebecca, singing on the porch at dusk. "In the gloaming, oh my darling," a song that carried Monty back to home in Iowa, and the zigzag rail fences; or she was at his elbow during the milking hour, an ever-growing task; or in the fields. She could work, that girl; and he told her mother it would not take long for her to earn the money she had squandered in town.

Sunday after Sunday passed, with the usual host of merry callers, and no word was ever spoken of Rebecca having passed a night on the desert with a gentile. So that specter died, except in an occasional mocking look she gave him, which he took to mean that she still could betray herself and him if she took the notion.

In June came the first cutting of alfalfa—fifty acres with an enormous yield. The rich, green, fragrant hay stood knee high. Monty tried to contain himself. But it did seem marvelous that the few simple changes he had made could produce such a rich harvest.

Monty worked late, and a second bell did not deter him. He wanted to finish this last great stack of alfalfa. Then he saw Rebecca running along the trail, calling. Monty let her call. It somehow tickled him, pretending not to hear. So she came out into the field and up to him.

"Sam, are you deaf? Ma rang twice. And then she sent me."

"Wal, I reckon I been feelin' orful good about this alfalfa," he replied.

"Oh, it is lovely. So dark and green—so sweet to smell! . . . Sam, I'll just have to slide down that haystack."

"Don't you dare," called Monty in alarm.

But she ran around to the lower side and presently appeared on top, her face flushed, full of fun and the desire to torment him.

"Please, Rebecca, don't slide down. You'll topple it over, an' I'll have all the work to do over again."

"Sam, I just have to, the way I used to when I was a kid."

"You're a kid right now," he retorted. "An' go back an' get down careful."

She shrieked and let herself go and came sliding down, somewhat at the expense of modesty. Monty knew he was angry, but he feared that he was some other things too.

"There! You see how slick I did it? I could always beat the girls—and boys, too."

"Wal, let thet do," growled Monty.

"Just one more, Sam."

He dropped his pitchfork and made a lunge for her, catching only the air. How quick she was! He controlled an impulse to run after her. Soon she appeared on top again, with something added to her glee.

"Rebecca, if you slide down heah again you'll be sorry," he shouted warningly.

"What'll *you* do?"

"I'll spank you."

"Sam Hill! . . . You wouldn't dare."

"So help me heaven, I will."

She did not in the least believe him, but it was evident that his threat made her project only the more thrilling. There was at least a possibility of excitement.

"Look out. I'm acoming," she cried, with a wild, sweet trill of laughter.

As she slid down Monty leaped to intercept her. A scream escaped from Rebecca, but it was only because of her unruly skirts. That did not deter Monty. He caught her and stopped her high off the ground, and there he pinioned her.

Whatever Monty's intent had been it now escaped him. A winged flame flicked at every fiber of his being. He had her arms spread, and it took all his strength and weight to hold her there, feet off the ground. She was not in the least frightened at this close contact, though a wonderful look of speculation sparkled in her big gray eyes.

"You caught me. Now what?" she said challengingly.

Monty kissed her square on the mouth.

"Oh!" she cried, obviously startled. Then a wave of scarlet rushed up from the rich gold swell of her neck to her forehead. She struggled. "Let me down—you—you gentile cowpuncher!"

Monty kissed her again, longer, harder than before. Then when she tried to scream he stopped her lips again.

"You—little Mormon—devil!" he panted. "This heah—was shore—comin' to you!"

"I'll kill you!"

"Wal, it'll be worth—dyin' fer, I reckon." Then Monty kissed her again and again until she gasped for breath, and when she sagged limp and unresisting into his arms he kissed her cheeks, her eyes, her hair, and like a madman whose hunger had been augmented by what it fed on he went back to her red parted lips.

Suddenly the evening sky appeared to grow dark. A weight carried him down with the girl. The top of the alfalfa stack had slid down upon them. Monty floundered out and dragged Rebecca from under the fragrant mass of hay. She did not move. Her eyes were closed. With trembling hand he brushed the chaff and bits of alfalfa off her white face. But her hair was full of them.

"My Gawd, I've played hob now," he whispered, as the enormity of his offense suddenly dawned upon him. Nevertheless, he felt a tremendous thrill of joy as he looked down at her. Only her lips bore a vestige of color. Suddenly her eyes opened wide. From the sheer glory of them Monty fled.

v

His first wild impulse, as he ran, was to get out of the canyon, away from the incomprehensible forces that had worked such sudden havoc with his life. His second thought was to rush to Mrs. Keetch and confess everything to her, before Rebecca could damn him forever in that good woman's estimation. Then by the time he had reached his cabin and thrown himself on the porch bench, both of these impulses had given place to still others. But it was not Monty's nature to remain helpless for long. Presently he sat up, wringing wet with sweat, and still shaking.

"Aw, what could have come over me?" he breathed hoarsely. And suddenly he realized that nothing so terrible had happened after all. He had been furious with Rebecca and meant to chastise her. But when he held her close and tight, with those challenging eyes and lips right before him, all else except the sweetness of momentary possession had been forgotten. He loved the girl and had not before felt any realization of the full magnitude of his love. He believed that he could explain to Mrs. Keetch, so that she would not drive him away. But of course he would be as dirt under Rebecca's feet from that hour on. Yet even in his mournful acceptance of this fate his spirit rose in wonderment over what this surprising Mormon girl must be thinking of him now.

Darkness had almost set in. Down the lane Monty saw a figure approaching, quite some distance away, and he thought he heard a low voice singing. It could not be Rebecca. Rebecca would be weeping.

"Re-becca," called Mrs. Keetch from the porch, in her mellow, far-reaching voice.

"Coming, Ma," replied the girl.

Monty sank into the shadow of his little cabin. He felt small enough to be unseen, but dared not risk it. And he watched in fear and trepidation. Suddenly Rebecca's low contralto voice rang on the quiet sultry air.

> In the gloaming, Oh my darling!
> When the lights are dim and low—
> And the quiet shadows falling,
> Softly come and softly go.

Monty's heart swelled almost to bursting. Did she realize the truth and was she mocking him? He was simply flabbergasted. But how the sweet voice filled the canyon and came back in echo from the walls!

Rebecca, entering the square between the orchards and the cottonwoods, gave Monty's cabin a wide berth.

"Isn't Sam with you?" called Mrs. Keetch from the porch.

"Sam? . . . No, he isn't."

"Where is he? Didn't you call him? Supper is getting cold."

"I haven't any idea where Sam is. Last I saw of him he was running like mad," rejoined Rebecca with a giggle.

That giggle saved Monty from a stroke of apoplexy.

"Running? What for?" asked the mother, as Rebecca mounted the porch.

"Ma, it was the funniest thing. I called Sam, but he didn't hear. I went out to tell him supper was ready. He had a great high stack of alfalfa up. Of course I wanted to climb it and slide down. Well, Sam got mad and ordered me not to do any such thing. Then I *had* to do it. Such fun! Sam growled like a bear. Well, I couldn't resist climbing up for another slide. . . . Do you know, Mother, Sam got perfectly furious. He has a terrible temper. He commanded me not to slide off that stack. And when I asked him what he'd do if I did—he declared he'd spank me. Imagine! I only meant to tease him. I wasn't going to slide at all. Then, you can see I *had* to. . . . So I did. . . . I—oh dear!—I fetched the whole top of the stack down on us—and when I got out from under the smothering hay—and could see—there was Sam running for dear life."

"Well, for the land's sake!" exclaimed Mrs. Keetch dubiously, and then she laughed. "You drive the poor fellow wild with your pranks. Rebecca, will you never grow up?"

Whereupon she came out to the porch rail and called, "Sam."

Monty started up, opened his door to let it slam and replied, in what he thought a perfectly normal voice, "Hello?"

"Hurry to supper."

Monty washed his face and hands, brushed his hair, while his mind whirled. Then he sat down bewildered. "Doggone me!— Can you beat thet gurl? She didn't give me away—she didn't lie, yet she never tole. . . . She's not goin' to tell. . . . Must have been funny to her. . . . But shore it's a daid safe bet she never got kissed thet way before. . . . I jist cain't figger her out."

Presently he went to supper and was grateful for the dim light. Still he felt the girl's eyes on him. No doubt she was now appreciating him at last as a real Arizona cowboy. He pretended weariness, and soon hurried away to his cabin, where he spent a night of wakefulness and of conflicting emotions. Remorse, however, had died a natural death after hearing Rebecca's story to her mother.

With dawn came the blessed work into which Monty plunged, finding relief in tasks which kept him away from the ranch house.

For two whole weeks Rebecca did not speak a single word to him. Mrs. Keetch finally noticed the strange silence and reproved her daughter for her attitude.

"Speak to *him?*" asked Rebecca, with a sniff. "Maybe—when he crawls on his knees!"

"But, daughter, he only threatened to spank you. And I'm sure you gave him provocation. You must always forgive. We cannot live at enmity here," she said. "Sam is a good man, and we owe him much."

Then she turned to Monty.

"Sam, you know Rebecca has passed eighteen and she feels an exaggerated sense of her maturity. Perhaps if you'd tell her you were sorry—"

"What about?" asked Monty, when she hesitated.

"Why, about what offended Rebecca."

"Aw, shore. I'm orful sorry," drawled Monty, his keen eyes on the girl. "Turrible sorry—but it's about not sayin' an' doin' *more*—an' then spankin' her to boot."

Mrs. Keetch looked aghast, and when Rebecca ran away from the table hysterical with mirth, the good woman seemed positively nonplused.

"That girl! Why, Sam, I thought she was furious with you. But she's not. It's all sham."

"Wal, I reckon she's riled all right, but it doesn't matter. An' see heah, ma'am," he went on, lowering his voice. "I'm confidin' in you, an' if you give me away—wal, I'll leave the ranch. . . . I reckon you've forgot how once you told me I'd lose my haid over Rebecca. Wal, I've lost it, clean an' plumb an' otherwise. An' sometimes I do queer things. Jist remember thet's why. This won't make no difference. I'm happy heah. Only I want you to understand me."

"Sam Hill!" she whispered in amazement. "So that's what ails you. . . . Now all will be well."

"Wal, I'm glad you think so," replied Monty shortly. "An' I reckon it will be—when I get over these growin' pains."

She leaned toward him. "My son, I understand now. Rebecca has been in love with you for a long time. Just let her alone. All will be well."

Monty gave her one mute, incredulous stare and then he fled. In the darkness of his cabin he persuaded himself of the absurdity of the sentimental Mrs. Keetch's claim. That night he could sleep. But when day came again he found that the havoc had been wrought. He found himself living in a kind of dream, and he was always watching for Rebecca.

Straightway he began to make some discoveries. Gradually she appeared to come out of her icy shell. She worked as usual, and apparently with less discontent, especially in the mornings when she had time to sew on the porch. She would fetch lunch to the men out in the fields. Once or twice Monty saw her on top of a haystack, but he always quickly looked away. She climbed the wall trail; she gathered armloads of wild flowers; she helped where her help was not needed.

On Sunday mornings she went to church at White Sage and in the afternoon entertained callers. But it was noticeable that her Mormon courters grew fewer as the summer advanced. Monty missed in her the gay allure, the open coquetry, the challenge that had once been so marked.

All this was thought-provoking enough for Monty, but nothing to the discovery that Rebecca watched him from afar and from near at hand. Monty could scarcely believe it. Only more proof of his addled brain! However, the eyes which had made Monty Smoke Bellew a great shot and tracker, wonderful out on the range, could not be deceived. When he himself took to spying upon Rebecca, he had learned the staggering truth.

In the mornings and evenings while he was at work near the barn or resting on his porch she watched him, believing herself unseen. She

peered from behind her window curtain, through the leaves, above her
sewing, from the open doors—from everywhere her great gray hungry
eyes sought him. It began to get on Monty's nerves. Did she hate him
so much that she was planning some dire revenge? But the eyes that
watched him in secret seldom or never met his own any more.
Sometimes he would recall Mrs. Keetch's strangely tranquil words,
and then he would have to battle fiercely with himself to recover his
equanimity. The last asinine thing Smoke Bellew would ever do
would be to believe that Rebecca loved him.

One noonday Monty returned to his cabin to find a magical
change in his single room. He could not recognize it. Clean and tidy
and colorful, it met his eye as he entered. There were Indian rugs on
the clay floor, Indian ornaments on the log walls, curtains at his
windows, a scarf on his table, and a bright bedspread on his bed. In a
little Indian vase on the table stood some stalks of golden daisies and
purple asters.

"What happened around heah this mawnin'?" he drawled at
meal hour. "My cabin is spruced up fine as a parlor."

"Yes, it does look nice," replied Mrs. Keetch complacently.
"Rebecca has had that in mind to do for some time."

"Wal, it was turrible good of her," said Monty.

"Oh, nonsense," returned Rebecca, with a swift blush. "Ma
wanted you to be more comfortable, that's all."

Monty escaped somehow, as he always managed to escape when
catastrophe impended. But one August night when the harvest moon
rose white and huge above the black canyon rim he felt such a strange
impelling presentiment that he could not bear to leave his porch and
go into bed. It had been a hard day—one in which the accumulated
cut of alfalfa had been heavy. Canyon Walls Ranch, with its soil and
water and sun, was beyond doubt a gold mine. All over southern Utah
the ranchers were clamoring for that record alfalfa crop.

The hour was late. The light in Rebecca's room had long been
out. Frogs and owls and nighthawks had ceased their lonely calls. Only
the insects hummed in the melancholy stillness.

A rustle startled Monty. Was it a leaf falling from a cottonwood?
A dark form crossed the barred patches of moonlight. Rebecca! She
passed close to him as he lounged on the porch steps. Her face flashed
white. She ran down the lane and then stopped to look back.

"Doggone! Am I drunk or crazy or just moonstruck?" said Monty
rising. "What is the gurl up to? . . . Shore she seen me heah. . . .
Shore she did!"

He started down the lane and when he came out of the shadow
of the cottonwoods into the moonlight she began to run with the
speed of a deer. Monty stalked after her. He was roused now. He

would see this thing through. If this was just another of her hoydenish tricks! But there seemed to be something mysterious in this night flight out into the canyon under the full moon.

Monty lost sight of her at the end of the lane. But when he reached it and turned into the field he saw her on the other side, lingering, looking back. He could see her moon-blanched face. She ran on and he followed.

That side of the canyon lay clear in the silver light. On the other the looming canyon wall stood up black, with its level rim moon-fired against the sky. The alfalfa shone bright, and the scent of it in the night air was overpowering in its sweetness.

Rebecca was making for the upper end where that day the alfalfa had been cut. She let Monty gain on her, but at last with a burst of laughter she ran to the huge silver-shining haystack and began to climb it.

Monty did not run: he slowed down. He did not know what was happening to him, but his state seemed to verge upon lunacy. One of his nightmares! He would awaken presently. But there was the white form scrambling up the steep haystack. That afternoon he had finished this mound of alfalfa, with the satisfaction of an artist.

When he reached it Rebecca had not only gained the top, but was lying flat, propped on her elbows. Monty went closer—until he was standing right up against the stack. He could see her distinctly now, scarcely fifteen feet above his head. The moonlight lent her form an air of witchery. But it was the mystery of her eyes that completed the bewitchment of Monty. Why had he followed her? He could do nothing. His former threat was but an idle memory. His anger would not rise. She would make him betray his secret and then, alas! Canyon Walls could no longer be a home for him.

"Howdy, Sam," she said, in a tone that he could not comprehend.

"Rebecca, what you doin' out heah?"

"Isn't it a glorious night?"

"Yes. But you ought to be in your bed. An' you could have watched from your window."

"Oh, no. I had to be out in it. . . . Besides, I wanted to make you follow me."

"Wal, you shore have. I was plumb scared, I reckon. An'—an' I'm glad it was only in fun. . . . But why did you want me to follow you?"

"For one thing, I wanted you to see me climb your new haystack."

"Yes? Wal, I've seen you. So come down now. If your mother should ketch us out heah—"

"And I wanted you to see me slide down *this* one."

As he looked up at her he realized how helpless he was in the hands of this strange girl. He kept staring, not knowing what she would do next.

"And *I* wanted to see—terribly—what you'd do," she went on, with a seriousness that surely must have been mockery.

"Rebecca, honey, I don't aim to do—nothin'," replied Monty almost mournfully.

She got to her knees, and leaned over as if to see more clearly. Then she turned round to sit down and slide to the very edge. Her hands were clutched deep in the alfalfa.

"You won't spank me, Sam?" she asked, in impish glee.

"No. Much as I'd like to—an' as you shore need it—I cain't."

"Bluffer . . . Gentile cowpuncher . . . showing yellow . . . marble-hearted fiend!"

"Not thet last, Rebecca. For all my many faults, not that," he said sadly.

She seemed fighting to let go of something that the mound of alfalfa represented only in symbol. Surely the physical effort for Rebecca to hold her balance there could not account for the look of strain on her body and face. And, in addition, all the mystery of Canyon Walls and the beauty of the night hovered over her.

"Sam, dare me to slide," she taunted.

"No," he retorted grimly.

"Coward!"

"Shore. You hit me on the haid there."

Then ensued a short silence. He could see her quivering. She was moving, almost imperceptibly. Her eyes, magnified by the shadow and light, transfixed Monty.

"Gentile, dare me to slide—into your arms," she cried a little quaveringly.

"Mormon tease! Would you—"

"Dare me!"

"Wal, I dare—you, Rebecca . . . but so help me Gawd I won't answer for the consequences."

Her laugh, like the sweet, wild trill of a night bird, rang out, but this time it was full of joy, of certainty, of surrender. And she let go her hold, to spread wide her arms and come sliding on an avalanche of silver hay down upon him.

VI

Next morning Monty found work in the fields impossible. He roamed about like a man possessed, and at last went back to the cabin. It was just before the noonday meal. In the ranch house Rebecca hummed a tune while she set the table. Mrs. Keetch sat in her rocker, busy with work on her lap. There was no charged atmosphere. All seemed serene.

Monty responded to the girl's shy glance by taking her hand and leading her up to her mother.

"Ma'am," he began hoarsely, "you've knowed long how my feelin's are for Rebecca. But it seems she—she loves me, too. . . . How thet come about I cain't say. It's shore the wonderfullest thing. . . . Now I ask you—fer Rebecca's sake most—what can be done about this heah trouble?"

"Daughter, is it true?" asked Mrs. Keetch, looking up with serene and smiling face.

"Yes, Mother," replied Rebecca simply.

"You love Sam?"

"Oh, I do."

"Since when?"

"Always, I guess. But I never knew till this June."

"I am very glad, Rebecca," replied the mother, rising to embrace her. "Since you could not or would not love one of your own creed it is well that you love this man who came a stranger to our gates. He is strong, he is true, and what his religion is matters little."

Then she smiled upon Monty. "My son, no man can say what guided your steps to Canyon Walls. But I always felt God's intent in it. You and Rebecca shall marry."

"Oh, Mother," murmured the girl rapturously, and she hid her face.

"Wal, I'm willin' an' happy," stammered Monty. "But I ain't worthy of her, ma'am, an' you know thet old—"

She silenced him. "You must go to White Sage and be married at once."

"At once!— When?" faltered Rebecca.

"Aw, Mrs. Keetch, I—I wouldn't hurry the gurl. Let her have her own time."

"No, why wait? She has been a strange, starved creature. . . . Tomorrow you must take her to be wed, Sam."

"Wal an' good, if Rebecca says so," said Monty with wistful eagerness.

"Yes," she whispered. "Will you go with us, Ma?"

"Yes," suddenly cried Mrs. Keetch, as if inspired. "I will go. I will cross the Utah line once more before I am carried over. . . . But not White Sage. We will go to Kanab. You shall be married by the bishop."

In the excitement and agitation that possessed mother and daughter at that moment, Monty sensed a significance more than just the tremendous importance of impending marriage. Some deep, strong motive was urging Mrs. Keetch to go to Kanab, there to have the bishop marry Rebecca to a gentile. One way or another it did not matter to Monty. He rode in the clouds. He could not believe in his good luck. Never in his life had he touched such happiness as he was experiencing now.

The womenfolk were an hour late in serving lunch, and during the meal the air of vast excitement permeated their every word and action. They could not have tasted the food on their plates.

"Wal, this heah seems like a Sunday," said Monty, after a hasty meal. "I've loafed a lot this mawnin'. But I reckon I'll go back to work now."

"Oh, Sam—don't—when—when we're leaving so soon," remonstrated Rebecca shyly.

"When are we leavin'?"

"Tomorrow—early."

"Wal, I'll get thet alfalfa up anyhow. It might rain, you know— Rebecca, do you reckon you could get up at daylight fer this heah ride?"

"I could stay up all night, Sam."

Mrs. Keetch laughed at them. "There's no rush. We'll start after breakfast, and get to Kanab early enough to make arrangements for the wedding next day. It will give Sam time to buy a respectable suit of clothes to be married in."

"Doggone! I hadn't thought of thet," replied Monty ruefully.

"Sam Hill, you don't marry *me* in a ten-gallon hat, a red shirt and blue overalls, and boots," declared Rebecca.

"How about wearin' my gun?" drawled Monty.

"Your gun!" exclaimed Rebecca.

"Shore. You've forgot how I used to pack it. I might need it there to fight off them Mormons who're so crazy about you."

"Heavens! You leave that gun home."

Next morning when Monty brought the buckboard around, Mrs. Keetch and Rebecca appeared radiant of face, gorgeous of apparel. But for the difference in age anyone might have mistaken the mother for the intended bride.

The drive to Kanab, with fresh horses and light load, took six hours. And the news of the wedding spread over Kanab like wildfire in dry prairie grass. For all Monty's keen eyes he never caught a jealous look, nor did he hear a critical word. That settled with him for all time the status of the Keetches' Mormon friends. The Tyler brothers came into town and made much of the fact that Monty would soon be one of them. And they planned another fall hunt for wild mustangs and deer. This time Monty would surely bring in Rebecca's wild pony. Waking hours sped by and sleeping hours were few. Almost before Monty knew what was happening he was in the presence of the Mormon bishop.

"Will you come into the Mormon Church?" asked the bishop.

"Wal, sir, I cain't be a Mormon," replied Monty in perplexity. "But I shore have respect fer you people an' your Church. I reckon I never had no religion. I can say I'll never stand in Rebecca's way, in anythin' pertainin' to hers."

"In the event she bears you children you will not seek to raise them gentiles?"

"I'd leave thet to Rebecca," replied Monty quietly.

"And the name Sam Hill, by which you are known, is a middle name?"

"Shore, jist a cowboy middle name."

So they were married. Monty feared they would never escape from the many friends and the curious crowd. But at last they were safely in the buckboard, speeding homeward. Monty sat in the front seat alone. Mrs. Keetch and Rebecca occupied the rear seat. The girl's expression of pure happiness touched Monty and made him swear deep in his throat that he would try to deserve her love. Mrs. Keetch had evidently lived through one of the few great events of her life. What dominated her feelings Monty could not divine, but she had the look of a woman who asked no more of life. Somewhere, at some time, a monstrous injustice or wrong had been done the Widow Keetch. Recalling the bishop's strange look at Rebecca—a look of hunger—Monty pondered deeply.

The ride home, being downhill, with a pleasant breeze off the desert, and that wondrous panorama coloring and spreading in the setting sun, seemed all too short for Monty. He drawled to Rebecca, when they reached the portal of Canyon Walls and halted under the gold-leaved cottonwoods: "Wal, wife, heah we are home. But we shore ought to have made thet honeymoon drive a longer one."

That suppertime was the only one in which Monty ever saw the Widow Keetch bow her head and give thanks to the Lord for the salvation of these young people so strangely brought together, for the home overflowing with milk and honey, for the hopeful future.

They had their fifth cutting of alfalfa in September, and it was in the nature of an event. The Tyler boys rode over to help, fetching Sue to visit Rebecca. And there was much merrymaking. Rebecca would climb every mound of alfalfa and slide down screaming her delight. And once she said to Monty, "Young man, you should pray under every haystack you build."

"Ahuh. An' what fer should I pray, Rebecca?" he drawled.

"To give thanks for all this sweet-smelling alfalfa has brought you."

The harvest god smiled on Canyon Walls that autumn. Three

wagons plied between Kanab and the ranch for weeks, hauling the produce that could not be used. While Monty went off with the Tyler boys for their hunt in Buckskin Forest, the womenfolk and their guests, and the hired hands applied themselves industriously to the happiest work of the year—preserving all they could of the luscious fruit yield of the season.

Monty came back to a home such as had never been his even in his happiest dreams. Rebecca was incalculably changed, and so happy that Monty trembled as he listened to her sing, as he watched her at work. The mystery never ended for him, not even when she whispered that they might expect a little visitor from the angels next spring. But Monty's last doubt faded, and he gave himself over to work, to his loving young wife, to walks in the dusk under the canyon walls, to a lonely pipe beside his little fireside.

The winter passed, and spring came, doubling all former activities. They had taken over the canyon three miles to the westward, which once cleared of brush and cactus and rock promised well. The problem had been water and Monty solved it by extending a new irrigation ditch from the same brook that watered the home ranch. Good fortune had attended his every venture.

Around the middle of April, when the cottonwoods began to be tinged with green and the peach trees with pink, Monty began to grow restless about the coming event. It uplifted him one moment, appalled him the next. In that past which seemed so remote to him now, he had snuffed out life. Young, fiery, grim Smoke Bellew! And by some incomprehensible working out of life he was now about to bring life into being.

On the seventeenth of May, some hours after breakfast, he was hurriedly summoned from the fields. His heart appeared to be choking him.

Mrs. Keetch met him at the porch. He scarcely knew her.

"My son, do you remember this date?"

"No," replied Monty wonderingly.

"Two years ago today you came to us. . . . And Rebecca has just borne you a son."

"Aw—my Gawd!— How—how is she, ma'am?" he gasped.

"Both well. We could ask no more. It has all been a visitation of God. . . . Come."

Some days later the important matter of christening the youngster came up.

"Ma wants one of those jaw-breaking Biblical names," said Rebecca pouting. "But I like just plain Sam."

"Wal, it ain't much of a handle fer sech a wonderful little feller."

"It's your name. I love it."

"Rebecca, you kinda forget Sam Hill was jist a—a sort of a middle name. It ain't my real name."

"Oh, yes, I remember now," replied Rebecca, her great eyes lighting. "At Kanab—the bishop asked about Sam Hill. Mother had told him that was your nickname."

"Darlin', I had another nickname once," he said sadly.

"So, my man with a mysterious past. And what was that?"

"They called me Smoke."

"How funny! . . . Well, I may be Mrs. Monty Smoke Bellew, according to the law and the Church, but *you*, my husband, will always be Sam Hill to me!"

"An' the boy?" asked Monty enraptured.

"Is Sam Hill, too."

An anxious week passed and then all seemed surely well with the new mother and baby. Monty ceased to tiptoe around. He no longer awoke with a start in the dead of night.

Then one Saturday as he came out on the wide porch, he heard a hallo from someone, and saw four riders coming through the portal. A bolt shot back from a closed door of his memory. Arizona riders! How well he knew the lean faces, the lithe forms, the gun belts, the mettlesome horses!

"Nix, fellers," called the foremost rider, as Monty came slowly out.

An instinct followed by a muscular contraction that had the speed of lightning passed over Monty. Then he realized he packed no gun and was glad. Old habit might have been too strong. His hawk eye saw lean hands drop from hips. A sickening feeling of despair followed his first reaction.

"Howdy, Smoke," drawled the foremost rider.

"Wal, doggone! If it ain't Jim Sneed," returned Monty, as he recognized the sheriff, and he descended the steps to walk out and offer his hand, quick to see the swift, penetrating eyes run over him.

"Shore, it's Jim. I reckoned you'd know me. Hoped you would, as I wasn't too keen about raisin' your smoke."

"Ahuh. What you all doin' over heah, Jim?" asked Monty, with a glance at the three watchful riders.

"Main thing I come over fer was to buy stock fer Strickland. An' he said if it wasn't out of my way I might fetch you back. Word come thet you'd been seen in Kanab. An' when I made inquiry at White Sage I shore knowed who Sam Hill was."

"I see. Kinda tough it happened to be Strickland. Doggone! My luck jist couldn't last."

"Smoke, you look uncommon fine," said the sheriff with another appraising glance. "You shore haven't been drinkin'. An' I seen fust off you wasn't totin' no gun."

"Thet's all past fer me, Jim."

"Wal, I'll be damned!" exclaimed Sneed, and fumbled for a cigarette. "Bellew, I jist don't savvy."

"Reckon you wouldn't. . . . Jim, I'd like to ask if my name ever got linked up with thet Green Valley deal two years an' more ago?"

"No, it didn't, Smoke, I'm glad to say. Your pards Slim an' Cuppy pulled thet. Slim was killed coverin' Cuppy's escape."

"Ahuh . . . So Slim—wal, wal—" sighed Monty, and paused a moment to gaze into space.

"Smoke, tell me your deal heah," said Sneed.

"Shore. But would you mind comin' indoors?"

"Reckon I wouldn't. But Smoke, I'm still figgerin' you the cowboy."

"Wal, you're way off. Get down an' come in."

Monty led the sheriff into Rebecca's bedroom. She was awake, playing with the baby by her side on the bed.

"Jim, this is my wife an' youngster," said Monty feelingly. "An' Rebecca, this heah is an old friend of mine, Jim Sneed, from Arizona."

That must have been a hard moment for the sheriff—the cordial welcome of the blushing wife, the smiling mite of a baby who was clinging to his finger, the atmosphere of unadulterated joy in the little home.

At any rate, when they went out again to the porch Sneed wiped his perspiring face and swore at Monty, "—— cowboy, have you gone an' double-crossed thet sweet gurl?"

Monty told him the few salient facts of his romance, and told it with trembling eagerness to be believed.

"So you've turned Mormon?" said the sheriff.

"No, but I'll be true to these women. . . . An' one thing I ask, Sneed. Don't let it be known in White Sage or heah *why* I'm with you. . . . I can send word to my wife I've got to go to Arizona . . . then afterward I'll come back."

"Smoke, I wish I had a stiff drink," replied Sneed. "But I reckon you haven't anythin'?"

"Only water an' milk."

"Good Lawd! For an Arizonian!" Sneed halted at the head of the porch steps and shot out a big hand. His cold eyes had warmed.

"Smoke, may I tell Strickland you'll send him some money now an' then—till thet debt is paid?"

Monty stared and faltered, "Jim—you shore can."

"Fine," returned the sheriff in a loud voice, and he strode down the steps to mount his horse. "Adios, cowboy. Be good to thet little woman."

Monty could not speak. He watched the riders down the lane, out into the road, and through the wide canyon gates to the desert beyond. His heart was full. He thought of Slim and Cuppy, those young firebrand comrades of his range days. He could remember now without terror. He could live once more with his phantoms of the past. He could see lean, lithe Arizona riders come into Canyon Walls, if that event ever chanced again, and be glad of their coming.

QUESTIONS

1. "Canyon Walls" is one of the many Western stories that have pastoral settings; it is laid in a kind of Shangri La valley where placid streams flow through an unspoiled canyon. How does the setting contribute to the hero's reformation and triumph?

2. Mormons frequently figured as villains in Zane Grey novels. How are Mormons and the Mormon faith portrayed in this story?

3. Some critics claim that most Western stories have been written by male chauvinists. Does the portrayal of women in this story support the accusation? Explain.

4. Zane Grey was an enormously popular writer. If this story is representative of his work, what elements or characteristics of it might account for his popularity?

5. This story is unlike most of the work of Zane Grey in that it contains neither gun play nor other violence. Does it lack interest because it lacks overt conflict?

VARDIS FISHER
THE SCARECROW

We were threshing on the ranch of Jon Weeg and when we went to the machine one morning we discovered that a stray animal had been to the piled sacks of grain and had ripped several of them wide open. Around the pile were the hoofprints of a horse. We searched the yard and the outlying land, expecting to find the beast foundered; but there was no trace of it. In the evening of this day we built around the stacks of wheat a fence of barbed wire. "That'll hold him," we said.

But on the next morning we found another half-dozen sacks torn open; for the prowler had returned during the night, had leapt our three-wire fence, and had gone. In this evening we added two wires to the fence. It was now chin-high and we didn't think that even an elk could jump it. Our astonishment on the third morning left us speechless. The beast had come again, had vaulted our five-wire fence, and had plundered another half-dozen sacks. On the top wire was a little hair but that was all. And it was at this point that the matter began to be a little unreal for all of us. For Joe Burt, a huge and feeble-witted youth, it was nothing less than a miracle. Because ordinarily, as in turn we declared to one another, an animal does not gorge itself upon grain without foundering; does not come slyly under cover of darkness and vanish before daylight; and does not leap a five-wire fence.

"Mebbe it's a mule," said Curt Obbing. We searched and found tracks but they were not the tracks of a mule.

"I'm going to sleep out here," I said. "I'll find out."

And on the third night I laid my bed in the grain yard and waited for the thief. I fell asleep; and later was awakened by a terrific screeching of wire; and upon looking up, I saw a very tall gaunt horse caught on the fence. In the moonlight it seemed to be nothing but hide and bones and eyes. It had jumped and now stood with its front legs over the wire and with the taunt wire under its belly; and a more forlorn and helpless creature I had never seen. I rose and went over to it, intending to flog the ungainly beast off the place, but something in its eyes made me pause. It was a kind of sad resignation, a hopeless surrender, mixed with shame for having got into such a predicament. And instead of flogging the thief I patted its gaunt and ancient head and looked at its eyes. "You old fool," I said. "Don't you know enough to keep off a wire fence?" I went over and stirred the torn sacks of wheat and watched the beast's eyes, but it gave no sign. It did not even lift an ear or turn its eyes to watch me. Then I put a halter on it and cut the wires to get it off the fence and tied it to a post.

On the next morning the men walked around the drooping skeleton and wondered what should be done. There was no agreement among us. Joe Burt wanted to tie cans to its tail and set the dogs on it; Curt wanted to turpentine it; and Jack Brody wanted to put a girth around it, with sharp nails set to the flesh and turn it loose. And as they spoke, the men smote the beast or cuffed its ears, but it did not flinch. It seemed to be a dead horse, tied to a post. I persuaded the men to let me take it down the road and point its nose valleyward. "It's a good Christian practice," I said, "to give all pests to your neighbors."

And I took the creature a mile down the road and threw clubs at it and as far as I could see that horse, it was going patiently westward and out of sight. But on the next morning, there that beast was, stuffed and contented, before those bags of grain. Even my patience was gone now.

"I suppose," Curt said, "you wanta play with it some more."

"Let me fix him," said Jack Brody. "Put a spiked cinch around him and then give him all the water he'n drink. He'll move plenty fast."

"No, if we're going to do anything we'll kill it."

We talked of the matter and decided it would be best to kill it; and in this night, which was very dark, we got Jon Weeg's double-barreled shotgun and led the horse into a patch of timber. And now all of us, I observed, were very quiet and mysterious, as if we plotted some crime. Joe Burt laughed queerly a time or two but none of us said a word. Curt took the horse and we followed in single file. The old beast led easily, never drawing back or turning aside, as if he had spent all his years on the end of a rope. I think it was his dumb surrender to our wish, the almost eager way in which he went with us, that explains what happened later.

Because after Curt stopped in a dark recess of the woods none of us wanted to be the executioner. This in itself was rather unusual; for we had all slain animals before and none of us thought anything of twisting the head off a rooster or putting pups in a sack with stones and throwing them into water. This execution was different somehow, and I am still at a loss to explain the difference. I don't know why we hesitated as if there would be guilt on our souls. We seemed to share a common friendliness for this old vagabond that had outraged our fence and another's property. Or perhaps it was because Joe began to whimper and put his hands to his ears.

No matter: I am convinced now that none of us would have slain this animal if there had been a protest. If Curt had led him back to the yard, I imagine we would have set food and drink to the thief. But we had brought this horse out to murder and none of us would confess any weakness or any change of mind. We were men and we were doing a man's job. And when Curt said, "Who's got the gun?" we all stepped forward, as though eager to slay the beast; but we did not look at one another.

One of the men stepped forward with the gun and there was another pause. We were waiting for a volunteer.

"Well," said Curt, "who's to blow his head off?"

"It don't make any difference," Jack Brody said.

But Joe Burt, shaking from head to feet, put his hands to his ears and chattered:

"It's—it's a cinch I don't want to!"

This declaration made us hesitate again. Then Curt swore a mighty oath and said we were a fine bunch of men.

"What's the matter you guys? Give me that gun!"

We all stepped back and Curt loaded both barrels. He took the halter off and threw it at our feet and then dug into a pocket for his tobacco and bit off a huge quid. He tongued the tobacco for a moment and looked at us and then raised the gun to his shoulder. We all stepped farther back and Joe, with fingers thrust into his ears, began to babble.

"I can't see the sights!" Curt shouted. "Someone light a match."

"You don't have to see," said Jack. "Just put it against his head."

"Light a match!"

I struck a match and in its feeble light we saw the horse like a gaunt shadow, waiting patiently with his head drooping. The match sputtered and went out. I struck another. We could all see the gleaming barrel of the gun and Curt squinting along the sights. Then there was a thundering roar, the match went out, and we stood in overwhelming darkness. I struck another match and we saw the beast, standing there as if propped, with blood running down its face. I stepped forward quickly with the light and Curt fired the other barrel. The horse squealed and dropped to earth.

On our way back we said nothing. Curt went ahead, with gun smoking on his shoulder; and as before, we followed him in single file. After we had gone fifty yards I stopped and listened but could hear no sound. We took our several ways to bed and I lay sleepless for a long while, thinking of that dead beast out in the woods.

What happened later is very strange and a little incredible and I am not sure that I can make it clear. On the next morning we went to the yard and found that horse again within our fence, standing forlornly before the bags of wheat. Still, this is not exactly the way it happened. As a matter of fact, Joe Burt went out first and made the discovery. He came running to the house, pale and gibbering; and like a frenzied fellow he tried to tell us what he had seen. "He's been dreaming," we said; and we jested with him and did not believe his story at all.

"You're all cracked," Curt said. "You big simple lubber, stop that shakun around!" And Joe babbled at us and his teeth chattered.

And when we did go out, still unconvinced, we saw that creature before the grain. We all stopped and looked at him and looked at one another. He had not torn any sacks or eaten any wheat. Blood from his skull had run down to the bags, suggesting that he had been here most of the night: and the upper part of his head seemed to be a mass of clotted blood. One eye had been shot out and one ear had been blown off.

It is of what happened next that I cannot be certain, because it all seemed strange to me then and it seems strange to me now. None of us ate much breakfast and none of us said anything after our first amazement. I went to the timber to be sure that this was the horse we had shot. I found signs of a terrific struggle, as if it had taken the beast a long while to recover its legs; and I found the bloody trail back to the yard. I also found the halter which in our excitement we had forgotten.

On this day we did not work and for hours we did not talk. We sat in the yard, smoking cigarettes one after another; or looking with fresh astonishment at the horse; or with shame at the world around us. For it seemed to be a new world and we did not understand it. And all the while the animal stood there without moving, and apparently without pain, like a horrible apparition from the dead. More than his return, I think, was the way he stood that filled us with strange emotion. He possessed the yard and the pile of grain in spite of all opposition. He seemed to have a serene, an almost unearthly, unconcern about his victory; and he looked as if he would stand there forever, having by some privilege unknown to us claimed his heritage and his rights.

Harold Dow sat on the doorstep with his chin in his hands. It occurred to me, time and again while walking around, that the whole situation was more comic than tragic; but Dow would not look at me, nor would Curt or Jack, when I passed them. Curt, in fact, pretended to be very busy tinkering with machinery in the yard. Jack lay in the sun with his hands under his head. But it was Joe Burt who acted most queerly and who made us all feel queer. During the whole forenoon he hid behind the bags of wheat and peered at that horse, his big round face like a moon against the sky. The big lubber with his stricken eyes and gibbering tongue made us all feel disembodied and lost. I have wondered since if what took place later would have happened if Joe had not been with us. I don't know. I do know that something persistent and inexplicable was busy in our minds and hearts; a notion which slowly took hold of us; the same thought. And when at last I said, "Fellows, let's get busy," they all knew what I meant. They all rose and followed me as if we had talked of the matter and planned what to do; and we went to the horse and looked at it. For a long moment we did not speak, but I knew that every one of us was thinking the same thing. And it is this part of the experience that baffles me. I've no idea why we wanted to save that creature's life; for it was worthless and homeless and a nuisance to everybody. But here we were, who had suggested one torture and another, who had tried to blow its head off, now resolved to save its life. It may be that our experience—the attempt to kill the beast and then fetch it back to health—became in some strange way symbolic: a struggle between ourselves and all the blind forces of life which we did not understand. Death was our enemy, too, and against it we matched all our cunning and all our skill. And the fight we made here was more than a fight on the Antelope Hills. It was infinitely more than that to every one of us.

For three days and three nights we labored to save that horse's life. Not one of us suggested that we should call a veterinarian: this was our fight, our small epic of cunning and devotion, and we did not want professional skill. If a doctor had come the matter would not have been the same at all. There would not have been those tremendous implications that made silent men of us and chastened our hearts and hands. And so we devoted ourselves to this struggle and everything else in our lives stood aside and waited. With a pile of empty sacks we made a bed and forced the horse to lie; and we put liniments and salves on the wound and bandaged it; and hunted in coves for tender grass. We took turns sitting up with the creature, as if it were a human being, as if our whole life and happiness depended on it. And in everything that we did we moved and felt in common and were driven by the same overwhelming desire. In these three days we achieved the deepest kinship that I have ever known to exist among men.

On my night with the horse I did not sleep at all. I sat by it and looked at the sick eye and wondered what else I could do to relieve the pain and bring healing blood to the wound. Early in the morning Jack called to me from the bunkhouse where the men slept.

"How is he?"

"Better, I think."

"Does he—seem to be in much pain?"

"No, he's resting easily."

And then Curt appeared. "You say he's all right?"

"Yes, I think so."

At break of day they all left the bunkhouse and came to the yard. They looked at the horse and patted his lean hide or studied the sick eye. Jack went away and returned with an armful of grass, though the beast had not in forty-eight hours eaten a mouthful; and Curt warmed a pail of water. The horse drank on this morning and we were sure it was better. We smiled at one another and said the horse would be well soon; and when we sat to breakfast we ate with a little of our former appetites.

But in spite of all our efforts the animal died on the fourth day. Joe Burt wept; and the eyes of the other men, I observed, were as misty as my own. We ate no breakfast on this morning. Upon all of us there fell a depressing sadness; a great loneliness that ached in our throats, as if everything good and beautiful had been taken from life. Out in the woods we searched for a spot to dig a grave; and Curt said, "Here," and upon the ground where we had shot the horse we dug a grave. We did not drag it to the grave, as is the custom, with a log chain around its neck. We rolled it to some planks and hauled it to the grave; and over the unsightly skull we placed a box, so that nothing would strike the wound; and upon the carcass we let the earth fall gently. . . .

And then as one man we returned to the yard and tore the fence down.

QUESTIONS

1. "The Scarecrow" is laid in the West, but it is not a "Western story." What essential is missing: a hero, a heroine, a villain, or a human conflict?

2. Joe Burt is characterized as "feeble-witted"; yet he takes an important part at every turn of the story. How does he act in a way to represent all the characters who are not feeble-witted?

3. Remembering the old horse being led to its "execution," the narrator says, "I think it was his dumb surrender to our wish, the almost eager way in which he went with us, that explains what happened later." Why?

4. What shared emotions bound the men together as they cared for the wounded horse? Guilt? Shame? Pity? Explain.

5. What meanings are suggested by the title "The Scarecrow"?

6. Like many stories laid in the West, this one is about men without women. How might the story have been different if a woman had been with the threshing crew?

ERNEST HAYCOX

STAGE TO LORDSBURG

This was one of those years in the Territory when Apache smoke signals spiraled up from the stony mountain summits and many a ranch cabin lay as a square of blackened ashes on the ground and the departure of a stage from Tonto was the beginning of an adventure that had no certain happy ending. . . .

The stage and its six horses waited in front of Weilner's store on the north side of Tonto's square. Happy Stuart was on the box, the ribbons between his fingers and one foot teetering on the brake. John Strang rode shotgun guard and an escort of ten cavalrymen waited behind the coach, half asleep in their saddles.

At four-thirty in the morning this high air was quite cold, though the sun had begun to flush the sky eastward. A small crowd stood in the square, presenting their final messages to the passengers now entering the coach. There was a girl going down to marry an infantry officer, a whisky drummer from St. Louis, an Englishman all length and bony corners and bearing with him an enormous sporting rifle, a gambler, a solid-shouldered cattleman on his way to New Mexico and a blond young man upon whom both Happy Stuart and the shotgun guard placed a narrow-eyed interest.

This seemed all until the blond man drew back from the coach door; and then a girl known commonly throughout the Territory as Henriette came quietly from the crowd. She was small and quiet, with a touch of paleness in her cheeks and her quite dark eyes lifted at the blond man's unexpected courtesy, showing surprise. There was this moment of delay and then the girl caught up her dress and stepped into the coach.

Men in the crowd were smiling but the blond one turned, his motion like the swift cut of a knife, and his attention covered that group until the smiling quit. He was tall, hollow-flanked, and definitely stamped by the guns slung low on his hips. But it wasn't the guns alone; something in his face, so watchful and so smooth, also showed his trade. Afterwards he got into the coach and slammed the door.

Happy Stuart kicked off the brakes and yelled, "Hi!" Tonto's people were calling out their last farewells and the six horses broke

into a trot and the stage lunged on its fore and aft springs and rolled
from town with dust dripping off its wheels like water, the cavalrymen
trotting briskly behind. So they tipped down the long grade, bound on
a journey no stage had attempted during the last forty-five days. Out
below in the desert's distance stood the relay stations they hoped to
reach and pass. Between lay a country swept empty by the quick raids
of Geronimo's men.

The Englishman, the gambler and the blond man sat jammed
together in the forward seat, riding backward to the course of the
stage. The drummer and the cattleman occupied the uncomfortable
middle bench; the two women shared the rear seat. The cattleman
faced Henriette, his knees almost touching her. He had one arm
hooked over the door's window sill to steady himself. A huge gold
nugget slid gently back and forth along the watch chain slung across
his wide chest and a chunk of black hair lay below his hat. His eyes
considered Henriette, reading something in the girl that caused him
to show her a deliberate smile. Henriette dropped her glance to the
gloved tips of her fingers, cheeks unstirred.

They were all strangers packed closely together, with nothing in
common save a destination. Yet the cattleman's smile and the
boldness of his glance were something as audible as speech, noted by
everyone except the Englishman, who sat bolt upright with his stony
indifference. The army girl, tall and calmly pretty, threw a quick side
glance at Henriette and afterwards looked away with a touch of color.
The gambler saw this interchange of glances and showed the
cattleman an irritated attention. The whisky drummer's eyes narrowed a little and some inward cynicism made a faint change on his
lips. He removed his hat to show a bald head already beginning to
sweat; his cigar smoke turned the coach cloudy and ashes kept
dropping on his vest.

The blond man had observed Henriette's glance drop from the
cattleman; he tipped his hat well over his face and watched her—not
boldly but as though he were puzzled. Once her glance lifted and
touched him. But he had been on guard against that and was quick to
look away.

The army girl coughed gently behind her hand, whereupon the
gambler tapped the whisky drummer on the shoulder. "Get rid of
that." The drummer appeared startled. He grumbled, "Beg pardon,"
and tossed the smoke through the window.

All this while the coach went rushing down the ceaseless turns of
the mountain road, rocking on its fore and aft springs, its heavy wheels
slamming through the road ruts and whining on the curves. Occasionally the strident yell of Happy Stuart washed back. "Hi, Nellie! By
God—!" The whisky drummer braced himself against the door and
closed his eyes.

Three hours from Tonto the road, making a last round sweep, let them down upon the flat desert. Here the stage stopped and the men got out to stretch. The gambler spoke to the army girl, gently: "Perhaps you would find my seat more comfortable." The army girl said "Thank you," and changed over. The cavalry sergeant rode up to the stage, speaking to Happy Stuart.

"We'll be goin' back now—and good luck to ye."

The men piled in, the gambler taking the place beside Henriette. The blond man drew his long legs together to give the army girl more room, and watched Henriette's face with a soft, quiet care. A hard sun beat fully on the coach and dust began to whip up like fire smoke. Without escort they rolled across a flat earth broken only by cacti standing against a dazzling light. In the far distance, behind a blue heat haze, lay the faint suggestion of mountains.

The cattleman reached up and tugged at the ends of his mustache and smiled at Henriette. The army girl spoke to the blond man. "How far is it to the noon station?" The blond man said courteously: "Twenty miles." The gambler watched the army girl with the strictness of his face relaxing, as though the run of her voice reminded him of things long forgotten.

The miles fell behind and the smell of alkali dust got thicker. Henriette rested against the corner of the coach, her eyes dropped to the tips of her gloves. She made an enigmatic, disinterested shape there; she seemed past stirring, beyond laughter. She was young, yet she had a knowledge that put the cattleman and the gambler and the drummer and the army girl in their exact places; and she knew why the gambler had offered the army girl his seat. The army girl was in one world and she was in another, as everyone in the coach understood. It had no effect on her for this was a distinction she had learned long ago. Only the blond man broke through her indifference. His name was Malpais Bill and she could see the wildness in the corners of his eyes and in the long crease of his lips; it was a stamp that would never come off. Yet something flowed out of him toward her that was different than the predatory curiosity of other men; something unobtrusively gallant, unexpectedly gentle.

Upon the box Happy Stuart pointed to the hazy outline two miles away. "Injuns ain't burned that anyhow." The sun was directly overhead, turning the light of the world a cruel brass-yellow. The crooked crack of a dry wash opened across the two deep ruts that made this road. Johnny Strang shifted the gun in his lap. "What's Malpais Bill ridin' with us for?"

"I guess I wouldn't ask him," returned Happy Stuart and studied the wash with a troubled eye. The road fell into it roughly and he got a tighter grip on his reins and yelled: "Hang on! Hi, Nellie! God damn you, hi!" The six horses plunged down the rough side of the wash and for a moment the coach stood alone, high and lonely on the break, and then went reeling over the rim. It struck the gravel with a roar, the front wheels bouncing and the back wheels skewing around. The horses faltered but Happy Stuart cursed at his leaders and got them into a run again. The horses lunged up the far side of the wash two and two, their muscles bunching and the soft dirt flying in yellow clouds. The front wheels struck solidly and something cracked like a pistol shot; the stage rose out of the wash, teetered crosswise and then fell ponderously on its side, splintering the coach panels.

Johnny Strang jumped clear. Happy Stuart hung to the handrail with one hand and hauled on the reins with the other; and stood up while the passengers crawled through the upper door. All the men, except the whisky drummer, put their shoulders to the coach and heaved it upright again. The whisky drummer stood strangely in the bright sunlight shaking his head dumbly while the others climbed back in. Happy Stuart said, "All right, brother, git aboard."

The drummer climbed in slowly and the stage ran on. There was a low, gray dobe relay station squatted on the desert dead ahead with a scatter of corrals about it and a flag hanging limp on a crooked pole. Men came out of the dobe's dark interior and stood in the shade of the porch gallery. Happy Stuart rolled up and stopped. He said to a lanky man: "Hi, Mack. Where's the God-damned Injuns?"

The passengers were filing into the dobe's dining room. The lanky one drawled: "You'll see 'em before tomorrow night." Hostlers came up to change horses.

The little dining room was cool after the coach, cool and still. A fat Mexican woman ran in and out with the food platters. Happy Stuart said: "Ten minutes," and brushed the alkali dust from his mouth and fell to eating.

The long-jawed Mack said: "Catlin's ranch burned last night. Was a troop of cavalry around here yesterday. Came and went. You'll git to the Gap tonight all right but I do' know about the mountains beyond. A little trouble?"

"A little," said Happy, briefly, and rose. This was the end of rest. The passengers followed, with the whisky drummer straggling at the rear, reaching deeply for wind. The coach rolled away again, Mack's voice pursuing them. "Hit it a lick, Happy, if you see any dust rollin' out of the east."

Heat had condensed in the coach and the little wind fanned up by the run of the horses was stifling to the lungs; the desert floor projected its white glitter endlessly away until lost in the smoky haze. The cattleman's knees bumped Henriette gently and he kept watching her, a celluloid toothpick drooped between his lips. Happy Stuart's voice ran back, profane and urgent, keeping the speed of the coach constant through the ruts. The whisky drummer's eyes were round and strained and his mouth was open and all the color had gone out of his face. The gambler observed this without expression and without care; and once the cattleman, feeling the sag of the whisky drummer's shoulder, shoved him away. The Englishman sat bolt upright, staring emotionlessly at the passing desert. The army girl spoke to Malpais Bill: "What is the next stop?"

"Gap Creek."

"Will we meet soldiers there?"

He said: "I expect we'll have an escort over the hills into Lordsburg."

And at four o'clock of this furnace-hot afternoon the whisky drummer made a feeble gesture with one hand and fell forward into the gambler's lap.

The cattleman shrugged his shoulders and put a head through the window, calling up to Happy Stuart: "Wait a minute." When the stage stopped everybody climbed out and the blond man helped the gambler lay the whisky drummer in the sweltering patch of shade created by the coach. Neither Happy Stuart nor the shotgun guard bothered to get down. The whisky drummer's lips moved a little but nobody said anything and nobody knew what to do—until Henriette stepped forward.

She dropped to the ground, lifting the whisky drummer's shoulders and head against her breasts. He opened his eyes and there was something in them that they could all see, like relief and ease, like gratefulness. She murmured: "You are all right," and her smile was soft and pleasant, turning her lips maternal. There was this wisdom in her, this knowledge of the fears that men concealed behind their manners, the deep hungers that rode them so savagely, and the loneliness that drove them to women of her kind. She repeated, "You are all right," and watched this whisky drummer's eyes lose the wildness of what he knew.

The army girl's face showed shock. The gambler and the cattleman looked down at the whisky drummer quite impersonally. The blond man watched Henriette through lids half closed, but the flare of a powerful interest broke the severe lines of his cheeks. He held a cigarette between his fingers; he had forgotten it.

Happy Stuart said: "We can't stay here."

The gambler bent down to catch the whisky drummer under the arms. Henriette rose and said, "Bring him to me," and got into the coach. The blond man and the gambler lifted the drummer through the door so that he was lying along the back seat, cushioned on Henriette's lap. They all got in and the coach rolled on. The drummer groaned a little, whispering: "Thanks—thanks," and the blond man, searching Henriette's face for every shred of expression, drew a gusty breath.

They went on like this, the big wheels pounding the ruts of the road while a lowering sun blazed through the coach windows. The mountain bulwarks began to march nearer, more definite in the blue fog. The cattleman's eyes were small and brilliant and touched Henriette personally, but the gambler bent toward Henriette to say: "If you are tired—"

"No," she said. "No. He's dead."

The army girl stifled a small cry. The gambler bent nearer the whisky drummer, and then they were all looking at Henriette; even the Englishman stared at her for a moment, faint curiosity in his eyes. She was remotely smiling, her lips broad and soft. She held the drummer's head with both her hands and continued to hold him like that until, at the swift fall of dusk, they rolled across the last of the desert floor and drew up before Gap Station.

The cattleman kicked open the door and stepped out, grunting as his stiff legs touched the ground. The gambler pulled the drummer up so that Henriette could leave. They all came out, their bones tired from the shaking. Happy Stuart climbed from the box, his face a gray mask of alkali and his eyes bloodshot. He said: "Who's dead?" and looked into the coach. People sauntered from the station yard, walking with the indolence of twilight. Happy Stuart said, "Well, he won't worry about tomorrow," and turned away.

A short man with a tremendous stomach shuffled through the dusk. He said: "Wasn't sure you'd try to git through yet, Happy."

"Where's the soldiers for tomorrow?"

"Other side of the mountains. Everybody's chased out. What ain't forted up here was sent into Lordsburg. You men will bunk in the barn. I'll make out for the ladies somehow." He looked at the army girl and he appraised Henriette instantly. His eyes slid on to Malpais Bill standing in the background and recognition stirred him then and made his voice careful. "Hello, Bill. What brings you this way?"

Malpais Bill's cigarette glowed in the gathering dusk and Henriette caught the brief image of his face, serene and watchful. Malpais Bill's tone was easy, it was soft. "Just the trip."

They were moving on toward the frame house whose corners seemed to extend indefinitely into a series of attached sheds. Lights glimmered in the windows and men moved around the place, idly talking. The unhitched horses went away at a trot. The tall girl walked into the station's big room, to face a soldier in a disheveled uniform.

He said: "Miss Robertson? Lieutenant Hauser was to have met you here. He is at Lordsburg. He was wounded in a brush with the Apaches last night."

The tall army girl stood very still. She said: "Badly?"

"Well," said the soldier, "yes."

The fat man came in, drawing deeply for wind. "Too bad—too bad. Ladies, I'll show you the rooms, such as I got."

Henriette's dove-colored dress blended with the background shadows. She was watching the tall army girl's face whiten. But there was a strength in the army girl, a fortitude that made her think of the soldier. For she said quietly, "You must have had a bad trip."

"Nothing—nothing at all," said the soldier and left the room. The gambler was here, his thin face turning to the army girl with a strained expression, as though he were remembering painful things. Malpais Bill had halted in the doorway, studying the softness and the humility of Henriette's cheeks. Afterwards both women followed the fat host of Gap Station along a narrow hall to their quarters.

Malpais Bill wheeled out and stood indolently against the wall of this desert station, his glance quick and watchful in the way it touched all the men loitering along the yard, his ears weighing all the night-softened voices. Heat died from the earth and a definite chill rolled down the mountain hulking so high behind the house. The soldier was in his saddle, murmuring drowsily to Happy Stuart.

"Well, Lordsburg is a long ways off and the damn' mountains are squirmin' with Apaches. You won't have any cavalry escort tomorrow. The troops are all in the field."

Malpais Bill listened to the hoofbeats of the soldier's horse fade out, remembering the loneliness of a man in those dark mountain passes, and went back to the saloon at the end of the station. This was a low-ceilinged shed with a dirt floor and whitewashed walls that once had been part of a stable. Three men stood under a lantern in the middle of this little place, the light of the lantern palely shining in the rounds of their eyes as they watched him. At the far end of the bar the cattleman and the gambler drank in taciturn silence. Malpais Bill took his whisky when the bottle came, and noted the barkeep's obscure glance. Gap's host put in his head and wheezed, "Second table," and the other men in here began to move out. The barkeep's words rubbed together, one tone above a whisper. "Better not ride into Lordsburg. Plummer and Shanley are there."

Malpais Bill's lips were stretched to the long edge of laughter and there was a shine like wildness in his eyes. He said, "Thanks, friend," and went into the dining room.

When he came back to the yard night lay wild and deep across the desert and the moonlight was a frozen silver that touched but could not dissolve the world's incredible blackness. The girl Henriette walked along the Tonto road, swaying gently in the vague shadows. He went that way, the click of his heels on the hard earth bringing her around.

Her face was clear and strange and incurious in the night, as though she waited for something to come, and knew what it would be.

But he said: "You're too far from the house. Apaches like to crawl down next to a settlement and wait for strays."

She was indifferent, unafraid. Her voice was cool and he could hear the faint loneliness in it, the fatalism that made her words so even. "There's a wind coming up, so soft and good."

He took off his hat, long legs braced, and his eyes were both attentive and puzzled. His blond hair glowed in the fugitive light.

She said in a deep breath: "Why do you do that?"

His lips were restless and the sing and rush of strong feeling was like a current of quick wind around him. "You have folks in Lordsburg?"

She spoke in a direct, patient way as though explaining something he should have known without asking. "I run a house in Lordsburg."

"No," he said, "it wasn't what I asked."

"My folks are dead—I think. There was a massacre in the Superstition Mountains when I was young."

He stood with his head bowed, his mind reaching back to fill in that gap of her life. There was a hardness and a rawness to this land and little sympathy for the weak. She had survived and had paid for her survival, and looked at him now in a silent way that offered no explanations or apologies for whatever had been; she was still a pretty girl with the dead patience of all the past years in her eyes, in the expressiveness of her lips.

He said: "Over in the Tonto Basin is a pretty land. I've got a piece of a ranch there—with a house half built."

"If that's your country why are you here?"

His lips laughed and the rashness in him glowed hot again and he seemed to grow taller in the moonlight. "A debt to collect."

"That's why you're going to Lordsburg? You will never get through collecting those kind of debts. Everybody in the Territory knows you. Once you were just a rancher. Then you tried to wipe out a grudge and then there was a bigger one to wipe out—and the debt kept growing and more men are waiting to kill you. Someday a man will. You'd better run away from the debts."

His bright smile kept constant, and presently she lifted her shoulders with resignation. "No," she murmured, "you won't run." He could see the sweetness of her lips and the way her eyes were sad for him; he could see in them the patience he had never learned.

He said, "We'd better go back," and turned her with his arm. They went across the yard in silence, hearing the undertone of men's drawling talk roll out of the shadows, seeing the glow of men's pipes in the dark corners. Malpais Bill stopped and watched her go through the station door; she turned to look at him once more, her eyes all dark and her lips softly sober, and then passed down the narrow corridor to her own quarters. Beyond her window, in the yard, a man was murmuring to another man: "Plummer and Shanley are in Lordsburg. Malpais Bill knows it." Through the thin partition of the adjoining room she heard the army girl crying with a suppressed, uncontrollable regularity. Henriette stared at the dark wall, her shoulders and head bowed; and afterwards returned to the hall and knocked on the army girl's door and went in.

Six fresh horses fiddled in front of the coach and the fat host of Gap Station came across the yard swinging a lantern against the dead, bitter black. All the passengers filed sleep-dulled and miserable from the house. Johnny Strang slammed the express box in the boot and Happy Stuart gruffly said: "All right, folks."

The passengers climbed in. The cattleman came up and Malpais Bill drawled: "Take the corner spot, mister," and got in, closing the door. The Gap host grumbled: "If they don't jump you on the long grade you'll be all right. You're safe when you get to Al Schrieber's ranch." Happy's bronze voice shocked the black stillness and the coach lurched forward, its leather springs squealing.

They rode for an hour in this complete darkness, chilled and uncomfortable and half asleep, feeling the coach drag on a heavy-climbing grade. Gray dawn cracked through, followed by a sunless light rushing all across the flat desert now far below. The road looped from one barren shoulder to another and at sunup they had reached the first bench and were slamming full speed along a boulder-strewn flat. The cattleman sat in the forward corner, the left corner of his mouth swollen and crushed, and when Henriette saw that her glance slid to Malpais Bill's knuckles. The army girl had her eyes closed, her shoulders pressing against the Englishman, who remained bolt upright with the sporting gun between his knees. Beside Henriette the gambler seemed to sleep, and on the middle bench Malpais Bill watched the land go by with a thin vigilance.

At ten they were rising again, with juniper and scrub pine showing on the slopes and the desert below them filling with the powdered haze of another hot day. By noon they reached the summit of the range and swung to follow its narrow rock-ribbed meadows. The gambler, long motionless, shifted his feet and caught the army girl's eyes.

"Schrieber's is directly ahead. We are past the worst of it."

The blond man looked around at the gambler, making no comment; and it was then that Henriette caught the smell of smoke in the windless air. Happy Stuart was cursing once more and the brake blocks began to cry. Looking through the angled vista of the window panel Henriette saw a clay and rock chimney standing up like a gaunt skeleton against the day's light. The house that had been there was a black patch on the ground, smoke still rising from pieces that had not been completely burnt.

The stage stopped and all the men were instantly out. An iron stove squatted on the earth, with one section of pipe stuck upright to it. Fire licked lazily along the collapsed fragments of what had been a trunk. Beyond the location of the house, at the foot of a corral, lay two nude figures grotesquely bald, with deliberate knife slashes marking their bodies. Happy Stuart went over there and had his look; and came back.

"Schriebers. Well—"

Malpais Bill said: "This morning about daylight." He looked at the gambler, at the cattleman, at the Englishman who showed no emotion. "Get back in the coach." He climbed to the coach's top, flattening himself full length there. Happy Stuart and Strang took their places again. The horses broke into a run.

The gambler said to the army girl: "You're pretty safe between those two fellows," and hauled a .44 from a back pocket and laid it over his lap. He considered Henriette more carefully than before, his taciturnity breaking. He said: "How old are you?"

Her shoulders rose and fell, which was the only answer. But the gambler said gently, "Young enough to be my daughter. It is a rotten world. When I call to you, lie down on the floor."

The Englishman had pulled the rifle from between his knees and laid it across the sill of the window on his side. The cattleman swept back the skirt of his coat to clear the holster of his gun.

The little flinty summit meadows grew narrower, with shoulders of gray rock closing in upon the road. The coach wheels slammed against the stony ruts and bounced high and fell again with a jar the springs could not soften. Happy Stuart's howl ran steadily above this rattle and rush. Fine dust turned all things gray.

Henriette sat with her eyes pinned to the gloved tips of her fingers, remembering the tall shape of Malpais Bill cut against the moonlight of Gap Station. He had smiled at her as a man might smile at any desirable woman, with the sweep and swing of laughter in his voice; and his eyes had been gentle. The gambler spoke very quietly and she didn't hear him until his fingers gripped her arm. He said again, not raising his voice: "Get down."

Henriette dropped to her knees, hearing gunfire blast through the rush and run of the coach. Happy Stuart ceased to yell and the army girl's eyes were round and dark. The walls of the canyon had tapered off. Looking upward through the window on the gambler's side, Henriette saw the weaving figure of an Apache warrior reel nakedly on a calico pony and rush by with a rifle raised and pointed in his bony elbows. The gambler took a cool aim; the stockman fired and aimed again. The Englishman's sporting rifle blasted heavy echoes through

the coach, hurting her ears, and the smell of powder got rank and
bitter. The blond man's boots scraped the coach top and round small
holes began to dimple the paneling as the Apache bullets struck. An
Indian came boldly abreast the coach and made a target that couldn't
be missed. The cattleman dropped him with one shot. The wheels
screamed as they slowed around the sharp ruts and the whole heavy
superstructure of the coach bounced high into the air. Then they were
rushing downgrade.

The gambler said quietly, "You had better take this," handing
Henriette his gun. He leaned against the door with his small hands
gripping the sill. Pallor loosened his cheeks. He said to the army girl:
"Be sure and keep between those gentlemen," and looked at her with
a way that was desperate and forlorn and dropped his head to the
window's sill.

Henriette saw the bluff rise up and close in like a yellow wall.
They were rolling down the mountain without brake. Gunfire fell off
and the crying of the Indians faded back. Coming up from her knees
then she saw the desert's flat surface far below, with the angular
pattern of Lordsburg vaguely on the far borders of the heat fog. There
was no more firing and Happy Stuart's voice lifted again and the
brakes were screaming on the wheels, and going off, and screaming
again. The Englishman stared out of the window sullenly; the army
girl seemed in a deep desperate dream; the cattleman's face was
shining with a strange sweat. Henriette reached over to pull the
gambler up, but he had an unnatural weight to him and slid into the
far corner. She saw that he was dead.

At five o'clock that long afternoon the stage threaded
Lordsburg's narrow streets of dobe and frame houses, came upon the
center square and stopped before a crowd of people gathered in the
smoky heat. The passengers crawled out stiffly. A Mexican boy ran up
to see the dead gambler and began to yell his news in shrill Mexican.
Malpais Bill climbed off the top, but Happy Stuart sat back on his
seat and stared taciturnly at the crowd. Henriette noticed then that
the shotgun messenger was gone.

A gray man in a sleazy white suit called up to Happy. "Well, you
got through."

Happy Stuart said: "Yeah. We got through."

An officer stepped through the crowd, smiling at the army girl.
He took her arm and said, "Miss Robertson, I believe. Lieutenant
Hauser is quite all right. I will get your luggage—"

The army girl was crying then, definitely. They were all standing
around, bone-weary and shaken. Malpais Bill remained by the wheel
of the coach, his cheeks hard against the sunlight and his eyes riveted
on a pair of men standing under the board awning of an adjoining
store. Henriette observed the manner of their waiting and knew why

they were here. The blond man's eyes, she noticed, were very blue and flame burned brilliantly in them. The army girl turned to Henriette, tears in her eyes. She murmured: "If there is anything I can ever do for you—"

But Henriette stepped back, shaking her head. This was Lordsburg and everybody knew her place except the army girl. Henriette said formally, "Good-by," noting how still and expectant the two men under the awning remained. She swung toward the blond man and said, "Would you carry my valise?"

Malpais Bill looked at her, laughter remote in his eyes, and reached into the luggage pile and got her battered valise. He was still smiling as he went beside her, through the crowd and past the two waiting men. But when they turned into an anonymous and dusty little side street of the town, where the houses all sat shoulder to shoulder without grace or dignity, he had turned sober. He said: "I am obliged to you. But I'll have to go back there."

They were in front of a house no different from its neighbors; they had stopped at its door. She could see his eyes travel this street and comprehend its meaning and the kind of traffic it bore. But he was saying in that gentle, melody-making tone:

"I have watched you for two days." He stopped, searching his mind to find the thing he wanted to say. It came out swiftly. "God made you a woman. The Tonto is a pretty country."

Her answer was quite barren of feeling. "No. I am known all through the Territory. But I can remember that you asked me."

He said: "No other reason?" She didn't answer but something in her eyes pulled his face together. He took off his hat and it seemed to her he was looking through this hot day to that far-off country and seeing it fresh and desirable. He murmured: "A man can escape nothing. I have got to do this. But I will be back."

He went along the narrow street, made a quick turn at the end of it, and disappeared. Heat rolled like a heavy wave over Lordsburg's housetops and the smell of dust was very sharp. She lifted her valise, and dropped it and stood like that, mute and grave before the door of her dismal house. She was remembering how tall he had been against the moonlight at Gap Station.

There were four swift shots beating furiously along the sultry quiet, and a shout, and afterwards a longer and longer silence. She put one hand against the door to steady herself, and knew that those shots marked the end of a man, and the end of a hope. He would never come back; he would never stand over her in the moonlight with the long gentle smile on his lips and with the swing of life in his casual tone. She was thinking of all that humbly and with the patience life had beaten into her. . . .

She was thinking of all that when she heard the strike of boots on

the street's packed earth; and turned to see him, high and square in
the muddy sunlight, coming toward her with his smile.

QUESTIONS

1. "Stage to Lordsburg" has become a famous story because it was the
   basis for John Ford's classic Western film "Stagecoach." If you
   were making a new movie based on this short story, what actor or
   actress would you choose for each part? Explain.

2. This story is a good example of an "adult Western." How does the
   heroine differ from those in other stories in this book? How does
   she differ from the army girl?

3. One of Ernest Haycox's most effective strengths as a writer was his
   use of understatement—his ability to suggest much with few words.
   How is this technique used in this story?

4. How do the illness and death of the drummer contribute to the
   development of other characters in the story?

5. How does the character of Malpais Bill prove to be more complex
   than that of a merely fearless gunfighter? Explain.

MAX BRAND

WINE ON THE DESERT

There was no hurry, except for the thirst, like clotted salt, in the back of his throat, and Durante rode on slowly, rather enjoying the last moments of dryness before he reached the cold water in Tony's house. There was really no hurry at all. He had almost twenty-four hours' head start, for they would not find his dead man until this morning. After that, there would be perhaps several hours of delay before the sheriff gathered a sufficient posse and started on his trail. Or perhaps the sheriff would be fool enough to come alone.

Durante had been able to see the wheel and fan of Tony's windmill for more than an hour, but he could not make out the ten acres of the vineyard until he had topped the last rise, for the vines had been planted in a hollow. The lowness of the ground, Tony used to say, accounted for the water that gathered in the well during the wet season. The rains sank through the desert sand, through the gravels beneath, and gathered in a bowl of clay hardpan far below.

In the middle of the rainless season the well ran dry but, long before that, Tony had every drop of the water pumped up into a score of tanks made of cheap corrugated iron. Slender pipe lines carried the water from the tanks to the vines and from time to time let them sip enough life to keep them until the winter darkened overhead suddenly, one November day, and the rain came down, and all the earth made a great hushing sound as it drank. Durante had heard that whisper of drinking when he was here before; but he never had seen the place in the middle of the long drought.

The windmill looked like a sacred emblem to Durante, and the twenty stodgy, tar-painted tanks blessed his eyes; but a heavy sweat broke out at once from his body. For the air of the hollow, unstirred by wind, was hot and still as a bowl of soup. A reddish soup. The vines were powdered with thin red dust, also. They were wretched, dying things to look at, for the grapes had been gathered, the new wine had been made, and now the leaves hung in ragged tatters.

Durante rode up to the squat adobe house and right through the entrance into the patio. A flowering vine clothed three sides of the little court. Durante did not know the name of the plant, but it had large white blossoms with golden hearts that poured sweetness on the air. Durante hated the sweetness. It made him more thirsty.

He threw the reins of his mule and strode into the house. The water cooler stood in the hall outside the kitchen. There were two jars made of a porous stone, very ancient things, and the liquid which distilled through the pores kept the contents cool. The jar on the left held water; that on the right contained wine. There was a big tin dipper hanging on a peg beside each jar. Durante tossed off the cover of the vase on the left and plunged it in until the delicious coolness closed well above his wrist.

"Hey, Tony," he called. Out of his dusty throat the cry was a mere groaning. He drank and called again, clearly, "Tony!"

A voice pealed from the distance.

Durante, pouring down the second dipper of water, smelled the alkali dust which had shaken off his own clothes. It seemed to him that heat was radiating like light from his clothes, from his body, and the cool dimness of the house was soaking it up. He heard the wooden leg of Tony bumping on the ground, and Durante grinned; then Tony came in with that hitch and side-swing with which he accommodated the stiffness of his artificial leg. His brown face shone with sweat as though a special ray of light were focused on it.

"Ah, Dick!" he said. "Good old Dick! . . . How long since you came last! . . . Wouldn't Julia be glad! Wouldn't she be glad!"

"Ain't she here?" asked Durante, jerking his head suddenly away from the dripping dipper.

"She's away at Nogalez," said Tony. "It gets so hot. I said, 'You go up to Nogalez, Julia, where the wind don't forget to blow.' She cried, but I made her go."

"Did she cry?" asked Durante.

"Julia . . . that's a good girl," said Tony.

"Yeah. You bet she's good," said Durante. He put the dipper quickly to his lips but did not swallow for a moment; he was grinning too widely. Afterward he said: "You wouldn't throw some water into that mule of mine, would you, Tony?"

Tony went out with his wooden leg clumping loud on the wooden floor, softly in the patio dust. Durante found the hammock in the corner of the patio. He lay down in it and watched the color of sunset flush the mists of desert dust that rose to the zenith. The water was soaking through his body; hunger began, and then the rattling of pans in the kitchen and the cheerful cry of Tony's voice:

"What you want, Dick? I got some pork. You don't want pork. I'll make you some good Mexican beans. Hot. Ah ha, I know that old Dick. I have plenty of good wine for you, Dick. Tortillas. Even Julia can't make tortillas like me. . . . And what about a nice young rabbit?"

"All blowed full of buckshot?" growled Durante.

"No, no. I kill them with the rifle."

"You kill rabbits with a rifle?" repeated Durante, with a quick interest.

"It's the only gun I have," said Tony. "If I catch them in the sights, they are dead. . . . A wooden leg cannot walk very far. . . . I must kill them quick. You see? They come close to the house about sunrise and flop their ears. I shoot through the head."

"Yeah? Yeah?" muttered Durante. "Through the head?" He relaxed, scowling. He passed his hand over his face, over his head.

Then Tony began to bring the food out into the patio and lay it on a small wooden table; a lantern hanging against the wall of the house included the table in a dim half circle of light. They sat there and ate. Tony had scrubbed himself for the meal. His hair was soaked in water and sleeked back over his round skull. A man in the desert might be willing to pay five dollars for as much water as went to the soaking of that hair.

Everything was good. Tony knew how to cook, and he knew how to keep the glasses filled with his wine.

"This is old wine. This is my father's wine. Eleven years old," said Tony. "You look at the light through it. You see that brown in the red? That's the soft that time puts in good wine, my father always said."

"What killed your father?" asked Durante.

Tony lifted his hand as though he were listening or as though he were pointing out a thought.

"The desert killed him. I found his mule. It was dead, too. There was a leak in the canteen. My father was only five miles away when the buzzards showed him to me."

"Five miles? Just an hour. . . . Good Lord!" said Durante. He stared with big eyes. "Just dropped down and died?" he asked.

"No," said Tony. "When you die of thirst, you always die just one way. . . . First you tear off your shirt, then your undershirt. That's to be cooler. . . . And the sun comes and cooks your bare skin. . . . And then you think . . . there is water everywhere, if you dig down far enough. You begin to dig. The dust comes up your nose. You start screaming. You break your nails in the sand. You wear the flesh off the tips of your fingers, to the bone." He took a quick swallow of wine.

"Without you seen a man die of thirst, how d'you know they start to screaming?" asked Durante.

"They got a screaming look when you find them," said Tony. "Take some more wine. The desert never can get to you here. My father showed me the way to keep the desert away from the hollow. We live pretty good here? No?"

"Yeah," said Durante, loosening his shirt collar. "Yeah, pretty good."

Afterward he slept well in the hammock until the report of a rifle waked him and he saw the color of dawn in the sky. It was such a great, round bowl that for a moment he felt as though he were above, looking down into it.

He got up and saw Tony coming in holding a rabbit by the ears, the rifle in his other hand.

"You see?" said Tony. "Breakfast came and called on us!" He laughed.

Durante examined the rabbit with care. It was nice and fat and it had been shot through the head. Through the middle of the head. Such a shudder went down the back of Durante that he washed gingerly before breakfast; he felt that his blood was cooled for the entire day.

It was a good breakfast, too, with flapjacks and stewed rabbit with green peppers, and a quart of strong coffee. Before they had finished, the sun struck through the east window and started them sweating.

"Gimme a look at that rifle of yours, Tony, will you?" Durante asked.

"You take a look at my rifle, but don't you steal the luck that's in it," laughed Tony. He brought the fifteen-shot Winchester.

"Loaded right to the brim?" asked Durante.

"I always load it full the minute I get back home," said Tony.

"Tony, come outside with me," commanded Durante.

They went out from the house. The sun turned the sweat of Durante to hot water and then dried his skin so that his clothes felt transparent.

"Tony, I gotta be damn mean," said Durante. "Stand right there where I can see you. Don't try to get close. . . . Now listen. . . . The sheriff's gunna be along this trail some time to-day, looking for me. He'll load up himself and all his gang with water out of your tanks. Then he'll follow my sign across the desert. Get me? He'll follow if he finds water on the place. But he's not gunna find water."

"What you done, poor Dick?" said Tony. "Now look. . . . I could hide you in the old wine cellar where nobody . . ."

"The sheriff's not gunna find any water," said Durante. "It's gunna be like this."

He put the rifle to his shoulder, aimed, fired. The shot struck the base of the nearest tank, ranging down through the bottom. A semicircle of darkness began to stain the soil near the edge of the iron wall.

Tony fell on his knees, "No, no, Dick! Good Dick!" he said.

"Look! All the vineyard. It will die. It will turn into old, dead wood, Dick . . ."

"Shut your face," said Durante. "Now I've started, I kinda like the job."

Tony fell on his face and put his hands over his ears. Durante drilled a bullet hole through the tanks, one after another. Afterward, he leaned on the rifle.

"Take my canteen and go in and fill it with water out of the cooling jar," he said. "Snap into it, Tony!"

Tony got up. He raised the canteen, and looked around him, not at the tanks from which the water was pouring so that the noise of the earth drinking was audible, but at the rows of his vineyard. Then he went into the house.

Durante mounted his mule. He shifted the rifle to his left hand and drew out the heavy Colt from his holster. Tony came dragging back to him, his head down. Durante watched Tony with a careful revolver but he gave up the canteen without lifting his eyes.

"The trouble with you, Tony," said Durante, "is you're yellow. I'd of fought a tribe of wildcats with my bare hands, before I'd let 'em do what I'm doin' to you. But you sit back and take it."

Tony did not seem to hear. He stretched out his hands to the vines.

"Ah, my God," said Tony. "Will you let them all die?"

Durante shrugged his shoulders. He shook the canteen to make sure that it was full. It was so brimming that there was hardly room for the liquid to make a sloshing sound. Then he turned the mule and kicked it into a dog-trot.

Half a mile from the house of Tony, he threw the empty rifle to the ground. There was no sense packing that useless weight, and Tony with his peg leg would hardly come this far.

Durante looked back, a mile or so later, and saw the little image of Tony picking up the rifle from the dust, then staring earnestly after his guest. Durante remembered the neat little hole clipped through the head of the rabbit. Wherever he went, his trail never could return again to the vineyard in the desert. But then, commencing to picture to himself the arrival of the sweating sheriff and his posse at the house of Tony, Durante laughed heartily.

The sheriff's posse could get plenty of wine, of course, but without water a man could not hope to make the desert voyage, even with a mule or a horse to help him on the way. Durante patted the full, rounding side of his canteen. He might even now begin with the first sip but it was a luxury to postpone pleasure until desire became greater.

He raised his eyes along the trail. Close by, it was merely dotted

with occasional bones, but distance joined the dots into an unbroken
chalk line which wavered with a strange leisure across the Apache
Desert, pointing toward the cool blue promise of the mountains. The
next morning he would be among them.

A coyote whisked out of a gully and ran like a gray puff of dust on
the wind. His tongue hung out like a little red rag from the side of his
mouth; and suddenly Durante was dry to the marrow. He uncorked
and lifted his canteen. It had a slightly sour smell; perhaps the sacking
which covered it had grown a trifle old. And then he poured a great
mouthful of lukewarm liquid. He had swallowed it before his senses
could give him warning.

It was wine!

He looked first of all toward the mountains. They were as calmly
blue, as distant as when he had started that morning. Twenty-four
hours not on water, but on wine!

"I deserve it," said Durante. "I trusted him to fill the canteen.
. . . I deserve it. Curse him!" With a mighty resolution, he quieted
the panic in his soul. He would not touch the stuff until noon. Then
he would take one discreet sip. He would win through.

Hours went by. He looked at his watch and found it was only ten
o'clock. And he had thought that it was on the verge of noon! He
uncorked the wine and drank freely and, corking the canteen, felt
almost as though he needed a drink of water more than before. He
sloshed the contents of the canteen. Already it was horribly light.

Once, he turned the mule and considered the return trip; but he
could remember the head of the rabbit too clearly, drilled right
through the center. The vineyard, the rows of old twisted, gnarled
little trunks with the bark peeling off . . . every vine was to Tony like
a human life. And Durante had condemned them all to death!

He faced the blue of the mountains again. His heart raced in his
breast with terror. Perhaps it was fear and not the suction of that dry
and deadly air that made his tongue cleave to the roof of his mouth.

The day grew old. Nausea began to work in his stomach, nausea
alternating with sharp pains. When he looked down, he saw that there
was blood on his boots. He had been spurring the mule until the red
ran down from its flanks. It went with a curious stagger, like a rocking
horse with a broken rocker; and Durante grew aware that he had been
keeping the mule at a gallop for a long time. He pulled it to a halt. It
stood with wide-braced legs. Its head was down. When he leaned from
the saddle, he saw that its mouth was open.

"It's gunna die," said Durante. "It's gunna die . . . what a fool I
been. . . ."

The mule did not die until after sunset. Durante left everything
except his revolver. He packed the weight of that for an hour and
discarded it, in turn. His knees were growing weak. When he looked

up at the stars they shone white and clear for a moment only, and then whirled into little racing circles and scrawls of red.

He lay down. He kept his eyes closed and waited for the shaking to go out of his body, but it would not stop. And every breath of darkness was like an inhalation of black dust.

He got up and went on, staggering. Sometimes he found himself running.

Before you die of thirst, you go mad. He kept remembering that. His tongue had swollen big. Before it choked him, if he lanced it with his knife the blood would help him; he would be able to swallow. Then he remembered that the taste of blood is salty.

Once, in his boyhood, he had ridden through a pass with his father and they had looked down on the sapphire of a mountain lake, a hundred thousand million tons of water as cold as snow. . . .

When he looked up, now, there were no stars; and this frightened him terribly. He never had seen a desert night so dark. His eyes were failing, he was being blinded. When the morning came, he would not be able to see the mountains, and he would walk around and around in a circle until he dropped and died.

No stars, no wind; the air as still as the waters of a stale pool, and he in the dregs at the bottom. . . .

He seized his shirt at the throat and tore it away so that it hung in two rags from his hips.

He could see the earth only well enough to stumble on the rocks. But there were no stars in the heavens. He was blind: he had no more hope than a rat in a well. Ah, but Italian devils know how to put poison in wine that will steal all the senses or any one of them: and Tony had chosen to blind Durante.

He heard a sound like water. It was the swishing of the soft deep sand through which he was threading; sand so soft that a man could dig it away with his bare hands. . . .

Afterward, after many hours, out of the blind face of that sky the rain began to fall. It made first a whispering and then a delicate murmur like voices conversing, but after that, just at the dawn, it roared like the hoofs of ten thousand charging horses. Even through that thundering confusion the big birds with naked heads and red, raw necks found their way down to one place in the Apache Desert.

QUESTIONS

1. A short story or novel is written from one or more points of view—that of one character, that of several characters, that of an invisible observer who sees and hears the action much as an

audience would view a play, or that of an omniscient creator who knows the thoughts and feelings and destinies of all his characters. Which point of view is used in all but the last paragraph of this story? What point of view is used in the last paragraph?

2. What is dramatic irony? What is the irony of the first sentence of the story?

3. What is the purpose of Tony's telling of his father's death in the desert? (This kind of interpolation is called "preparation"; some writers refer to it as a "plant.")

4. Why is the shooting of the rabbit also a "plant," a kind of preparation for later action in the story?

5. According to Edgar Allan Poe, there should be no wasted sentences or extraneous details in a short story: everything must be directed toward a certain calculated effect. Does this story conform to Poe's prescription? Explain.

JOHN M. CUNNINGHAM

THE TIN STAR

Sheriff Doane looked at his deputy and then down at the daisies he had picked for his weekly visit, lying wrapped in newspaper on his desk. "I'm sorry to hear you say that, Toby. I was kind of counting on you to take over after me."

"Don't get me wrong, Doane," Toby said, looking through the front window. "I'm not afraid. I'll see you through this shindig. I'm not afraid of Jordan or young Jordan or any of them. But I want to tell you now. I'll wait till Jordan's train gets in. I'll wait to see what he does. I'll see you through whatever happens. After that, I'm quitting."

Doane began kneading his knuckles, his face set against the pain as he gently rubbed the misshapen, twisted bones. Using his fists all these years hadn't helped the gout. He said nothing.

Toby looked around, his brown eyes troubled in his round, olive-skinned face. "What's the use of holding down a job like this? Look at you. What'd you ever get of it? Enough to keep you eating. And what for?"

Doane stopped kneading his arthritic hands and looked down at the star on his shirt front. He looked from it to the smaller one on Toby's. "That's right," he said. "They don't even hang the right ones. You risk your life catching somebody, and the damned juries let them go so they can come back and shoot at you. You're poor all your life, you got to do everything twice, and in the end they pay you off in lead. So you can wear a tin star. It's a job for a dog, son."

Toby's voice did not rise, but his eyes were a little wider in his round, gentle face. "Then why keep on with it? What for? I been working for you for two years—trying to keep the law so sharp-nosed money-grabbers can get rich, while we piddle along on what the county pays us. I've seen men I used to bust playing marbles going up and down this street on four-hundred-dollar saddles, and what've I got? Nothing. Not a damned thing."

There was a little smile around Doane's wide mouth. "That's right, Toby. It's all for free. The headaches, the bullets and everything, all for free. I found that out long ago." The mock-grave look vanished. "But somebody's got to be around and take care of things." He looked out of the window at the people walking up and down the crazy boardwalks. "I like it free. You know what I mean?

You don't get a thing for it. You've got to risk everything. And you're free inside. Like the larks. You know the larks? How they get up in the sky and sing when they want to? A pretty bird. A very pretty bird. That's the way I like to feel inside."

Toby looked at him without expression. "That's the way you look at it. I don't see it. I've only got one life. You talk about doing it all for nothing, and that gives you something. What? What've you got now, waiting for Jordan to come?"

"I don't know yet. We'll have to wait and see."

Toby turned back to the window. "All right, but I'm through. I don't see any sense in risking your neck for nothing."

"Maybe you will," Doane said, beginning to work on his hands again.

"Here comes Mettrick. I guess he don't give up so easy. He's still got that resignation in his hand."

"I guess he doesn't," Doane said. "But I'm through listening. Has young Jordan come out of the saloon yet?"

"No," Toby said, and stepped aside as the door opened. Mettrick came in. "Now listen, Doane," he burst out, "for the last time—"

"Shut up, Percy," Doane said. "Sit down over there and shut up or get out."

The flare went out of the mayor's eyes. "Doane," he moaned, "you are the biggest—"

"Shut up," Doane said. "Toby, has he come out yet?"

Toby stood a little back from the window, where the slant of golden sunlight, swarming with dust, wouldn't strike his white shirt.

"Yes. He's got a chair. He's looking this way, Doane. He's still drinking. I can see a bottle on the porch beside him."

"I expected that. Not that it makes much difference." He looked down at the bunch of flowers.

Mettrick, in the straight chair against the wall, looked up at him, his black eyes scornful in his long, hopeless face.

"Don't make much difference? Who the hell do you think you are, Doane? God? It just means he'll start the trouble without waiting for his stinking brother, that's all it means." His hand was shaking, and the white paper hanging listlessly from his fingers fluttered slightly. He looked at it angrily and stuck it out at Doane. "I gave it to you. I did the best I could. Whatever happens, don't be blaming me, Doane. I gave you a chance to resign, and if—" He left off and sat looking at the paper in his hand as though it were a dead puppy of his that somebody had run a buggy over.

Doane standing with the square almost chisel-pointed tips of his fingers just touching the flowers, turned slowly with the care of movement he would have used around a crazy horse. "I know you're my friend, Percy. Just take it easy, Percy. If I don't resign, it's not because I'm ungrateful."

"Here comes Staley with the news," Toby said from the window. "He looks like somebody just shot his grandma."

Percy Mettrick laid his paper on the desk, and began smoothing it out carefully. "It's not as though it were dishonorable, Doane. You should have quit two years ago, when your hands went bad. It's not dishonorable now. You've still got time."

He glanced up at the wall clock. "It's only three. You've got an hour before it gets in, you can take your horse . . ." As he talked to himself, Doane looked slantwise at him with his little smile. He grew more cheerful. "Here." He jabbed a pen out at Doane. "Sign it and get out of town."

The smile left Doane's mouth. "This is an elective office. I don't have to take orders, even if you are mayor." His face softened. "It's simpler than you think, Percy. When they didn't hang Jordan, I knew this day would come. Five years ago, I knew it was coming, when they gave him that silly sentence. I've been waiting for it."

"But not to commit suicide," Mettrick said in a low voice, his eyes going down to Doane's gouty hands. Doane's knobby, twisted fingers closed slowly into fists, as though hiding themselves; his face flushed slightly. "I may be slow, but I can still shoot."

The mayor stood up and went slowly over to the door.

"Goodbye, Doane."

"I'm not saying goodbye, Percy. Not yet."

"Goodbye," Mettrick repeated. He went out of the door.

Toby turned from the window. His face was tight around the mouth. "You should have resigned like he said, Doane. You ain't a match for one of them, much less two of them together. And if Pierce and Frank Colby come, too, like they was all together before—"

"Shut up, shut up," Doane said. "For God's sake, shut up." He sat down suddenly at the desk and covered his face with his hands. "Maybe the pen changes a man." He was sitting stiff, hardly breathing.

"What are you going to do, Doane?"

"Nothing. I can't do anything until they start something. I can't do a thing. . . . Maybe the pen changes a man. Sometimes it does. I remember—"

"Listen, Doane," Toby said, his voice, for the first time, urgent. "It maybe changes some men, but not Jordan. It's already planned, what they're going to do. Why else would young Jordan be over there, watching? He's come three hundred miles for this."

"I've seen men go in the pen hard as rock and come out peaceful and settle down. Maybe Jordan—"

Toby's face relapsed into dullness. He turned back to the window listlessly. Doane's hands dropped.

"You don't think that's true, Toby?"

Toby sighed. "You know it isn't so, Doane. He swore he'd get you. That's the truth."

Doane's hands came up again in front of his face, but this time he was looking at them, his big gray eyes going quickly from one to the other, almost as though he were afraid of them. He curled his fingers slowly into fists, and uncurled them slowly, pulling with all his might, yet slowly. A thin sheen on his face reflected the sunlight from the floor. He got up.

"Is he still there?" he asked.

"Sure, he's still there."

"Maybe he'll get drunk. Dead drunk."

"You can't get a Jordan that drunk."

Doane stood with feet apart, looking at the floor, staring back and forth along one of the cracks. "Why didn't they hang him?" he asked the silence in the room.

"Why didn't they hang him?" he repeated, his voice louder.

Toby kept his post by the window, not moving a muscle in his face, staring out at the man across the street. "I don't know," he said. "For murder, they should, I guess they should, but they didn't."

Doane's eyes came again to the flowers, and some of the strain went out of his face. Then suddenly his eyes closed and he gave a long sigh, and then, luxuriously, stretched his arms. "Good God!" he said, his voice easy again. "It's funny how it comes over you like that." He shook his head violently. "I don't know why it should. It's not the first time. But it always does."

"I know," Toby said.

"It just builds up and then it busts."

"I know."

"The train may be late."

Toby said nothing.

"You never can tell," Doane said, buckling on his gun belt. "Things may have changed with Jordan. Maybe he won't even come. You never can tell. I'm going up to the cemetery as soon as we hear from Staley."

"I wouldn't. You'd just tempt young Jordan to start something."

"I've been going up there every Sunday since she died."

"We'd best both just stay in here. Let them make the first move."

Feet sounded on the steps outside and Doane stopped breathing for a second. Staley came in, his face pinched, tight and dead, his eyes on the floor. Doane looked him over carefully.

"Is it on time?" he asked steadily.

Staley looked up, his faded blue eyes, distant, pointed somewhere over Doane's head. "Mr. Doane, you ain't handled this thing right. You should of drove young Jordan out of town." His hand went to his chest and he took off the deputy's badge.

"What are you doing?" Doane asked sharply.

"If you'd of handled it right, we could have beat this," Staley said, his voice louder.

"You know nobody's done nothing yet," Toby said softly, his gentle brown eyes on Staley. "There's nothing we can do until they start something."

"I'm quitting, Mr. Doane," Staley said. He looked around for someplace to put the star. He started for the desk, hesitated, and then awkwardly, with a peculiar diffidence, laid the star gently on the window sill.

Doane's jaw began to jut a little. "You still haven't answered my question. Is the train on time?"

"Yes. Four ten. Just on time." Staley stood staring at Doane, then swallowed. "I saw Frank Colby. He was in the livery putting up his horse. He'd had a long ride on that horse. I asked him what he was doing in town—friendly like." He ducked his head and swallowed again. "He didn't know I was a deputy. I had my star off." He looked up again. "They're all meeting together, Mr. Doane. Young Jordan, and Colby and Pierce. They're going to meet Jordan when he comes in. The same four."

"So you're quitting," Doane said.

"Yes, sir. It ain't been handled right."

Toby stood looking at him, his gentle eyes dull. "Get out," he said, his voice low and tight.

Staley looked at him, nodded and tried to smile, which was too weak to last. "Sure."

Toby took a step toward him. Staley's eyes were wild as he stood against the door. He tried to back out of Toby's way.

"Get out," Toby said again, and his small brown fist flashed out. Staley stepped backward and fell down the steps in a sprawling heap, scrambled to his feet and hobbled away. Toby closed the door slowly. He stood rubbing his knuckles, his face red and tight.

"That didn't do any good," Doane said softly.

Toby turned on him. "It couldn't do no harm," he said acidly, throwing the words into Doane's face.

"You want to quit, too?" Doane asked, smiling.

"Sure, I want to quit," Toby shot out. "Sure. Go on to your blasted cemetery, go on with your flowers, old man—" He sat down suddenly on the straight chair. "Put a flower up there for me, too."

Doane went to the door. "Put some water on the heater, Toby. Set out the liniment that the vet gave me. I'll try it again when I get back. It might do some good yet."

Then he let himself out and stood in the sunlight on the porch, the flowers drooping in his hand, looking against the sun across the street at the dim figure under the shaded porch.

Then he saw the two other shapes hunkered against the front of the saloon in the shade of the porch, one on each side of young Jordan, who sat tilted back in a chair. Colby and Pierce. The glare of the sun beat back from the blinding white dust and fought shimmering in the air.

Doane pulled the brim of his hat farther down in front and stepped slowly down to the board sidewalk, observing just as carefully, avoiding any pause which might be interpreted as a challenge.

Young Jordan had the bottle to his lips as Doane came out. He held it there for a moment motionless, and then, as Doane reached the walk, he passed the bottle slowly sideward to Colby and leaned forward, away from the wall, so that the chair came down softly. He sat there, leaning forward slightly, watching while Doane untied his horse. As Doane mounted, Jordan got up. Colby's hand grabbed one of his arms. He shook it off and untied his own horse from the rail.

Doane's mouth tightened and his eyes looked a little sad. He turned his horse, and holding the flowers so the jog would not rattle off the petals, headed up the street, looking straight ahead.

The hoofs of his horse made soft, almost inaudible little plops in the deep dust. Behind him he heard a sudden stamping of hoofs and then the harsh splitting and crash of wood. He looked back. Young Jordan's horse was up on the sidewalk, wild-eyed and snorting with young Jordan leaning forward half out of the saddle, pushing himself back from the horse's neck, back off the horn into the saddle, swaying insecurely. And as Jordan managed the horse off the sidewalk Doane looked quickly forward again, his eyes fixed distantly ahead and blank.

He passed men he knew, and out of the corner of his eye he saw their glances slowly follow him, calm, or gloomy, or shrewdly speculative. As he passed, he knew their glances were shifting to the man whose horse was softly coming up behind him. It was like that all the way up the street. The flowers were drooping markedly now.

The town petered out with a few Mexican shacks, the road dwindled to broad ruts, and the sage was suddenly on all sides of him, stretching away toward the heat-obscured mountains like an infinite multitude of gray-green sheep. He turned off the road and began the slight ascent up the little hill whereon the cemetery lay. Grasshoppers thrilled invisibly in the sparse, dried grass along the track, silent as he came by, and shrill again as he passed, only to become silent again as the other rider came.

He swung off at the rusty barbed wire Missouri gate and slipped the loop from the post, and the shadow of the other slid tall across his path and stopped. Doane licked his lips quickly and looked up, his grasp tightening on the now sweat-wilted newspaper. Young Jordan was sitting his horse, open-mouthed, leaning forward with his hands on the pommel to support himself, his eyes vague and dull. His lips were wet and red, and hung in a slight smile.

A lark made the air sweet over to the left, and then Doane saw it, rising into the air. It hung in the sun, over the cemetery. Moving steadily and avoiding all suddenness, Doane hung his reins over the post.

"You don't like me, do you?" young Jordan said. A long thread of saliva descended from the corner of his slackly smiling mouth.

Doane's face set into a sort of blank preparedness. He turned and started slowly through the gate, his shoulders hunched up and pulled backward.

Jordan got down from the saddle, and Doane turned toward him slowly. Jordan came forward straight enough, with his feet apart, braced against staggering. He stopped three feet from Doane, bent forward, his mouth slightly open.

"You got any objections to me being in town?"

"No," Doane said, and stood still.

Jordan thought that over, his eyes drifting idly sideways for a moment. Then they came back, to a finer focus this time, and he said, "Why not?" hunching forward again, his hands open and held away from the holsters at his hips.

Doane looked at the point of his nose. "You haven't done anything, Jordan. Except get drunk. Nothing to break the law."

"I haven't done nothing," Jordan said, his eyes squinting away at one of the small, tilting tombstones. "By God, I'll do something. Whadda I got to do?" He drew his head back, as though he were farsighted, and squinted. "Whadda I got to do to make you fight, huh?"

"Don't do anything," Doane said quietly, keeping his voice even. "Just go back and have another drink. Have a good time."

"You think I ain't sober enough to fight?" Jordan slipped his right gun out of its holster, turning away from Doane. Doane stiffened. "Wait, mister," Jordan said.

He cocked the gun. "See that bird?" He raised the gun into the air, squinting along the barrel. The bright nickel of its finish gleamed in the sun. The lark wheeled and fluttered. Jordan's arm swung unsteadily in a small circle.

He pulled the trigger and the gun blasted. The lark jumped in the air, flew away about twenty feet, and began circling again, catching insects.

"Missed 'im," Jordan mumbled, lowering his arm and wiping sweat off his forehead. "Damn it, I can't see!" He raised his arm again.

Again the heavy blast cracked Doane's ears. Down in the town, near the Mexican huts, he could see tiny figures run out into the street.

The bird didn't jump this time, but darted away out of sight over the hill.

"Got him," Jordan said, scanning the sky. His eyes wandered over the graveyard for a moment, looking for the bird's body. "Now you see?" he said, turning to Doane, his eyes blurred and watering with the sun's glare. "I'm going down and shoot up the damned town. Come down and stop me, you old—"

He turned and lurched sideways a step, straightened himself out and walked more steadily toward his horse, laughing to himself. Doane turned away, his face sick, and trudged slowly up the hill, his eye on the ground.

He stopped at one of the newer graves. The headstone was straight on this one. He looked at it, his face changing expression. "Here lies Cecelia Doane, born 1837, died 1885, the loyal wife . . ."

He stopped and pulled a weed from the side of the grave, then pulled a bunch of withered stems from a small green funnel by the headstone, and awkwardly took the fresh flowers out of the newspaper. He put the flowers into the funnel, wedging them firmly down into the bottom, and set it down again. He stood up and moved back, wiping sweat from his eyes.

A sudden shout came from the gate, and the sharp crack of a quirt. Doane turned with a befuddled look.

Jordan was back on his horse, beating Doane's. He had looped the reins over its neck so that it would run free. It was tearing away down the slope headed back for town.

Doane stood with his hat in his hand, his face suddenly beet red. He took a step after Jordan, and then stood still, shaking a little. He stared fixedly after him, watching him turn into the main road and toward the main street again. Then, sighing deeply, he turned back to the grave. Folding the newspaper, he began dusting off the heavy slab, whispering to himself. "No, Cissie, I could have gone. But, you know—it's my town."

He straightened up, his face flushed, put on his hat, and slapping the folded paper against his knee, started down the path. He got to the Missouri gate, closed it, and started down the ruts again.

A shot came from the town, and he stopped. Then there were two more, sharp spurts of sound coming clear and definite across the sage. He made out a tiny figure in a blue shirt running along a sidewalk.

He stood stock-still, the grasshoppers singing in a contented chorus all around him in the bright yellow glare. A train whistle came faint from off the plain, and he looked far across it. He made out the tiny trailed plume of smoke.

His knees began to quiver very slightly and he began to walk, very slowly, down the road.

Then suddenly there came a splatter of shots from below. The train whistle came again, louder, a crying wail of despair in the burning, brilliant, dancing air.

He began to hurry, stumbling a little in the ruts. And then he stopped short, his face open in fear. "My God, my empty horse, those shots—Toby, no!" He began to run, shambling, awkward and stumbling, his face ashen.

From the end of the street, as he hobbled panting past the tight-shut Mexican shanties, he could see a blue patch in the dust in front of the saloon, and shambled to a halt. It wasn't Toby, whoever it was, lying there face down: face buried in the deep, pillowing dust, feet still on the board sidewalk where the man had been standing.

The street was empty. None of the faces he knew looked at him now. He drew one of his guns and cocked it and walked fast up the walk, on the saloon side.

A shot smashed ahead of him and he stopped, shrinking against a store front. Inside, through the glass door, he could see two pale faces in the murk. Blue powder smoke curled out from under the saloon porch ahead of him.

Another shot smashed, this time from his office. The spurt of smoke, almost invisible in the sunlight, was low down in the doorway. Two horses were loose in the street now, his own, standing alert up past the saloon, and young Jordan's half up on the boardwalk under one of the porches.

He walked forward, past young Jordan's horse, to the corner of the saloon building. Another shot slammed out of his office door, the bullet smacking the window ahead of him. A small, slow smile grew on his mouth. He looked sideways at the body in the street. Young Jordan lay with the back of his head open to the sun, crimson and brilliant, his bright nickel gun still in his right hand, its hammer still cocked, unfired.

The train whistle moaned again, closer.

"Doane," Toby called from the office door, invisible. "Get out of town." There was a surge of effort in the voice, a strain that made it almost a squeal. "I'm shot in the leg. Get out before they get together."

A door slammed somewhere. Doane glanced down between the saloon and the store beside it. Then he saw, fifty yards down the street, a figure come out of another side alley and hurry away down the walk toward the station. From the saloon door another shot slammed across the street. Toby held his fire.

Doane peered after the running figure, his eyes squinting thoughtfully. The train's whistle shrieked again like the ultimatum of an approaching conqueror at the edge of town, and in a moment the ground under his feet began to vibrate slightly and the hoarse roar of braking wheels came up the street.

He turned back to young Jordan's horse, petted it around the head a moment and then took it by the reins close to the bit. He guided it across the street, keeping its body between him and the front of the saloon, without drawing fire, and went on down the alley beside his office. At the rear door he hitched the horse and went inside.

Toby was on the floor, a gun in his hand, his hat beside him, peering out across the sill. Doane kept low, beneath the level of the window, and crawled up to him. Toby's leg was twisted peculiarly and blood leaked steadily out from the boot top onto the floor. His face was sweating and very pale, and his lips were tight. "I thought he got you," Toby said keeping his eyes on the saloon across the street. "I heard those shots and then your horse came bucketing back down the street. I got Jordan. Colby got me in the leg before I got back inside."

"Never mind about that. Come on, get on your feet if you can and I'll help you on the horse in back. You can get out of town and I'll shift for myself."

"I think I'm going to pass out. I don't want to move. It won't hurt no worse getting killed than it does now. The hell with the horse! Take it yourself."

Doane looked across the street, his eyes moving over the door and the windows carefully, inch by inch.

"I'm sorry I shot him," Toby said. "It's my fault. And it's my fight now, Doane. Clear out."

Doane turned and scuttled out of the back. He mounted the horse and rode down behind four stores. He turned up another alley, dashed across the main street, down another alley, then back up behind the saloon.

He dismounted, his gun cocked in his hand. The back door of the place was open and he got through it quickly, the sound of his boot heels dimmed under the blast of a shot from the front of the saloon. From the dark rear of the room, he could see Pierce, crouched behind the bar, squinting through a bullet hole in the stained-glass bottom half of the front window.

There was a bottle of whisky standing on the bar beside Pierce; he reached out a hand and tilted the bottle up to his mouth, half turning toward Doane as he did so. Pierce kept the bottle to his lips, pretending to drink, and, with his right hand invisible behind the bar, brought his gun into line with Doane.

The tip of Pierce's gun came over the edge of the bar, the rest of him not moving a hair and Doane, gritting his teeth, squeezed slowly and painfully on his gun trigger. The gun flamed and bucked in his hand, and he dropped it, his face twisting in agony. The bottle fell out of Pierce's hand and spun slowly on the bar. Pierce sat there for a moment before his head fell forward and he crashed against the edge of the bar and slipped down out of sight.

Doane picked up his gun with his left hand and walked forward to the bar, holding his right hand like a crippled paw in front of him. The bottle had stopped revolving. Whisky inside it, moving back and forth, rocked it gently. He righted it and took a short pull at the neck, and in a moment the pain lines relaxed in his face. He went to the bat-wing doors and pushed one of them partly open.

"Toby!" he called.

There was no answer from across the street, and then he saw the barrel of a revolver sticking out of his office door, lying flat, and behind it one hand, curled loosely and uselessly around the butt.

He looked down the street. The train stood across it. A brakeman moved along the cars slowly, his head down. There was nobody else in sight.

He started to step out, and saw then two men coming up the opposite walk, running fast. Suddenly one of them stopped, grabbing the other by the arm, and pointed at him. He stared back for a moment, seeing Jordan clearly now, the square, hard face unchanged except for its pallor, bleak and bony as before.

Doane let the door swing to and continued to watch them over the top of it. They talked for a moment. Then Colby ran back down the street—well out of effective range—sprinted across it and disappeared. Down the street the engine, hidden by some building, chuffed angrily, and the cars began to move again. Jordan stood still, leaning against the front of a building, fully exposed, a hard smile on his face.

Doane turned and hurried to the back door. It opened outward. He slammed and bolted it, then hurried back to the front and waited, his gun ready. He smiled as the back door rattled, turned, fired a shot at it and listened. For a moment there was no sound. Then something solid hit it, bumped a couple of times and silence came again.

From the side of the building, just beyond the corner where Pierce's body lay, a shot crashed. The gun in the office door jumped out of the hand and spun wildly. The hand lay still.

He heard Jordan's voice from down the street, calling, the words formed slowly, slightly spaced.

"Is he dead?"

"Passed out," Colby called back.

"I'm going around back to get him. Keep Doane inside." Jordan turned and disappeared down an alley.

Doane leaned across the bar, knocked bottles off the shelves of the back bar and held his pistol on the corner of the wall, about a foot above the floor.

"Pierce," he said.

"Throw out your guns," Pierce answered.

Doane squinted at the corner, moved his gun slightly and fired. He heard a cry of pain, then curses; saw the bat-wing doors swing slightly. Then he turned and ran for the back door. He threw back the bolt and pushed on the door. It wouldn't give. He threw himself against it. It gave a little at the bottom. Colby had thrown a stake up against it to keep him locked in.

He ran back to the front.

Across the street, he could see somebody moving in his office, dimly, beyond the window. Suddenly the hand on the floor disappeared.

"Come on out, you old—" Pierce said, panting. "You only skinned me." His voice was closer than before, somewhere between the door and the corner of the building, below the level of the stained glass.

Then Doane saw Toby's white shirt beyond the window opposite. Jordan was holding him up, and moving toward the door. Jordan came out on the porch, hugging Toby around the chest, protecting himself with the limp body. With a heave he sent Toby flying down the steps, and jumped back out of sight. Toby rolled across the sidewalk and fell into the street, where he lay motionless.

Doane looked stupidly at Toby, then at young Jordan, still lying with his feet cocked up on the sidewalk.

"He ain't dead, Doane," Jordan called. "Come and get him if you want him alive." He fired through the window. Dust jumped six inches from Toby's head. "Come on out, Doane, and shoot it out. You got a chance to save him." The gun roared again, and dust jumped a second time beside Toby's head, almost in the same spot.

"Leave the kid alone," Doane called. "This fight's between you and me."

"The next shot kills him, Doane."

Doane's face sagged white and he leaned against the side of the door. He could hear Pierce breathing heavily in the silence, just outside. He pushed himself away from the door and drew a breath through clenched teeth. He cocked his pistol and strode out, swinging around. Pierce fired from the sidewalk, and Doane aimed straight into the blast and pulled as he felt himself flung violently around by Pierce's bullet.

Pierce came up from the sidewalk and took two steps toward him, opening and shutting a mouth that was suddenly full of blood, his eyes wide and wild, and then pitched down at his feet.

Doane's right arm hung useless, his gun at his feet. With his left hand he drew his other gun and stepped out from the walk, his mouth wide open, as though he were gasping for breath or were about to scream, and took two steps toward Toby as Jordan came out of the office door, firing. The slug caught Doane along the side of his neck, cutting the shoulder muscle, and his head fell over to one side. He staggered on, firing. He saw Toby trying to get up, saw Jordan fall back against the building, red running down the front of his shirt, and the smile gone.

Jordan stood braced against the building, holding his gun in both hands, firing as he slid slowly down. One bullet took Doane in the stomach, another in the knee. He went down, flopped forward and dragged himself up to where Toby lay trying to prop himself up on one elbow. Doane knelt there like a dog, puking blood into the dust, blood running out of his nose, but his gray eyes almost indifferent, as though there were one man dying and another watching.

He saw Jordan lift his gun with both hands and aim it toward Toby, and as the hammer fell, he threw himself across Toby's head and took it in the back. He rolled off onto his back and lay staring into the sky.

Upside down, he saw Toby take his gun and get up on one elbow, level it at Jordan and fire, and then saw Toby's face, over his, looking down at him as the deputy knelt in the street.

They stayed that way for a long moment, while Doane's eyes grew more and more dull and the dark of his blood in the white dust grew broader. His breath was coming hard, in small sharp gasps.

"There's nothing in it, kid," he whispered. "Only a tin star. They don't hang the right ones. You got to fight everything twice. It's a job for a dog."

"Thank you, Doane."

"It's all for free. You going to quit, Toby?"

Toby looked down at the gray face, the mouth and chin and neck crimson, the grey eyes dull. Toby shook his head. His face was hard as a rock.

Doane's face suddenly looked a little surprised, his eyes went past Toby to the sky. Toby looked up. A lark was high above them, circling and fluttering, directly overhead. "A pretty bird," Doane mumbled. "A very pretty bird."

His head turned slowly to one side, and Toby looked down at him and saw him as though fast asleep.

He took Doane's gun in his hand, and took off Doane's star, and sat there in the street while men slowly came out of stores and circled about them. He sat there unmoving, looking at Doane's half-averted face, holding the two things tightly, one in each hand, like a child with a broken toy, his face soft and blurred, his eyes unwet.

After a while the lark went away. He looked up at the men, and saw Mettrick.

"I told him he should have resigned," Mettrick said, his voice high. "He could have taken his horse—"

"Shut up," Toby said. "Shut up or get out." His eyes were sharp and his face placid and set. He turned to another of the men. "Get the doc," he said. "I've got a busted leg. And I've got a lot to do."

The man looked at him, a little startled, and then ran.

QUESTIONS

1. "The Tin Star" is one of many Western stories about outlaws or lawmen who have grown old and slow. Indeed it has been said that the hero of a Western story is either old or young—rarely middle aged. Why may this be?

2. What is the significance of the lark? What does it symbolize?

3. Why does Doane stay on the job if he thinks "it's a job for a dog"? Why does Toby?

4. In the picture "High Noon," which was based on "The Tin Star," the character of Staley becomes representative of all the deputies and all the townspeople, none of whom will help the sheriff. The sheriff survives the battle, but then he throws his star into the dust of the street, disgusted with all the town's citizens, and drives away. How do these changes affect the tone and meaning of the story?

5. Why would a plot like this one be improbable or even impossible in a modern detective story?

CLAY FISHER

THE TRAP

Canady felt the horse beginning to go rough beneath him. He had
been expecting it. On this rocky going no mount could make it for
long when he was already ridden out in coming to it. "Easy, easy," he
said to the laboring animal. "It's only a posse." The horse seemed to
understand the tone of the words, for it slowed and went better and
steadier for a ways. "We'll rest on the rise ahead," Canady said, "I can
see back a few miles and you can catch some wind and we'll go on.
We'll make it."

He knew they wouldn't. He knew it before they came to the rise
and he got down and walked out on the overhanging spur of
gray-black basalt that gave view down the canyon behind them for ten
miles. It wasn't a canyon, really, but a narrowing valley. The canyon
proper lay before them. Canady grinned and wiped his streaming face.
It was hot, and going to get hotter. "Hoss," he said, "they're pushing.
They mean to take up. They must know the country ahead. They
don't ride like there's any hurry." The horse, now, did not respond
with its ears and a turning of its soft eyes, as it had before. It stood,
head-down, blowing out through its distended nostrils. Canady came
back and squatted down and put his hand below the nose of the
horse, where the moisture of its pained breathing would strike his
palm. "Damn," he said softly. "Blood."

He got his field glasses from the saddle pocket and examined the
pursuers through them. "Eight," he said aloud, "and six ropes. I
wonder how come it is that they always fetch so many ropes? Never
saw a posse yet didn't feel they'd each of them ought to have a rope."

His fingers went to his sunburned neck. They felt it tenderly, and
he grinned again. "Son of a gun," he said, "it could happen."

Canady's grins were not the grimaces of a fool, or of an unfeeling
man. They were the grins of a gambler. And of an outlaw. And a thief.
Canady knew where he was and where he had been and, most
apparently, where he was going. It did not frighten him. He would
grin when they put the loop over his head. That was his kind. He
wouldn't curse or revile, and he wouldn't pray. Not out loud, anyway.

"Hoss," he said, "what do you think?"

The animal, slightly recovered, moved its ears and whickered
gruntingly. Canady nodded, turning his back to the approaching posse

and glassing the country ahead. "Me too," he agreed. "A grunt and a whicker is all she's worth. We haven't got no place to go." He tensed, as he said it, the glasses freezing on an opening in the rearing base rock of the closing valley. It was to their right. A good horse, fresh and sound, could take a man up to that gap in the cliff. The spill of detritus and ages-old fan of boulders and stunted pine that lay below its lips would permit of perilous mounted passage. There was water up there, too, for Canady could see the small white ribbon of the stream splashing down a rainbow falls to mist up upon the lower rocks in a spume of red and yellow and turquoise green lights, splendid with beauty in the early sun. "I take it back," he said. "Maybe we do have a place to go. Pretty, too, and handy to town. You can't beat that."

Directly ahead was a level sunlit flat, dotted with tall pines and scrub juniper and house-sized boulders. The clear stream from the high hole in the right-side valley wall watered the flat, growing good mountain hay upon its sandy red loam and making a ride across it a thing to pleasure the heart of any Western man.

"Come on," said Canady to his horse. "You canter me across the flat and I'll climb the fan afoot leaving you to pack up nothing but the saddle and the grub sack. You game? Least we can do is make those birds scratch for their breakfast. And who knows? Our luck might change. We might get up there and into that hole-in-the-wall before they come up to the rise, here, and spot us. If we can do that, there's a chance they'll ride on by, up the valley, and we can double back tonight and make it free."

He was talking to Canady, now, not to the horse. It was the way of men much alone and when they needed to do some figuring. They would do it out loud, the way Canady was doing. It sounded better thay way, more convincing, and more as though it might really come off. Canady even swung into the saddle believing his own advice, telling himself what he wanted to know, then accepting it as a very good chance indeed. Again, it was his way. A man didn't live by the gun and the good fast horse without acquiring a working philosophy with lots of elastic in it.

"Move out," he repeated to the horse. "It's your part to get us across the flat in time."

The little mustang humped its back and shook itself like a wet dog. Running sweat, and caked, as well, flew from its streaked hide. Its gathering of itself in response to the rider's words was a visible thing. The horse was like the man. It wouldn't quit short of the last second, or step, or shot. They were of a kind with the country around them. It was all the edge they had ever needed.

Canady panted. He wiped the perspiration from his eyes and started upward again. Behind him, the little horse came on, unled, the reins looped over the horn so as not to trail and be stepped on. He followed the man like a dog, panting with him, struggling where he struggled, sliding where he slid, and lunging on as he did, after each setback.

They had made nearly the top of the fan of fallen rock below and leading into the opening of the side canyon. In another four or five minutes they would be clear of the climb. They would be off the slide and safely into the notch in the high wall of the valley. They would be out of sight of the posse, and the posse still had not come into view of them on the rise back across the pine flat.

"Easy, hoss," gasped Canady. "We're going to make it."

But Canady was wrong. Thirty yards from the top, the mustang put its slender foreleg into a rock crevice and drew back quickly. The movement set the slide moving and caught the leg and crushed it like a matchstick below the knee. When the horse had freed itself and was standing hunched and trembling behind Canady, the shattered leg hung sickeningly a'swing and free of the ground, and Canady cursed with tears in his eyes. It was not the luck of it that brought his angry words, but the shame of it. It was his pity and his feeling for a gallant companion that had given its all and almost found it enough.

The hesitation, the wait there near the top of the slide, near the safety of the hole-in-the-wall, was the natural thing for a Western man. His horse was hurt. It was hopelessly hurt. He would have to leave it, but not like that. Not standing there on three legs hunched up in the middle with pain and fright. Not standing there watching him with those liquid brown eyes. No, he couldn't leave his horse like that.

But how else? He couldn't shoot the mustang, for the noise would key the posse to his location. Had he had a knife he could cut its throat. Or had he an ax he could have crushed its skull above the eye-socket and put the poor devil down painlessly. With a rock he might be able to stun the brave little brute, but he could not be sure of killing it cleanly. The same held true for the butt of his Colt or the steel-shod heel of his Winchester. He could stun the horse, likely put it to its knees, but not, still, be able to go on knowing it would not recover and try to get up again and go on, and so suffer as no horse-riding man could think to let his mount suffer. But, damn it, this was *his* life he was arguing with himself about. It wasn't the damned horse's life. If he didn't do something and do it quick, the posse would be over the rise and he and the horse could go to hell together. Well, he would use the Colt butt. He knew he could hit the exhausted animal hard enough with it to put it down for the necessary time for himself to get on into the hole-in-the-wall and for the posse to ride by and on up the valley. That was all the time he needed, or at least it was all he could ask for. He pulled the Colt and started back to the horse, sliding and stumbling in his hurry to get to the trembling beast and knock it down. But when he got up to its side, when he looked into those dark eyes, he couldn't do it. He had to be sure. "The hell with the posse," he said to the little horse, and spun the Colt in the air and caught it by the handle and put it behind the ragged ear and pulled the trigger. The smoke from the shot was still curling upward, and the little pony just going slowly down, when the first of the pursuing riders came up over the rise across the flat and yelled excitedly back to his comrades that the game was in sight, and on foot.

Canady went up the little stream. Behind him, where it fed the rainbow falls leaping outward into the main valley, the possemen were just topping the detritus fan and closing in on "the hole." Back there Canady had made a decision. It was not to stay and fight from the entrance cleft of the hole, where the little rivulet went out of the side canyon. He did not know what lay on up the side canyon, and feared there might be a way by which the possemen, familiar with this territory, could ride a circle and come in behind him. He could not risk that, he believed, and must go on up the creek as far as he could, hoping it would be far enough to find a place here he could put his back to the wall and fight without their being able to get behind him.

Now, going along, the way becoming steeper and narrower and the creek bank little more than wide enough to pass a good horse and rider, he saw ahead of him a basalt dike, or cross dam of rock, which cut across the narrowing floor of the side canyon. Here the stream took another plunge, this of about thirty feet. Above the dike, Canady could see the boles of pine trees and hence knew that the ground above the dike lay fairly level. The cross-lying of rock apparently served as a barrier against which the winter erosions of snow, ice and thaw had worked with the spring floodings of the creek to bring down and build up a tiny flat.

Canady's gray eyes lit up. His brown face relaxed and he said aloud, "By God, maybe this is it," and went on with renewed strength and some hope of keeping his life a little longer. Up there, above that rock cross-bank, a man with a good carbine and plenty of shells could hold down most eight-man posses for several afternoons. Well, two or three, anyway. Or one. For certain, until nightfall. Twelve, fifteen hours, say. It was better than nothing.

His luck held. There was a good angling trail going up that thirty-foot vertical face of rock. It was a game trail, and somewhat of a cow trail, too. He made out the droppings of elk, blacktail deer, range steers and, then, suddenly and strangely, a fairly fresh piling of horse sign. This latter find sent a chill through him. He was on his knees in the instant of the sighting, but then he straightened, grinning. It was all right. The pony was unshod. Moreover, he suspected, from the hard round prints that it left, that it never had been shod and was one of a bunch of broomtails—wild mustangs—that came into the rocky depth for the water that flowed so green and cool in the stream.

Clearing the top of the stone dam, Canady's grin widened. The flat above lay precisely as he had imagined it did. He laughed softly, as a man will who is alone. Now, then, it would be a little different from the way those hungry lawmen had planned it. This was perfect. At the apex of the triangle of the flat he saw the thick stand of sycamore and cottonwood, aspen, laurel and willow, and he knew that the water headed there. A moment later, he made out the source of the stream, a large artesian spring gushing from the native rock under great pressure. The spring was set above the grove some few feet, its stream falling rapidly to plunge into the foliage. Likely it pooled up there under the trees and at the foot of the down-plunge. That's what lured in the wild horses and the other game and the cattle, too, what few of the latter were hardy enough to come this far into the mountains for feed. All a man would need to do, now, was hole up in those boulders that girded the spring, up there above the trees, and he could command with his Winchester the whole of the small, open flat between the spring grove and the stone cross-dam that Canady had just clambered up. Taking a deep breath, the fugitive started across the flat, toward the spring and its hole-up boulders. It was not until he had climbed safely into this haven at the canyon head and laid down pantingly to look back on his trail and get ready for the possemen, that he saw where he had come.

Below him in the trees the spring pooled up exactly as he had expected it would. Also the rim of the pool showed the centuries of wear of the hoofed animals coming to its banks for water. But there was something else—two other things—that he had not expected to see there, and his grin faded and his gray eyes grew taut and tired and empty.

The first thing was the wild horse. It had not gone on up out of the little side canyon as Canady had hoped, showing him the way to follow its tracks and escape over the rim where no mounted man might follow. It was still in the grove of trees that sheltered the spring-pool waterhole, and it wasn't still there because of its thirst. Beyond the trees, back where Canady had come from, and so skillfully blended and built into the natural cover of the canyon that even his range-wise eyes had missed them, were the two woven brush and pole wings of the second thing Canady had not dreamed to find there. Those were the man-made wings of a mustang corral down there. Canady had stumbled into a wild horse trap. And he was caught there, with this unfortunate lone mustang that now cowered in the trees and could not get out of the trap any more than could he, and for the same reason—the posse and the box canyon.

"Steady on," Canady called down softly to the terrified horse. "We'll think of something."

Two hours after high noon the sun was gone from the canyon. Canady could see its light splashing the far side of the main valley still, but in the side canyon all was soft shade, and hot. Canady drank enough water to keep himself from drying out, yet not enough to log him. He noted that the wild mustang did the same thing. It knew, as Canady knew, that to be ready to fight or fly called for an empty belly. "Smart," said Canady, "smart as hell." The horse heard him and looked up. "*Coo-ee, coo-ee,*" Canady called to him reassuringly. "Don't fret; I'll figure something for us." But it was a lie and he knew it was a lie.

He had gone down, right after he first lay up in the spring boulders and saw the trap and the wild broomtail in it, and closed off the narrow gate of the funnel-winged corral with his lariat. He had done that in a hurry, before the posse had worked up into the canyon and taken its position along the top of the crossdam. His one thought had been that the broomtail was a horse, wild or not, and that so long as a man had a horse he wasn't out of it in that country. And he had wanted to keep hidden from the posse the fact that he did have a horse up there in that headwaters timber. The mustang had played with him in that last part of it, lying up shy and quiet as a deer in the trees and brush, not wanting any more than Canady wanted for the men to know that it was there. "It" in this case was a scrubby little stallion, probably too small and old to hold a band of mares. The little horse had not only the fixtures but the temperament of the mongrel stud animal. Watching him lie still in the spring brush and keep his eyes following every move of the men below him, as well as of the single man above him, Canady knew that he and the trapped horse were friends. The only problem was proving it to the horse.

Sometimes these old scrub studs had been ridden long ago and would remember man's smell and voice. He tried a dozen times to talk the mustang up toward his end of the spring pool. But the animal gave no sign that the sight, scent or sound of mankind was familiar to him, or welcome. He bared his teeth silently and pinned his ears and squatted in the haunches ready to kick like a pack mule on a cold morning. He did this every time Canady said more than three or four words to him, or accompanied his talk with any movement that might mean he was coming down to see the horse, if the horse would not come up to see him.

What possible good the horse could do him, even if, by some miracle Canady might gentle him down and put his saddle and bridle on him, Canady didn't know. Then, even in thinking that far, he laughed and shrugged. His saddle and bridle were down there on that rock slide below the hole-in-the-wall. He'd had no time and no reason to take them off his dead mount. So if he went out of there astride that broomtail it would be bareback, and that was about as good a bet as that the crafty old stallion would sprout wings and fly up out of the canyon. A bridle, of sorts, he could rig from splitting and unraveling a short length of his lariat. It would be sort of a breaking hackamore arrangement and might do to give simple directions of right and left and who-up. But even if he rigged this Sioux headstall and got it on the shaggy little horse, then what? That was, even if the rascal wanted to be good, or had been ridden in the past, and remembered it of a sudden? Nothing. Not a damned thing. Canady couldn't ride out of that canyon if he had the best saddle mount in Montana waiting and eager to make the try with him. It was all crazy, thinking of that wild stud. But just finding any horse up there was bound to start a man's mind going. Especially when he had just shot his own mount and was fixing to put his back to the best rock he could find and go down with lead flying. But it was crazy all the same. All Canady could do was what the old broomtail stud could do—fight the rope to the last breath he had in him, then kill himself, if he could, before the others did it for him.

The afternoon wore on. The heat in the deep-walled little canyon was enormous. The deerflies swarmed at the spring pool and bit like mad cats. They nearly drove Canady wild, but he fought them with hand and mind and swathed neckband and, when evening came, they lifted up out of the canyon on the first stir of the night wind. In the early part of the waiting there had been some desultory talk between the posse and Canady, talk of Canady coming out peacefully and getting a fair trial, but the fugitive had not bothered to take that offer seriously. He knew the trial he would get. The posse had its own witnesses with it. They would bring up these two or three men who had "seen" the shooting and say to them, "Is that him?" and the men would say, "Yes, that's him," and the trial would be over. Witnesses! thought Canady. God, how he hated them. It wasn't that he minded being identified if he was the man. In his business no feeling was held against the witness who *had* seen something. It was those devils, like the ones with the posse, who had *not* seen the job and yet who were always ready to raise their right hands and be sworn, who were the ones Canady hated. There had not been any witnesses as to what passed between him and that teller. All the other bank people had been on the floor behind the cage, and there had been no customers in the bank, or out in front of it. The shooting had happened and Canady had made it to his horse in back of the bank, and made it away down the alley and into the sagebrush south of town before he had passed a living soul. Then, it was two farm wagons, both carrying kids and driven by women, that he had ridden by well out of Gray's Landing. How those good folks—and they were the only real witnesses, save the cashier and the other teller on the bank floor—how they could identify him as anything other than a horseman not of that area, Canady did not know. As for the three shots that had killed the teller, and they must have killed him or the posse would not have pushed so hard, those shots had been fired *after* both barrels of the .36 caliber derringer that the teller brought up out of the cash drawer had been triggered and put their slugs, one in Canady's chest, and one in the ceiling of the Second National Bank of Gray's Landing, Montana. But the only witness to that fact was dead. Canady had reacted as all men with guns in their hands react to other men with guns in their hands. He had fired by instinct, by pure conditioned reflex of long experience, when that first .36 bullet went into the pectoral muscles of his left chest.

Armed robbery? Certainly. Twenty years in the Territorial Prison? Of course. A man expected that. But to be run down like a mad dog and cornered and starved out and then strung up on a naked cottonwood like a damned Indian drunk or a common horse thief was not right or fair. Murder? Could you call it murder when the other man was a professional in his business and he could see that you were a professional in yours? When you told him he would be killed if he tried anything funny? Then, when on top of the fair warning, you gave him the first shot? Could you call it murder, then, if you shot in answer to his try at killing you? Self-defense was the actual verdict, but of course an armed robber could not plead self-defense. But he was not guilty of murder, or even of assault with a deadly weapon, or even of intent to commit murder, or of a damned thing, really, but to sack that cash drawer and clear out of Gray's Landing just as fast and peaceably as he and the old horse might manage.

Canady grinned, even as he exonerated himself.

It was no good. He knew it was no good. A man had to be honest with himself. If he was in another business he wouldn't need a gun to conduct his trade. Needing and using a gun, he was always in the peril of being forced to use it. The teller was an honest man. Frank Canady was a crook. The teller was a dead honest man and Canady was a live dishonest man. Canady was a killer.

"No!" he yelled down to the posse. "I won't do it; I shot second; I didn't mean to harm that fellow. He pulled on me and shot first. But he's dead, ain't he? Sure he is. And you say to me to come on down peaceable and you'll see I get a fair trial? With a dead teller back there on the floor of the Second National. That's rich. Really rich."

The possemen were startled. It had been two hours since the fugitive had made a sound. Previously he had refused to come down and they had thought he meant it. Now, did they detect a change? Was it that he wanted to reconsider and was only protecting his ego by the defiant outburst?

"That's right, you heard us right," the leader of the posse called up to him. "You come down here and we'll guarantee to take you back to Gray's Landing and get you to either Cheyenne or Miles City, wherever the court is sitting, by train and under armed guard. You'll get a trial we promised, and the protection beforehand." He waited a significant moment, then demanded, "What do you say? There's no use any more people getting hurt."

Canady's gray eyes grew tired again.

"That's so," he called back. "It includes me too. I don't want to see anybody else get it, either. 'Specially me. No thanks, Mr. Posseman. I'll stay up here. I don't fancy that you brung along all them ropes just to tie me up for the ride back to Gray's Landing."

There was a silence from below the cross-dam of rock in the upper throat of the canyon that lasted perhaps two, perhaps three stretching minutes. Then the posseman called back. "All right," he said, "you'll have it your way. When it's full dark we're going to come for you, and you know what that will mean. There are eight of us, all good shots, and you won't have the chance of a rat in an oatbin. We've got bulls-eye lanterns to light you out. We will set them up behind boulders where you can't snipe them, and yet where they will throw light up there around you like it was bright moonlight. We mean to stomp you out. There will be no trial and no talk of a trial. You're dead right now."

Canady sank back behind his breastwork of basalt and gray-green granite. He hawked the cottony spittle from his throat and spat grimacingly down toward the mustang stud. The animal had been crouching and listening to the exchange of voices intelligently like some big gaunt sandy-maned dog. Seeing him, and noting his apparent interest, Canady managed a trace of his quiet grin.

"What do *you* say, amigo?" he asked.

The horse looked up at him. It was the first time in all the long hours that Canady had tried gentle-talking to him that the animal had made a direct and not spooked response to the man's voice. Now he stomped a splayed and rock-split forehoof and whickered softly and gruntingly in his throat, precisely as Canady's old horse had done.

"All right," said Canady, for some reason feeling mightily warmed by the mustang's action, "so we've each got one friend in the world. That isn't too bad. As long as you have a friend you have a chance. Rest easy; let me think. We'll still make it, you and me. . . ."

It was dusk when the old steer came down the cliff trail. He was a ladino, one of those mossy-horned old rascals that had successfully

hidden out from the gathers of a dozen years. He was old and crafty
and cautious as any wild animal, but he had to have water and he was
coming down to the spring pool to get it. He certainly saw the men of
the posse, and winded their mounts, but they did not see him and he
knew that they did not. His yellow buckskin hide with the dark "cruz"
or cross-stripe on the shoulders, and the dark brown legs and feet,
blended perfectly into the weathered face of the cliff, and he made no
more sound coming down that hidden trail than a mountain doe
might have made. But he had failed to see Canady or to separate his
scent, or the scent of the mustang stud, from the other horse and man
scents coming from below. He came on, carefully, silently, yet quickly
down the wall of the canyon from the rim above and Canady, seeing
him, was suddenly lifted in mind and heart. He had been right in the
first place. There *was* a trail up out of that blind box of a side canyon.
A track up that dizzy sheer cliff, up there, that would pass a desperate
man, or a catlike wild mustang, but not a mounted man or a man
going afoot leading his tamed and trained saddle mount. "Come on,
come on," he heard himself whispering to the old outlaw steer.
"Come on down here and let me see how you do it. Let me see how
and where you get off that damned wall and down here where we are."

He grinned when he said that, when he said "we," meaning
himself and the wild stud, without thinking about it. It was funny how
a man took to anything for a friend when he had run out of the real
McCoy and was in his last corner. He supposed that if a sidewinder
crawled along at the final minute and that was all he had to talk to, a
man would find some excuse to think kindly of the snake tribe. Well,
anyway, he was thinking with deep kindness about the animal
kingdom just then. Especially the horse and cow part of it. And
extraspecially about the latter half. "Come on, keep coming on, don't
slip, for God's sake," he said to the gaunt dun steer. "Easy, easy. Let
me see you do it, just don't fall or spook or get a bad smell and change
your mind. That's it, that's it. Easy, easy. . . ."

He talked the steer down that cliff trail as though his life
depended on it, and it did. And the steer made it. He made it in a way
that caused Canady to suck in his breath and shake his head in
wonderment. He made it in a way that even caused Canady to think
for a moment about there being something to the idea of a divine
providence, for it was the sort of thing no man could have figured out
by himself, the weird, crazy, wonderful kind of a last-second reprieve
that no force but God Almighty could have sent to a man in Canady's
place. It was a miracle.

The dun steer performed it with an easy quickness that defied
belief, too. He came to that place on his side of the canyon where it
seemed to Canady that the trail must end. The man could see the

sheer face of the rock dropping sixty feet to the creek bed. A giant
outcropping of granite hid the exact end of the rightside trail, but
Canady could see, and with absolute certainty, that the trail did not
continue downward past that outcrop that hid its actual terminus. But
as he watched the steer disappear behind the outcrop and as he
wondered what would happen next, he saw the lean yellow body
launch itself in a graceful leap from behind the outer edge of the
outcrop, and sail outward through the thin air of the canyon's dark
throat. It appeared as though the leap would smash the ribby brute
into the rearing face of the opposite, left-hand canyon wall, which lay
not more than fifteen or twenty feet from the right-side wall. But
again the steer disappeared, this time seemingly into the very face of
the opposing cliff.

There was a tricky turn in the rock wall of the canyon's left side
at just that point, however, and while Canady could see the creek's
raggedly broken bottom, he could not see where the steer hit into the
wall. All he was sure of for the moment was that the animal had made
his landing somewhere other than in the creek bottom. Difficult as it
might be to accept, that old outlaw steer had somehow made it from
one side of the wall to the other. But, even so, then what? Where was
he now? The questions were soon answered when the missing steer
appeared to walk right out of the waterfall that came down from
Canady's elevated vantage to strike into and begin following the brief
section of creek bed into the pool grove. While Canady gaped, the
animal stole swiftly to the pool, drank sparingly, returned and
disappeared again behind the curtain of misty water cascading down
from the spring above.

So that was it. As simple and as remarkable as that. A trail ran
from behind the waterfall up the left-hand wall. At a point opposite
the right-side trail's end, it too, terminated. But it was obvious that
there was room enough for a running jump and opposite landing, to
and from either wall, with both takeoff and landing spots completely
masked from the lower canyon.

Gaging the distance of the jump, Canady knew that he could
make it. With his boots off and laced about his neck, or better,
thrown over with his Colt and the saddlebags with the bank money,
the Winchester being slung on his back, alone, he could make that
distance through the air. But, then, what of that? He made the jump
safely and went on up the right-side cliff trail behind the ladino steer
and gained the rim; then what? He would still be afoot in a hostile
land in midsummer's blazing heat without food, water, or a mount.
That was the rub. Even if he made that jump and the cliff climb
beyond it and got to the rim, he would have to have a horse.
Otherwise, the possemen, within an hour or two of dark, having come

for him and found him gone, would go back out and climb out of the main valley and cut for his sign on both rims of the side canyon, and they would still get him. They would get him easy, with them mounted and he afoot.

No, he had to take that broomy studhorse with him.

Somehow, he had to get that mustang to go with him up the cliff. If he could do that, could get the little horse to make the jump with him on its back—it would have to be that way for he could never trust the brute to follow him or to wait for him if he allowed it to jump first—if he could make that gap in the canyon on the back of that little wild horse, then stay with him, hand-leading him up the cliff trail, then oh then, by the dear good Lord, he would make it. He and the horse would make it together. Just as he had promised the raunchy little devil. Up on the rim, he would remount the tough wiry mustang and together they would race away and Canady would have his life and the broomtail stud would have his freedom and the Gray's Landing posse would have their ropes unstretched and their vengeance unadministered and left to God where it belonged.

The thought of the Almighty came very strong to Canady in that moment of desperate hope. He turned his face upward to peer out of the narrow slit of late twilight far above him where the walls of the Canyon seemed almost to touch at the top and where, far, far up there, he could now see the yellow steer climbing the last few steps of the steep trail and humping himself over the rim and losing himself to canyon's view. Canady nodded and said to the dusk-hushed stillness about him: "If you'll let me make it, too, Lord, me and that little hoss down yonder, I will try to set things as right as I can. I'll take this money, Lord, the bank don't need it and I won't want it any more after this night, and I will give this money to the widow of that poor teller. I will figure some way to do it, Lord, that she don't know where it came from. And I'll turn loose this little wild hoss, if you will let me gentle him enough to get on him and push him to that jump, up yonder. I'm going to try it, Lord. I'm going down there to the pool and try putting my loop on him right now. You reckon you could help me? I surely hope so, as I think you wouldn't send that ladino steer down here to show a man the way out, and then not help him to make it. Nor likewise do I think you would put that little old mustang studhorse down there in that trap by the pool unless you wanted him used. It looks to me, Lord, as if you truly wanted to pull me out of this here trap, and if that's the way it is, why thank You and I'll do my best. . . ."

In the little light remaining, Canady went down from his rocks by the spring to try for the trapped wild horse. He took his rope from the trap gate and closed the gate, instead, with brush and poles, hoping it would turn the stud should he break past him when he came at him with the lariat.

The actual catching went, as such things perversely will, with a strange easiness. Oh, the little horse fought that loop when he felt it settle on him, but he did not do so viciously. The very fact that he permitted Canady to come close enough to dab the loop on him to begin with was peculiarly simple. It made the matter suspicious to Canady and he thought the little stud was merely stalling on him, was trying to tempt him in close where he could use his teeth and hooves on him. He knew the small mustangs would do this. They would fight like panthers in close, using their teeth like carnivorous animals, and their feet with all the savagery of elk or moose fighting off wolves. But this was not the case with the tattered broomtail in the mustang trap. When Canady got up near enough to him, he saw the reason why, or thought that he did. The telltale white marks of the cinch and saddle, the places where white hair had grown in to replace the original claybank sorrel hairs, showed clearly in the darkening twilight. Canady's first thought that this horse had been handled before was now assured. And it certainly explained the change in the animal the moment the man snugged the loop high up on his neck, under the jaw, in a way that showed the horse he meant to hold him hard and fast, and to handle him again as he had been handled years before. Memory is a strong force. The stud made Canady throw him on the ground, using the loose end of the rope to make a figure-8 snake and roll it around the front legs to bring the little pony down, but once he had been thrown and permitted to stand up again, it was all over. This man had gentled many horses. He had spent his life with them. Their smell had become his smell. The very sound of his voice had a horse sound in it. The mustang had heard it the first word of the day. He had sensed his kinship with this particular man, then, and he sensed his mastery of the horsekind, now. He submitted to Canady and stood quietly, if still trembling, while the man stroked him and sweet-whispered to him and got him to ease and to stand without shaking, and without dread or apprehension.

Then Canady cut and wove the makeshift breaking halter, the Plains Indian's simple rope rein and bridle arrangement, continuing to talk all the while to the small mustang. When, in half an hour more, it was full dark and the split-ear hackamore-bridle and its short reining rope were finished and put upon the horse, the animal was to all practical purposes reduced to a useable saddle horse. It was a piece of the greatest luck, Canady knew, that he had been able to catch and work the little brute. But it was not so entirely luck that it had no sense or possibility to it, and his success only made the fugitive believe that his hunch of higher help was a true one, and this thought, in turn, strengthened him and made his spirits rise.

"Come on," he murmured to the little horse, "it's time we got shut of here. Come along, *coo-ee, coo-ee*, little hoss. That's good, that's real good. Easy, easy. . . ."

They went in behind the creek falls, as the yellow ladino steer had done. The mustang pulled back a bit at the water but once it had hit him he steadied down and followed Canady's urging pull on the lariat as well and as obediently as any horse would have done in similar straits. Beyond the sheet of the falls, the left-hand trail went sharply but safely upward and around the trunklike bulge of the canyon's wall which had hidden it from Canady's view at the spring. Around the turn was the expected straight run at the leapover. It was better, even, than Canady hoped. There was some actual soil in its track and here and there, some clumps of tough wire grass to give footing and power for the jump.

"Steady, now," said Canady, and eased up onto the crouching mustang. The little mount flinched and deepened his crouch, but he did not break. Canady sighed gratefully and nodded upward to that power which clearly was helping him now. He took his grip on the rope rein and put the pressure of his bowed knees to the mustang's ribs. Beneath him, he felt the little horse squat and gather himself. Then he touched him, just touched him, with his left bootheel. The wild stud uncoiled his tensed muscles, shot down the runway of the trail, came up to the jump-across as though he had been trained to it since colthood. Canady felt his heart soar with the mighty upward spring in the small brute's wiry limbs. He laughed with the sheer joy of it. He couldn't help it. He had never in his life felt a triumph such as this one; this sailing over that hell's pit of blackness down there beneath him; this gliding spring, this arching, floating burst of power that was carrying him high above those deadly rock fangs so far below, and was carrying him, too, up and away from those blood-hungry possemen and their winking, glaring, prying bull's-eye lanterns, which he could just see now, from an eye-corner, coming into view down-canyon of his deserted place at the spring above the pool and the peaceful grove of mountain ash and alder and willow there at the head of Rainbow Creek in Blind Canyon, sixty and more miles from the Second National Bank and that fool of a dead teller in Gray's Landing, Montana. Oh, what a wondrous, heady thing was life! And, oh! what a beholden and humble man was Frank Canady for this gift, this chance, this answer to his fumbling prayer. He would never forget it. Never, never, never.

They came down very hard at the far end of the jump. The concussion of the horse hitting the ground rattled Canady's teeth and cracked his jaws together as loud as a pistol shot. He saw lights behind his eyes and heard wild and strange sounds, but only for a second or two. Then all was clear again and he and the little horse were going together up the right-side cliff trail, Canady leading the way, the little horse following faithful as a pet dog behind him. It seemed no more than a minute before they were where it had taken the yellow steer half an hour to climb, and it seemed only a breath later that they had topped out on the rim and were free.

Canady cried then. The tears came to his eyes and he could not help himself. He didn't think that the little mustang would care, though, and he was right. When he put his arms about the shaggy, warm neck and hugged the skinny old stud, the mustang only whickered deep in his throat and leaned into Frank Canady and rested his homely jughead over the man's shoulder. They were of a kind. They belonged to each other, and with each other, and that was true; for that was the way that the possemen found them when they came probing carefully up the bed of the creek in its brief run from the deserted pool grove to the foot of the spring's waterfall. The horse had fallen with the man beneath him, and neither had known a flash or a spark or a hint of thought, in the instant their lives had been crushed out among the granite snags of the creek bed below the jumping place of the yellow ladino steer.

QUESTIONS

1. How does the author succeed in creating sympathy for Canady, a man described as a gambler, an outlaw, a thief, and a murderer?

2. Canady discovers the cliffside trail when he watches an old ladino steer come down it. "Ladino" is a Western word for *wild* or *outlaw;* why is its use ironic in this story?

3. *Rationalization* is the word we use to describe specious or illogical self-justification. Does Canady indulge in rationalization? If so, does he deceive himself with it?

4. Compare "The Trap" with "All Gold Canyon" (p. 73) and "The Indian Well" (p. 290). In one of these stories only one character is human; and in two the leading characters spend most of their time talking to themselves or to the animals they depend on. Why is this technique of story development almost unique to the Western story? What elements replace other human characters?

5. "The Trap" is a short story with a "trick" ending, one borrowed from a Civil War story by Ambrose Bierce: "An Occurrence at Owl

Creek Bridge." Read this famous story (it has been widely anthologized) and compare it with Fisher's. Does your comparison help to bear out the old critical commonplace that there are no new plots—only new characters and new situations?

LUKE SHORT

TOP HAND

Gus Irby was out on the boardwalk in front of the Elite, giving his swamper hell for staving in an empty beer barrel, when the kid passed on his way to the feed stable. His horse was a good one and it was tired, Gus saw, and the kid had a little hump in his back from the cold of a mountain October morning. In spite of the ample layer of flesh that Gus wore carefully like an uncomfortable shroud, he shivered in his shirt sleeves and turned into the saloon, thinking without much interest *Another fiddle-footed dry-country kid that's been paid off after round-up.*

Later, while he was taking out the cash for the day and opening up some fresh cigars, Gus saw the kid go into the Pride Café for breakfast, and afterward come out, toothpick in mouth, and cruise both sides of Wagon Mound's main street in aimless curiosity.

After that, Gus wasn't surprised when he looked around at the sound of the door opening, and saw the kid coming toward the bar. He was in a clean and faded shirt and looked as if he'd been cold for a good many hours. Gus said good morning and took down his best whisky and a glass and put them in front of the kid.

"First customer in the morning gets a drink on the house," Gus announced.

"Now I know why I rode all night," the kid said, and he grinned at Gus. He was a pleasant-faced kid with pale eyes that weren't shy or sullen or bold, and maybe because of this he didn't fit readily into any of Gus' handy character pigeonholes. Gus had seen them young and fiddle-footed before, but they were the tough kids, and for a man with no truculence in him, like Gus, talking with them was like trying to pet a tiger.

Gus leaned against the back bar and watched the kid take his whisky and wipe his mouth on his sleeve, and Gus found himself getting curious. Half a lifetime of asking skillful questions that didn't seem like questions at all, prompted Gus to observe now, "If you're goin' on through you better pick up a coat. This high country's cold now."

"I figure this is far enough," the kid said.

"Oh, well, if somebody sent for you, that's different." Gus reached around lazily for a cigar.

The kid pulled out a silver dollar from his pocket and put it on the bar top, and then poured himself another whisky, which Gus was sure he didn't want, but which courtesy dictated he should buy. "Nobody sent for me, either," the kid observed. "I ain't got any money."

Gus picked up the dollar and got change from the cash drawer and put it in front of the kid, afterward lighting his cigar. This was when the announcement came.

"I'm a top hand," the kid said quietly, looking levelly at Gus. "Who's lookin' for one?"

Gus was glad he was still lighting his cigar, else he might have smiled. If there had been a third man here, Gus would have winked at him surreptitiously; but since there wasn't, Gus kept his face expressionless, drew on his cigar a moment, and then observed gently, "You look pretty young for a top hand."

"The best cow pony I ever saw was four years old," the kid answered pointedly.

Gus smiled faintly and shook his head. "You picked a bad time. Round-up's over."

The kid nodded, and drank down his second whisky quickly, waited for his breath to come normally. Then he said, "Much obliged. I'll see you again," and turned toward the door.

A mild cussedness stirred within Gus, and after a moment's hesitation he called out, "Wait a minute."

The kid hauled up and came back to the bar. He moved with an easy grace that suggested quickness and work-hardened muscle, and for a moment Gus, a careful man, was undecided. But the kid's face, so young and without caution, reassured him, and he folded his heavy arms on the bar top and pulled his nose thoughtfully. "You figure to hit all the outfits, one by one, don't you?"

The kid nodded, and Gus frowned and was silent a moment, and then he murmured, almost to himself, "I had a notion—oh, hell, I don't know."

"Go ahead," the kid said, and then his swift grin came again. "I'll try anything once."

"Look." Gus said, as if his mind were made up. "We got a newspaper here—the Wickford County Free Press. Comes out every Thursday, that's today." He looked soberly at the kid. "Whyn't you put a piece in there and say 'Top hand wants a job at forty dollars a month'? Tell 'em what you can do and tell 'em to come see you here if they want a hand. They'll all get it in a couple days. That way you'll save yourself a hundred miles of ridin'. Won't cost much either."

The kid thought awhile and then asked, without smiling, "Where's this newspaper at?"

Gus told him and the kid went out. Gus put the bottle away and doused the glass in water, and he was smiling slyly at his thoughts. Wait till the boys read that in the Free Press. They were going to have some fun with that kid, Gus reflected.

Johnny McSorley stepped out into the chill thin sunshine. The last silver dollar in his pants pocket was a solid weight against his leg, and he was aware that he'd probably spend it in the next few minutes on the newspaper piece. He wondered about that, and figured shrewdly it had an off chance of working.

Four riders dismounted at a tie rail ahead and paused a moment, talking. Johnny looked them over and picked out their leader, a tall, heavy, scowling man in his middle thirties who was wearing a mackinaw unbuttoned.

Johnny stopped and said, "You know anybody lookin' for a top hand?" and grinned pleasantly at the big man.

For a second Johnny thought he was going to smile. He didn't think he'd have liked the smile, once he saw it, but the man's face settled into the scowl again. "I never saw a top hand that couldn't vote," he said.

Johnny looked at him carefully, not smiling, and said, "Look at one now, then," and went on, and by the time he'd taken two steps he thought, *Voted, huh? A man must grow pretty slow in this high country.*

He crossed the street and paused before a window marked WICKFORD COUNTY FREE PRESS. JOB PRINTING. D. MELAVEN, ED. AND PROP. He went inside, then. A girl was seated at a cluttered desk, staring at the street, tapping a pencil against her teeth. Johnny tramped over to her, noting the infernal racket made by one of two men at a small press under the lamp behind the railed-off office space.

Johnny said "Hello," and the girl turned tiredly and said, "Hello, bub." She had on a plain blue dress with a high bodice and a narrow lace collar, and she was a very pretty girl, but tired, Johnny noticed. Her long yellow hair was worn in braids that crossed almost atop her head, and she looked, Johnny thought, like a small kid who has pinned her hair up out of the way for her Saturday night bath. He thought all this and then remembered her greeting, and he reflected without rancor, *Damn, that's twice,* and he said, "I got a piece for the paper, sis."

"Don't call me sis," the girl said. "Anybody's name I don't know, I call him bub. No offense. I got that from pa, I guess."

That's likely, Johnny thought, and he said amiably, "Any girl's name I don't know, I call her sis. I got that from ma."

The cheerful effrontery of the remark widened the girl's eyes. She held out her hand now and said with dignity, "Give it to me. I'll see it gets in next week."

"That's too late," Johnny said. "I got to get it in this week."

"Why?"

"I ain't got money enough to hang around another week."

The girl stared carefully at him. "What is it?"

"I want to put a piece in about myself. I'm a top hand, and I'm lookin' for work. The fella over there at the saloon says why don't I put a piece in the paper about wantin' work, instead of ridin' out lookin' for it."

The girl was silent a full five seconds and then said, "You don't look that simple. Gus was having fun with you."

"I figured that," Johnny agreed. "Still, it might work. If you're caught short-handed, you take anything."

The girl shook her head. "It's too late. The paper's made up." Her voice was meant to hold a note of finality, but Johnny regarded her curiously, with a maddening placidity.

"You D. Melaven?" he asked.

"No. That's pa."

"Where's he?"

"Back there. Busy."

Johnny saw the gate in the rail that separated the office from the shop and he headed toward it. He heard the girl's chair scrape on the floor and her urgent command, "Don't go back there. It's not allowed."

Johnny looked over his shoulder and grinned and said, "I'll try anything once," and went on through the gate, hearing the girl's swift steps behind him. He halted alongside a square-built and solid man with a thatch of stiff hair more gray than black, and said, "You D. Melaven?"

"Dan Melaven, bub. What can I do for you?"

That's three times, Johnny thought, and he regarded Melaven's square face without anger. He liked the face; it was homely and stubborn and intelligent, and the eyes were both sharp and kindly. Hearing the girl stop beside him, Johnny said, "I got a piece for the paper today."

The girl put in quickly, "I told him it was too late, pa. Now you tell him, and maybe he'll get out."

"Cassie," Melaven said in surprised protest.

"I don't care. We can't unlock the forms for every out-at-the-pants puncher that asks us. Besides, I think he's one of Alec Barr's bunch." She spoke vehemently, angrily, and Johnny listened to her with growing amazement.

"Alec who?" he asked.

"I saw you talking to him, and then you came straight over here from him," Cassie said hotly.

"I hit him for work."

"I don't believe it."

"Cassie," Melaven said grimly, "come back here a minute." He took her by the arm and led her toward the back of the shop, where they halted and engaged in quiet, earnest conversation.

Johnny shook his head in bewilderment, and then looked around him. The biggest press, he observed, was idle. And on a stone-topped table where Melaven had been working was a metal form almost filled with lines of type and gray metal pieces of assorted sizes and shapes. Now, Johnny McSorley did not know any more than the average person about the workings of a newspaper, but his common sense told him that Cassie had lied to him when she said it was too late to accept his advertisement. Why, there was space and to spare in that form for the few lines of type his message would need. Turning this over in his mind, he wondered what was behind her refusal.

Presently, the argument settled, Melaven and Cassie came back to him, and Johnny observed that Cassie, while chastened, was still mad.

"All right, what do you want printed, bub?" Melaven asked.

Johnny told him and Melaven nodded when he was finished, said, "Pay her," and went over to the type case.

Cassie went back to the desk and Johnny followed her, and when she was seated he said, "What do I owe you?"

Cassie looked speculatively at him, her face still flushed with anger. "How much money have you got?"

"A dollar some."

"It'll be two dollars," Cassie said.

Johnny pulled out his lone silver dollar and put it on the desk. "You print it just the same; I'll be back with the rest later."

Cassie said with open malice, "You'd have it now, bub, if you hadn't been drinking before ten o'clock."

Johnny didn't do anything for a moment, and then he put both hands on the desk and leaned close to her. "How old are you?" he asked quietly.

"Seventeen."

"I'm older'n you," Johnny murmured. "So the next time you call me 'bub' I'm goin' to take down your pigtails and pull 'em. I'll try anything once."

Once he was in the sunlight, crossing toward the Elite, he felt better. He smiled—partly at himself but mostly at Cassie. She was a real spitfire, kind of pretty and kind of nice, and he wished he knew what her father said to her that made her so mad, and why she'd been mad in the first place.

Gus was breaking out a new case of whisky and stacking bottles against the back mirror as Johnny came in and went up to the bar. Neither of them spoke while Gus finished, and Johnny gazed absently at the poker game at one of the tables and now yawned sleepily.

Gus said finally, "You get it in all right?"

Johnny nodded thoughtfully and said, "She mad like that at everybody?"

"Who? Cassie?"

"First she didn't want to take the piece, but her old man made her. Then she charges me more for it than I got in my pocket. Then she combs me over like I got my head stuck in the cookie crock for drinkin' in the morning. She calls me bub, to boot."

"She calls everybody bub."

"Not me no more," Johnny said firmly, and yawned again.

Gus grinned and sauntered over to the cash box. When he came back he put ten silver dollars on the bar top and said, "Pay me back when you get your job. And I got rooms upstairs if you want to sleep."

Johnny grinned. "Sleep, hunh? I'll try anything once." He took the money, said "Much obliged" and started away from the bar and then paused. "Say, who's this Alec Barr?"

Johnny saw Gus's eyes shift swiftly to the poker game and then shuttle back to him. Gus didn't say anything.

"See you later," Johnny said.

He climbed the stairs whose entrance was at the end of the bar, wondering why Gus was so careful about Alec Barr.

A gunshot somewhere out in the street woke him. The sun was gone from the room, so it must be afternoon, he thought. He pulled on his boots, slopped some water into the washbowl and washed up, pulled a hand across his cheek and decided he should shave, and went downstairs. There wasn't anybody in the saloon, not even behind the bar. On the tables and on the bar top, however, were several newspapers, all fresh. He was reminded at once that he was in debt to the Wickford County Free Press for the sum of one dollar. He pulled one of the newspapers toward him and turned to the page where all the advertisements were.

When, after some minutes, he finished, he saw that his advertisement was not there. A slow wrath grew in him as he thought of the girl and her father taking his money, and when it had come to full flower, he went out of the Elite and cut across toward the newspaper office. He saw, without really noticing it, the group of men clustered in front of the store across from the newspaper office. He swung under the tie rail and reached the opposite boardwalk just this side of the newspaper office and a man who was lounging against the building. He was a puncher and when he saw Johnny heading up the walk he said, "Don't go across there."

Johnny said grimly, "You stop me," and went on, and he heard the puncher say, "All right, getcher head blown off."

His boots crunched broken glass in front of the office and he came to a gingerly halt, looking down at his feet. His glance raised to the window, and he saw where there was a big jag of glass out of the window, neatly wiping out the Wickford except for the W on the sign and ribboning cracks to all four corners of the frame. His surprise held him motionless for a moment, and then he heard a voice calling from across the street, "Clear out of there, son."

That makes four times, Johnny thought resignedly, and he glanced across the street and saw Alec Barr, several men clotted around him, looking his way.

Johnny went on and turned into the newspaper office and it was like walking into a dark cave. The lamp was extinguished.

And then he saw the dim forms of Cassie Melaven and her father back of the railing beside the job press, and the reason for his errand came back to him with a rush. Walking through the gate, he began firmly, "I got a dollar owed—" and ceased talking and halted abruptly. There was a six-shooter in Dan Melaven's hand hanging at his side. Johnny looked at it, and then raised his glance to Melaven's face and found the man watching him with a bitter amusement in his eyes. His glance shuttled to Cassie, and she was looking at him as if she didn't see him, and her face seemed very pale in that gloom. He half gestured toward the gun and said, "What's that for?"

"A little trouble, bub," Melaven said mildly. "Come back for your money?"

"Yeah," Johnny said slowly.

Suddenly it came to him, and he wheeled and looked out through the broken window and saw Alec Barr across the street in conversation with two men, his own hands, Johnny supposed. That explained the shot that wakened him. A little trouble.

He looked back at Melaven now in time to hear him say to Cassie, "Give him his money."

Cassie came past him to the desk and pulled open a drawer and opened the cash box. While she was doing it, Johnny strolled soberly over to the desk. She gave him the dollar and he took it, and their glances met. *She's been crying*, he thought, with a strange distress.

"That's what I tried to tell you," Cassie said. "We didn't want to take your money, but you wouldn't have it. That's why I was so mean."

"What's it all about?" Johnny asked soberly.

"Didn't you read the paper?"

Johnny shook his head in negation, and Cassie said dully, "It's right there on page one. There's a big chunk of Government land out on Artillery Creek coming up for sale. Alec Barr wanted it, but he didn't want anybody bidding against him. He knew pa would have to publish a notice of sale. He tried to get pa to hold off publication of the date of sale until it would be too late for other bidders to make it. Pa was to get a piece of the land in return for the favor, or money. I guess we needed it all right, but pa told him no."

Johnny looked over at Melaven, who had come up to the rail now and was listening. Melaven said, "I knew Barr'd be in today with his bunch, and they'd want a look at a pull sheet before the press got busy, just to make sure the notice wasn't there. Well, Cassie and Dad Hopper worked with me all last night to turn out the real paper, with the notice of sale and a front-page editorial about Barr's proposition to me, to boot."

"We got it printed and hid it out in the shed early this morning," Cassie explained.

Melaven grinned faintly at Cassie, and there was a kind of open admiration for the job in the way he smiled. He said to Johnny now, "So what you saw in the forms this mornin' was a fake, bub. That's why Cassie didn't want your money. The paper was already printed." He smiled again, that rather proud smile. "After you'd gone, Barr came in. He wanted a pull sheet and we gave it to him, and he had a man out front watching us most of the morning. But he pulled him off later. We got the real paper out of the shed onto the Willow Valley stage, and we got it delivered all over town before Barr saw it."

Johnny was silent a moment, thinking this over. Then he nodded toward the window. "Barr do that?"

"I did," Melaven said quietly. "I reckon I can keep him out until someone in this town gets the guts to run him off."

Johnny looked down at the dollar in his hand and stared at it a moment and put it in his pocket. When he looked up at Cassie, he surprised her watching him, and she smiled a little, as if to ask forgiveness.

Johnny said, "Want any help?" to Melaven, and the man looked at him thoughtfully and then nodded. "Yes. You can take Cassie home."

"Oh, no," Cassie said. She backed away from the desk and put her back against the wall, looking from one to the other. "I don't go. As long as I'm here, he'll stay there."

"Sooner or later, he'll come in," Melaven said grimly. "I don't want you hurt."

"Let him come," Cassie said stubbornly. "I can swing a wrench better than some of his crew can shoot."

"Please go with him."

Cassie shook her head. "No, pa. There's some men left in this town. They'll turn up."

Melaven said "Hell," quietly, angrily, and went back into the shop. Johnny and the girl looked at each other for a long moment, and Johnny saw the fear in her eyes. She was fighting it, but she didn't have it licked, and he couldn't blame her. He said, "If I'd had a gun on me, I don't reckon they'd of let me in here, would they?"

"Don't try it again," Cassie said. "Don't try the back either. They're out there."

Johnny said, "Sure you won't come with me?"

"I'm sure."

"Good," Johnny said quietly. He stepped outside and turned up-street, glancing over at Barr and the three men with him, who were watching him wordlessly. The man leaning against the building straightened up and asked, "She comin' out?"

"She's thinkin' it over," Johnny said.

The man called across the street to Barr, "She's thinkin' it over," and Johnny headed obliquely across the wide street toward the Elite. *What kind of a town is this, where they'd let this happen?* he thought angrily, and then he caught sight of Gus Irby standing under the wooden awning in front of the Elite, watching the show. Everybody else was doing the same thing. A man behind Johnny yelled, "Send her out, Melaven," and Johnny vaulted up onto the boardwalk and halted in front of Gus.

"What do you aim to do?" he asked Gus.

"Mind my own business, same as you," Gus growled, but he couldn't hold Johnny's gaze.

There was shame in his face, and when Johnny saw it his mind was made up. He shouldered past him and went into the Elite and saw it was empty. He stepped behind the bar now and, bent over so he could look under it, slowly traveled down it. Right beside the beer taps he found what he was looking for. It was a sawed-off shotgun and he lifted it up and broke it and saw that both barrels were loaded. Standing motionless, he thought about this now, and presently he moved on toward the back and went out the rear door. It opened onto an alley, and he turned left and went up it, thinking, *It was brick, and the one next to it was painted brown, at least in front.* And then he saw it up ahead, a low brick store with a big loading platform running across its rear.

He went up to it, and looked down the narrow passageway he'd remembered was between this building and the brown one beside it. There was a small areaway here, this end cluttered with weeds and bottles and tin cans. Looking through it he could see a man's elbow and segment of leg at the boardwalk, and he stepped as noiselessly as he could over the trash and worked forward to the boardwalk.

At the end of the areaway, he hauled up and looked out and saw Alec Barr some ten feet to his right and teetering on the edge of the high boardwalk, gun in hand. He was engaged in low conversation with three other men on either side of him. There was a supreme insolence in the way he exposed himself, as if he knew Melaven would not shoot at him and could not hit him if he did.

Johnny raised the shotgun hip high and stepped out and said quietly, "Barr, you goin' to throw away that gun and get on your horse or am I goin' to burn you down?"

The four men turned slowly, not moving anything except their heads. It was Barr whom Johnny watched, and he saw the man's bold baleful eyes gauge his chances and decline the risk, and Johnny smiled. The three other men were watching Barr for a clue to their moves.

Johnny said "Now," and on the heel of it he heard the faint clatter of a kicked tin can in the areaway behind him. He lunged out of the areaway just as a pistol shot erupted with a savage roar between the two buildings.

Barr half turned now with the swiftness with which he lifted his gun across his front, and Johnny, watching him, didn't even raise the shotgun in his haste; he let go from the hip. He saw Barr rammed off the high boardwalk into the tie rail, and heard it crack and splinter and break with the big man's weight, and then Barr fell in the street out of sight.

The three other men scattered into the street, running blindly for the opposite sidewalk. And at the same time, the men who had been standing in front of the buildings watching this now ran toward Barr, and Gus Irby was in the van. Johnny poked the shotgun into the areaway and without even taking sight he pulled the trigger and listened to the bellow of the explosion and the rattling raking of the buckshot as it caromed between the two buildings. Afterward, he turned down street and let Gus and the others run past him, and he went into the Elite.

It was empty, and he put the shotgun on the bar and got himself a glass of water and stood there drinking it, thinking, *I feel some different, but not much.*

He was still drinking water when Gus came in later. Gus looked at him long and hard, as he poured himself a stout glass of whisky and downed it. Finally, Gus said, "There ain't a right thing about it, but they won't pay you a bounty for him. They should."

Johnny didn't say anything, only rinsed out his glass.

"Melaven wants to see you," Gus said then.

"All right." Johnny walked past him and Gus let him get past him ten feet, and then said, "Kid, look."

Johnny halted and turned around and Gus, looking sheepish, said, "About that there newspaper piece. That was meant to be a rawhide, but damned if it didn't backfire on me."

Johnny just waited, and Gus went on. "You remember the man

that was standing this side of Barr? He works for me, runs some cows for me. Did, I mean, because he stood there all afternoon sickin' Barr on Melaven. You want his job? Forty a month, top hand."

"Sure," Johnny said promptly.

Gus smiled expansively and said, "Let's have a drink on it."

"Tomorrow," Johnny said. "I don't aim to get a reputation for drinkin' all day long."

Gus looked puzzled, and then laughed. "Reputation? Who with? Who knows——" His talk faded off, and then he said quietly, "Oh."

Johnny waited long enough to see if Gus would smile, and when Gus didn't, he went out. Gus didn't smile after he'd gone either.

QUESTIONS

1. The plots of many Western stories require a country in which there is no effective police officer, or in which the law is corrupt, or in which the hero himself represents the law. Which of these situations exists in this story?

2. Many short stories are told from the point of view of a single character. This selection, however, begins from the point of view of one character and then shifts to that of another. Who are the two characters, and when does the shift take place?

3. Why is it important to the story to establish that Gus is "a man with no truculence in him"?

4. Is there any relationship between Johnny's italicized thoughts (*"Damn, that's twice . . . . That's three times . . . . That makes four times."*) and the last sentence of the story?

5. The story of a boy who proves himself a man is one of the oldest plots in all literature. Young King Arthur, for instance, drew a sword from a stone when no other man could do so. How does Johnny prove himself a man? What recognition does he receive?

6. The prices and wages in this story are those of the last half of the nineteenth century. When they are compared to prices and wages of today, are they evidences of modern inflation? Or deflation?

ALLAN BOSWORTH

STAMPEDE

Nobody ever found out how Ma Collins managed to locate the camp that night before we threw the herd out on the long trail. There had been a heavy fog in the evening when we bedded down on the prairie maybe fifteen miles from San Antone, and at two o'clock in the morning it was still so thick you couldn't see your horse's ears. I know, because from midnight until two I rode my very first night herd, singing to the longhorns in a voice that hadn't decided whether to be soprano or baritone.

But the fog must have lifted just before daylight. Ed Schuler got up then to rustle breakfast. He went around the chuck wagon to get some wood, and the first thing I heard was when he let out a surprised whistle and came over by my bed to shake McQuiston's shoulder and tell him we had company. Bat McQuiston was the Bar 9 trail boss.

I wish I could make you see how everything was. Maybe the mornings were younger, those days, and the earth hadn't been scarred so much by plows and fences and roads; maybe at fifteen you see with clearer eyes. I raised my head from the saddle and smelled the dew-fresh dawn and the trampled grass, and a little breeze bringing the clean, sweet scent of cattle; and then I caught a whiff of mesquite-wood smoke and knew it was nearly breakfast time. Three or four big stars still blazed overhead, but it was getting light in the east above the dark rim of prairie. I rubbed dreams out of my eyes and looked that way under the wagon, and saw Ma Collins.

She was like an old-fashioned cutout, one of those silhouette pictures done in black against a pale gold background. She was sitting in a buggy, just watching the camp. Her sunbonnet came up to a starched peak against the sky, and her gaunt, patient shoulders made angles. The reins were half-hitched around the whip socket, as if she had been there a long time, waiting with her hands folded in her lap and the team of little Spanish mules asleep. It wasn't until Ed Schuler went back to put wood on the fire that she moved at all, and by then McQuiston was stamping into his boots and going out to see what she wanted.

"Mornin', ma'am!" he called. "Get yourself lost in the fog?"

"No, don't reckon I did," she said. Her voice was soft and tired. "Ain't this the Bar Nine outfit?"

"Yes'm, it is."

"And you're trailing these cows all the way to Dodge City?"

"Yes'm, if we can hold 'em together that long."

She gathered up her skirts and got down out of the buggy. "Well," she said, "I'm Ma Collins, and I'm going up the trail with you."

Bat McQuiston's eyes kind of bugged out. The way she said that, you'd have thought she was talking about hitching up and driving to San Antone for a couple of yards of calico.

"Well, now, that's quite a ways," McQuiston said, laughing. "But we'd be proud to have you come into camp and have a cup of coffee."

Ma reached into the buggy and lifted out a rusty bucket with a little green shrub growing in it. "I'm going," she said. "If you don't think it's all right for me to go, you just ask Sam Murray."

Sam Murray owned the Bar 9 and a couple of other Texas brands, but he was already up the trail about ten days ahead of us, and there wasn't any way of asking him. McQuiston started getting uneasy.

"Sam ain't here, ma'am," he said. "But you just couldn't hardly go. It ain't no place for a lady. There's rivers to cross, and dry drives, and maybe Comanche trouble. Besides—"

"I know all about them things," Ma Collins told him, starting for the wagon. "Could you spare a little water for my rosebush? The sun was mighty hot on it yesterday."

Everybody was up by then, and maybe enjoying seeing Bat McQuiston run into something he couldn't boss around. I forget some of the names; we had nearly twenty-five hundred head of cattle, and there were about ten men besides the wrangler and the cook. The wrangler was Scotty Andrews, and I remember Curly Spence and Bill Ike Parrish and Tennessee Jones. There were myself—Bud Rogers— and Dan Robie, who was a colored boy about nineteen, and one of the best riders I ever saw. It was a long time ago.

Ma Collins was about forty; her hair was turning gray, and she had that dried-up, sun-and-wind look of the frontier woman. She didn't take much notice of anybody after the introductions. She watched the fire, not moving when the wind changed and smoke blew her way. But she picked up the bucket holding her little rosebush and put it behind the bedding roll out of the smoke.

Ed Schuler poured her a tin cup of coffee, and Bat McQuiston watched her and started walking up and down. It was nearly sunup, and the cattle were beginning to move out and graze. They were headed in the direction we wanted them to go, but they were spreading out too much.

"Now, Miz Collins," McQuiston said firmly, "we're just goin' to have to get movin'. I'm mighty sorry, but we can't take you along."

"I'll drive my own team," Ma Collins said, sipping the coffee. "I've got bedding, and a little tent to put up if the weather gets bad."

"I mean," McQuiston said, "we just can't——We—well, why do you want to go up the trail, anyway? Like I said, it ain't no place for a lady!"

"I reckon I can stand it," Ma said. "And you couldn't stop me if I just tagged along."

McQuiston poured himself a cup of coffee and choked on it. He got red in the face and told Curly and Dan Robie and me to saddle up and relieve the last night herd and string the cattle out. Ma Collins looked up at me as I went by.

"How old are you, child?" she asked.

I could see Curly grinning, and knew they'd all hooraw me about being called that. I blushed and told her I was going on sixteen.

"Does your mother know you're going up the trail?"

"Yes'm," I said. "I had to do some tall talking. She didn't want me to go yet, but pa said I had to go sometime."

"Yes," Ma Collins said. "Yes, they all have to go, sooner or later. Seems like it's in their blood."

Curly and Dan Robie and I went out to the remuda to saddle up, and McQuiston came that way, cussing softly behind his hand.

"Be careful, Bat," Curly told him. "This child will hear you!"

McQuiston didn't think he was funny. "What can I do?" he asked. "I'm bossin' this outfit, but she ain't on the payroll, and she's bound and determined to tag along. What could anybody do?"

"You tell me," Curly grinned. "I hear it's a free country."

He was right; it was mighty free and wide and wild, and it belonged to any man who could saddle a horse and ride. But it wasn't a woman's country for a thousand miles in the direction we were headed. We didn't expect to see another woman until we hit Dodge City.

"What you suppose she wants to go for?" I asked Dan Robie, when we fell back in the drag.

Dan was pretty smart. He'd been up the trail twice, and to New Orleans, and all over. Like I said, he was one of the best riders I ever saw, and he went to a lot of trouble to teach me things about handling cattle. I know, now, that Dan turned to me out of loneliness; the others didn't have much to do with him on account of his color. Sometimes I caught him watching their horseplay around camp with a wistful, pleading look, like a dog's. I always liked him without thinking about the color of his skin.

"There's a man somewhere up there," Dan said. "A woman goes traipsin' way off somewhere like this, there's always a man."

I thought about that awhile, and decided that whoever the man was, he just might as well give up. There was something about the set of Ma's shoulders that showed she was going to hang on till she found him. It wasn't spunk exactly, or even determination; it was just the kind of slow patience that wears mountains down.

Ma Collins was there that night when we made camp at Leon Springs, and there wasn't anything McQuiston could do except ask her to sit down and have supper with us. Then, later, he told Dan Robie to help her set up that little tent, because it looked like it might rain.

"She'll get tired," McQuiston predicted. "She'll get enough of it a long time before we get to Red River."

But she didn't show any signs of getting tired. I remember our watering places; we camped on the Cibolo, and at Boerne, and we hit the Guadalupe at Comfort, and went on up to the Llano and the San Saba. Ma Collins was always there when we bedded the herd down for the night.

It wasn't any kind of trick for a buggy and a team of mules to keep up with the outfit. Bat McQuiston aimed to get the Bar 9's to Dodge City weighing more than they did when we slapped the trail brand on them, and we averaged about ten miles a day. It took a little while to get the herd trail-broke; after that a couple of big, powerful line-backed steers from the Nueces brush stepped out every morning and took the lead, and the others fell into accustomed places all down the line. I tell you, a big herd of Texas longhorns on the trail was something to see. It was like an army on the march, with dust clouds for banners and the gleam of proud, sun-tipped horns for bayonets. Sometimes the cattle would be strung out for a mile or more, threading the hill passes or winding through the post-oak country; sometimes, where the grass was good, we let them bunch and feed on a wide front.

In open country Ma Collins sometimes drove her buggy along at the side of the herd, and McQuiston worried for a while because none of those longhorns had ever seen a buggy before. But they got used to it, and we didn't have any trouble on that account. More often, she drove behind the drag, and I felt sorry for her then, because she got all the dust.

But when she drove there, I saw her more often. Dan Robie and I brought up the drag—Dan because he was a colored boy, and I because I was so green that Curly Spence was always asking McQuiston how many trading stamps he swapped for me. The drag was the orneriest spot in the herd; we not only had to eat dust but all the mean scalawag steers dropped back there and kept lagging or trying to break away into the brush.

But I wouldn't have traded jobs with President Rutherford B.

Hayes. I was learning how to handle cattle; I was out in the open and riding a horse. And at night there was always the shine of firelight on a wind-flapped wagon tarp, and a million stars overhead, and sometimes another campfire away out on the prairie, as if one of the stars had fallen out of the sky. There was always somebody to tell a big windy in the evening before we turned in to our bedding rolls, although for the first few nights Ma Collins was with us the boys acted mighty bashful.

She didn't talk much. I thought it was because McQuiston was still letting her know that she wasn't exactly welcome, even if he did have to invite her to supper with us. Then, after the boys got used to having her around, and watching their talk and maybe even slicking up a little because she was there, she would sometimes act like she was a thousand miles away. The night we camped by the Colorado, Ed Schuler got out his old fiddle and played a few tunes, and The Parson, who had a good tenor voice, started singing. I remember that The Parson was singing When the Work's All Done This Fall when Ma got up all of a sudden and went to her tent.

McQuiston had stepped out of the firelight to look at the sky for weather signs, and he saw her go. He came back into the camp, pitching mad.

"One of you jaspers say somethin' you hadn't ought to say before a lady?" he demanded. "Talk up! The one that done it is fired!"

"Now, don't get ringy," Bill Ike Parrish told him. "We don't know what made her leave, unless she couldn't stand The Parson's warbling."

McQuiston looked around and cooled off a little. He said, "Dan, you go out to her tent and ask her if she'd like a cup of coffee before she goes to bed. And here, take her some water for that rosebush. I didn't see her water it tonight."

I wasn't but fifteen, but I knew how it was with Bat McQuiston. He was a big man, and tough as whitleather, and they said he had killed a couple of men once in a saloon fight at Laredo. But under his hide he was soft as a baby.

Only he wasn't going to let anybody think he was soft. He unrolled his bed tarp, and said, "Of course we can't have her tagging along all through the Indian Nation, nursing that rosebush. I've seen the time on this trail when there ain't water enough to wet your tongue." He sat down, grunting as he pulled off his boots. "So I wrote a letter to Sam Murray, in care of Doan's store. Told him we're goin' to have to send her packin' back home."

He fixed his saddle for a pillow and slid into his tarp. I saw Dan Robie come back from Ma Collins' tent and put his bed down where he always slept, a little way out from everybody else. The lantern light winked out in her tent, and there wasn't anything but the dying fire and the stars; there was just the lonesome sound of the wind, and now and then a few notes of the night herders' song to the longhorn cattle.

Clear Fork—that was where they ran. It came up a thunder-and-lightning storm about one o'clock in the morning. Dan Robie and Tennessee Jones had the night herd, and they said one minute everything was peaceful, and the next there was a clap of thunder, and hell just blew the lid off. It was my first stampede; I woke up to feel the whole earth shaking and to hear McQuiston yelling for us to hit the saddle.

I didn't have my boots on before the herd came right through the edge of the camp. It began to rain, and there was a zigzag streak of lightning flashing clear across the sky, mighty low, and I saw the cattle like a dark rolling wave, splitting into two streams past Ma Collins' buggy and her little tent. The tent was under a post-oak tree that night, and I reckon that helped; the leaders went around it all right, but the press of cattle behind and on both sides pushed some of the steers right into the tent and wrecked it.

You hear a lot about cowboys getting killed in stampedes, but nine times out of ten it was when horses fell and rolled on their riders, and not because of getting trampled by the steers. A longhorn would always try to jump over anything lying on the ground. McQuiston knew that, but he was scared to death until the cattle thinned out and another flash of lightning showed Ma Collins hugging the tree.

He ran out and grabbed her by the arm. "Get in the wagon and stay there till we get back!" he ordered.

"You wait a minute!" Ma said. She jerked her arm free and began digging around in what was left of the tent. "You wait till I find my rosebush!"

"The hell with your rosebush!" McQuiston yelled. But he couldn't boss her around. He said, "Excuse me, ma'am. . . . Come on, boys!"

They ran for an hour, and it was nine o'clock in the morning before we rounded up all the scattered bunches and tallied them again. We got them pointed north, and went back to get the wagon. Ed Schuler was in the saddle like the rest of us, so nobody expected anything but coffee for breakfast.

But it was there. Hot biscuits and bacon and blackstrap sorghum molasses. And when Ma Collins learned nobody was hurt, I saw her smile for the first time.

What could you do with a woman like that? I think McQuiston was ready to give up trying to send her home, because he said if she wasn't with the Bar 9 she'd just tie onto some other outfit. But he swore he wasn't going to be bothered helping her cross the Red River. From what we heard, it was running bank full, and there would be trouble enough floating the chuck wagon over.

I remember our watering places, because in those days you

measured progress up the trail by the rivers crossed and left behind—the shining rivers with the singing names. Elm Creek and Brazos, Pony Creek, Wichita and Beaver, Paradise and Pease—all running clear before plows broke the plains, all washing the dust from hoofs and wheels. And I remember the Red, biggest of all, gleaming like a pink ribbon in the sunshine when we sighted it from away off.

We camped a couple of miles out from Doan's store, which was a kind of disappointment to me, because at that time it was made of buffalo hides and wagon tarps stretched over a frame of poles. There were three other herds waiting for the river to drop before they tried to cross, and one of them was Sam Murray's other northbound outfit.

He rode out to our camp that first evening. Dusk was gray, and it began to rain slowly, and you could smell wet hides and saddle leather, and wood smoke beaten down to earth. Sam Murray got down from his horse and came into the firelight, a big man wearing the same kind of flop-brimmed hat and ducking jumper and scuffed boots as anybody else, although I reckon he was worth a couple of hundred thousand dollars.

"Howdy, boys," he said, and tipped his hat to Ma Collins. "Howdy, Mary."

She spoke to him, and then there was a silence, and everybody felt awkward and maybe afraid that he was going to tell Ma she had to go home. It was somehow worse because of the rain; the Bar 9 camp was a good place to be, with its warmth and flickering light, and the music of rain on the wagon tarp Ed Schuler had rigged as a fly.

"Well," Ma Collins said, "I haven't got so far to go now. You tell him I can go on with the outfit, Sam."

"Well, I sure wouldn't try to stop you, after what happened," Sam Murray said gently. "But you hadn't ought to have come, Mary. What good will it do?"

Ma Collins looked out beyond the shelter of the fly, where that rusty bucket was setting so the rosebush would get the rain.

"I want to see my boy's grave," she said. "I want to see it just once."

We heard her, and all of us were afraid to look at her. But she wasn't going to cry, because she was past all crying. We heard what she said, and then there was just the sound of the rain on the wagon tarp for a minute, and the hiss and sputter of wet wood in the fire.

"It ain't right for him to be buried up there so far away from home," she went on in that tired voice. "In such a lonesome place. They told me it was out on the prairie, miles from anywhere."

"Yes'm," Sam Murray said.

"I brought a little rosebush along, Sam. From the yard at home. He used to like the roses there. He was a good boy."

Sam Murray cleared his throat. "A fine boy, Mary. But . . . well, it's been two years . . . nearly three. I ain't so sure you could find his—the place, I mean."

"It's just across the Cimarron, they said. Just on the other side of the Cimarron crossing."

"I know," Sam nodded. "But nesters have come into that country. The crossing ain't in the same place now. Every time you drive a herd up north the fences and the plowed fields have pushed the trail a little farther west."

Ma Collins folded her hands in her lap, and I couldn't see her face for the shadow of her sunbonnet. I looked at McQuiston, and knew he was sorry he had written that letter.

"I'll find it," Ma said patiently. "I've scrimped and saved for two years to make this trip, and I'll feel better when the rosebush is planted there. It's a hardy variety, and it'll grow."

Nobody on the trail knew how to handle cattle any better than Bat McQuiston. He let the other outfits throw their herds across the river first, and they lost some steers doing it. McQuiston waited a week after the rain stopped, and we cut dry cottonwood timbers and lashed them to the running gear of the wagon and the buggy, so they could be rafted over. And then the day before the crossing he saw to it that the herd wasn't watered at all.

That way the longhorns came down to the river thirsty, and McQuiston timed it to get them there in the heat of the day. The water was down some, showing scarred red banks and the pale roots of undermined trees on both sides, but it was still mighty wide, with flecks of foam the size of wagon sheets riding along with the current. Dan Robie said that was because the snow was melting way up in New Mexico.

Dan and I didn't see the lead steers hit the river, but we kept the drag closing in, and everything seemed to be working out smoothly enough. By the time we got to the riverbank, there was the wagon already on the other side, and Ma Collins' buggy beside it; and the Bar 9's were swimming across in an almost unbroken stream that bent with the current and came out in Indian Territory a couple of hundred yards below.

Even the scalawags were thirsty enough to wade belly-deep into the water. Curly Spence and Tennessee Jones were there to help, and we crowded the steers in the shallows, slapping ropes' ends on their rumps. They tried to turn and couldn't. They began to swim.

Dan put his horse just downstream from mine, and I felt better because I knew he was keeping an eye on me. He said, "Give your horse his head, and slip your feet out of the stirrups. If you have to, you can slide back into the water and hold on to his tail."

The Red River spilled cold into my boots and I said good-by to Texas.

"A couple more big ones to cross, Bud!" Curly called over to me. And then he yelled, "Look out for that tree, kid!"

I remember how it looked. It was all like a dream from then on—like a nightmare that won't end. It was a great big cottonwood, drifting down the current, trunk first, like a battering ram, and at the other end the branches fanned out, half of them submerged; and the whole tree was rolling a little. I didn't do a thing; I was too scared. But my horse got out of the way just by inches, and then the butt end of the trunk glanced against a swimming longhorn in a way that turned the whole tree. The current caught it, and it swung broadside and really started to roll.

Curly and Tennessee shouted a warning to Dan Robie, but there wasn't time for him to get clear. The nightmare was frozen now. I can still see Dan's face, and that pleading in his eyes, and then a submerged limb tangled with his horse's legs, throwing him on his side. We saw Dan spill out of the saddle, and a branch as thick as a man's leg swung over and slapped hard against the back of his neck.

He went under. Tennessee and Curly had their ropes out, and Curly made a throw, but the whole tree was in between and he only snagged a limb. I saw Dan's horse swimming toward the shore, and then Dan came up a long way downriver, floating face down beside one of those big patches of foam. The nightmare broke and I began to cry like I was a baby.

There must have been hundreds of pitiful little buryings like that one, up and down the whole dusty, wind-swept reaches of the Texas cattle trail before the settlements came. So many things could happen to a man between the Nueces and Dodge City or Abilene; and when they did, there wasn't much anybody could do. We didn't have any lumber for a coffin; we wrapped Dan Robie in his bed tarp, like a sailor going to his last rest at sea, and we dug a shallow grave on the lonesome prairie.

The picture is still in my mind like it was yesterday: the longhorn cattle strung out and moving slowly with an undertone of complaining bawls and bellowings, and killdeers running along the bank of the Red River with shrill, mournful cries; and big Bat McQuiston standing in awkward embarrassment that amounted to shame as he tried to remember something out of the Bible. I remember the cloud shadows moving lazily across the grass, and the smell of freshly turned earth, and the way Tennessee and Curly put Dan down into the grave, wanting to be tender and wanting to get it over and done with.

The wind was whipping at the wagon tarp, slapping it against the bows; the wind was bending the prairie grass. And there was Ma Collins standing by McQuiston's side with the wind ruffling her calico dress and her sunbonnet framing her pinched face, and the old heartbreak hard and dry in her eyes. I knew then, and I know now, how many mothers of Texas boys went up the long trail without ever leaving home.

"Our Father—" It was McQuiston, and I had never heard his voice like that before. "Our Father, there ain't much we can say. You know what happened down here, and you know Dan was a mighty good hand. We're turning him into Your keeping, Amen."

Then there was just the murmur of the wind, and the first dry whisper of earth on Dan's bed tarp. And Ma Collins' tired voice asking, "Do you know where to write his folks?"

McQuiston shook his head. That was why he was ashamed; that was the reason all of us felt the same sense of guilt. We had lived with Dan Robie for a couple of months without ever really knowing him, without ever asking where his home was.

"No, ma'am," McQuiston said. "I don't know whether Dan had any folks or not."

We stood there, and Ed Schuler went away and came back with the end gate of the wagon. He said, "This is the only thing we got for a marker. I can whittle his name on it."

"We got to get moving," McQuiston said. He shifted his weight restlessly and looked up at the cattle scattering across the prairie to the north. "Bud, you and Bill Ike—"

"Wait a minute," said Ma Collins. She walked over to her buggy, with its wheels washed yellow again by the Red River, and came back, carrying the rosebush. She got down on her knees by the mound of fresh earth and scooped a little hole there with her patient hands, and all at once she began to cry. She had needed to cry for a long, long time.

McQuiston was kind of choked up himself. He said, "Bud, you and Bill Ike ride down by the river and drag up some cottonwoods. We'll have to make a picket fence to keep the cattle off."

It was morning before we moved the Bar 9's out on the trail again, into Indian Territory, where spring ran like a tide over the rolling prairies. When we got to the Cimarron and crossed it, we saw what was happening to the land, changing it so that it would never be the same, and we knew that the old trail and the wild, free ways were dying. We spent two days looking around the old crossing for something that would mark the grave of Ma Collins' boy. There wasn't anything but bare, dun fields, with furrows running where the longhorns used to walk.

But I don't think it mattered as much to Ma Collins any more. She had planted her Texas rose with loving hands, and watered it with a mother's tears. It was for her own boy, and for Dan Robie, and for every other gallant rider who ever went up the trail with the longhorn cattle. It would keep their memory green.

QUESTIONS

1. What effects does the author achieve by telling the story as it was experienced by a fifteen-year-old boy? How would the story be different if it were told by McQuiston, the trail boss, or by Ma Collins herself?

2. This is one of the very few works of Western fiction in which a black cowboy plays an important part. Yet we know that more than five thousand black cowboys rode the trails north from Texas during the thirty years after the Civil War. Why, then, are there so few black cowboys in Western fiction and film?

3. Much of Western fiction is nostalgic. How does the author of this story show his love of a vanished past?

4. What evidence of race discrimination among Texas cowboys is given in this story?

5. What does the stampede tell the reader about McQuiston? About Ma Collins? What do critics of fiction mean by saying that character is best shown in action?

THOMAS THOMPSON

GUN JOB

He was married in June and he gave up his job as town marshal the following September, giving himself time to get settled on the little ranch he bought before the snows set in. That first winter was mild, and now, with summer in the air, he walked down the main street of the town and thought of his own calf crop and of his own problems, a fine feeling after fifteen years of thinking of the problems of others. He wasn't Marshal Jeff Anderson any more. He was Jeff Anderson, private citizen, beholden to no man, and that was the way he wanted it.

He gave the town his quick appraisal, a tall, well-built man who was nearing forty and beginning to think about it, and every building and every alley held a memory for him, some amusing, some tragic. The town had a Sunday morning peacefulness on it, a peacefulness Jeff Anderson had worked for. It hadn't always been this way. He inhaled deeply, a contented man, and he caught the scent of freshly sprinkled dust that came from the dampened square of street in front of the ice-cream parlor. There was a promise of heat in the air and already the thick, warm scent of the tar weed was drifting down from the yellow slopes in back of the town. He kept to the middle of the street, enjoying his freedom, not yet free of old habits, and he headed for the marshal's office, where the door was closed, the shade drawn.

This was his Sunday morning pleasure, this brief tour of the town that had claimed him so long. It was the same tour he had made every Sunday morning for fifteen years; but now he could enjoy the luxury of knowing he was making it because he wanted to, not because it was his job. A man who had built a bridge or a building could sit back and look at his finished work, remembering the fun and the heartache that had gone into it, but he didn't need to chip away personally at its rust or take a pot of paint to its scars.

In front of the marshal's office Anderson paused, remembering it all, not missing it, just remembering; then he turned and pushed open the door, the familiarity of the action momentarily strong on him. The floor was worn and his own boot heels had helped wear it; the desk was scarred and some of those spur marks were as much his own as his own initials would have been. He grinned at the new marshal and said, "Caught any criminals lately?"

The man behind the desk glanced up, his face drawn, expressionless, his eyes worried. He tried to joke. "How could I?" he said. "You ain't been in town since last Sunday." He took one foot off the desk and kicked a straight chair toward Jeff. "How's the cow business?"

"Good," Jeff said. "Mighty good." He sat down heavily and stretched his long legs, pushed his battered felt hat back on his thinning, weather-bleached hair and made himself a cigarette. He saw the papers piled on the desk and glancing at the clock he knew it was nearly time to let the two or three prisoners exercise in the jail corridor. A feeling of well-being engulfed him. These things were another man's responsibility now, not Jeff Anderson's. "How's it with you, Billy?" he asked.

The answer came too quickly, the answer of a man who was nervous or angry, or possibly both. "You ought to know, Jeff. The mayor and the council came to see you, didn't they?"

Annoyance clouded Jeff Anderson's gray eyes. He hadn't liked the idea of the city fathers going behind the new marshal's back. If they didn't like the job Billy was doing they should have gone to Billy, not to Jeff. But that was typical of the city council. Jeff had known three mayors and three different councils during his long term in office and they usually ran to a pattern. A few complaints and they got panicky and started going off in seven directions at once. They seemed to think that because Jeff had recommended Billy for this job the job was still Jeff's responsibility— "They made the trip for nothing, Billy," Jeff said. "If you're worried about me wanting your job you can forget it. I told them that plain."

"They'll keep asking you, Jeff."

"They'll keep getting 'no' for an answer," Jeff said.

Billy Lang sat at his desk and stared at the drawn shade of the front window, the thumb of his left hand toying nervously with the badge on his calfskin vest. He was a small man with eternally pink cheeks and pale blue eyes. He wore a full, white mustache and there was a cleft in his chin. He was married and had five children, and most of his life he had clerked in a store. When Jeff Anderson recommended him for this job Billy took it because it paid more and because the town was quiet. But now there was trouble and Billy was sorry he had ever heard of the job. He said, "You can't blame them for wanting you back, Jeff. You did a good job."

There was no false modesty in Jeff Anderson. He had done a good job here and he knew it. He had handled his job exactly the way he felt it should be handled and he had backed down to no one. But it hadn't been all roses, either. He grinned. "Regardless of what a man does, there's some who won't like it."

"Like Hank Fetterman?"

Jeff shrugged. Hank Fetterman was a cattleman. Sometimes Hank got the idea that he ought to take this town over and run it the way he once had. Hank hadn't gotten away with it when Jeff was marshal. Thinking about it now, it didn't seem to matter much to Jeff one way or the other, and it was hard to remember that his fight with Hank Fetterman had once been important. It had been a long time ago and things had changed— "Hank's not a bad sort," Jeff said.

"He's in town," Billy Lang said. "Did you know that?"

Jeff felt that old, familiar tightening of his stomach muscles, the signal of trouble ahead. He inhaled deeply, let the smoke trickle from his nostrils, and the feeling went away. Hank Fetterman was Jeff Anderson's neighbor now and Jeff was a rancher, not a marshal. "I'm in town too," he said. "So are fifty other people. There's no law against it."

"You know what I mean, Jeff," Billy Lang said. "You talked to Rudy Svitac's boy."

Jeff moved uneasily in his chair. Billy Lang was accusing him of meddling, and Jeff didn't like it. Jeff had never had anything to do with the marshal's job since his retirement, and he had promised himself he never would. It was Billy's job, and Billy was free to run it his own way. But when a twelve-year-old kid who thought you were something special asked you a straight question you gave him a straight answer. It had nothing to do with the fact that you had once been a marshal—

"Sure, Billy," Jeff said. "I talked to Rudy's boy. He came to see me about it just the way he's been coming to see me about things ever since he was big enough to walk. The kid needs somebody to talk to, I guess, so he comes to me. He's not old-country, like his folks. He was born here; he thinks American. I guess it's hard for the boy to understand them. I told him to have his dad see you, Billy."

"He took your advice," Billy Lang said. "Three days ago." He turned over a paper. "Rudy Svitac came in and swore out a warrant against Hank Fetterman for trespassing. He said his boy told him it was the thing to do."

Jeff had a strange feeling that he was suddenly two people. One was Jeff Anderson, ex-marshal, the man who had recommended Billy Lang for this job. As such, he should offer Billy some advice right here and now. The other person was Jeff Anderson, private citizen, a man with a small ranch and a fine wife and a right to live his own life. And that was the Jeff Anderson that was important. Jeff Anderson, the rancher, grinned. "Hank pawin' and bellerin' about it, is he?"

"I don't know, Jeff," Billy Lang said. "I haven't talked to Hank about it. I'm not sure I'm going to."

Jeff glanced quickly at the new marshal, surprised, only half believing what he had heard. He had recommended Billy for this job because he figured he and Billy thought along the same lines. Surely Billy knew that if you gave Hank Fetterman an inch he would take a mile—

He caught himself quickly, realizing suddenly that it was none of his business how Billy Lang thought. There were plenty of business-men in town who had argued loudly and openly that Jeff Anderson's methods of law enforcement had been bad for their cash registers. They had liked the old days when Hank Fetterman was running things and the town was wide open. Maybe they wanted it that way again. Every man was entitled to his own opinion and Billy Lang was entitled to handle his job in his own way. This freedom of thought and action that Jeff prized so highly had to work for everyone. He stood up and clapped a hand affectionately on Billy Lang's shoulder, anxious to change the conversation. "That's up to you, Billy," he said. "It's sure none of my affair." His grin widened. "Come on over to the saloon and I'll buy you a drink."

Billy Lang stared at the drawn shade, and he thought of Hank Fetterman, a man who was big in this country, waiting over at the saloon. Hank Fetterman knew there was a warrant out for his arrest; the whole town knew it by now. You didn't need to tell a thing like that. It just got around. And before long people would know who the law was in this town, Hank Fetterman or Billy Lang. Billy colored slightly, and there was perspiration on his forehead. "You go ahead and have your drink, Jeff," he said. "I've got some paperwork to do—" He didn't look up.

Jeff went outside and the gathering heat of the day struck the west side of the street and brought a resinous smell from the old boards of the false-fronted buildings. He glanced at the little church, seeing Rudy Svitac's spring wagon there, remembering that the church hadn't always been here; then he crossed over toward the saloon, the first business building this town had erected. He had been in a dozen such towns, and it was always the same. The saloons and the deadfalls came first, the churches and the schools later. Maybe that proved something. He didn't know. He had just stepped onto the board sidewalk when he saw the druggist coming toward him. The druggist was also the mayor, a sanctimonious little man, dried up by his own smallness. "Jeff, I talked to Billy Lang," the mayor said. His voice was thin and reedy. "I wondered if you might reconsider—"

"No," Jeff Anderson said. He didn't break his stride. He walked by the mayor and went into the saloon. Two of Hank Fetterman's riders were standing by the piano, leaning on it, and one of them was fumbling out a one-finger tune, cursing when he missed a note. Hank Fetterman was at the far end of the bar, and Jeff went and joined him. A little cow talk was good of a Sunday morning and Hank Fetterman knew cows. The two men at the piano started to sing.

Hank Fetterman's glance drifted lazily to Jeff Anderson and then away. His smile was fleeting. "How are you, Jeff?"

"Good enough," Jeff said. "Can I buy you a drink?"

"You twisted my arm," Hank Fetterman said.

Hank Fetterman was a well-built man with a weathered face. His brows were heavy and they pinched together toward the top, forming a perfect diamond of clean, hairless skin between his deep-set eyes. His voice was quiet, his manner calm. Jeff thought of the times he had crossed this man, enforcing the no-gun ordinance, keeping Hank's riders in jail overnight to cool them off— He had no regrets over the way he had handled Hank in the past. It had nothing to do with his feeling toward Hank now or in the future. He saw that Hank was wearing a gun and he smiled inwardly. That was like Hank. Tell him he couldn't do something and that was exactly what he wanted to do. "Didn't figure on seeing you in town," Jeff said. "Thought you and the boys were on roundup."

"I had a little personal business come up," Hank Fetterman said. "You know about it?"

Jeff shrugged. "Depends on what it is."

The pale smile left Hank Fetterman's eyes but not his lips. "Rudy Svitac is telling it around that I ran a bunch of my cows through his corn. He claims I'm trying to run him out of the country."

Jeff had no trouble concealing his feelings. It was a trick he had learned a long time ago. He leaned his elbows on the bar and turned his shot glass slowly in its own wet circle. Behind him Hank Fetterman's two cowboys broke into a boisterous, ribald song. The bartender wiped his face with his apron and glanced out the front window across toward the marshal's office. Jeff Anderson downed his drink, tossed the shot glass in the air and caught it with a down sweep of his hand. "You're used to that kind of talk, Hank." He set the shot glass on the bar.

"You're pretty friendly with the Svitacs, aren't you, Jeff?" Hank Fetterman asked. He was leaning with his back to the bar, his elbows behind him. His position made the holstered gun he wore obvious.

Again, just for a moment, Jeff Anderson was two people. He remembered the man he wanted to be. "I don't reckon anybody's very friendly with the Svitacs," he said. "They're hard to know. I think a lot of their boy. He's a nice kid."

Slowly the smile came back into Hank Fetterman's amber eyes. He turned around and took the bottle and poured a drink for himself and one for Jeff. "That forty acres of bottom land you were asking me about for a calf pasture," he said. "I've been thinking about it. I guess I could lease it to you all right."

"That's fine, Hank," Jeff Anderson said. "I can use it." He doffed his glass to Hank and downed his drink. It didn't taste right but he downed it anyway. The two cowboys started to scuffle and one of them collided with a table. It overturned with a crash.

"Please, Hank," the bartender said. "They're gonna get me in trouble—" His voice trailed off and his eyes widened. A man had come through the door. He stood there, blinking the bright sun out of his eyes. Jeff Anderson felt his heart start to pump heavily, slowly, high in his chest. "Morning, Mr. Svitac," the bartender mumbled.

Rudy Svitac stood in the doorway, a thick, dull man with black hair and brows that met across the bridge of his nose and a forehead that sloped. Jeff saw the rusty suit the man wore on Sundays, the suit that had faint soil stains on the knees because this man could not leave the soil alone, even on Sundays. He had to kneel down and feel the soil with his fingers, feeling the warmth and the life of it; for the soil was his book and his life and it was the only thing he understood completely and perhaps the only thing that understood him. He looked at Jeff, not at Hank Fetterman. "Is no good," Rudy Svitac said. "My son says I must talk to Billy Lang. I talk to Billy Lang but he does nothing. Is no good."

A thick silence settled in the room and the two cowboys who had been scuffling quit it now and stood there looking at the farmer. Hank Fetterman said, "Say what's on your mind, Svitac."

"You broke my fence," Rudy Svitac said. "You drive your cows in my corn and spoil my crop. All winter I wait to plant my crop and now is grow fine and you drive your cows in."

"Maybe you're mistaken, Svitac," Hank Fetterman said.

"My boy says is for judge to decide," Rudy Svitac said. "My boy tell me to go to Billy Lang and he will make a paper and judge will decide. My boy says is fair. Is America." Rudy Svitac stared unblinkingly. He shook his head slowly. "Is not so. I want my money. You broke my fence."

"You're a liar, Svitac," Hank Fetterman said. He moved away from the bar, slowly. He looked steadily at Jeff Anderson, then he glanced across the street toward the marshal's office. The door was still closed, the shade still drawn. Hank Fetterman smiled. He walked forward and gripped Rudy Svitac by the shirt front. For a moment he held the man that way, pulling him close, then he shoved and Rudy Svitac stumbled backward, out through the door, and his heel caught on a loose board in the sidewalk. He fell hard and for a long time he lay there, his dull, steady eyes staring at Jeff Anderson; then he turned and pushed himself up and he stood there looking at the dust on his old suit. He dropped his head and looked at the dust and he reached with his fingers and touched it. One of Hank Fetterman's cowboys started to laugh.

Across the street Jeff Anderson saw the blind on the window of the marshal's office move aside and then drop back into place, and immediately the door opened and Billy Lang was hurrying across the street. He came directly to Rudy Svitac and put his hand on Svitac's arm and jerked him around. "What's going on here?" Billy Lang demanded.

"Svitac came in looking for trouble," Hank Fetterman said. "I threw him out." Hank was standing in the doorway, directly alongside Jeff. For a brief moment Hank Fetterman's amber eyes met Jeff's gaze and Jeff saw the challenge. If you don't like it, do something about it, Hank Fetterman was saying. I want to know how you stand in this thing and I want to know now—

There was a dryness in Jeff Anderson's mouth. He had backed Hank Fetterman down before; he could do it again. But for what? One hundred and fifty dollars a month and a chance to get killed? Jeff had had fifteen years of that. A man had a right to live his own life. He looked up toward the church and the doors were just opening and people were coming out to stand on the porch, a small block of humanity suddenly aware of trouble. Jeff saw his wife Elaine, and he knew her hand was at her throat, twisting the fabric of her dress the way she did. He thought of the little ranch and of the things he and Elaine had planned for the future, and then he looked at Billy Lang and he knew Billy wasn't going to buck Hank Fetterman. So Jeff could make a stand, and it would be his own stand and he would be right back into it again just the way he had been for fifteen years. There was a thick line of perspiration on Jeff's upper lip. "That's the way it was, Billy," Jeff said.

He saw the quick smile cross Hank Fetterman's face, the dull acceptance and relief in Billy Lang's eyes. "Get out of town, Svitac," Billy Lang said. "I'm tired of your troublemaking. If Hank's cows got in your corn, it was an accident."

"Is no accident," Rudy Svitac said stubbornly. "Is for judge to decide. My son says—"

"It was an accident," Billy Lang said. "Make your fences stronger." He didn't look at Jeff. He glanced at Hank Fetterman and made his final capitulation. "Sorry it happened, Hank."

For a long moment Rudy Svitac stared at Billy Lang, at the star on Billy's vest, remembering that this star somehow had a connection with the stars in the flag. His son Anton had explained it, saying that Jeff Anderson said it was so, so it must be so. But it wasn't so. Hank Fetterman wasn't in jail. They weren't going to do anything about the ruined corn. The skin wrinkled between Rudy Svitac's eyes and there was perspiration on his face and his lips moved thickly but no sound came out. He could not understand. Thirteen years he had lived in this America, but still he could not understand. His son had tried to tell him the things they taught in the schools and the things Jeff Anderson said were so; but Rudy had his soil to work and his crops to plant, and when a man's back was tired his head did not work so good. Rudy Svitac knew only that if the jimson weed grew in the potato patch, you cut it out. And the wild morning-glory must be pulled out by the roots. No one came to do these things for a man. A man did these chores himself. He turned and walked solidly up the street toward where he had left his spring wagon by the church.

His wife Mary was there, a thick, tired woman who never smiled nor ever complained, and watching them, Jeff saw Anton, their son, a boy of twelve with an old man's face, a boy who had always believed every word Jeff Anderson said. Jeff saw young Anton looking down the street toward him and he remembered the boy's serious brown eyes and the thick, black hair that always stood out above his ears and lay rebelliously far down his neck. He remembered the hundred times he had talked to young Anton, patiently explaining things so Anton would understand, learning his own beliefs from the process of explaining them in simple words. And Anton would listen and then repeat to his parents in Bohemian, telling them this was so because Jeff Anderson said it was so. A bright boy with an unlimited belief in the future, in a household where there was no future. At times it seemed to Jeff almost as if God had looked upon Rudy and Mary Svitac and wanted to compensate in some way, so he had given them Anton.

Jeff saw Rudy reaching into the bed of the wagon. He saw Mary protest once; then Mary stood there, resigned, and now the boy had his father's arm and there was a brief struggle. The father shook the boy off, and now Rudy had a rifle and he was coming back down the street, walking slowly, down the middle of the street, the rifle in the crook of his arm.

Billy Lang moved. He met Rudy halfway, and he held out his hand. Jeff saw Rudy hesitate, take two more steps; and now Billy was saying something and Rudy dropped his head and let his chin lay on his chest. The boy came running up, and he took the rifle out of his father's hand and the crowd in front of the saloon expelled its breath. Jeff felt the triumph come into Hank Fetterman. He didn't need to look at the man. He could feel it.

The slow, wicked anger was inside Hank Fetterman, goaded by his ambition, his sense of power, and the catlike eagerness was in his eyes. "No Bohunk tells lies about me and gets away with it," he murmured. "No Bohunk comes after me with a gun and gets a second chance." His hand dropped and rested on the butt of his holstered six-shooter, and then the thumb of his left hand touched Jeff Anderson's arm. "Have a drink with me, Jeff?"

Jeff saw Elaine standing in front of the church and he could feel her anxiety reaching through the hot, troubled air. And he saw the boy there in the street, the gun in his hand, his eyes, bewildered, searching Jeff Anderson's face. "I reckon I won't have time, Hank," Jeff said. He walked up the street and now the feeling of being two people was strong in him, and there was a responsibility to Billy Lang that he couldn't deny. He had talked Billy into taking this job. It was a lonely job, and there was never a lonelier time than when a man was by himself in the middle of the street. He came close to Billy and he said, "Look, Billy, if you can take a gun away from one man you can take a gun away from another."

Billy looked at him. Billy's hands were shaking, and there was sweat on his face. "A two-year-old kid could have taken that gun away from Rudy, and you know it," he said. He reached up swiftly and unpinned the badge from his vest. He handed it across. "You want it?"

Jeff looked at that familiar piece of metal and he could feel the boy's eyes on him; and then he looked up and he saw Elaine there on the church porch, and he thought of his own dreams and of the plans he and Elaine had made for the future. "No, Billy," he said. "I don't want it."

"Then let it lay there," Billy Lang said. He dropped the badge into the dust of the street and hurried off, a man who had met defeat and accepted it, a man who could now go back to the clothing store and sell shirts and suits and overalls because that was the job he could do best. There was no indignity in Billy Lang's defeat. He had taken a role that he wasn't equipped to handle, and he was admitting it.

The boy said, "Mr. Jeff, I don't understand. You told me once—"

"We'll talk about it later, Anton," Jeff said. "Tell your dad to go home." He walked swiftly toward Elaine, swallowing against the sourness in his throat.

They drove out of town, Jeff and Elaine Anderson, toward their own home and their own life; and now the full heat of the day lay on the yellow slopes and the dry air crackled with the smell of dust and the cured grass, and the leather seat of the buggy was hot to the touch. A mile out of town Jeff stopped in the shade of a sycamore, and put up the top. He moved with dull efficiency, pausing momentarily to glance up as Hank Fetterman and his two riders passed on their way back to the ranch. He got back into the buggy and unwrapped the lines from the whipstock, and Elaine said, "If there's anything you want to say, Jeff—"

How could he say it? He couldn't, for the thing that was most in his mind had nothing to do with the matter at hand, and yet it had everything to do with it and it couldn't be explained. For he was thinking not of Hank Fetterman nor of Rudy Svitac, but of a colored lithograph, a town promotion picture that had once hung on every wall in this town. It showed wide, tree-lined streets, a tremendous town house with a flag half as large as the building flying from a mast, and lesser pennants, all mammoth, rippling from every building. Tiny men in cutaway coats and top hats leisurely strolled the avenues, and high-wheeled bicycles rolled elegantly past gleaming black victorias on the street of exclusive shops, while three sleek trains chuffed impatiently at the station. The railroad had put on a large land promotion around here when the road was first built. They had offered excursion trips free so that people could see the charms of New Canaan. They had handed out these lithos of the proposed town by the bushel. For a while New Canaan bustled with activity, and men bought town lots staked out in buffalo grass. And then the bubble burst and New Canaan settled back to what it was before—a place called Alkali at the edge of open cattle range. And young Anton Svitac had come to see Marshal Jeff Anderson for the first time and he had come about that picture—

Jeff remembered how the boy had looked that day, no more than six years old, his eyes too large for his old-man's face, his voice a mirror of the seriousness of thought that was so much a part of him. He had come to Jeff Anderson because Jeff Anderson was authority, and already young Anton had learned that in America authority was for everyone. "My father and mother do not understand," he said. "They do not speak English—" He unrolled the lithograph and put his finger on it, and then indicated the town of Alkali with a spread hand. "Is not the same," he said. "Is not so."

There were dreams in that boy's eyes, and they were about to be snuffed out; and Jeff Anderson didn't want it to happen. "Sure it's so, Anton," he heard himself saying. "It's not what it is today, it's what's going to be tomorrow, see?" He remembered the trouble he had had with the words, and then it was all there and he was telling it to Anton, telling it so this boy could go home and tell it to a work-bent man and a tired woman. "It's like America, see? Some of the things aren't right where you can touch them. Maybe some of the things you see are ugly. But the picture is always there to look at, and you keep thinking about the picture, and you keep working and making things better all the time, see? America isn't something you cut off like a piece of cake and say there it is. You keep on looking ahead to what it's going to be, and you keep working hard for it all the time, and you keep right on knowing it's going to be good because you've got the picture there to look at. You never stop working and say 'Now the job is done,' because it never is. You see that, Anton?"

The boy hadn't smiled. This was a big thing and a boy didn't smile about big things. He rolled the lithograph carefully. "I see," he said. "Is good. I will tell my father. We will keep the picture—"

Those were Jeff Anderson's thoughts, and how could he tell them, even to Elaine; for they had so little to do with the matter at hand and yet they had everything to do with it.

And Elaine, looking at her husband now, respected his silence. She remembered the three long years she was engaged to this man before they were married, years in which she had come to know him so well because she loved him so well. She knew him even better now. He was a man who was born to handle trouble, and a piece of tin on his vest or a wife at his side couldn't change the man he was born to be. She knew that and she didn't want to change him, but a woman couldn't help being what she was either and a woman could be afraid, especially at a time like this when there was so much ahead. She wanted to help him. "Maybe the Svitacs would be better off some place else," she said. "They never have made the place pay."

And that was exactly the same argument he had used on himself; but now, hearing it put into words, he didn't like the sound of it and he wanted to argue back. His voice was rough. "I reckon they look on it as home," he said. "The boy was born there. I reckon it sort of ties you to a place if your first one is born there."

She closed her eyes tightly, knowing that she was no longer one person but three, knowing the past was gone and the future would always be ahead, and it was her job to help secure that future as much as it was Jeff's job. She opened her eyes and looked at her husband, still afraid, for that was her way; but somehow prouder and older now. She folded her hands in her lap and the nervousness was gone. "I suppose we'll feel that way too, Jeff," she said. "It will always be our town after our baby is born here. I talked to the doctor yesterday—"

He felt the hard knot in the pit of his stomach. Then the coldness ran up his spine, and it was surprise and fear and a great swelling pride; and the feeling crawled up his neck, and every hair on his head was an individual hair, and the hard lump was in his throat— He moved on the seat, suddenly concerned for her comfort. "You feel all right, honey? Is there anything I can do?"

She didn't laugh at him any more than Anton had laughed at him that day in the office. She reached over and put her hand on his hand, and she smiled. As they drove down the lane the great pride was inside him, swelling against him until he felt that the seat of the buggy was no longer large enough to contain him. He helped her out of the buggy, his motions exaggerated in their kindness; and he took her arm and helped her up the front steps.

The coolness of the night still lingered in the little ranch house, for she had left the shades drawn; and now she went to the west windows and lifted the shades slightly, and she could see down the lane and across the small calf pasture where a thin drift of dust from their buggy wheels still lingered. There was a loneliness to Sunday after church, a stillness on the ranch. She glanced toward the barn and Jeff was unharnessing the mare and turning her into the corral, his back broad, his movements deliberate; and she saw him stand for a moment and look down the creek toward where Rudy Svitac's place cornered on Hank Fetterman's huge, unfenced range.

He came into the house later, into the cool living room, and he sat down in his big chair with a gusty sigh, and pulled off his boots and stretched his legs. "Good to be home," he said. "Good to have nothing to do." He raised his eyes to meet hers and they both knew he was lying. There was always something to do.

The moment he was sure she knew it was easier for him, but he still had to be positive that she understood that now it was different. Once he made this move there would be no turning back. She had to see that. An hour ago the town had been a town, nothing more; and if certain merchants felt business would be better with Hank Fetterman running things that was their business; and if Billy Lang wanted to go along with that thinking or go back to the clothing store, that was his business. Jeff Anderson hadn't needed the town. It was a place to shop and nothing more, and a man could shop as well with Hank Fetterman running things as he could with Jeff Anderson running things. But now, suddenly, that had changed, and there was tomorrow to think about, and it was exactly as he had explained it to Anton. Now, one day soon, Jeff Anderson might be explaining the same things to his own son; and a man had to show his son that he believed what he said, for if he didn't there was nothing left— "I was wrong about Billy Lang," Jeff Anderson said. "He's not going to stand up to Hank Fetterman."

She looked into his eyes and saw the deep seriousness and knew his every thought, and in this moment they were closer than they had ever been before; and she remembered thinking so many times of men and women who had been married for fifty years or more and of how they always looked alike. She said, "I have some curtains I promised Mary Svitac. Will you take them to her when you go?"

She didn't trust herself to say more and she didn't give him a lingering embrace as a woman might who was watching her man go off to danger; but she pretended to be busy and turned her head so that his lips just brushed her temple, and it was as casual as if he were only going to his regular day's work. "And thank her for the pickles," she said.

He stalked out of the house as if he didn't like having his Sunday disturbed by such woman nonsense, but when he was halfway to the barn his stride lengthened and she saw the stiffness of his back and the set of his shoulders. She sat down then and cried.

Anton, the boy, was pouring sour milk into a trough for the pigs when Jeff rode into the Svitac yard. The world could collapse but pigs had to be fed, and the boy was busy with his thoughts and did not see Jeff ride up. The door of the little house that was half soddy, half dugout, opened, and Mary Svitac called something in Bohemian. The boy looked up, startled, and Jeff smiled. "Will you ride my horse over and tie him in the shade, Anton?"

The flood of hope that filled the boy's eyes was embarrassing to a man, and Jeff dismounted quickly, keeping his head turned. He took the bundle of curtains from behind the saddle, and handed the reins to the boy; then walked on to the sod house where Mary Svitac stood, the shawl tied under her chin framing her round, expressionless face. He handed her the curtains. "Those pickles you gave us were fine, Mrs. Svitac. Elaine wanted me to bring these curtains over."

Mary Svitac let her rough fingers caress the curtain material. "I will give you all the pickles," she said. "We don't need the curtains. We don't stay here no more."

Rudy's thick voice came from the dark interior of the sod house; and now Jeff could see him there, sitting in a chair, a man dulled with work and disappointments, a man with a limited knowledge of English who had come to a new country with a dream, and found grasshoppers and drought and blizzards and neighbors who tried to drive him out. He looked up. "We don't stay," he said.

"Can I come in for a minute, Mrs. Svitac?" Jeff asked.

"I make coffee," she said.

He stooped to pass through the low door, and he took off his hat and sat down. Now that his eyes were accustomed to the darkness of the room, he saw the big lithograph there on the wall, the only decoration. Rudy Svitac stared unblinkingly at the floor, and a tear ran unashamed down the side of his nose. "We don't stay," he said.

"Sure, Rudy," Jeff Anderson said softly. "You stay."

Mary Svitac started to cry. There were no tears, for the land had taken even that away from her. There were just sobs—dry, choking sounds as she made the coffee—but they were woman sounds, made for her man; and she was willing to give up fifteen years of work if her man would be safe. "They will fight with us," she said. "They put cows in my Rudolph's corn. They tear down our fence. Soon they come to break my house. Is too much. Rudolph does not know fight. Rudolph is for plant the ground and play wiolin—"

"You stay, Rudy," Jeff Anderson said. "The law will take care of you. I promise you that."

Rudy Svitac shook his ponderous head. "Law is for Hank Fetterman," he said. "Is not for me."

"It's not so, Rudy," Jeff said. "You ask Anton. He knows."

"I ask Anton," Rudy Svitac said. "He says I am right. Law is for Hank Fetterman."

The boy came to the door and stood there, peering inside the room. His face was white, drawn with worry; but the hope was still in his eyes and a confidence was there. He didn't say anything. He didn't need to. Jeff could hear the sound of horses approaching—Jeff stood up and the feeling that was in him was an old and familiar feeling—a tightening of all his muscles. He went to the corner of the room and took Rudy Svitac's rifle from its place, and he levered in a shell, leaving the rifle at full cock. He stepped through the door then, and he put his hand on the boy's head. "You explain again to your father about the law," he said. "You know, Anton, like we talked before."

"I know," Anton Svitac said.

Jeff stepped swiftly through the door into the sunlight, and he saw Hank Fetterman and the same two riders who had been with him at the saloon coming toward the soddy. Only Hank was armed, and this could be handy later, when Hank talked to the judge. If we had expected trouble all three of us would have been armed, Judge, Hank Fetterman could say— They rode stiffly, holding their horses in. Jeff Anderson stood the cocked rifle by the fence post, placing it carefully. He pushed his hat back on his head and felt the sun on his back as he leaned there, one foot on a fence rail, watching the pigs eat the sour milk.

He knew when the riders were directly beside him, and he turned, his elbows leaning on the top rail of the fence behind him. His hat was pushed back but his face was in shade, for he had moved to where he was between the sun and the riders. Hank Fetterman said, "We're seeing a lot of each other, neighbor."

"Looks that way," Jeff said.

Hank Fetterman quieted his horse with a steady hand. His eyes never left Jeff Anderson's face. "I asked you once today if you was a friend of the Bohunks," he said. "Maybe I better ask it again."

"Maybe it depends on what you've got on your mind, Hank."

"The Bohunk's been eating my beef," Fetterman said. "I'm sick of it."

"You sure that's it, Hank?" Jeff asked quietly. "Or is it just that there's something that eats on you and makes you want to tear down things other folks have taken years to build up?"

There were small, white patches on either side of Hank Fetterman's mouth. "I said the Bohunk was eating my beef," Hank Fetterman said. His lips didn't move. "You doubting my word?"

"No," Jeff said. "I'm calling you a liar."

He saw the smoldering anger in Hank Fetterman, the sore, whiskey-nursed anger, and then the cattleman felt the full shock as the flat insult in Jeff's voice reached through to him. He cursed and half twisted in the saddle, blinking directly into the sun. "You forgetting you ain't a lawman any more?" he demanded.

"You decide, Hank," Jeff said.

They looked at each other, two men who had killed before and knew the meaning of it, two men who respected a gun and understood a gun. They said nothing and yet they spoke a silent language, and the man who had been a lawman said, I'm telling you to back down, Fetterman, and the man who wanted to be king said, You'll have to be big enough to make me. No actual words, and yet they knew; and they faced each other with muscles tense and faces drawn, and appeared at ease. Jeff Anderson had dealt himself into the game, and he had checked the bet.

Hank Fetterman saw the rifle by the post. He knew it was cocked and loaded. He wondered if Jeff Anderson was actually as quick and as accurate as men said he was; and because he was Hank Fetterman he had to know, because if he backed down now it was over for him and he knew it. He jerked his horse around, trying to avoid that direct glare of the sun, and he made his decision. His hand went for his gun.

Jeff Anderson saw the move coming. It seemed to him that he had plenty of time. He had placed the rifle carefully and now he held it, hip high, gripping it with one hand, tilting it up and pulling the trigger all at the same time. He didn't hear the sound of the rifle's explosion. You never did, he remembered; but he saw the thin film of gun smoke and he saw Hank Fetterman's mouth drop open, saw the man clawing at his chest. He didn't feel the sickness. Not yet—

Time passed as if through a film of haze, and nothing was real. Then they were gone and a canvas was stretched over the still form of Hank Fetterman and Rudy Svitac was whipping his team toward town to get the coroner. Now the sickness came to Jeff Anderson. He stood by the barn, trembling, and he heard the boy come up behind him. The boy said, "This was in the street in town, Mr. Anderson." The boy held out the tin star. "I told my father how the law was for everybody in America. Now he knows."

Jeff Anderson took the tin star and dropped it into his pocket.

Elaine saw him through the front window. She had been watching a long time and she had been praying, silently; and now she said, "Thank God," and she went and sat down, and she was like that when he came into the room. She wanted to ask him about it, but her throat kept choking; and then he was kneeling there, his head in her lap, and he was crying deep inside, not making a sound. "It's all right, Jeff," she said. "It's all right."

For that was the thing he had to know—that it was all right with her. He had to know that she loved him for the man he was and not for the man he had tried to become. He couldn't change any more than Billy Lang could change. She had never told him to take off his gun—not in words—but she had wanted him to, and he had understood, and he had tried. No woman could ask for greater love than that a man try to change himself. And no woman need be afraid when she had such love. She thought of young Anton Svitac and of her own son who was to be, and she was calm and sure.

A long time later she picked up Jeff's coat and laid it across her arm. The tin star fell to the floor. For a long time she looked at it, then she bent her knees and reached down and picked it up and put it back into the coat pocket. She went into the bedroom then and hung the coat carefully. From the bureau drawer she took a clean, white, pleated-front shirt and laid it out where he could see it. Marshal Jeff Anderson had worn a clean, white, pleated-front shirt to the office on Monday morning for as long back as she could remember. She didn't expect him to change his habits now.

QUESTIONS

1. Elaine Anderson knew that her husband was "a man born to handle trouble, and a piece of tin on his vest or a wife at his side couldn't change the man he was born to be." This statement is true of almost all heroes of Western stories. Is it true of many men you know?

2. At the end of the story, Anton Svitac says, "I told my father how the law was for everybody in America. Now he knows." Does the action of this story really support the boy's statement?

3. What is the effect of making the Svitacs foreigners who do not fully understand American customs and legal procedures?

4. Does Jeff Anderson's explanation (that America is a dream to work for) justify the lying lithograph published by the railroad to sell lots in the town of New Canaan?

5. Compare "Gun Job" with "The Tin Star" (p. 209). How are the two stories similar? How are they dissimilar?

DONALD HAMILTON

THE GUNS OF
WILLIAM LONGLEY

We'd been up north delivering a herd for old man Butcher the
summer I'm telling about. I was nineteen at the time. I was young and
big, and I was plenty tough, or thought I was, which amounts to the
same thing up to a point. Maybe I was making up for all the years of
being that nice Anderson boy, back in Willow Fork, Texas. When
your dad wears a badge, you're kind of obliged to behave yourself
around home so as not to shame him. But Pop was dead now, and this
wasn't Texas.

Anyway, I was tough enough that we had to leave Dodge City in
something of a hurry after I got into an argument with a fellow who, it
turned out, wasn't nearly as handy with a gun as he claimed to be. I'd
never killed a man before. It made me feel kind of funny for a couple
of days, but like I say, I was young and tough then, and I'd seen men I
really cared for trampled in stampedes and drowned in rivers on the
way north. I wasn't going to grieve long over one belligerent stranger.

It was on the long trail home that I first saw the guns one evening
by the fire. We had a blanket spread on the ground, and we were
playing cards for what was left of our pay—what we hadn't already
spent on girls and liquor and general hell-raising. My luck was in, and
one by one the others dropped out, all but Waco Smith, who got
stubborn and went over to his bedroll and hauled out the guns.

"I got them in Dodge," he said. "Pretty, ain't they? Fellow I
bought them from claimed they belonged to Bill Longley."

"Is that a fact?" I said, like I wasn't much impressed. "Who's
Longley?"

I knew who Bill Longley was, all right, but a man's got a right to
dicker a bit, and besides I couldn't help deviling Waco now and then.
I liked him all right, but he was one of those cocky little fellows who
ask for it. You know the kind. They always know everything.

I sat there while he told me about Bill Longley, the giant from
Texas with thirty-two killings to his credit, the man who was hanged
twice. A bunch of vigilantes strung him up once for horse-stealing he
hadn't done, but the rope broke after they'd ridden off and he
dropped to the ground, kind of short of breath but alive and kicking.

Then he was tried and hanged for a murder he had done, some

years later in Giddings, Texas. He was so big that the rope gave way again and he landed on his feet under the trap, making six-inch-deep footprints in the hard ground—they're still there in Giddings to be seen, Waco said, Bill Longley's footprints—but it broke his neck this time and they buried him nearby. At least a funeral service was held, but some say there's just an empty coffin in the grave.

I said, "This Longley gent can't have been so much, to let folks keep stringing him up that way."

That set Waco off again, while I toyed with the guns. They were pretty, all right, in a big carved belt with two carved holsters, but I wasn't much interested in leatherwork. It was the weapons themselves that took my fancy. They'd been used but someone had looked after them well. They were handsome pieces, smooth-working, and they had a good feel to them. You know how it is when a firearm feels just right. A fellow with hands the size of mine doesn't often find guns to fit him like that.

"How much do you figure they're worth?" I asked, when Waco stopped for breath.

"Well, now," he said, getting a sharp look on his face, and I came home to Willow Fork with the Longley guns strapped around me. If that's what they were.

I got a room and cleaned up at the hotel. I didn't much feel like riding clear out to the ranch and seeing what it looked like with Ma and Pa gone two years and nobody looking after things. Well, I'd put the place on its feet again one of these days, as soon as I'd had a little fun and saved a little money. I'd buckle right down to it, I told myself, as soon as Junellen set the date, which I'd been after her to do since before my folks died. She couldn't keep saying forever we were too young.

I got into my good clothes and went to see her. I won't say she'd been on my mind all the way up the trail and back again, because it wouldn't be true. A lot of the time I'd been too busy or tired for dreaming, and in Dodge City I'd done my best *not* to think of her, if you know what I mean. It did seem like a young fellow engaged to a beautiful girl like Junellen Barr could have behaved himself better up there, but it had been a long dusty drive and you know how it is.

But now I was home and it seemed like I'd been missing Junellen every minute since I left, and I couldn't wait to see her. I walked along the street in the hot sunshine feeling light and happy. Maybe my leaving my guns at the hotel had something to do with the light feeling, but the happiness was all for Junellen, and I ran up the steps to the house and knocked on the door. She'd have heard we were back and she'd be waiting to greet me, I was sure.

I knocked again and the door opened and I stepped forward eagerly. "Junellen—" I said, and stopped foolishly.

"Come in, Jim," said her father, a little turkey of a man who owned the drygoods store in town. He went on smoothly: "I understand you had quite an eventful journey. We are waiting to hear all about it."

He was being sarcastic, but that was his way, and I couldn't be bothered with trying to figure what he was driving at. I'd already stepped into the room, and there was Junellen with her mother standing close as if to protect her, which seemed kind of funny. There was a man in the room, too, Mister Carmichael from the bank, who'd fought with Pa in the war. He was tall and handsome as always, a little heavy nowadays but still dressed like a fashion plate. I couldn't figure what he was doing there.

It wasn't going at all the way I'd hoped, my reunion with Junellen, and I stopped, looking at her.

"So you're back, Jim," she said. "I heard you had a real exciting time. Dodge City must be quite a place."

There was a funny hard note in her voice. She held herself very straight, standing there by her mother, in a blue-flowered dress that matched her eyes. She was a real little lady, Junellen. She made kind of a point of it, in fact, and Martha Butcher, old man Butcher's kid, used to say about Junellen Barr that butter wouldn't melt in her mouth, but that always seemed like a silly saying to me, and who was Martha Butcher anyway, just because her daddy owned a lot of cows?

Martha'd also remarked about girls who had to drive two front names in harness as if one wasn't good enough, and I'd told her it surely wasn't if it was a name like Martha, and she'd kicked me on the shin. But that was a long time ago when we were all kids.

Junellen's mother broke the silence, in her nervous way: "Dear, hadn't you better tell Jim the news?" She turned to Mister Carmichael. "Howard, perhaps you should—"

Mister Carmichael came forward and took Junellen's hand. "Miss Barr has done me the honor to promise to be my wife," he said.

I said, "But she can't. She's engaged to me."

Junellen's mother said quickly, "It was just a childish thing, not to be taken seriously."

I said, "Well, I took it seriously!"

Junellen looked up at me. "Did you, Jim? In Dodge City, did you?" I didn't say anything. She said breathlessly, "It doesn't matter. I suppose I could forgive. . . . But you have killed a man. I could never love a man who has taken a human life."

Anyway, she said something like that. I had a funny feeling in my stomach and a roaring sound in my ears. They talk about your heart breaking, but that's where it hit me, the stomach and the ears. So I can't tell you exactly what she said, but it was something like that.

I heard myself say, "Mister Carmichael spent the war peppering Yanks with a pea-shooter, I take it."

"That's different—"

Mister Carmichael spoke quickly. "What Miss Barr means is that there's a difference between a battle and a drunken brawl, Jim. I am glad your father did not live to see his son wearing two big guns and shooting men down in the street. He was a fine man and a good sheriff for this county. It was only for his memory's sake that I agreed to let Miss Barr break the news to you in person. From what we hear of your exploits up north, you have certainly forfeited all right to consideration from her."

There was something in what he said, but I couldn't see that it was his place to say it. "You agreed?" I said. "That was mighty kind of you, sir, I'm sure." I looked away from him. "Junellen—"

Mister Carmichael interrupted. "I do not wish my fiancée to be distressed by a continuation of this painful scene. I must ask you to leave, Jim."

I ignored him. "Junellen," I said, "is this what you really—"

Mister Carmichael took me by the arm. I turned my head to look at him again. I looked at the hand with which he was holding me. I waited. He didn't let go. I hit him and he went back across the room and kind of fell into a chair. The chair broke under him. Junellen's father ran over to help him up. Mr. Carmichael's mouth was bloody. He wiped it with a handkerchief.

I said, "You shouldn't have put your hand on me, sir."

"Note the pride," Mr. Carmichael said, dabbing at his cut lip. "Note the vicious, twisted pride. They all have it, all these young toughs. You are too big for me to box, Jim, and it is an undignified thing, anyway. I have worn a sidearm in my time. I will go to the bank and get it, while you arm yourself."

"I will meet you in front of the hotel, sir," I said, "if that is agreeable to you."

"It is agreeable," he said, and went out.

I followed him without looking back. I think Junellen was crying, and I know her parents were saying one thing and another in high, indignant voices, but the funny roaring was in my ears and I didn't pay too much attention. The sun was very bright outside. As I started for the hotel, somebody ran up to me.

"Here you are, Jim." It was Waco, holding out the Longley guns in their carved holsters. "I heard what happened. Don't take any chances with the old fool."

I looked down at him and asked, "How did Junellen and her folks learn about what happened in Dodge?"

He said, "It's a small town, Jim, and all the boys have been drinking and talking, glad to get home."

"Sure," I said, buckling on the guns. "Sure."

It didn't matter. It would have got around sooner or later, and I wouldn't have lied about it if asked. We walked slowly toward the hotel.

"Dutch LeBaron is hiding out back in the hills with a dozen men," Waco said. "I heard it from a man in a bar."

"Who's Dutch LeBaron?" I asked. I didn't care, but it was something to talk about as we walked.

"Dutch?" Waco said. "Why Dutch is wanted in five states and a couple of territories. Hell, the price on his head is so high now even Fenn is after him."

"Fenn?" I said. He sure knew a lot of names. "Who's Fenn?"

"You've heard of Old Joe Fenn, the bounty hunter. Well, if he comes after Dutch, he's asking for it. Dutch can take care of himself."

"Is that a fact?" I said, and then I saw Mr. Carmichael coming, but he was a ways off yet and I said, "You sound like this Dutch fellow was a friend of yours—"

But Waco wasn't there any more. I had the street to myself, except for Mr. Carmichael, who had a gun strapped on outside his fine coat. It was an army gun in a black army holster with a flap, worn cavalry style on the right side, butt forward. They wear them like that to make room for the saber on the left, but it makes a clumsy rig.

I walked forward to meet Mr. Carmichael, and I knew I would have to let him shoot once. He was a popular man and a rich man and he would have to draw first and shoot first or I would be in serious trouble. I figured it all out very coldly, as if I had been killing men all my life. We stopped, and Mr. Carmichael undid the flap of the army holster and pulled out the big cavalry pistol awkwardly and fired and missed, as I had known, somehow, that he would.

Then I drew the right-hand gun, and as I did so I realized that I didn't particularly want to kill Mr. Carmichael. I mean, he was a brave man coming here with his old cap-and-ball pistol, knowing all the time that I could outdraw and outshoot him with my eyes closed. But I didn't want to be killed, either, and he had the piece cocked and was about to fire again. I tried to aim for a place that wouldn't kill him, or cripple him too badly, and the gun wouldn't do it.

I mean, it was a frightening thing. It was like I was fighting the Longley gun for Mr. Carmichael's life. The old army revolver fired once more and something rapped my left arm lightly. The Longley gun went off at last, and Mr. Carmichael spun around and fell on his face in the street. There was a cry, and Junellen came running and went to her knees beside him.

"You murderer!" she screamed at me. "You hateful murderer!"

It showed how she felt about him, that she would kneel in the dust like that in her blue-flowered dress. Junellen was always very careful of her pretty clothes. I punched out the empty and replaced it. Dr. Sims came up and examined Mr. Carmichael and said he was shot in the leg, which I already knew, being the one who had shot him there. Dr. Sims said he was going to be all right, God willing.

Having heard this, I went over to another part of town and tried to get drunk. I didn't have much luck at it, so I went into the place next to the hotel for a cup of coffee. There wasn't anybody in the place but a skinny girl with an apron on.

I said, "I'd like a cup of coffee, ma'am," and sat down.

She said, coming over, "Jim Anderson, you're drunk. At least you smell like it."

I looked up and saw that it was Martha Butcher. She set a cup down in front of me. I asked, "What are you doing here waiting tables?"

She said, "I had a fight with Dad about . . . well, never mind what it was about. Anyway, I told him I was old enough to run my own life and if he didn't stop trying to boss me around like I was one of the hands, I'd pack up and leave. And he laughed and asked what I'd do for money, away from home, and I said I'd earn it, so here I am."

It was just like Martha Butcher, and I saw no reason to make a fuss over it like she probably wanted me to.

"Seems like you are," I agreed. "Do I get sugar, too, or does that cost extra?"

She laughed and set a bowl in front of me. "Did you have a good time in Dodge?" she asked.

"Fine," I said. "Good liquor. Fast games. Pretty girls. Real pretty girls."

"Fiddlesticks," she said. "I know what you think is pretty. Blonde and simpering. You big fool. If you'd killed him over her they'd have put you in jail, at the very least. And just what are you planning to use for an arm when that one gets rotten and falls off? Sit still."

She got some water and cloth and fixed up my arm where Mr. Carmichael's bullet had nicked it.

"Have you been out to your place yet?" she asked.

I shook my head. "Figure there can't be much out there by now. I'll get after it one of these days."

"One of these days!" she said. "You mean when you get tired of strutting around with those big guns and acting dangerous—" She stopped abruptly.

I looked around, and got to my feet. Waco was there in the doorway, and with him was a big man, not as tall as I was, but wider. He was a real whiskery gent, with a mat of black beard you could have used for stuffing a mattress. He wore two gunbelts, crossed, kind of sagging low at the hips.

Waco said, "You're a fool to sit with your back to the door, Jim. That's the mistake Hickok made, remember? If instead of us it had been somebody like Jack McCall—"

"Who's Jack McCall?" I asked innocently.

"Why, he's the fellow shot Wild Bill in the back . . ." Waco's face reddened. "All right, all right. Always kidding me. Dutch, this big joker is my partner, Jim Anderson, Jim, Dutch LeBaron. He's got a proposition for us."

I tried to think back to where Waco and I had decided to become partners, and couldn't remember the occasion. Well, maybe it happens like that, but it seemed like I should have had some say in it.

"Your partner tells me you're pretty handy with those guns," LeBaron said, after Martha'd moved off across the room. "I can use a man like that."

"For what?" I asked.

"For making some quick money over in New Mexico Territory," he said.

I didn't ask any fool questions, like whether the money was to be made legally or illegally. "I'll think about it," I said.

Waco caught my arm. "What's to think about? We'll be rich, Jim!"

I said, "I'll think about it, Waco."

LeBaron said, "What's the matter, sonny, are you scared?"

I turned to look at him. He was grinning at me, but his eyes weren't grinning, and his hands weren't too far from those low-slung guns.

I said, "Try me and see."

I waited a little. Nothing happened. I walked out of there and got my pony and rode out to the ranch, reaching the place about dawn. I opened the door and stood there, surprised. It looked just about the way it had when the folks were alive, and I half expected to hear Ma yelling at me to beat the dust off outside and not bring it into the house. Somebody had cleaned the place up for me, and I thought I knew who. Well, it certainly was neighborly of her, I told myself. It was nice to have somebody show a sign they were glad to have me home, even if it was only Martha Butcher.

I spent a couple of days out there, resting up and riding around. I didn't find much stock. It was going to take money to make a going ranch of it again, and I didn't figure my credit at Mr. Carmichael's bank was anything to count on. I couldn't help giving some thought to Waco and LeBaron and the proposition they'd put before me. It was funny, I'd think about it most when I had the guns on. I was out back practicing with them one day when the stranger rode up.

He was a little, dry, elderly man on a sad-looking white horse he must have hired at the livery stable for not very much, and he wore his gun in front of his left hip with the butt to the right for a cross draw. He didn't make any noise coming up. I'd fired a couple of times before I realized he was there.

"Not bad," he said when he saw me looking at him. "Do you know a man named LeBaron, son?"

"I've met him," I said.

"Is he here?"

"Why should he be here?"

"A bartender in town told me he'd heard you and your sidekick, Smith, had joined up with LeBaron, so I thought you might have given him the use of your place. It would be more comfortable for him than hiding out in the hills."

"He isn't here," I said. The stranger glanced toward the house. I started to get mad, but shrugged instead. "Look around if you want to."

"In that case," he said, "I don't figure I want to." He glanced toward the target I'd been shooting at, and back to me. "Killed a man in Dodge, didn't you, son? And then stood real calm and let a fellow here in town fire three shots at you, after which you laughed and pinked him neatly in the leg."

"I don't recall laughing," I said. "And it was two shots, not three."

"It makes a good story, however," he said. "And it is spreading. You have a reputation already, did you know that, Anderson? I didn't come here just to look for LeBaron. I figured I'd like to have a look at you, too. I always like to look up fellows I might have business with later."

"Business?" I said, and then I saw that he'd taken a tarnished old badge out of his pocket and was pinning it on his shirt. "Have you a warrant, sir?" I asked.

"Not for you," he said. "Not yet."

He swung the old white horse around and rode off. When he was out of sight, I got my pony out of the corral. It was time I had a talk with Waco. Maybe I was going to join LeBaron and maybe I wasn't, but I didn't much like his spreading it around before it was true.

I didn't have to look for him in town. He came riding to meet me with three companions, all hard ones if I ever saw any.

"Did you see Fenn?" he shouted as he came up. "Did he come this way?"

"A little old fellow with some kind of a badge?" I said. "Was that Fenn? He headed back to town, about ten minutes ahead of me. He didn't look like much."

"Neither does the devil when he's on business," Waco said. "Come on, we'd better warn Dutch before he rides into town."

I rode along with them, and we tried to catch LeBaron on the trail, but he'd already passed with a couple of men. We saw their dust ahead and chased it, but they made it before us, and Fenn was waiting in front of the cantina that was LeBaron's hangout when he was in town.

We saw it all as we came pounding after LeBaron, who dismounted and started into the place, but Fenn came forward, looking small and inoffensive. He was saying something and holding out his hand. LeBaron stopped and shook hands with him, and the little man held onto LeBaron's hand, took a step to the side, and pulled his gun out of that cross-draw holster left-handed, with a kind of twisting motion.

Before LeBaron could do anything with his free hand, the little old man had brought the pistol barrel down across his head. It was as neat and coldblooded a thing as you'd care to see. In an instant, LeBaron was unconscious on the ground, and Old Joe Fenn was covering the two men who'd been riding with him.

Waco Smith, riding beside me, made a sort of moaning sound as if he'd been clubbed himself. "Get him!" he shouted, drawing his gun. "Get the dirty sneaking bounty hunter!"

I saw the little man throw a look over his shoulder, but there wasn't much he could do about us with those other two to handle. I guess he hadn't figured us for reinforcements riding in. Waco fired and missed. He never could shoot much, particularly from horseback. I reached out with one of the guns and hit him over the head before he could shoot again. He spilled from the saddle.

I didn't have it all figured out. Certainly it wasn't a very nice thing Mr. Fenn had done, first taking a man's hand in friendship and then knocking him unconscious. Still, I didn't figure LeBaron had ever been one for giving anybody a break; and there was something about the old fellow standing there with his tarnished old badge that reminded me of Pa, who'd died wearing a similar piece of tin on his chest. Anyway, there comes a time in a man's life when he's got to make a choice, and that's the way I made mine.

Waco and I had been riding ahead of the others. I turned my pony fast and covered them with the guns as they came charging up—as well as you can cover anybody from a plunging horse. One of them had his pistol aimed to shoot. The left-hand Longley gun went off, and he fell to the ground. I was kind of surprised. I'd never been much at shooting left-handed. The other two riders veered off and headed out of town.

By the time I got my pony quieted down from having that gun go off in his ear, everything was pretty much under control. Waco had disappeared, so I figured he couldn't be hurt much; and the new sheriff was there, old drunken Billy Bates who'd been elected after

Pa's death by the gambling element in town, who hadn't liked the strict way Pa ran things.

"I suppose it's legal," Old Billy was saying grudgingly. "But I don't take it kindly, Marshal, your coming here to serve a warrant without letting me know."

"My apologies, Sheriff," Fenn said smoothly. "An oversight, I assure you. Now, I'd like a wagon. He's worth seven-hundred and fifty dollars over in New Mexico Territory."

"No decent person would want that kind of money," Old Billy said sourly, swaying on his feet.

"There's only one kind of money," Fenn said. "Just as there's only one kind of law, even though there's different kinds of men enforcing it." He looked at me as I came up. "Much obliged, son."

"*Por nada,*" I said. "You get in certain habits when you've had a badge in the family. My daddy was sheriff here once."

"So? I didn't know that." Fenn looked at me sharply. "Don't look like you're making any plans to follow in his footsteps. That's hardly a lawman's rig you're wearing."

I said, "Maybe, but I never yet beat a man over the head while I was shaking his hand, Marshal."

"Son," he said, "my job is to enforce the law and maybe make a small profit on the side, not to play games with fair and unfair." He looked at me for a moment longer. "Well, maybe we'll meet again. It depends."

"On what?" I asked.

"On the price," he said. "The price on your head."

"But I haven't got—"

"Not now," he said. "But you will, wearing those guns. I know the signs. I've seen them before, too many times. Don't count on having me under obligation to you, when your time comes. I never let personal feelings interfere with business. . . . Easy, now," he said, to a couple of fellows who were lifting LeBaron, bound hand and foot, into the wagon that somebody had driven up. "Easy. Don't damage the merchandise. I take pride in delivering them in good shape for standing trial, whenever possible."

I decided I needed a drink, and then I changed my mind in favor of a cup of coffee. As I walked down the street, leaving my pony at the rail back there, the wagon rolled past and went out of town ahead of me. I was still watching it, for no special reason, when Waco stepped from the alley behind me.

"Jim!" he said. "Turn around, Jim!"

I turned slowly. He was a little unsteady on his feet, standing there, maybe from my hitting him, maybe from drinking. I thought it was drinking. I hadn't hit him very hard. He'd had time for a couple of quick ones, and liquor always got to him fast.

"You sold us out, you damn traitor!" he cried. "You took sides with the law!"

"I never was against it," I said. "Not really."

"After everything I've done for you!" he said thickly. "I was going to make you a great man, Jim, greater than Longley or Hardin or Hickok or any of them. With my brains and your size and speed, nothing could have stopped us! But you turned on me! Do you think you can do it alone? Is that what you're figuring, to leave me behind now that I've built you up to be somebody?"

"Waco," I said, "I never had any ambitions to be—"

"You and your medicine guns!" he sneered. "Let me tell you something. Those old guns are just something I picked up in a pawnshop. I spun a good yarn about them to give you confidence. You were on the edge, you needed a push in the right direction, and I knew once you started wearing a flashy rig like that, with one killing under your belt already, somebody'd be bound to try you again, and we'd be on our way to fame. But as for their being Bill Longley's guns, don't make me laugh!"

I said, "Waco—"

"They's just metal and wood like any other guns!" he said. "And I'm going to prove it to you right now! I don't need you, Jim! I'm as good a man as you, even if you laugh at me and make jokes at my expense. . . . *Are you ready, Jim?*"

He was crouching, and I looked at him, Waco Smith, with whom I'd ridden up the trail and back. I saw that he was no good and I saw that he was dead. It didn't matter whose guns I was wearing, and all he'd really said was that he didn't know whose guns they were. But it didn't matter, they were my guns now, and he was just a little runt who never could shoot for shucks, anyway. He was dead, and so were the others, the ones who'd come after him, because they'd come, I knew that.

I saw them come to try me, one after the other, and I saw them go down before the big black guns, all except the last, the one I couldn't quite make out. Maybe it was Fenn and maybe it wasn't. . . .

I said, "To hell with you, Waco. I've got nothing against you, and I'm not going to fight you. Tonight or any other time."

I turned and walked away. I heard the sound of his gun behind me an instant before the bullet hit me. Then I wasn't hearing anything for a while. When I came to, I was in bed, and Martha Butcher was there.

"Jim!" she breathed. "Oh, Jim . . . !"

She looked real worried, and kind of pretty, I thought, but of course I was half out of my head. She looked even prettier the day I asked her to marry me, some months later, but maybe I was a little out of my head that day, too. Old Man Butcher didn't like it a bit. It seems his fight with Martha had been about her cleaning up my place, and his ordering her to quit and stay away from that young troublemaker, as he'd called me after getting word of all the hell we'd raised up north after delivering his cattle.

He didn't like it, but he offered me a job, I suppose for Martha's sake. I thanked him and told him I was much obliged but I'd just accepted an appointment as Deputy U.S. Marshal. Seems like somebody had recommended me for the job, maybe Old Joe Fenn, maybe not. I got my old gun out of my bedroll and wore it tucked inside my belt when I thought I might need it. It was a funny thing how seldom I had any use for it, even wearing a badge. With that job, I was the first in the neighborhood to hear about Waco Smith. The news came from New Mexico Territory. Waco and a bunch had pulled a job over there, and a posse had trapped them in a box canyon and shot them to pieces.

I never wore the other guns again. After we moved into the old place, I hung them on the wall. It was right after I'd run against Billy Bates for sheriff and won that I came home to find them gone. Martha looked surprised when I asked about them.

"Why," she said, "I gave them to your friend, Mr. Williams. He said you'd sold them to him. Here's the money."

I counted the money, and it was a fair enough price for a pair of second-hand guns and holsters, but I hadn't met any Mr. Williams.

I started to say so, but Martha was still talking. She said, "He certainly had an odd first name, didn't he? Who'd christen anybody Long Williams? Not that he wasn't big enough. I guess he'd be as tall as you, wouldn't he, if he didn't have that trouble with his neck?"

"His neck?" I said.

"Why, yes," she said. "Didn't you notice when you talked to him, the way he kept his head cocked to the side? Like this."

She showed me how Long Williams had kept his head cocked to the side. She looked real pretty doing it, and I couldn't figure how I'd ever thought her plain, but maybe she'd changed. Or maybe I had. I kissed her and gave her back the gun money to buy something for herself, and went outside to think. Long Williams, William Longley. A man with a wry neck and a man who was hanged twice. It was kind of strange, to be sure, but after a time I decided it was just a coincidence. Some drifter riding by just saw the guns through the window and took a fancy to them.

I mean, if it had really been Bill Longley, if he was alive and had his guns back, we'd surely have heard of him by now down at the sheriff's office, and we never have.

QUESTIONS

1. This story is written in the first person, and yet the author manages to have the narrator communicate knowledge to the reader that is not yet consciously known to the narrator himself. How, for instance, do you learn early that Jim is not really in love with Junellen?

2. The pull between two women—one straitlaced, the other understanding—is a staple device of many Western stories. Compare the two young women of this story with the two young women in "Stage to Lordsburg" (p. 188). Are there similarities between the pairs? What are the dissimilarities?

3. The guns of William Longley clearly have quasi-magical qualities. Are they a force for good or for evil? Why does Jim Anderson hang them up after he becomes a lawman?

4. How does the old bounty hunter anticipate the choices the hero will have to make?

5. What is added to the story by the appearance of Long Williams and his twisted neck?

WALTER VAN TILBURG CLARK

THE INDIAN WELL

In this dead land, like a vast relief model, the only allegiance was to sun. Even night was not strong enough to resist; earth stretched gratefully under it, but had no hope that day would not return. Such living things as hoarded a little juice at their cores were secret about it, and only the most ephemeral existences, the air at dawn and sunset, the amethyst shadows in the mountains, had any freedom. The Indian Well alone, of lesser creations, was in constant revolt. Sooner or later all minor, breathing rebels came to its stone basin under the spring in the cliff, and from its overflow grew a meadow delta and two columns of willows and aspens holding a tiny front against the valley. The pictograph of a starving, ancient journey, cut in rock above the basin, a sun-warped shack on the south wing of the canyon, and an abandoned mine above it, were the last minute and practically contemporary tokens of man's participation in the cycles of the well's resistance, each of which was an epitome of centuries, and perhaps of the wars of the universe.

The day before Jim Suttler came up in the early spring to take his part in one cycle was a busy day. The sun was merely lucid after four days of broken showers and one rain of an hour with a little cold wind behind it, and under the separate cloud shadows sliding down the mountain and into the valley, the canyon was alive. A rattler emerged partially from a hole in the mound on which the cabin stood, and having gorged in the darkness, rested with his head on a stone. A road-runner, stepping long and always about to sprint, came down the morning side of the mound, and his eye, quick to perceive the difference between the live and the inanimate of the same color, discovered the coffin-shaped head on the stone. At once he broke into a reaching sprint, his neck and tail stretched level, his beak agape with expectation. But his shadow arrived a step before him. The rattler recoiled, his head scarred by the sharp beak but his eye intact. The road-runner said nothing, but peered warily into the hole without stretching his neck, then walked off stiffly, leaning forward again as if about to run. When he had gone twenty feet he turned, balanced for an instant, and charged back, checking abruptly just short of the hole. The snake remained withdrawn. The road-runner paraded briefly before the hole, talking to himself, and then ran angrily up to the spring, where he drank at the overflow, sipping and stretching his neck, lifting his feet one at a time, ready to go into immediate action. The road-runner lived a dangerous and exciting life.

In the upper canyon the cliff swallows, making short sharp notes, dipped and shot between the new mud under the aspens and their high community on the forehead of the cliff. Electrical bluebirds appeared to dart the length of the canyon at each low flight, but turned up tilting half way down. Lizards made similar unexpected flights and stops on the rocks, and when they stopped did rapid push-ups, like men exercising on a floor. They were variably pugnacious and timid.

Two of them arrived simultaneously upon a rock below the road-runner. One of them immediately skittered to a rock two feet off, and they faced each other, exercising. A small hawk coming down over the mountain, but shadowless under a cloud, saw the lizards. Having overfled the difficult target, he dropped to the canyon mouth swiftly and banked back into the wind. His trajectory was cleared of swallows but one of them, fluttering hastily up, dropped a pellet of mud between the lizards. The one who had retreated disappeared. The other flattened for an instant, then sprang and charged. The road-runner was on him as he struck the pellet, and galloped down the canyon in great, tense strides on his toes, the lizard lashing the air from his beak. The hawk swooped at the road-runner, thought better of it, and rose against the wind to the head of the canyon, where he turned back and coasted out over the desert, his shadow a little behind him and farther and farther below.

The swallows became the voice of the canyon again, but in moments when they were all silent the lovely smaller sounds emerged, their own feathering, the liquid overflow, the snapping and clicking of insects, a touch of wind in the new aspens. Under these lay still more delicate tones, erasing, in the most silent seconds, the difference between eye and ear, a white cloud shadow passing under the water of the well, a dark cloud shadow on the cliff, the aspen patterns on the stones. Deepest was the permanent background of the rocks, the lost on the canyon floor, and those yet strong, the thinking cliffs. When the swallows began again it was impossible to understand the cliffs, who could afford to wait.

At noon a red and white range cow with one new calf, shining and curled, came slowly up from the desert, stopping often to let the calf rest. At each stop the calf would try vigorously to feed, but the cow would go on. When they reached the well the cow drank slowly for a long time; then she continued to wrinkle the water with her muzzle, drinking a little and blowing, as if she found it hard to leave. The calf worked under her with spasmodic nudgings. When she was done playing with the water, she nosed and licked him out from under her and up to the well. He shied from the surprising coolness and she put him back. When he stayed, she drank again. He put his nose into the water also, and bucked up as if bitten. She continued to pretend, and he returned, got water up his nostrils and took three jumps away. The cow was content and moved off toward the canyon wall, tonguing grass tufts from among the rocks. Against the cliff she rubbed gently and continuously with a mild voluptuous look, occasionally lapping her nose with a serpent tongue. The loose winter shag came off in tufts on the rock. The calf lost her, became panicked and made desperate noises which stopped prematurely, and when he discovered her, complicated her toilet. Finally she led him down to the meadow where, moving slowly, they both fed until he was full and went to sleep in a ball in the sun. At sunset they returned to the well, where the cow drank again and gave him a second lesson. After this they went back into the brush and northward into the dusk. The cow's size and relative immunity to sudden death left an aftermath of peace, rendered gently humorous by the calf.

Also at sunset, there was a resurgence of life among the swallows. The thin golden air at the cliff tops, in which there were now no clouds so that the eastern mountains and the valley were flooded with unbroken light, was full of their cries and quick maneuvers among a dancing myriad of insects. The direct sun gave them, when they perched in rows upon the cliff, a dramatic significance like that of men upon an immensely higher promontory. As dusk rose out of the canyon, while the eastern peaks were still lighted, the swallows gradually became silent creatures with slightly altered flight, until, at twilight, the air was full of velvet, swooping bats.

In the night jack-rabbits multiplied spontaneously out of the brush of the valley, drank in the rivulet, their noses and great ears continuously searching the dark, electrical air, and played in fits and starts on the meadow, the many young hopping like rubber, or made thumping love among the aspens and the willows.

A coyote came down canyon on his belly and lay in the brush with his nose between his paws. He took a young rabbit in a quiet spring and snap, and went into the brush again to eat it. At the slight rending of his meal the meadow cleared of leaping shadows and lay empty in the starlight. The rabbits, however, encouraged by newcomers, returned soon, and the coyote killed again and went off heavily, the jack's great hind legs dragging.

In the dry-wash below the meadow an old coyote, without family, profited by the second panic, which came over him. He ate what his loose teeth could tear, leaving the open remnant in the sand, drank at the basin and, carefully circling the meadow, disappeared into the dry wilderness.

Shortly before dawn, when the stars had lost luster and there was no sound in the canyon but the rivulet and the faint, separate clickings of mice in the gravel, nine antelope in loose file, with three silently flagging fawns, came on trigger toe up the meadow and drank at the well, heads often up, muzzles dripping, broad ears turning. In the meadow they grazed and the fawns nursed. When there was as much gray as darkness in the air, and new wind in the canyon, they departed, the file weaving into the brush, merging into the desert, to nothing, and the swallows resumed the talkative day shift.

Jim Suttler and his burro came up into the meadow a little after noon, very slowly, though there was only a spring-fever warmth. Suttler walked pigeon-toed, like an old climber, but carefully and stiffly, not with the loose walk natural to such a long-legged man. He stopped in the middle of the meadow, took off his old black sombrero, and stared up at the veil of water shining over the edge of the basin.

"We're none too early, Jenny," he said to the burro.

The burro had felt water for miles, but could show no excitement. She stood with her head down and her four legs spread unnaturally, as if to postpone a collapse. Her pack reared higher than Suttler's head, and was hung with casks, pails, canteens, a pick, two shovels, a crowbar and a rifle in a sheath. Suttler had the cautious uncertainty of his trade. His other burro had died two days before in the mountains east of Beatty, and Jenny and he bore its load.

Suttler shifted his old six shooter from his rump to his thigh, and studied the well, the meadow, the cabin and the mouth of the mine as if he might choose not to stay. He was not a cinema prospector. If he looked like one of the probably mistaken conceptions of Christ, with his red beard and red hair to his shoulders, it was because he had been long away from barbers and without spare water for shaving. He was unlike Christ in some other ways also.

"It's kinda run down," he told Jenny, "but we'll take it."

He put his sombrero back on, let his pack fall slowly to the ground, showing the sweat patch in his bleached brown shirt, and began to unload Jenny carefully, like a collector handling rare vases, and put everything into one neat pile.

"Now," he said, "we'll have a drink." His tongue and lips were so swollen that the words were unclear, but he spoke casually, like a club-man sealing a minor deal. One learns to do business slowly with deserts and mountains. He picked up a bucket and started for the well. At the upper edge of the meadow he looked back. Jenny was still standing with her head down and her legs apart. He did not particularly notice her extreme thinness for he had seen it coming on gradually. He was thinner himself, and tall, and so round-shouldered that when he stood his straightest he seemed to be peering ahead with his chin out.

"Come on, you old fool," he said. "It's off you now."

Jenny came, stumbling in the rocks above the meadow, and stopping often as if to decide why this annoyance recurred. When she became interested, Suttler would not let her get to the basin, but for ten minutes gave her water from his cupped hands, a few licks at a time. Then he drove her off and she stood in the shade of the canyon wall watching him. He began on his thirst in the same way, a gulp at a time, resting between gulps. After ten gulps he sat on a rock by the spring and looked at the little meadow and the big desert, and might have been considering the courses of the water through his body, but noticed also the antelope tracks in the mud.

After a time he drank another half dozen gulps, gave Jenny half a pailful, and drove her down to the meadow, where he spread a dirty blanket in the striped sun and shadow under the willows. He sat on the edge of the blanket, rolled a cigarette and smoked it while he watched Jenny. When she began to graze with her rump to the canyon, he flicked his cigarette onto the grass, rolled over with his back to the sun and slept until it became chilly after sunset. Then he woke, ate a can of beans, threw the can into the willows and led Jenny up to the well, where they drank together from the basin for a long time. While she resumed her grazing, he took another blanket and his rifle from the pile, removed his heel-worn boots, stood his rifle against a fork, and, rolling up in both blankets, slept again.

In the night many rabbits played in the meadow in spite of the strong sweat and tobacco smell of Jim Suttler lying under the willows, but the antelope, when they came in the dead dark before dawn, were nervous, drank less, and did not graze but minced quickly back across the meadow and began to run at the head of the dry wash. Jenny slept with her head hanging, and did not hear them come or go.

Suttler woke lazy and still red-eyed, and spent the morning drinking at the well, eating and dozing on his blanket. In the afternoon, slowly, a few things at a time, he carried his pile to the cabin. He had a bachelor's obsession with order, though he did not mind dirt, and puttered until sundown making a brush bed and arranging his gear. Much of this time, however, was spent studying the records, on the cabin walls, of the recent human life of the well. He had to be careful, because among the still legible names and dates, after Frank Davis, 1893, Willard Harbinger, 1893, London, England, John Mason, June 13, 1887, Bucksport, Maine, Matthew Kenling from Glasgow, 1891, Penelope and Martin Reave, God Guide Us, 1885, was written Frank Hayward, 1492, feeling my age. There were other wits too. John Barr had written, Giv it back to the injuns, and Kenneth Thatcher, two years later, had written under that, Pity the noble redskin, while another man, whose second name was Evans, had written what was already a familiar libel, since it was not strictly true: Fifty miles from water, a hundred miles from wood, a million miles from God, three feet from hell. Someone unnamed had felt differently, saying, God is kind. We may make it now. Shot an antelope here July 10, 188—and the last number blurred. Arthur Smith, 1881, had recorded, Here berried my beloved wife Semantha, age 22, and my soul. God let me keep the child. J.M. said cryptically, Good luck, John, and Bill said, Ralph, if you come this way, am trying to get to Los Angeles. B. Westover said he had recovered from his wound there in 1884, and Galt said, enigmatically and without date, Bart and Miller burned to death in the Yellow Jacket. I don't care now. There were poets too, of both parties. What could still be read of Byron Cotter's verses, written in 1902, said,

> . . . here alone
> Each shining dawn I greet,
> The Lord's wind on my forehead
> And where he set his feet
> One mark of heel remaining
> Each day filled up anew,
> To keep my soul from burning,
> With clear, celestial dew.
> Here in His Grace abiding
> The mortal years and few
> I shall . . .

but you can't tell what he intended, while J.A. had printed,

> My brother came out in '49
> I came in '51
> At first we thought we liked it fine
> But now, by God, we're done.

Suttler studied these records without smiling, like someone reading a funny paper, and finally, with a heavy blue pencil, registered, Jim and Jenny Suttler, damn dried out, March—and paused, but had no way of discovering the day—1940.

In the evening he sat on the steps watching the swallows in the golden upper canyon turn bats in the dusk, and thought about the antelope. He had seen the new tracks also, and it alarmed him a little that the antelope could have passed twice in the dark without waking him.

Before false dawn he was lying in the willows with his carbine at ready. Rabbits ran from the meadow when he came down, and after that there was no movement. He wanted to smoke. When he did see them at the lower edge of the meadow, he was startled, yet made no quick movement, but slowly pivoted to cover them. They made poor targets in that light and backed by the pale desert, appearing and disappearing before his eyes. He couldn't keep any one of them steadily visible, and decided to wait until they made contrast against the meadow. But his presence was strong. One of the antelope advanced onto the green, but then threw its head up, spun, and ran back past the flank of the herd, which swung after him. Suttler rose quickly and raised the rifle, but let it down without firing. He could hear the light rattle of their flight in the wash, but had only a belief that he could see them. He had few cartridges, and the report and ponderous echo under the cliffs would scare them off for weeks.

His energies, however, were awakened by the frustrated hunt. While there was still more light than heat in the canyon, he climbed to the abandoned mine tunnel at the top of the alluvial wing of the cliff. He looked at the broken rock in the dump, kicked up its pack with a boot toe, and went into the tunnel, peering closely at its sides, in places black with old smoke smudges. At the back he struck two matches and looked at the jagged dead end and the fragments on the floor, then returned to the shallow beginning of a side tunnel. At the second match here he knelt quickly, scrutinized a portion of the rock, and when the match went out at once lit another. He lit six matches, and pulled at the rock with his hand. It was firm.

"The poor chump," he said aloud.

He got a loose rock from the tunnel and hammered at the projection with it. It came finally, and he carried it into the sun on the dump.

"Yessir," he said aloud, after a minute.

He knocked his sample into three pieces and examined each minutely.

"Yessir, yessir," he said with malicious glee, and, grinning at the tunnel, "The poor chump."

Then he looked again at the dump, like the mound before a gigantic gopher hole. "Still, that's a lot of digging," he said.

He put sample chips into his shirt pocket, keeping a small, black, heavy one that had fallen neatly from a hole like a borer's, to play with in his hand. After trouble he found the claim pile on the side hill south of the tunnel, its top rocks tumbled into the shale. Under the remaining rocks he found what he wanted, a ragged piece of yellowed paper between two boards. The writing was in pencil, and not diplomatic. "I hereby clame this whole damn side hill as far as I can shoot north and south and as far as I can dig in. I am a good shot. Keep off. John Barr, April 11, 1897."

Jim Suttler grinned. "Tough guy, eh?" he said.

He made a small ceremony of burning the paper upon a stone from the cairn. The black tinsel of ash blew off and broke into flakes.

"O.K., John Barr?" he asked.

"O.K., Suttler," he answered himself.

In blue pencil, on soiled paper from his pocket, he slowly printed, "Becus of the lamented desease of the late clament, John Barr, I now clame these diggins for myself and partner Jenny. I can shoot too." And wrote rather than printed, "James T. Suttler, March—" and paused.

"Make it an even month," he said, and wrote, "11, 1940." Underneath he wrote, "Jenny Suttler, her mark," and drew a skull with long ears.

"There," he said, and folded the paper, put it between the two boards, and rebuilt the cairn into a neat pyramid above it.

In high spirit he was driven to cleanliness. With scissors, soap and razor he climbed to the spring. Jenny was there, drinking.

"When you're done," he said, and when she lifted her head, pulled her ears and scratched her.

"Maybe we've got something here Jenny," he said.

Jenny observed him soberly and returned to the meadow.

"She doesn't believe me," he said, and began to perfect himself. He sheared off his red tresses in long hanks, then cut closer, and went over yet a third time, until there remained a brush, of varying density, of stiff red bristles, through which his scalp shone whitely. He sheared the beard likewise, then knelt to the well for mirror and shaved painfully. He also shaved his neck and about his ears. He arose younger and less impressive, with jaws as pale as his scalp, so that his sunburn was a red domino. He burned tresses and beard ceremoniously upon a sage bush, and announced, "It is spring."

He began to empty the pockets of his shirt and breeches onto a flat stone, yelling, "In the spring a young man's fancy," to a kind of tune, and paused, struck by the facts.

"Oh, yeah?" he said. "Fat chance."

"Fat," he repeated with obscene consideration. "Oh, well," he said, and finished piling upon the rock notebooks, pencil stubs, cartridges, tobacco, knife, stump pipe, matches, chalk, samples, and three wrinkled photographs. One of the photographs he observed at length before weighting it down with a .45 cartridge. It showed a round, blonde girl with a big smile on a stupid face, in a patterned calico house dress, in front of a blossoming rhododendron bush.

He added to this deposit his belt and holster with the big .45.

Then he stripped himself, washed and rinsed his garments in the spring, and spread them upon stones and brush, and carefully arranged four flat stones into a platform beside the trough. Standing there he scooped water over himself, gasping, made it a lather, and at last, face and copper bristles also foaming, gropingly entered the basin, and submerged, flooding the water over in a thin and soapy sheet. His head emerged at once. "My God," he whispered. He remained under, however, till he was soapless, and goose pimpled as a file, when he climbed out cautiously onto the rock platform and performed a dance of small, revolving patterns with a great deal of up and down.

At one point in his dance he observed the pictograph journey upon the cliff, and danced nearer to examine it.

"Ignorant," he pronounced. "Like a little kid," he said.

He was intrigued, however, by more recent records, names smoked and cut upon the lower rock. One of these, in script, like a gigantic handwriting deeply cut, said ALVAREZ BLANCO DE TOLDEO, Anno Di 1624. A very neat, upright cross was chiseled beneath it.

Suttler grinned. "Oh, yeah?" he asked, with his head upon one side. "Nuts," he said, looking at it squarely.

But it inspired him, and with his jack-knife he began scraping beneath the possibly Spanish inscription. His knife, however, made scratches, not incisions. He completed a bad Jim and Jenny and quit, saying, "I should kill myself over a phony wop."

Thereafter, for weeks, while the canyon became increasingly like a furnace in the daytime and the rocks stayed warm at night, he drove his tunnel farther into the mountain and piled the dump farther into the gully, making, at one side of the entrance, a heap of ore to be worked, and occasionally adding a peculiarly heavy pebble to the others in his small leather bag with a draw string. He and Jenny thrived upon this fixed and well-watered life. The hollows disappeared from his face and he became less stringy, while Jenny grew round, her battleship-gray pelt even lustrous and its black markings distinct and ornamental. The burro found time from her grazing to come to the cabin door in the evenings and attend solemnly to Suttler playing with his samples and explaining their future.

"Then, old lady," Suttler said, "you will carry only small children, one at a time, for never more than half an hour. You will have a bedroom with French windows and a mattress, and I will paint your feet gold.

"The children," he said, "will probably be redheaded, but maybe blonde. Anyway, they will be beautiful.

"After we've had a holiday, of course," he added. "For one hundred and thirty-three nights," he said dreamily. "Also," he said, "just one hundred and thirty-three quarts. I'm no drunken bum.

"For you, though," he said, "for one hundred and thirty-three nights a quiet hotel with other old ladies. I should drag my own mother in the gutter." He pulled her head down by the ears and kissed her loudly upon the nose. They were very happy together.

Nor did they greatly alter most of the life of the canyon. The antelope did not return, it is true, the rabbits were fewer and less playful because he sometimes snared them for meat, the little, clean mice and desert rats avoided the cabin they had used, and the road-runner did not come in daylight after Suttler, for fun, narrowly missed him with a piece of ore from the tunnel mouth. Suttler's violence was disproportionate perhaps, when he used his .45 to blow apart a creamy rat who did invade the cabin, but the loss was insignificant to the pattern of the well, and more than compensated when he one day caught the rattler extended at the foot of the dump in a drunken stupor from rare young rabbit, and before it could recoil held it aloft by the tail and snapped its head off, leaving the heavy body to turn slowly for a long time among the rocks. The dominant voices went undisturbed, save when he sang badly at his work or said beautiful things to Jenny in a loud voice.

There were, however, two more noticeable changes, one of which, at least, was important to Suttler himself. The first was the execution of the range cow's calf in the late fall, when he began to suggest a bull. Suttler felt a little guilty about this because the calf might have belonged to somebody, because the cow remained near the meadow bawling for two nights, and because the calf had come to meet the gun with more curiosity than challenge. But when he had the flayed carcass hung in the mine tunnel in a wet canvas, the sensation of providence overcame any qualms.

The other change was more serious. It occurred at the beginning of such winter as the well had, when there was sometimes a light rime on the rocks at dawn, and the aspens held only a few yellow leaves. Suttler thought often of leaving. The nights were cold, the fresh meat was eaten, his hopes had diminished as he still found only occasional nuggets, and his dreams of women, if less violent, were more nostalgic. The canyon held him with a feeling he would have called lonesome but at home, yet he probably would have gone except for this second change.

In the higher mountains to the west, where there was already snow, and at dawn a green winter sky, hunger stirred a buried memory in a cougar. He had twice killed antelope at the well, and felt there had been time enough again. He came down from the dwarfed trees and crossed the narrow valley under the stars, sometimes stopping abruptly to stare intently about, like a house-cat in a strange room. After each stop he would at once resume a quick, noiseless trot. From the top of the mountain above the spring he came down very slowly on his belly, but there was nothing at the well. He relaxed, and leaning on the rim of the basin, drank, listening between laps. His nose was clean with fasting, and he knew of the man in the cabin and Jenny in the meadow, but they were strange, not what he remembered about the place. But neither had his past made him fearful. It was only habitual hunting caution which made him go down into the willows carefully, and lie there head up, watching Jenny, but still waiting for antelope, which he had killed before near dawn. The strange smells were confusing and therefore irritating. After an hour he rose and went silently to the cabin, from which the strangest smell came strongly, a carnivorous smell which did not arouse appetite, but made him bristle nervously. The tobacco in it was like pins in his nostrils. He circled the cabin, stopping frequently. At the open door the scent was violent. He stood with his front paws up on the step, moving his head in serpent motions, the end of his heavy tail furling and unfurling constantly. In a dream Suttler turned over without waking, and muttered. The cougar crouched, his eyes intent, his ruff lifting. Then he swung away from the door, growling a little, and after one pause, crept back down to the meadow again and lay in the willows, but where he could watch the cabin also.

When the sky was alarmingly pale and the antelope had not come, he crawled a few feet at a time, behind the willows, to a point nearer Jenny. Then he crouched, working his hind legs slowly under him until he was set, and sprang, raced the three or four jumps to the drowsy burro, and struck. The beginning of her mortal scream was severed, but having made an imperfect leap, and from no height, the cat did not at once break her neck, but drove her to earth, where her small hooves churned futilely in the sod, and chewed and worried until she lay still.

Jim Suttler was nearly awakened by the fragment of scream, but heard nothing after it, and sank again.

The cat wrestled Jenny's body into the willows, fed with uncertain relish, drank long at the well, and went slowly over the crest, stopping often to look back. In spite of the light and the beginning talk of the swallows, the old coyote also fed and was gone before Suttler woke.

When Suttler found Jenny, many double columns of regimented ants were already at work, streaming in and out of the interior and mounting like bridge workers upon the ribs. Suttler stood and looked down. He desired to hold the small muzzle in the hollow of his hand, feeling that this familiar gesture would get through to Jenny, but couldn't bring himself to it because of what had happened to that side of her head. He squatted and lifted one hoof on its stiff leg and held that. Ants emerged hurriedly from the fetlock, their lines of communication broken. Two of them made disorganized excursions on the back of his hand. He rose, shook them off, and stood staring again. He didn't say anything because he spoke easily only when cheerful or excited, but a determination was beginning in him. He followed the drag to the spot torn by the small hoofs. Among the willows again, he found the tracks of both the cougar and the coyote, and the cat's tracks again at the well and by the cabin doorstep. He left Jenny in the willows with a canvas over her during the day, and did not eat.

At sunset he sat on the doorstep, cleaning his rifle and oiling it until he could spring the lever almost without sound. He filled the clip, pressed it home, and sat with the gun across his knees until dark, when he put on his sheepskin, stuffed a scarf into the pocket, and went down to Jenny. He removed the canvas from her, rolled it up and held it under his arm.

"I'm sorry, old woman," he said. "Just tonight."

There was a little cold wind in the willows. It rattled the upper branches lightly.

Suttler selected a spot thirty yards down wind, from which he could see Jenny, spread the canvas and lay down upon it, facing toward her. After an hour he was afraid of falling asleep and sat up against a willow clump. He sat there all night. A little after midnight the old coyote came into the dry-wash below him. At the top of the wash he sat down, and when the mingled scents gave him a clear picture of the strategy, let his tongue loll out, looked at the stars for a moment with his mouth silently open, rose and trotted back into the desert.

At the beginning of daylight the younger coyote trotted in from the north, and turned up toward the spring, but saw Jenny. He sat down and looked at her for a long time. Then he moved to the west and sat down again. In the wind was only winter, and the water, and faintly the acrid bat dung in the cliffs. He completed the circle, but not widely enough, walking slowly through the willows, down the edge of the meadow and in again not ten yards in front of the following muzzle of the carbine. Like Jenny, he felt his danger too late. The heavy slug caught him at the base of the skull in the middle of the first jump, so that it was amazingly accelerated for a fraction of a second. The coyote began it alive, and ended it quite dead, but with a tense muscular movement conceived which resulted in a grotesque final leap and twist of the hindquarters alone, leaving them propped high against a willow clump while the head was half buried in the sand, red welling up along the lips of the distended jaws. The cottony underpelt of the tail and rump stirred gleefully in the wind.

When Suttler kicked the body and it did not move, he suddenly dropped his gun, grasped it by the upright hind legs, and hurled it out into the sage-brush. His face appeared slightly insane with fury for that instant. Then he picked up his gun and went back to the cabin, where he ate, and drank half of one of his last three bottles of whiskey.

In the middle of the morning he came down with his pick and shovel, dragged Jenny's much lightened body down into the dry-wash, and dug in the rock and sand for two hours. When she was covered, he erected a small cairn of stone, like the claim post, above her.

"If it takes a year," he said, and licked the salt sweat on his lips.

That day he finished the half bottle and drank all of a second one, and became very drunk, so that he fell asleep during his vigil in the willows, sprawled wide on the dry turf and snoring. He was not disturbed. There was a difference in his smell after that day which prevented even the rabbits from coming into the meadow. He waited five nights in the willows. Then he transferred his watch to a niche in the cliff, across from and just below the spring.

All winter, while the day wind blew long veils of dust across the desert, regularly repeated, like waves or the smoke of line artillery fire, and the rocks shrank under the cold glitter of night, he did not miss a watch. He learned to go to sleep at sundown, wake within a few minutes of midnight, go up to his post and become at once clear-headed and watchful. He talked to himself in the mine and the cabin, but never in the niche. His supplies ran low, and he ate less, but would not risk a startling shot. He rationed his tobacco, and when it was gone worked up to a vomiting sickness every three days for nine days, but did not miss a night in the niche. All winter he did not remove his clothes, bathe, shave, cut his hair or sing. He worked the dead mine only to be busy, and became thin again, with sunken eyes which yet were not the eyes he had come with the spring before. It was April, his food almost gone, when he got his chance.

There was a half moon that night, which made the canyon walls black, and occasionally gleamed on wrinkles of the overflow. The cat came down so quietly that Suttler did not see him until he was beside the basin. The animal was suspicious. He took the wind, and twice started to drink, and didn't, but crouched. On Suttler's face there was a set grin which exposed his teeth.

"Not even a drink, you bastard," he thought.

The cat drank a little though, and dropped again, softly, trying to get the scent from the meadow. Suttler drew slowly upon his soul in the trigger. When it gave, the report was magnified impressively in the canyon. The cougar sprang straight into the air and screamed outrageously. The back of Suttler's neck was cold and his hands trembled, but he shucked the lever and fired again. This shot ricocheted from the basin and whined away thinly. The first, however, had struck near enough. The cat began to scramble rapidly on the loose stone, at first without voice, then screaming repeatedly. It doubled upon itself snarling and chewing in a small furious circle, fell and began to throw itself in short, leaping spasms upon the stones, struck across the rim of the tank and lay half in the water, its head and shoulders raised in one corner and resting against the cliff. Suttler could hear it breathing hoarsely and snarling very faintly. The soprano chorus of swallows gradually became silent.

Suttler had risen to fire again, but lowered the carbine and advanced, stopping at every step to peer intently and listen for the hoarse breathing, which continued. Even when he was within five feet of the tank the cougar did not move, except to gasp so that the water again splashed from the basin. Suttler was calmed by the certainty of accomplishment. He drew the heavy revolver from his holster, aimed carefully at the rattling head, and fired again. The canyon boomed, and the east responded faintly and a little behind, but Suttler did not hear them, for the cat thrashed heavily in the tank, splashing him as with a bucket, and then lay still on its side over the edge, its muzzle and forepaws hanging. The water was settling quietly in the tank, but Suttler stirred it again, shooting five more times with great delibera-tion into the heavy body, which did not move except at the impact of the slugs.

The rest of the night, even after the moon was gone, he worked fiercely, slitting and tearing with his knife. In the morning, under the swallows, he dragged the marbled carcass, still bleeding a little in places, onto the rocks on the side away from the spring, and dropped it. Dragging the ragged hide by the neck, he went unsteadily down the canyon to the cabin, where he slept like a drunkard, although his whiskey had been gone for two months.

In the afternoon, with dreaming eyes, he bore the pelt to Jenny's grave, took down the stones with his hands, shoveled the earth from her, covered her with the skin, and again with earth and the cairn.

He looked at this monument. "There," he said.

That night, for the first time since her death, he slept through.

In the morning, at the well, he repeated his cleansing ritual of a year before, save that they were rags he stretched to dry, even to the dance upon the rock platform while drying. Squatting naked and clean, shaven and clipped, he looked for a long time at the grinning countenance, now very dirty, of the plump girl in front of the blossoming rhododendrons, and in the resumption of his dance he made singing noises accompanied by the words, "Spring, spring, beautiful spring." He was a starved but revived and volatile spirit.

An hour later he went south, his boot soles held on by canvas strips, and did not once look back.

The disturbed life of the spring resumed. In the second night the rabbits loved in the willows, and at the end of a week the rats played in the cabin again. The old coyote and a vulture cleaned the cougar, and his bones fell apart in the shale. The road-runner came up one day, tentatively, and in front of the tunnel snatched up a horned toad and ran with it around the corner, but no farther. After a month the antelope returned. The well brimmed, and in the gentle sunlight the new aspen leaves made a tiny music of shadows.

QUESTIONS

1. There is only one human character in this story, but one animal is given a name and a personality. Why is the description of this animal different from that of all the others in the canyon?

2. As the title implies, this is a story about a man and a place. Compare the canyon that contains the Indian well with the canyons in Jack London's "All Gold Canyon" (p. 73) and Zane Grey's "Canyon Walls" (p. 143).

3. How are contests between the road runner and the rattlesnake, the coyotes and the rabbits, and even the cougar and the burro different from the contest between Jim Suttler and the cougar? Explain.

4. The author says that Jim Suttler came up the canyon to take his part in one cycle "of the well's resistance, each of which was an epitome of centuries, and perhaps of the wars of the universe." What does this mean?

5. The author says that Jim Suttler, when he and Jenny first entered the canyon, "looked like one of the probably mistaken conceptions of Christ." But then he adds that Suttler was unlike Christ in several ways. What were they?

6. "One learns to do business slowly with deserts and mountains." Comment.

7. How is the loneliness of Jim Suttler typical of the essential loneliness of the heroes of most Western stories? Explain.

PART THREE

MYTH

One indication of the essentially mythic quality of the Western story is the almost continual consideration it has received from social historians, philosophers, sociologists, political scientists, psychologists, theologians, and critics of popular culture. Almost always these thinkers have considered the Western story as *one* myth—one representation of something peculiarly important to Americans and to American society.

Individual writers of Western novels complain of critical neglect. They say, with truth, that their books are rarely reviewed and that their individual achievements go uncelebrated, unremarked. Yet Western stories as a group have provoked millions of words of analysis and comment. Lawyers and political scientists have examined the nature of crime, violence, revenge, and law in literature, and some have found the Western hero to be the embodiment of racism, imperialism, or the virtues of free enterprise. Sociologists have found illustrations of American physical and social mobility, male chauvinism, and community formation. Psychologists have run wild through the purple sage, finding phallic symbols in six-guns, totemism in cattle brands, and sibling rivalry and Oedipus complexes operative in almost all Western heroes. Theologians have remarked the great attraction of ethical simplifications in many Westerns, yet they have often deplored a constant glorification of violence.

As early as 1902, when Frank Norris wrote "A Neglected Epic," critics believed that the development of the American West offered an unusually promising subject for fiction. Like Norris, too, they scoffed at the dime novels and sensational melodramas that had been written about the frontier.

At the same time, writers like Owen Wister were proclaiming the essential truth of their fiction. *The Virginian,* Wister said, was "of necessity historical." Other authors similarly maintained that their novels were "true to the West," and Zane Grey always insisted that his romances were "true." His "Foreword" to *To the Last Man* (1922) is in this respect typical of his statements about his work.

But critics have consistently denied the validity of such claims to historical or even spiritual truth. Like T. K. Whipple, they have seen Western heroes as primitive fictions. Or like Alexander Miller, they have seen Westerns as attractive oversimplifications of human problems. Some, like other writers reprinted here, have seen Western stories as glorifications of American strength or foreign policy, or as presentations of great ethical dilemmas, or as studies in life-styles and manners.

Taken together, the few essays reprinted here can illustrate only a small part of the diversity of criticism devoted to Western stories. Because of space limitations, many kinds of thought are necessarily unrepresented. There is no sampling, for instance, of psychoanalytic approaches to the actions and characters of the Western story. There are few suggestions of the many attempts to link Western stories with archetypal myths, legends, or folklore. And there are no studies of the transformation of oral tradition into full-blown legendry. All of these approaches, however, are represented in the suggested readings at the end of the book, and so they remain open to further exploration, study, and consideration by the student.

FRANK NORRIS

A NEGLECTED EPIC

As I have tried to point out once before in these pages, the Frontier has disappeared. The westward-moving course of empire has at last crossed the Pacific Ocean. Civilization has circled the globe and has come back to its starting point, the vague and mysterious East.

The thing has not been accomplished peacefully. From the very first it has been an affair of wars—of invasions. Invasions of the East by the West, and of raids north and south—raids accomplished by flying columns that dashed out from both sides of the main army. Sometimes even the invaders have fought among themselves, as for instance the Trojan War, or the civil wars of Italy, England and America; sometimes they have turned back on their tracks and, upon one pretext or another, reconquered the races behind them, as for instance Alexander's wars to the eastward, the Crusades, and Napoleon's Egyptian campaigns.

Retarded by all these obstacles, the march has been painfully slow. To move from Egypt to Greece took centuries of time. More centuries were consumed in the campaign that brought empire from Greece to Rome, and still more centuries passed before it crossed the Alps and invaded northern and western Europe.

But observe. Once across the Mississippi, the West—our Far West—was conquered in about forty years. In all the vast campaign from east to west here is the most signal victory, the swiftest, the completest, the most brilliant achievement—the wilderness subdued at a single stroke.

Now all these various fightings to the westward, these mysterious race-movements, migrations, wars and wanderings have produced their literature, distinctive, peculiar, excellent. And this literature we call epic. The Trojan War gave us the "Iliad," the "Odyssey" and the "Æneid"; the campaign of the Greeks in Asia Minor produced the "Anabasis"; a whole cycle of literature grew from the conquest of Europe after the fall of Rome—"The Song of Roland," "The Nibelungenlied," "The Romance of the Rose," "Beowulf," "Magnusson," "The Scotch Border Ballads," "The Poem of the Cid," "The Hemskringla," "Orlando Furioso," "Jerusalem Delivered," and the like.

On this side of the Atlantic, in his clumsy, artificial way, but yet recognized as a producer of literature, Cooper has tried to chronicle the conquest of the eastern part of our country. Absurd he may be in his ideas of life and character, the art in him veneered over with charlatanism; yet the man was solemn enough and took his work seriously, and his work is literature.

Also a cycle of romance has grown up around the Civil War. The theme has had its poets to whom the public have been glad to listen. The subject is vast, noble; is in a word epic, just as the Trojan War and the Retreat of the Ten Thousand were epic.

But when at last one comes to look for the literature that sprang from and has grown up around the last great epic event in the history of civilization, the event which in spite of stupendous difficulties was consummated more swiftly, more completely, more satisfactorily than any like event since the westward migration began—I mean the conquering of the West, the subduing of the wilderness beyond the Mississippi—What has this produced in the way of literature? The dime novel! The dime novel and nothing else. The dime novel and nothing better.

The Trojan War left to posterity the character of Hector; the wars with the Saracens gave us Roland; the folklore of Iceland produced Grettir; the Scotch border poetry brought forth the Douglas; the Spanish epic the Cid. But the American epic, just as heroic, just as elemental, just as important and as picturesque, will fade into history leaving behind no finer type, no nobler hero than Buffalo Bill.

The young Greeks sat on marble terraces overlooking the Aegean Sea and listened to the thunderous roll of Homer's hexameter. In the feudal castles the minstrel sang to the young boys, of Roland. The farm folk of Iceland to this very day treasure up and read to their little ones hand-written copies of the Gretla Saga chronicling the deeds and death of Grettir the Strong. But the youth of the United States learn of their epic by paying a dollar to see the "Wild West Show."

The plain truth of the matter is that we have neglected our epic—the black shame of it be on us—and no contemporaneous poet or chronicler thought it worth his while to sing the song or tell the tale of the West, because literature in the day when the West was being won was a cult indulged in by certain well-bred gentlemen in New England who looked eastward to the Old World, to the legends of England and Norway and Germany and Italy for their inspiration, and left the great, strong, honest, fearless, resolute deeds of their own countrymen to be defamed and defaced by the nameless hacks of the "yellow back" libraries.

One man—who wrote "How Santa Claus Came to Simpson's Bar"—one poet, one chronicler did, in fact, arise for the moment, who understood that wild, brave life and who for a time gave promise of bearing record of things seen.

One of the requirements of an epic—a true epic is that its action must devolve upon some great national event. There was no lack of such in those fierce years after '49. Just that long and terrible journey from the Mississippi to the ocean is an epic in itself. Yet no serious attempt has ever been made by an American author to render into prose or verse this event in our history as "national" in scope, in origin and in results as the Revolution itself. The prairie schooner is as large a figure in the legends as the black ship that bore Ulysses homeward from Troy. The sea meant as much to the Argonauts of the fifties as it did to the ten thousand.

And the Alamo! There is a trumpet-call in the word; and only the look of it on the printed page is a flash of fire. But the very histories slight the deed, and to many an American, born under the same flag that the Mexican rifles shot to ribbons on that splendid day, the word is meaningless. Yet Thermopylae was less glorious, and in comparison with that siege the investment of Troy was mere wanton riot. At the very least the Texans in that battered adobe church fought for the honor of their flag and the greater glory of their country, not for loot or the possession of the person of an adulteress. Young men are taught to consider the Iliad, with its butcheries, its glorification of inordinate selfishness and vanity, as a classic. Achilles, murderer, egoist, ruffian and liar, is a hero. But the name of Bowie, the name of the man who gave his life to his flag at the Alamo, is perpetuated only in the designation of a knife. Crockett is the hero only of a "funny story" about a sagacious coon; while Travis, the boy commander who did what Gordon with an empire back of him failed to do, is quietly and definitely ignored.

Because we have done nothing to get at the truth about the West, because our best writers have turned to the old country folklore and legends for their inspiration, because "melancholy harlequins" strut in fringed leggings upon the street corners, one hand held out for pennies, we have come to believe that our West, our epic, was an affair of Indians, road agents and desperadoes, and have taken no account of the brave men who stood for law and justice and liberty, and for those great ideas died by the hundreds, unknown and unsung; died that the West might be subdued, that the last stage of the march should be accomplished, that the Anglo-Saxon should fulfil his destiny and complete the cycle of the world.

The great figure of our neglected epic, the Hector of our ignored Iliad, is not, as the dime novels would have us believe, a lawbreaker, but a lawmaker; a fighter, it is true, as is always the case with epic figures, but a fighter for peace, a calm, grave, strong man who hated the lawbreaker as the hound hates the wolf.

He did not lounge in barrooms; he did not cheat at cards; he did not drink himself to maudlin fury; he did not "shoot at the drop of the hat." But he loved his horse, he loved his friend, he was kind to little children; he was always ready to side with the weak against the strong, with the poor against the rich. For hypocrisy and pretence, for shams and subterfuges, he had no mercy, no tolerance. He was too brave to lie and too strong to steal. The odds in that lawless day were ever against him; his enemies were many and his friends were few; but his face was always set bravely against evil, and fear was not in him even at the end. For such a man as this could die no quiet death in a land where law went no further than the statute books and life lay in the crook of my neighbor's forefinger.

He died in defense of an ideal, an epic hero, a legendary figure, formidable, sad. He died facing down injustice, dishonesty and crime; died "in his boots"; and the same world that has glorified Achilles and forgotten Travis finds none so poor to do him reverence. No literature has sprung up around him—this great character native to America. He is of all the world-types the one distinctive to us—peculiar, particular and unique. He is dead and even his work is misinterpreted and misunderstood. His very memory will soon be gone, and the American epic, which on the shelves of posterity should have stood shoulder to shoulder with the "Hemskringla" and the "Tales of the Nibelungen" and the "Song of Roland," will never be written.

QUESTIONS

1. Norris published this essay in the same year (1902) that Owen Wister's *The Virginian* was published. How does his description of "the great figure of our neglected epic" compare with the typical hero of the Western stories written after *The Virginian?*

2. Most of the epics cited by Norris are long narrative poems. Why, do you think, has so little poetry been written about the West and Westerners?

3. What were the "dime novels"? Why should Norris have been disappointed that in his day they had been almost the only literature about the West?

4. Although Western stories have been vastly popular, selling millions of copies and being adapted for hundreds of films, none has ever been generally accepted by critics as an important work of literature. Does this fact help to support Norris's belief that the American epic will never be written?

5. What do you understand a book review to mean if it says a novel has "epic sweep"? What do you expect when you go to see a movie that is described in advertisements as "an epic"?

ZANE GREY

foreword to
TO THE LAST MAN

It was inevitable that in my efforts to write romantic history of the great West I should at length come to the story of a feud. For long I have steered clear of this rock. But at last I have reached it and must go over it, driven by my desire to chronicle the stirring events of pioneer days.

Even to-day it is not possible to travel into the remote corners of the West without seeing the lives of people still affected by a fighting past. How can the truth be told about the pioneering of the West if the struggle, the fight, the blood be left out? It cannot be done. How can a novel be stirring and thrilling, as were those times, unless it be full of sensation? My long labors have been devoted to making stories resemble the times they depict. I have loved the West for its vastness, its contrast, its beauty and color and life, for its wildness and violence, and for the fact that I have seen how it developed great men and women who died unknown and unsung.

In this materialistic age, this hard, practical, swift, greedy age of realism, it seems there is no place for writers of romance, no place for romance itself. For many years all the events leading up to the great war were realistic, and the war itself was horribly realistic, and the aftermath is likewise. Romance is only another name for idealism; and I contend that life without ideals is not worth living. Never in the history of the world were ideals needed so terribly as now. Walter Scott wrote romance; so did Victor Hugo; and likewise Kipling, Hawthorne, Stevenson. It was Stevenson, particularly, who wielded a bludgeon against the realists. People live for the dream in their hearts. And I have yet to know anyone who has not some secret dream, some hope, however dim, some storied wall to look at in the dusk, some painted window leading to the soul. How strange indeed to find that the realists have ideals and dreams! To read them one would think their lives held nothing significant. But they love, they hope, they dream, they sacrifice, they struggle on with that dream in their hearts just the same as others. We all are dreamers, if not in the heavy-lidded wasting of time, then in the meaning of life that makes us work on.

It was Wordsworth who wrote, "The world is too much with us"; and if I could give the secret of my ambition as a novelist in a few words it would be contained in that quotation. My inspiration to write has always come from nature. Character and action are subordinated to setting. In all that I have done I have tried to make people see how the world is too much with them. Getting and spending they lay waste their powers, with never a breath of the free and wonderful life of the open!

So I come back to the main point of this foreword, in which I am trying to tell why and how I came to write the story of a feud notorious in Arizona as the Pleasant Valley War.

Some years ago Mr. Harry Adams, a cattleman of Vermajo Park, New Mexico, told me he had been in the Tonto Basin of Arizona and thought I might find interesting material there concerning this Pleasant Valley War. His version of the war between cattlemen and sheepmen certainly determined me to look over the ground. My old guide, Al Doyle of Flagstaff, had led me over half of Arizona, but never down into that wonderful wild and rugged basin between the Mogollon Mesa and the Mazatzal Mountains. Doyle had long lived on the frontier and his version of the Pleasant Valley War differed markedly from that of Mr. Adams. I asked other old timers about it, and their remarks further excited my curiosity.

Once down there, Doyle and I found the wildest, most rugged, roughest, and most remarkable country either of us had visited; and the few inhabitants were like the country. I went in ostensibly to hunt bear and lion and turkey, but what I really was hunting for was the story of that Pleasant Valley War. I engaged the services of a bear hunter who had three strapping sons as reserved and strange and aloof as he was. No wheel tracks of any kind had ever come within miles of their cabin. I spent two wonderful months hunting game and reveling in the beauty and grandeur of that Rim Rock country, but I came out knowing no more about the Pleasant Valley War. These Texans and their few neighbors, likewise from Texas, did not talk. But all I saw and felt only inspired me the more. This trip was in the fall of 1918.

The next year I went again with the best horses, outfit, and men the Doyles could provide. And this time I did not ask any questions. But I rode horses—some of them too wild for me—and packed a rifle many a hundred miles, riding sometimes thirty and forty miles a day, and I climbed in and out of the deep cañons, desperately staying at the heels of one of those long-legged Texans. I learned the life of those backwoodsmen, but I did not get the story of the Pleasant Valley War. I had, however, won the friendship of that hardy people.

In 1920 I went back with a still larger outfit, equipped to stay as long as I liked. And this time, without my asking it, different natives of the Tonto came to tell me about the Pleasant Valley War. No two of them agreed on anything concerning it, except that only one of the active participants survived the fighting. Whence comes my title, *To the Last Man.* Thus I was swamped in a mass of material out of which I could only flounder to my own conclusion. Some of the stories told me are singularly tempting to a novelist. But, though I believe them myself, I cannot risk their improbability to those who have no idea of the wildness of wild men at a wild time. There really was a terrible and bloody feud, perhaps the most deadly and least known in all the annals of the West. I saw the ground, the cabins, the graves, all so darkly suggestive of what must have happened.

I never learned the truth of the cause of the Pleasant Valley War, or if I did hear it I had no means of recognizing it. All the given causes were plausible and convincing. Strange to state, there is still secrecy and reticence all over the Tonto Basin as to the facts of this feud. Many descendents of those killed are living there now. But no one likes to talk about it. Assuredly many of the incidents told me really occurred, as, for example, the terrible one of the two women, in the face of relentless enemies, saving the bodies of their dead husbands from being devoured by wild hogs. Suffice it to say that this romance is true to my conception of the war, and I base it upon the setting I learned to know and love so well, upon the strange passions of primitive people, and upon my instinctive reaction to the facts and rumors that I gathered.

QUESTIONS

1. What does Grey mean by calling his melodramatic novels "romantic history"?

2. "My inspiration to write has always come from nature. Character and action are subordinated to setting." Is this statement by Grey borne out by his story "Canyon Walls" (p. 143)?

3. Grey says, "Romance is only another name for idealism; and I contend that life without ideals is not worth living." Does this statement mean that an idealist cannot write a realistic novel?

4. Feuds have usually been associated with the mountain people of Appalachia; there have been few family feuds in the American West. Why, then, was it "inevitable" that Grey should have to write a novel about one?

5. "In this materialistic age, this hard, practical, swift, greedy age of realism, it seems there is no place for writers of romance, no place for romance itself." Why does Grey, who achieved greater popularity than any other writer of his time, make this statement?

T. K. WHIPPLE

AMERICAN SAGAS

As everyone knows, the latest fad of the intelligentsia is discovering the United States. This is the cult of which Mr. Gilbert Seldes is high priest. He and his acolytes wax analytic and aesthetic over Charlie Chaplin, Fanny Brice, Krazy Kat, Ring Lardner, and "How Come You Do Me Like You Do Do Do." And, indeed, why not? The rest of us may be amused at the delighted surprise with which recent graduates of Harvard "discover" what everyone else has been familiar with since earliest childhood—but the fact remains that Mr. Seldes has secured for our popular arts a recognition that they never had before. Already jazz has invaded Carnegie Hall, and before long everyone may be attending recitals not of Lithuanian, Swedish, and Bantu folk songs only, but of American as well. The Negro spirituals have arrived; why not the ballads of cowboys, lumberjacks, and Kentucky mountaineers?

While the boom is on, I wish to put in a word for the tales of the American folk. In Paris, according to hearsay, one of the more recent literary finds is James Oliver Curwood, whose art is discussed at length in periodicals and reviews. My own nominee, however, for the position of American *tusitala* is not Mr. Curwood, but Zane Grey. Mr. Grey has received justice only from his millions of devoted readers— and some of them, I fear, have been shamefaced in their enthusiasm. The critics and reviewers have been persistently upstage in their treatment of Mr. Grey; they have lectured him for lacking qualities which there was no reason for him to possess, and have ignored most of the qualities in which he is conspicuous. The Boston *Transcript* complains that "he does not ask his readers to think for themselves"; Mr. Burton Rascoe asks sorrowfully: "Do Mr. Grey's readers believe in the existence of such people as Mr. Grey depicts; do they accept the code of conduct implicit in Mr. Grey's novels?"

One thing at least is clear: Mr. Grey himself emphatically believes in the truthfulness of his record. Above all else he prides himself upon his accuracy as a historian. In the foreword to *To the Last Man* he says: "My long labors have been devoted to making stories resemble the times they depict. I have loved the West for its vastness, its contrast, its beauty and color and life, for its wildness and violence, and for the fact that I have seen how it developed great men and women who died unknown and unsung." And he asks: "How can the truth be told about the pioneering of the West if the struggle, the fight, the blood be left out? How can a novel be stirring and thrilling, as were those times, unless it be full of sensation?" One must admire and be thankful for Mr. Grey's faith in his own veracity; but to share it is impossible. Zane Grey should never be considered as a realist. To Mr. Rascoe's questions, I can answer for only one reader, but I should say that I no more believe in the existence of such people as Mr. Grey's than I believe in the existence of the shepherds of Theocritus; I no more accept the code of conduct implicit in Mr. Grey's novels than I do the code of conduct implicit in Congreve's comedies. At the very start I grant that Mr. Grey does not portray the world as I know it, that he is not an expert psychologist, that his is no refined art in the subtle use of words—that in competition with Henry James, Jane Austen, George Eliot, and Laurence Sterne he is nowhere.

But what of it? There is no reason for comparing him with anyone, unless perhaps with competitors in his own genre. If he must be classified, however, let it be with the authors of *Beowulf* and of the Icelandic sagas. Mr. Grey's work is a primitive epic, and has the characteristics of other primitive epics. His art is archaic, with the traits of all archaic art. His style, for example, has the stiffness which comes from an imperfect mastery of the medium. It lacks fluency and facility; behind it always we feel a pressure toward expression, a striving for a freer and easier utterance. Herein lies much of the charm of all early art—in that the technique lags somewhat behind the impulse. On the whole, it is preferable to the later condition, when the technique is matured and the impulse meager. Mr. Grey's style has also the stiffness of traditional and conventional forms; his writing is encrusted with set phrases which may be called epic formulae, or, if you insist, clichés. These familiar locutions he uses as if they were new, to him at least—as if they were happy discoveries of his own. So behind all his impeded utterance there makes itself felt an effort toward truth of expression—truth, that is, to his own vision, for we must never ask of him truth to the actual world as we know it.

That Zane Grey has narrative power no one has denied, but not everyone is pleased with his type of story. To a reader whose taste has been formed on Howells and Bennett, Mr. Grey's tales seem somewhat strong. They are, of course, sensational melodrama, as "improbable" as plays by Elizabethan dramatists. They roar along over the mightiest stage that the author has been able to contrive for them. They tell of battle and bloodshed, of desperate pursuits and hairbreadth escapes, of mortal feuds and murder and sudden death, of adventures in which life is constantly the stake. These stories move on the grand scale; they are lavish in primitive, epic events. Mr. Grey does not dodge big scenes and crises, in which plot and passion come to a head; he has a distinct liking for intense situations, and he has the power which Stevenson so admired of projecting these high moments in memorable pictures. In *Riders of the Purple Sage*, when Lassiter throws his guns on the Mormon band and saves the Gentile youth, when Venters from his hiding place in the mysterious canyon watches the robbers ride through the waterfall, when at last Lassiter rolls the stone which crushes his pursuers and forever shuts the outlet from Surprise Valley—these are scenes which linger in the mind. Very different, obviously, is this art from Mrs. Wharton's when she condenses the tragedy of three lives into the breaking of a pickle dish, and from Sinclair Lewis' as he takes Babbitt through a typical day at the office. But what of that? Though melodrama is not in style at the moment, the human taste for tremendous happenings is not likely to die for some centuries yet. Mr. Grey has the courage of his innocence in tackling difficulties which cautious realists know enough to avoid.

And no more than in his stories does he dodge the heroic in his characters. His people are all larger than life size. They may be called cowpunchers, prospectors, ranchers, rangers, rustlers, highwaymen, but they are akin to Sigurd, Beowulf, and Robin Hood. Just at present, heroism, of all literary motifs, happens to be the most unfashionable, and disillusionment is all the cry. But it is tenable surely that the heroic is not incompatible with literary merit, and perhaps even that a naïve belief in human greatness is a positive asset to literature. Certainly of the writings in the past which humanity has singled out for special favor most have this element, notoriously strong in all early literature.

Of these heroic figures Mr. Grey's portrayal is crude and roughhewn. Their speech is often far from the talk of actual men and women; we are as much—and as little—conscious of the writer's working in a literary convention as when we read a play in blank verse. His characterization has no subtlety or finesse; but, like his style, it is true—again, of course, I mean true to the author's own conception. That conception of human nature is a simple one; he sees it as a battle of passions with one another and with the will, a struggle of love and hate, of remorse and revenge, of blood lust, honor, friendship, anger, grief—all on a grand scale and all incalculable and mysterious. The people themselves are amazed and incredulous at what they find in their own souls. A good illustration of Mr. Grey's psychological analysis is the following from *The Lone Star Ranger*:

> Then came realization. . . . He was the gunman, the gun-thrower, the gun-fighter, passionate and terrible. His father's blood, that dark and fierce strain, his mother's spirit, that strong and unquenchable spirit of the surviving pioneer—these had been in him; and the killings, one after another, the wild and haunted years, had made him, absolutely in spite

of his will, the gunman. He realized it now, bitterly, hopelessly. The thing he had intelligence enough to hate he had become. At last he shuddered under the driving, ruthless, inhuman blood-lust of the gunman.

In Zane Grey's conception of human nature nothing is more curious than his view of sex. In *Riders of the Purple Sage* a young man and a girl live alone together for weeks in a secret canyon; in *The Lone Star Ranger* the hero rescues an innocent girl from a gang of bandits and roams about Texas with her for a long time—and all as harmlessly as in *The Faerie Queene* Una and the Red Cross Knight go traveling together. Nothing shows more clearly how far away Mr. Grey's world is from actuality; his Texas is not in the Union, but in fairyland. His heroes, to be sure, have occasional fierce struggles with their "baser natures"—a difficulty, by the way, from which his heroines are exempt. Not all his women, however, are altogether pure; from time to time a seductress crosses the path of the hero, who usually regards her with indifference. These women, incidentally, are often among the best-drawn of Mr. Grey's characters. In his treatment of sex as in other respects Mr. Grey is simple and naïve; his conventions are as remote as those of the medieval Courts of Love, and must be taken for granted along with the other assumptions of his imaginary world.

Mr. Grey's heroic ideal looks a little strange in the twentieth century. It is; it belongs more naturally to the sixth century; it is the brutal ideal of the barbarian, of the Anglo-Saxons before they left their continental homes. Like them, Mr. Grey cares above all things for physical strength, for prowess in battle and expertness with weapons, for courage and fortitude and strength of will, for ability to control oneself and others. Where the Anglo-Saxon emphasized loyalty in thegn and generosity in earl, Mr. Grey more democratically insists on loyalty and generosity between friends, and on independence and self-reliance. And to this code he adds an element which is no doubt a kind of residuum from Christianity: he likes to see hatred and desire for vengeance supplanted by forgiveness and love. The process of purification or redemption is a favorite theme of his; sometimes it is brought about by the influence of a noble and unselfish man or by the love of a pure and innocent girl, but more often by the cleansing effect of nature in the rough. If one is to take Mr. Grey's ethics at all seriously, one must of course find fault with them; although such morals are better, no doubt, than those inculcated by Benjamin Franklin or Mr. Ben Hecht, still one would no more care to have one's sons adopt Mr. Grey's *beau idéal* than one would care to have one's sons adopt, say, the *Saga of Burnt Njal* as a program of life. Without wishing, however, to return to the human

ideals of the Bronze Age, we may insist that a storyteller's merit is not
dependent on the validity of the lessons which he teaches. There is
something of the savage in most of us, so that we can respond
imaginatively to Mr. Grey without our all rushing off to the wild to be
made men of.

Not that Mr. Grey regards nature as always a beneficent force.
Rather, he portrays it as an acid test of those elemental traits of
character which he admires. It kills off the weaklings, and among the
strong it makes the bad worse and the good better. Nature to him is
somewhat as God is to a Calvinist—ruthlessly favoring the elect and
damning the damned. Mr. Grey sees in nature the great primal force
which molds human lives. Not even Thomas Hardy lays more stress
on the effect of natural environment. The stories themselves are
subsidiary to the background: "My inspiration to write," says Mr.
Grey, "has always come from nature. Character and action are
subordinate to setting." This setting of desert, forest, mountain, and
canyon, great cliffs and endless plains, has been made familiar to us all
by the movies if not by travel; but as seen through Mr. Grey's
marveling and enhancing eyes it all takes on a fresh and unreal
greatness and wonder. For his descriptive power is as generally
recognized as his narrative skill; indeed, it would be hard for anyone
so overflowing with zest and with almost religious adoration to fail in
description. Mr. Grey's faculty of wonder, his sense of mystery, is
strong; it shows itself in his feeling for the strangeness of human
personality and also more outwardly in the air of strangeness with
which he invests his lonely wanderers or outlaws who from time to
time appear out of the unknown—but most of all it shows itself in his
feeling for the marvelous in nature. So far as he indicates a religion, it
is a form of nature worship; when he is face to face with the more
grandiose aspects of the earth's surface, he feels himself in the
presence of God.

Mr. Grey differs from many nature lovers, that is to say, in that
his fervor is altogether genuine. His enthusiasm is not assumed
because it is the proper thing; on the contrary, he feels much more
than he can manage to express. And here, I think, we come to the
secret of his superiority to most of his contemporaries and competitors: he is sincere and thoroughly in earnest. He really cares, he gets
excited about what he is writing. His books have not the look of
hackwork. It is true that they are uneven, that he has not been
immune to the influences of his own popularity and of the movies,
that he must often have worked hastily and carelessly—but he has
never written falsely. He is genuine and true to himself, an artist after
his fashion. Furthermore, he possesses a powerful imagination, of the
mythmaking type which glorifies and enlarges all that it touches, and
in his best work, such as *Riders of the Purple Sage*, he uses his

imagination to the utmost. The whole story, the situations and people and settings, are fully living in his mind, and he gets them into words as best he can. Of course he has an amazing, an incredible simplicity and unsophistication of mind, a childlike naïveté—but that is what makes him what he is, a fashioner of heroic myths. At the present moment, when the primitive is all the vogue in the arts, and Viennese and Parisian sculptors are doing their best to be archaic, in Zane Grey we have a real, not a would-be, primitive miraculously dropped among us; yet we accord him no recognition at all—except an astounding popularity.

If, that is, his popularity is astounding—if it is not, rather, what should be expected. Most Americans seem to have a strongly ingrained hankering for the primitive and a good deal of the childlike quality of mind, possibly as an inheritance from our three centuries of pioneering. Whenever a holiday comes along, we reproduce primitive conditions and play at pioneering as much as possible. The age of the pioneers, especially in the West, is taking on more and more the air of a heroic and mythic period. The glorification of the redblooded he-man, the pioneer ideal, is a national trait, and even those who have learned better cannot rid themselves of a sneaking respect for the brute in their hearts. If you doubt the simplicity and innocence of Americans, watch their reactions to Michael Arlen and Jean Cocteau and their forlorn efforts to imitate Ronald Firbank and to understand and admire *Ulysses*. They are like stray Vandals wandering bewildered through the streets of Byzantium. Only the pure in heart could be so impressed by decay and corruption, just as only a man from an Iowa village could have written *The Blind Bow-Boy*. No, the American forte is not sophisticated disillusion—it is much more likely to be something on the order of Zane Grey's work. Of course everyone is at liberty not to like such literature, which belongs by right to the infancy of the race, and to disagree with Mr. Grey's view of the world. Indeed, if one asks of books a valid criticism of life as we experience it, Mr. Grey has little to offer. But let us look at him for what he is, rather than what he is not. Then, whether or not we happen to care for his work, I think we must grant him a certain merit in his own way. We turn to him not for insight into human nature and human problems nor for refinements of art, but simply for crude epic stories, as we might to an old Norse skald, maker of the sagas of the folk.

QUESTIONS

1. Whipple quotes Zane Grey's foreword to *To the Last Man* and then concludes, "One must admire and be thankful for Mr. Grey's

faith in his own veracity; but to share it is impossible." Why is it impossible to believe that Grey told the truth about the pioneering of the West?

2. Why does Whipple believe that Grey has written the epics of the West that Frank Norris had hoped would be written?

3. Why does Whipple consider that in Zane Grey's conception of human nature "nothing is more curious than his view of sex"?

4. Whipple says that "we may insist that a storyteller's merit is not dependent on the validity of the lessons which he teaches." Does this mean that a great storyteller can teach immorality or treason?

5. How are the characters of Western stories like the shepherds of Theocritus or Virgil? What is a pastoral?

ALEXANDER MILLER

THE "WESTERN"—
A THEOLOGICAL NOTE

A while ago I had a week-end visit from a fellow theologian who made it clear early on the Saturday that he would accept no engagements that clashed with *Gunsmoke* on TV. Since I watch *Gunsmoke* myself, come hell or high water, I knew I had a kindred spirit as well as a fellow apostle. So we spent the early part of the evening analyzing the appeal of the show, which is not wholly to be explained by its undeniable quality. For not only do I find myself maneuvering to watch TV westerns of lesser quality than *Gunsmoke*, but I discover that through the long years I retain an unabated zest for every kind of western yarn, in print or in picture. And while I'm glad of quality when I can find it, a western has to be pretty bad before I find it intolerable. Enough for me if the hero runs to type, if there is the scent of sage and the squeak of saddle-leather, if the high hills are high enough.

At one level the attraction of the thing is obvious. I am professionally involved with the high matters of speculation and the deep matters of theology; and nothing is more relaxing after a bout with Hegel or Niebuhr than a vicarious ride into the sage. And there is the practical advantage that this particular escape-mechanism costs but twenty-five cents in paperback (plus one cent sales tax in some states). It's rarely necessary even to buy a new one. An old one will do equally well, since nothing of it sticks in the mind, and the formula is constant.

My friend wanted to go deeper. "If just once," said he, "I could stand in the dust of the frontier main street, facing an indubitably bad man who really deserved extermination, and with smoking six-gun actually exterminate him—shoot once and see him drop. Just once to face real and unqualified evil, plug it and see it drop . . ." None of this complex business of separating the sin from the sinner, of tempering justice with mercy, of remembering our own complicity in evil. To blow, just once, an actual and visible hole in the wall of evil, instead of beating the air with vain exhortation and the nicely calculated less and more of moral discrimination and doleful casuistry. To see something actually drop, as the gospel says Satan once fell as lightning from heaven.

Yet there must be more to it than that, and there *is* more to it than that. Another theologian friend of mine, whose specialty is Christian ethics, makes a point of reading the *Saturday Evening Post* from cover to cover, since, he says, it is a transcript of American folkways; and if the gospel is to be taken into all the world, the contemporary world into which it has to be taken is between the covers of the *Satevepost*. (I know other professional colleagues who find the same illumination in the funnies, but I don't read the funnies. I can't find time to master Pogo and Kingaroo, which appear to be theological staples; and in any event, when I'm worn out with Hegel everything is too strenuous except the westerns.) The western serial is standard in the *Post*, for the good and trite reason that it is *par excellence* the American folk tale.

The quality of "western" writing varies endlessly. Eugene Manlove Rhodes was a literary artist of high caliber. Ernest Haycox could and did write as well as the next man and better than most, but was apparently content to be, for the most part, the best of western hackwriters. He is only one of a number of highly competent operators. Then the stream runs out into a drab flatland of pedestrian writing (odd phrase for the horse opera!) which yet—at least for me—is never dull.

The so-called formula western is compact and predictable. It runs like this: Over the ridge of the high hills (or it may be against the backdrop of the desert) appears the maverick rider, he of the lean flanks, the taut, long-planed face, the lips stern yet capable of smiling, the dust of the trail in his clothes and on his horse. A single Colt, its butt hand-polished, hangs low on one hip (only lesser men carry two guns). His eyes miss nothing. Literally at random I take a paperback from a one-foot shelf of them:

> Cole Knapp rode through the dark-timbered passages of the La Sal Mountains and down into Paradox Valley with its high, bare walls, buff and red and white, bright-hued from the misty rain that was driven against them by a wind that was cool for June. Sage-brush, damp and dripping, gave off an odor both pungent and pleasant. A rock, loosened by rain, thundered off the rim to raise a low rumble on the valley floor.
>
> A big man, this Cole Knapp, but thin with riding and slim trail rations. Hide and bone and muscle, and travel-stained from the countless miles which lay between southern Arizona where he had started, and the western slope of Colorado where he now was.
>
> The gun at his right thigh was almost a part of him. . . . [Joseph Wayne: *Show-down at Stony Crest* (Dell), p. 5.]

As he drops over the last ridge, there on the flat or in the valley is the cattle town, a one-street town of clapboard—saloon, livery stable, store and sheriff's office, with a coffee-and-steak house in which the heroine (unless she is a cattleman's daughter) can be located handily, yet outside the saloon.

> Horse and rider came to a halt on the bluff overlooking Saddle-Up just as the sun dipped across the western line and began to sift into the canyon. The rider . . . hooked one leg over the saddle-horn and curled himself a cigarette, meanwhile surveying the dingy houses and the crooked dusty street of a town whose reputation was a by-word and a reproach all along the rolling leagues of two sovereign states. [Ernest Haycox: "The Bandit from Paloma County" in *Gun Talk* (Popular Library), p. 63.]

There is no reason why the rider should stop longer than to find vittles for himself and his cayuse. He is headed nowhere in particular, except that somewhere in the long distance lies the "spread" of his dreams. But he doubts that he will find it, or that he could settle if he did find it, for towns stifle him (he needs "a land where a man can breathe") and he knows no peace except under the stars. Yet his horse has no sooner catfooted it into town than he feels the tension in the place, "a full dozen pairs of eyes watching him from odd coverts." A shooting, the sight of a gratuitous beating, and he is hip-deep in the range war that is tearing the community apart.

Now there is nothing for it but to see it through, and see it through he does, surviving a half-dozen knock-down-drag-outs that would finish any normal man, snaking out the gun which is his pride and torment with a speed no man can match, and finally outdrawing the hired gunman brought in by the wicked cattle baron with the unsatisfied land-hunger. The ending is open: he may either marry the baron's daughter (or the local caterer who has feminine merits lacking in the baron's daughter) and find that "spread" on an unclaimed piece of bottom land; or he may take to the road again. In the first case he puts his gun away, as he had always longed to do. In the second case it stays strapped to his thigh, since in a world like this one there is always need for the law outside the law, the law embodied only in the strength of soul and speed of hand of the incorruptible man.

He is a philosopher after his fashion, but at no time does he understand the whys and the wherefores. Why not keep going? It's not his fight. And yet he cannot pass it up and "go on living with himself." "A man has to play the hand he's dealt." Yet now and then he takes time out to try to make sense of it all. But he's in a world that doesn't add up.

> Men were not meant for peace. Their minds, so filled with incessant wonder, would never let them alone, and their bodies were racked by feelings that eventually destroyed them; there was a form and a substance and a meaning somewhere, no doubt, but men died before

they knew what any of it was. [Ernest Haycox: *Long Storm* (Bantam Giant), p. 58.]

The pattern is worth analysis, if only because the flood of formula westerns grows greater all the time. I'm pretty sure that they now outnumber the sexy and salacious items on the pocket-book stands, and this is no doubt to the good. The TV channels are choked with them this fall, and this too is O.K. by me, both for their own sake and in view of the alternatives. But without being too heavy-handed about it, I would say that there must be some cultural symptoms here. It is not only the bulk of the phenomenon that requires explanation, but the pervasiveness of the appeal. My ten-year-old and I are radically unequal, I pride myself, in sophistication; yet we watch *Gunsmoke* or *Cheyenne* with equal absorption, and dang-bust it if I don't join him from time to time for *The Range-Rider.* Relaxing? Sure; and the sight of good horses against the skyline alone is worth the low price of admission. But one can, I think, without forcing it, find more in it than that: can find, in fact and in simplicity, most of the working philosophy, the bothersome confusions and the perplexed yearnings of the average 20th century American—maybe the average 20th century man, since you can find the same items in Charing Cross station as in Grand Central, and I myself am no American, but an amiable alien.

There is, for one thing, the eternal dialectic of pilgrimage and rest. The hero of this tale seeks his Shangri-la, his Tirna nOg—which for him is a place of good grass and free water: but he doubts if the world holds such a place; if it does, he doubts if he could bed down there in peace; and if his restlessness would let him stay, sure as shootin' the bad men wouldn't. This side of that six feet of earth which is the end of everything, he will keep moving or be kept moving, though he will never quite give up his dream. A longing for the home spread does battle with what T. S. Eliot calls a "distaste for beatitude" in a fashion which is of great Christian and theological interest.

There is a dialectic too of justice and mercy, of war and peace, and of war for the sake of peace. The gun is cruel but the gun is necessary. Good women hate it while good men wear it. A man wants nothing better than to hang it on the hook, but if he does then evil rides rampant, and the good things—including the good women—are not safe.

So a man does what he has to do, though never clear why he has to do it. "A man has to play the hand he's dealt." And since the things he has to do make curiously for a bad conscience, he uses the two human and perennial and contemporary "outs"—which are fatalism and moralism. The gunman has to die. But in the heart of the "good"

man who smokes him down there is no real enmity, for even the bad
man "does what he has to do."

> About all he could make out of it was that a man was meant for
> motion; he was meant to hope and to struggle, to be wrestling always
> with some sort of chains binding him. It was true of . . . Ringrose [the
> villain in this piece]; it was true of himself. [Ernest Haycox: *Long Storm*,
> p. 215.]

So each explosion of violence has about it an inevitability which
is in a way its justification. Or if it is not justified in this fatalistic
fashion, we pass over into moralism. The issues are so unambiguous,
the good so firmly fixed, the evil so clearly embodied, that the bad
man may be stamped out "like a sidewinder," without compunction
and without regret.

> Burro Yandle! The rusty-haired, rodent-faced destroyer. Dirty inside
> and out. But gifted with a malignant touch that ruined men and killed
> them. How long before . . . fundamental justice caught up with
> him . . . ? [L. P. Holmes: *High Starlight* (Pennant Books), p. 165.]

The range war becomes a Holy War.

"A man has to play the hand he's dealt." A man does what he has
to do, and justifies it one way or another. His is the incorrigible
yearning after virtue, the inevitable implication in sin, the irrepressible
inclination to self-justification. Every theological theme is here,
except the final theme, the deep and healing dimension of guilt and
grace.

Talking of self-justification, I have to ask myself, in respect of
westerns, whether I pretend to analyze them to have an excuse for
reading them, as a man might justify a visit to a burlesque house.
Could be. Anything could be, human nature being what it is, in
theologians as in other men. I can only protest unconvincingly that I
do read westerns and I don't go to burlesque houses—I *think* because
the former have more to offer.

QUESTIONS

1. One of the attractions of the Western story, says Miller, is its
   simplicity: "None of this complex business of separating the sin
   from the sinner, of tempering justice with mercy, of remembering
   our own complicity in evil." Compare any of the Western stories in
   this book with "The Scarecrow" (p. 181), which is not a "Western." Does the comparison prove Miller's point?

2. Miller says that Ernest Haycox "was apparently content to be . . . the best of western hackwriters." On the basis of a reading of "Stage to Lordsburg" (p. 188), would you describe Haycox as a "hackwriter"? Explain.

3. In summing up the action of many Western stories, Miller says, "So a man does what he has to do, though never clear why he has to do it." Is this true of "The Tin Star" (p. 209)? Of "The Indian Well" (p. 290)?

4. Miller finds in Western characters "the incorrigible yearning after virtue, the inevitable implication in sin, the irrepressible inclination to self-justification." How are these shown in the short story "The Trap" (p. 223)?

5. Why must a theologian find an excuse to read Western stories?

6. "A man has to play the hand he is dealt." Is this statement true in poker? In life?

HARRY SCHEIN

THE OLYMPIAN COWBOY

Translated from Swedish by Ida M. Alcock

When middle-brow people want to express their utter contempt for
films, they often cite the "Western" as typical of the idiocy they wish
to deprecate. Actually, the Western is the backbone, not the tail, of
the art of the film.

The Western, for that matter, is much more than a film. It offers
us the opportunity to experience the creation of folklore, to see how it
grows and takes form. The roots of the mythology of Europe and the
Far East are hidden in the past, and today can be only imperfectly
reconstructed. But the white man's America is no older than the
Gutenberg Bible. It attained economic independence and, therewith,
cultural independence about the time the novel achieved its artistic
and popular success. It is no accident that James Fenimore Cooper's
work stands as America's first significant contribution to literature. It
is just as natural that the film, at its very beginning, seized upon the
Western motif. In the life span of less than one generation, it has
developed from an apparently innocent, meaningless form into a
rigidly patterned and conventional mythology, into one body of
young America's folklore.

Of course, most of the Westerns of silent films were substantially
sideshows performed by puppets. But somewhere between William S.
Hart and Hopalong Cassidy, a change occurred. The simple, upright
and faithful cowboy became more and more decked out with silver
spurs and guitars; he sang much and drank little; he never worried
about women even while protecting them. Almost imperceptibly he
was changing into an omnipotent father symbol whose young
attendants consistently avoided heterosexual and other traps of an
unmanly nature.

The child is father to the man. The Western of the days of the
silent film already contained the material and the tendencies which,
little by little, as the element of sound consolidated the form of the
film, were deepened and rigidified. Folklore demands a rigid form. If
one is to feel the power of the gods, repetition is required. It is
precisely the rigid form of the Western which gives the contents

mythological weight and significance. This requires a ritualistic handling, with a rigid cast of characters similar to that of the *commedia dell'arte* and a strict orthodoxy like that of the Japanese Kabuki Theater.

Several years ago, when the Swedish state film censorship bureau wished to demonstrate the justification for its existence by showing what erotic and brutal shocks we escaped because of the intervention of the censor, it was found that these consisted to a great extent of saloon fights in the Westerns. The similarities among these fights, taken from perhaps ten different films, were astounding: the same bar counter, the same supernumeraries, the same groupings, the same choreography in the fights themselves. And when the Czech puppet-film director, Iri Trnka, decided to produce a satire on American films, it was natural that he chose the Western. It was simple enough to use puppets instead of human beings to make the rigid form and strict convention appear grotesque.

The movement in a stereotype is as obvious as the ticking of a clock in an otherwise absolute silence. The postwar shifts in perspective which the Western underwent did not disturb the mythological stability, but gave it a profound meaning aside from its aesthetic value. The genre has produced several good and many bad films, but even the stuttering priest can speak about God. Naturally, the Western does not lack aesthetic interest. Even in its role of nursery for American film directors it has a certain aesthetic significance. Moreover, the rigid form requires speed, action and movement, and, in propitious circumstances, can contribute to a dramatic conclusion. In addition, it creates an enormous demand for freshness within the limitations of the stereotype, an aesthetic stimulus as good as any.

Also characteristic of the Western is the public's relationship to it. The desire to experience the same thing time after time implies on the part of the public a ritualistic passivity similar to that which one finds in a congregation at divine service. It cannot be curiosity which drives the public to the Western; there is no wish for something different and unfamiliar, but a need for something old and well known. One can scarcely talk about escape from reality in the usual sense; it is a hypnotic condition rather than a complicated process of identification. The Western has the same bewitching strength as an incantation: the magic of repetition.

In the center stands the hero. He is always alone in the little community. He often lacks family and, not infrequently, is one of those exceptional human beings who seem never to have had a mother. Opposed to him are the bandits (there are always several) and their leader, an older, rich, often to all appearances respectable man in league with corrupt political bosses. The bandit, too, usually lacks a wife and only now and then does he have an unfortunate daughter.

Finally, there is the little community itself—respectable, timid and neutral in action.

The action often takes place in the period immediately after the Civil War. In such cases, the hero is often a Southern officer and his opponents are Northerners. The struggle between these two elements is an epilogue to the war, often with a reversed outcome. Uncle Sam is like a father figure, powerful and hateful, but at the same time filled with guilt feelings toward the ravished Southerners. Although the Western apparently takes revenge for the defeat of the South, the revenge is still illusory, a rebellious gesture which culminates in loyal submission and father-identification.

The hero is surrounded by a good woman and several bad saloon girls, who later either sing about love or dance the cancan. The good woman is usually a blonde and a specialist in making apple pie. The bad women are the kind one goes to bed with. Although the beds rarely appear in Western interiors, there is reason to assume that the saloon ladies are supposed to suggest those prostitutes who, during the enormous woman shortage of the eighteen-hundreds, were imported into the West and, through their kind actions, saw to it that not all the men shot one another to death. Of course, in more advanced films, the typical mixed-figure appears: an apparently bad woman who seems to be on the side of the bandits but who gradually shows herself to be innocent and finally helpful in their destruction.

The hero's relationship to women is very subtle. He shields them without actually being involved. In more and more Westerns a direct enmity toward women is displayed. Sadism is directed most often toward the bad women, but now and then even toward the mixed-type. "Duel in the Sun" offers the best example of this. Often a triangle drama appears (a woman and two men) which ends with the men becoming good friends and arriving at the realization that the woman is not worth having. In "The Outlaw," the young man, after prolonged abuse, humiliates the woman by choosing, in a tossup between her and a fine horse, the horse. In a priceless homosexual castration fantasy, the father figure of the film shoots off the ear lobes of the young man when he dares to defend himself. The pistol in Westerns is by now accepted as a phallic symbol.

In a series of films, the weapon stands in the center of the action—a bowie knife, a Winchester rifle, a Colt revolver. He who owns the weapon is unconquerable. The good men are the rightful owners from whom the bad men are trying to steal potency. To own the weapon is much more important than to own the woman. It is important how one draws the weapon. Bad men draw it too often but too slowly. Like Casanova, they shoot in all directions without finding their mark. The hero, who defends family and home—as an institution—draws his weapon quickly. He shoots seldom, but never misses.

As protector of the community, he cannot afford to be promiscuous. There must be an outcome of the shooting. A strong man is able to fire six shots without reloading.

So much for the rigid Western pattern, familiar even to the more occasional moviegoers. It may be of interest to determine what variations this pattern displays and particularly those tendencies that have been most pronounced since World War II. The question, in other words, is this: Is there a relation between America's politically dominant situation in the postwar period and a new arrangement of luminaries in its mythology?

Accepting the usual risks of generalization, one may speak of three basic elements in the Western: the symbolic, the psychological and the moral. If one bears in mind the fact that the Western is usually a mixture of these elements, it will not be too gross a simplification to discuss each of these factors separately.

It is said that Chaplin never had any inkling of his profundity until he began to read what various intellectuals wrote about him. Then he himself became intellectual. That is, of course, sheer nonsense. If, however, this kind of reasoning is applied to the symbolism of the Western, it probably has a certain correctness. In other words, the Western seems to have become conscious of its symbolic purport and, as a result of this consciousness, has become quite dreadfully symbolic.

That unconscious enmity toward women, formerly expressed more indirectly, with lipservice paid to chivalry while actions denoted inner indifference (placing on a pedestal always implies humiliation), now finds stronger and more direct expression. The hatred of women has become so obvious that it must give rise to speculation. Their ill-treatment in a physical and often purely sadistic sense is an increasingly common element not only in the Western but also in other American films such as "Gilda." "Winchester 73" is an outstanding example. "Colt 45" is a symbolic parody of this motif. Not only must the pistol be regarded from a symbolic point of view—it goes off with a louder bang than the rifle—but the villain in the film has a favorite position, teetering on a chair, half-sprawling, with his hands on his hips and the pistol profile following a naturalistic line. Even if this conscious smuggling in of symbols never can take in an artistically interested customs officer, it indicates an ambition to make more than a classical spectacle of the Western.

This ambition is made even clearer through the psychological element. Though Westerns are undoubtedly unpsychological for the most part, they have a predilection for dealing with the psychology of the villain. Even this is refreshing to an eye that yearns for some gray oases in the black and white desert.

Through trying to clarify the villain's behavior, the films muster a certain sympathy for him. He becomes a product of unfortunate circumstances, orphaned at an early age and brought up in a loveless milieu. He has, as a rule, suffered injustice and seeks revenge in a certain criminal but, in the deepest sense, forgivable way. Often, as stated before, he is a Southern officer whose home was devastated. The villain, of course, must die, but as a rule he dies happy, in a redeeming self-sacrifice through which the blessedness of the final kiss acquires a charmingly melancholy background.

These psychological efforts can give rise to important thematic rearrangements. A few years ago two films were made about Jesse James—a legendary Western figure who is well on the way to becoming America's Robin Hood. In one of these films, "The Great Missouri Raid," the James brothers are formidable enemies, but chivalrous supermen of steel, dutiful toward their mother. They are, of course, Southerners, and their enemy is a Northern general modeled after a hateful Gestapo type. The film is very well made, and belongs to the classical Western pattern. The other film, "I Shot Jesse James," seems more unpretentious. It concerns a man who shot his best—and oldest—friend in the back in order to obtain amnesty for himself and be able to marry a saloon girl (cf. Freud). The victim is the bandit sought by the law, the murderer the one who is protected by the law. The psychological complications caused by this rearrangement of boundaries between the territory of the villain and the hero are dealt with in two sections. The murderer is certainly free, but he is detested by public opinion. Even the girl is unkind enough not to trouble herself about him after the treachery which has been committed for her sake. The murderer, desiring to defy public opinion, accepts an offer from a traveling theatrical troupe to appear on the stage and show how he shot James in the back. In another part of the film, he forces a singer to render the ballad of the murder of Jesse James. Thus, as his crime is repeated again and again, the murderer returns to the mental scene of the crime and suffers an inner decay which leads to a new crime, this time unprotected by the law.

"I Shot Jesse James" is not the only Western which sets friend against friend. Very often the motif is family; now and then brother stands against brother, father against son. As a rule it is a woman who divides them. Something like Biblically elemental conflicts are deftly extracted from, or themselves extract, a taken moral stand. When form and conclusion are rigid, a fundamental moral problem can have some of the simple, primeval strength of the drama of fate, and thus prevent the repetitions from becoming mechanical.

These moral conflicts are undoubtedly the most interesting elements in the modern Western. They are evident in "The Gunfighter," a very fine film with far from ordinary psychological creativity, and in "High Noon," until now the genre's most outstanding artistic success.

"The Gunfighter" deals with a middle-aged and unglamorized gunman. No one in the entire West can handle a gun as he does. He is, therefore, challenged by all the young fighting cocks who wish to take over his reputation for being invincible. He is forced to kill them in self-defense. He flees from his home, but his reputation is swifter than his flight; he is always recognized and the killing is repeated time after time. Though he is fed up to the gills with it, there is always someone who will not leave him in peace. Finally there comes a man who draws the gun a fraction of a second more quickly than he. The gunfighter dies with what is almost relief, but at the same time he is filled with pity for his murderer: now it is *his* turn to take over this reputation as the foremost gunman of the West, his fate to kill and never to be able to flee from killing until he himself is killed.

The Western's moral problem revolves around the Fifth Commandment. One can understand that a country traditionally pacifist but suddenly transformed into the strongest military power in the history of the world must begin to consider how, with good conscience, it can take life. In somewhat awkward situations it is always good to take shelter behind the lofty example of the mythological gods.

I see "High Noon" as having an urgent political message. The little community seems to be crippled with fear before the approaching villains; seems to be timid, neutral and half-hearted, like the United Nations before the Soviet Union, China and North Korea; moral courage is apparent only in the very American sheriff. He is newly married; he wants to have peace and quiet. But duty and the sense of justice come first, in spite of the fact that he must suddenly stand completely alone. Even his wife, who is a Quaker and opposed on principle to killing, wishes to leave him, and only at the last moment does she understand that her duty to justice is greater than her duty to God. The point is, of course, that pacifism is certainly a good thing, but that war in certain situations can be both moral and unavoidable.

"High Noon," artistically, is the most convincing and, likewise, certainly the most honest explanation of American foreign policy. The mythological gods of the Western, who used to shoot unconcernedly, without any moral complications worth mentioning, are now grappling with moral problems and an ethical melancholy which could be called existentialist if they were not shared by Mr. Dulles.

This conscious symbolism, these psychological ambitions and moral statements of account give both color and relief to the mythological substratum. The anchorage in realism, for example, in the historical characters like Billy the Kid and Jesse James, or in the more and more ambitious and thoroughly worked out descriptions of milieux, contribute toward the creation of an impressive space before the footlights of the mythological scene. The native strength and possibilities of the Western are developed in the counterplay between American film production and American film critics. As witness thereof, take that farfetched but characteristic comparison between "High Noon" and "That Old Game about Everyman" of which Howard A. Burton is guilty in a recent number of *The Quarterly of Film, Radio, and Television.* His puzzle certainly does not fit together, but one still discerns an Olympian landscape-model, the Rocky Mountains—saturated with divine morality. Even satires on the Western, such as Bob Hope's "The Paleface," indicate a growing consciousness of the genre's true function.

An awareness of the mythological element is thus found not only among talentless writers, but also among talented directors like George Stevens. According to a statement in the English film magazine *Sight and Sound,* he is reported to have expressed his desire to "enlarge" the Western legend and to have said that the pioneers presented in the Western fill the same role for the Americans as King Arthur and his knights hold in English mythology. In Stevens' film "Shane," that ambition is entirely realized. As a matter of fact, the film incorporates the complete historical development of the Western, including the protest against the father and the identification with the father. It is, to be sure, an imperfect attempt—but still an attempt—at synthesis of the classical pattern, enriched with the three modern variations: symbolic, psychological, moral.

A large and fertile valley in the West is ruled by a powerful and greedy cattleman. With the help of his myrmidons, he carries on a private war of attrition against a handful of farmers who are struggling to bring the grazing lands under cultivation. To one of these small farms, Shane comes, dressed in romantic garb of leather, cartridge belt and gun. He takes a job there, becomes good friends with the farmer, his wife and their twelve-year-old boy, Joey. Shane has a mysterious past; he has been a gunman who now is trying to begin a new and peaceful life. He manages, for the longest time, to avoid being provoked by the cattleman's hirelings, but the terror of the farmers becomes unbearable. When one of them is shot down by an imported murderer, the others are willing to give up and move away. No one dares to meet terror with terror. Then Shane takes off his blue work-clothes and puts on his old leather outfit. He gets out the gun which he hoped he had laid down forever, rides forth to the saloon and kills the murderer. He has tried to begin a new life, but he has not succeeded. He has killed again and must ride away to the unknown from which he came.

"Shane" cannot, from an artistic point of view, be compared with

"High Noon," possibly because it has not an equally emphasized main point. It deals, as a matter of fact, with two motifs: Shane and the little family, and Shane and the community versus the dictatorial cattleman and his band. But the film is obviously strongly influenced by "High Noon." The tempo is equally slow and heavy with fate, the portrayal of the milieu equally penetrating. The action is one unbroken loading of a charge up to the climax. This is unusual for a Western, with its generally very rapid changes of scene.

Like the gunman in "The Gunfighter," Shane is the man marked by fate, he whom the gods set out to kill. The distance between him and Mr. Babbitt, the farmer, and the small-town dweller in "High Noon" is as great as the distance between Brooklyn and Korea. Only the woman lacks perception of the hovering air of fatefulness. She sees only what she can touch. Between Shane and her the atmosphere is tense with fear and eroticism, but only her husband can give her security.

The really original element in "Shane" is the relationship between Shane and the little boy, Joey. Joey cherishes a boundless, completely hysterical admiration for Shane, for his skill with the pistol. He himself is still not permitted to play with loaded weapons, but they occupy his imagination. He smacks his lips to imitate the sound of shooting; he catches sight of game without being able to press after it; he shoots imaginary enemies with imaginary bullets. His confidence in Shane is upset a trifle when Shane knocks his father unconscious. However, when the boy understands that Shane has not robbed his father of life, but only of potency (Shane wants to prevent him, less experienced in the art of shooting, from risking his life, and takes away his pistol), the boy identifies himself completely with Shane. He follows him to the saloon, witnesses the battle, and afterward takes leave of Shane, prepared to become his heir.

Shane, more than any other Western hero, is a mythological figure. This is partly because the film sees him so much through the eyes of Joey, looking upward. Shane's entry is as godlike as his exit; it is a higher being who comes, driven by fate-impregnated compulsion, to fulfill his mission. Shane is more than Robin Hood, more than Cinderella's prince. He is a suffering god, whose noble and bitter fate it is to sacrifice himself for others.

"Shane" is distinguished by a realism seldom worked out so thoroughly in Westerns. The film takes the time to portray the people in the valley, their everyday lives, their little festivities. A series of impressionistically bold details gives the production a sensitive and fine-grained texture. Its world is familiar and close to reality. Only Shane is alien. He is not Zeus who, disguised as a human being, visits the earth to cavort with its women, but an American saint, the cowboy who died in the Civil War and sits at God's right hand. He is a leather-bound angel with a gun, a mythological Boy Scout, always ready to keep the hands of true believers and the community unsullied by blood.

As a rule, of course, it is meaningless to discuss the degree of individual vision behind a work of art or a film with a mythological purport. Mythology rests on a collective foundation which also includes the creative artist.

When creative vision is expressed in the form of satire, it has quite obviously freed itself from the mythological substratum, but at the same time it strengthens the existence of that substratum—a puppet show which does not concern itself with the obvious is a paradox. As far as the Western is concerned, Bob Hope and the Marx Brothers demonstrate a blasphemous emancipation. Large sections of the American public, through television's mechanization of the Western, have become surfeited with the genre. Since "Shane" is neither mechanical nor satirical, it ought to be reckoned as the first offspring, and, through Stevens' statement, the first "documented" offspring of the new vision.

The question remains: Is this newly awakened mythological vision going to sabotage mythology itself by dispelling the cloud which carefully used to conceal the summit of Olympus? It is not altogether certain, since vision in and of itself does not preclude piety. Probably, however, these films are going to have a more and more strongly motivated central idea, whereby the distance between the hero of the Western and the rest of its cast is going to increase in proportion to the square of its consciousness. Most interesting, though, will be the future attempts to cram more and more current morality into the mythological pattern. When Shane's little Joey grows up and gets ammunition, he is not going to lack a target worth shooting at.

QUESTIONS

1. Schein finds "three basic elements in the Western: the symbolic, the psychological, and the moral." Choose a recent Western film and isolate and discuss these three elements. Or choose two or more stories from this collection and discuss the symbolism, the psychology, or the morality of one of the characters in each story.

2. The public, says Schein, views Western pictures with a kind of "ritualistic passivity." And Westerns have "the same bewitching strength as an incantation; the magic of repetition." Could the same thing be said of professional football or basketball? Why?

3. The author says that the film "High Noon" is the "most honest explanation of American foreign policy." Could the same thing be said of the story "The Tin Star" (p. 209), from which the basic plot of the film was taken?

4. What does Schein mean when he says that the cowboy hero is frequently "one of those exceptional human beings who seem never to have had a mother"? How would this characteristic make him different from the ordinary man who does have a mother?

5. Do you agree that hatred of women has become more and more obvious in recent Western films? Is any hatred of women revealed in ordinary American life?

ROBERT WARSHOW

THE WESTERNER

The two most successful creations of American movies are the gangster and the Westerner: men with guns. Guns as physical objects, and the postures associated with their use, form the visual and emotional center of both types of films. I suppose this reflects the importance of guns in the fantasy life of Americans; but that is a less illuminating point than it appears to be.

The gangster movie, which no longer exists in its "classical" form, is a story of enterprise and success ending in precipitate failure. Success is conceived as an increasing power to work injury, it belongs to the city, and it is of course a form of evil (though the gangster's death, presented usually as "punishment," is perceived simply as defeat). The peculiarity of the gangster is his unceasing, nervous activity. The exact nature of his enterprises may remain vague, but his commitment to enterprise is always clear, and all the more clear because he operates outside the field of utility. He is without culture, without manners, without leisure, or at any rate his leisure is likely to be spent in debauchery so compulsively aggressive as to seem only another aspect of his "work." But he is graceful, moving like a dancer among the crowded dangers of the city.

Like other tycoons, the gangster is crude in conceiving his ends but by no means inarticulate; on the contrary, he is usually expansive and noisy (the introspective gangster is a fairly recent development), and can state definitely what he wants: to take over the North Side, to own a hundred suits, to be Number One. But new "frontiers" will present themselves infinitely, and by a rigid convention it is understood that as soon as he wishes to rest on his gains, he is on the way to destruction.

The gangster is lonely and melancholy, and can give the impression of a profound worldly vision. He appeals most to adolescents with their impatience and their feeling of being outsiders, but more generally he appeals to that side of all of us which refuses to believe in the "normal" possibilities of happiness and achievement; the gangster is the "no" to that great American "yes" which is stamped so big over our official culture and yet has so little to do with the way we really feel about our lives. But the gangster's loneliness and melancholy are not "authentic"; like everything else that belongs to him, they are not honestly come by: he is lonely and melancholy not because life ultimately demands such feelings but because he has put himself in a position where everybody wants to kill him and eventually somebody will. He is wide open and defenseless, incomplete because unable to accept any limits or come to terms with his own nature, fearful, loveless. And the story of his career is a nightmare inversion of the values of ambition and opportunity. From the window of Scarface's bullet-proof apartment can be seen an electric sign proclaiming: "The World Is Yours," and, if I remember, this sign is the last thing we see after Scarface lies dead in the street. In the end it is the gangster's weakness as much as his power and freedom that appeals to us; the world is not ours, but it is not his either, and in his death he "pays" for our fantasies, releasing us momentarily both from the concept of success, which he denies by caricaturing it, and from the need to succeed, which he shows to be dangerous.

The Western hero, by contrast, is a figure of repose. He resembles the gangster in being lonely and to some degree melancholy. But his melancholy comes from the "simple" recognition that life is unavoidably serious, not from the disproportions of his own temperament. And his loneliness is organic, not imposed on him by his situation but belonging to him intimately and testifying to his completeness. The gangster must reject others violently or draw them violently to him. The Westerner is not thus compelled to seek love; he is prepared to accept it, perhaps, but he never asks of it more than it can give, and we see him constantly in situations where love is at best an irrelevance. If there is a woman he loves, she is usually unable to understand his motives; she is against killing and being killed, and he finds it impossible to explain to her that there is no point in being "against" these things: they belong to his world.

Very often this woman is from the East and her failure to understand represents a clash of cultures. In the American mind, refinement, virtue, civilization, Christianity itself, are seen as feminine, and therefore women are often portrayed as possessing some kind of deeper wisdom, while the men, for all their apparent self-assurance, are fundamentally childish. But the West, lacking the graces of civilization, is the place "where men are men"; in Western movies, men have the deeper wisdom and the women are children. Those women in the Western movies who share the hero's understanding of life are prostitutes (or, as they are usually presented, bar-room entertainers)—women, that is, who have come to understand in the most practical way how love can be an irrelevance, and therefore "fallen" women. The gangster, too, associates with prostitutes, but for him the important things about a prostitute are her passive availability and her costliness: she is part of his winnings. In

Western movies, the important thing about a prostitute is her quasi-masculine independence: nobody owns her, nothing has to be explained to her, and she is not, like a virtuous woman, a "value" that demands to be protected. When the Westerner leaves the prostitute for a virtuous woman—for love—he is in fact forsaking a way of life, though the point of the choice is often obscured by having the prostitute killed by getting into the line of fire.

The Westerner is *par excellence* a man of leisure. Even when he wears the badge of a marshal or, more rarely, owns a ranch, he appears to be unemployed. We see him standing at a bar, or playing poker—a game which expresses perfectly his talent for remaining relaxed in the midst of tension—or perhaps camping out on the plains on some extraordinary errand. If he does own a ranch, it is in the background; we are not actually aware that he owns anything except his horse, his guns, and the one worn suit of clothing which is likely to remain unchanged all through the movie. It comes as a surprise to see him take money from his pocket or an extra shirt from his saddlebags. As a rule we do not even know where he sleeps at night and don't think of asking. Yet it never occurs to us that he is a poor man; there is no poverty in Western movies, and really no wealth either: those great cattle domains and shipments of gold which figure so largely in the plots are moral and not material quantities, not the objects of contention but only its occasion. Possessions too are irrelevant.

Employment of some kind—usually unproductive—is always open to the Westerner, but when he accepts it, it is not because he needs to make a living, much less from any idea of "getting ahead." Where could he want to "get ahead" to? By the time we see him, he is already "there": he can ride a horse faultlessly, keep his countenance in the face of death, and draw his gun a little faster and shoot it a little straighter than anyone he is likely to meet. These are sharply defined acquirements, giving to the figure of the Westerner an apparent moral clarity which corresponds to the clarity of his physical image against his bare landscape; initially, at any rate, the Western movie presents itself as being without mystery, its whole universe comprehended in what we see on the screen.

Much of this apparent simplicity arises directly from those "cinematic" elements which have long been understood to give the Western theme its special appropriateness for the movies: the wide expanses of land, the free movement of men on horses. As guns constitute the visible moral center of the Western movie, suggesting continually the possibility of violence, so land and horses represent the movie's material basis, its sphere of action. But the land and the horses have also a moral significance: the physical freedom they represent belongs to the moral "openness" of the West—corresponding to the fact that guns are carried where they can be seen. (And, as we shall see, the character of land and horses changes as the Western film becomes more complex.)

The gangster's world is less open, and his arts not so easily identifiable as the Westerner's. Perhaps he too can keep his countenance, but the mask he wears is really no mask: its purpose is precisely to make evident the fact that he desperately wants to "get ahead" and will stop at nothing. Where the Westerner imposes himself by the appearance of unshakable control, the gangster's pre-eminence lies in the suggestion that he may at any moment lose control; his strength is not in being able to shoot faster or straighter than others, but in being more willing to shoot. "Do it first," says Scarface expounding his mode of operation, "and keep on doing it!" With the Westerner, it is a crucial point of honor *not* to "do it first"; his gun remains in its holster until the moment of combat.

There is no suggestion, however, that he draws the gun reluctantly. The Westerner could not fulfill himself if the moment did not finally come when he can shoot his enemy down. But because that moment is so thoroughly the expression of his being, it must be kept pure. He will not violate the accepted forms of combat though by doing so he could save a city. And he can wait. "When you call me that—smile!" the villain smiles weakly, soon he is laughing with horrible joviality, and the crisis is past. But it is allowed to pass because it must come again: sooner or later Trampas will "make his play," and the Virginian will be ready for him.

What does the Westerner fight for? We know he is on the side of justice and order, and of course it can be said he fights for these things. But such broad aims never correspond exactly to his real motives; they only offer him his opportunity. The Westerner himself, when an explanation is asked of him (usually by a woman), is likely to say that he does what he "has to do." If justice and order did not continually demand his protection, he would be without a calling. Indeed, we come upon him often in just that situation, as the reign of law settles over the West and he is forced to see that his day is over; those are the pictures which end with his death or with his departure for some more remote frontier. What he defends, at bottom, is the purity of his own image—in fact his honor. That is what makes him invulnerable. When the gangster is killed, his whole life is shown to have been a mistake, but the image the Westerner seeks to maintain can be presented as clearly in defeat as in victory: he fights not for advantage and not for the right, but to state what he is, and he must live in a world which permits that statement. The Westerner is the last gentleman, and the movies which over and over again tell his story are probably the last art form in which the concept of honor retains its strength.

Of course I do not mean to say that ideas of virtue and justice and courage have gone out of culture. Honor is more than these things: it is a style, concerned with harmonious appearances as much as with desirable consequences, and tending therefore toward the denial of life in favor of art. "Who hath it? he that died o' Wednesday." On the whole a world that leans to Falstaff's view is a more civilized and even, finally, a more graceful world. It is just the march of civilization that forces the Westerner to move on; and if we actually had to confront the question it might turn out that the woman who refuses to understand him is right as often as she is wrong. But we do not confront the question. Where the Westerner lives it is always about 1870—not the real 1870, either, or the real West—and he is killed or goes away when his position becomes problematical. The fact that he continues to hold our attention is evidence enough that, in his proper frame, he presents an image of personal nobility that is still real for us.

Clearly, this image easily becomes ridiculous: we need only look at William S. Hart or Tom Mix, who in the wooden absoluteness of their virtue represented little that an adult could take seriously; and doubtless such figures as Gene Autry or Roy Rogers are no better, though I confess I have seen none of their movies. Some film enthusiasts claim to find in the early, unsophisticated Westerns a "cinematic purity" that has since been lost; this idea is as valid, and finally as misleading, as T. S. Eliot's statement that *Everyman* is the only play in English that stays within the limitations of art. The truth is that the Westerner comes into the field of serious art only when his moral code, without ceasing to be compelling, is seen also to be imperfect. The Westerner at his best exhibits a moral ambiguity which darkens his image and saves him from absurdity; this ambiguity arises from the fact that, whatever his justifications, he is a killer of men.

In *The Virginian*, which is an archetypal Western movie as *Scarface* or *Little Caesar* are archetypal gangster movies, there is a lynching in which the hero (Gary Cooper), as leader of a posse, must supervise the hanging of his best friend for stealing cattle. With the growth of American "social consciousness," it is no longer possible to present a lynching in the movies unless the point is the illegality and injustice of the lynching itself; *The Ox-Bow Incident*, made in 1943, explicitly puts forward the newer point of view and can be regarded as a kind of "anti-Western." But in 1929, when *The Virginian* was made, the present inhibition about lynching was not yet in force; the justice, and therefore the necessity, of the hanging is never questioned—except by the schoolteacher from the East, whose refusal to understand serves as usual to set forth more sharply the deeper seriousness of the West. The Virginian is thus in a tragic dilemma where one moral absolute conflicts with another and the choice of either must leave a moral stain. If he had chosen to save his friend, he would have violated the image of himself that he had made essential to his existence, and the movie would have had to end with his death, for only by his death could the image have been restored. Having chosen instead to sacrifice his friend to the higher demands of the "code"— the only choice worthy of him, as even the friend understands—he is none the less stained by the killing, but what is needed now to set accounts straight is not his death but the death of the villain Trampas, the leader of the cattle thieves, who had escaped the posse and abandoned the Virginian's friend to his fate. Again the woman intervenes: Why must there be *more* killing? If the hero really loved her, he would leave town, refusing Trampas's challenge. What good will it be if Trampas should kill him? But the Virginian does once more what he "has to do," and in avenging his friend's death wipes out the stain on his own honor. Yet his victory cannot be complete: no death can be paid for and no stain truly wiped out; the movie is still a tragedy, for though the hero escapes with his life, he has been forced to confront the ultimate limits of his moral ideas.

This mature sense of limitation and unavoidable guilt is what gives the Westerner a "right" to his melancholy. It is true that the gangster's story is also a tragedy—in certain formal ways more clearly a tragedy than the Westerner's—but it is a romantic tragedy, based on a hero whose defeat springs with almost mechanical inevitability from the outrageous presumption of his demands: the gangster is *bound* to go on until he is killed. The Westerner is a more classical figure, self-contained and limited to begin with, seeking not to extend his dominion but only to assert his personal value, and his tragedy lies in the fact that even this circumscribed demand cannot be fully realized. Since the Westerner is not a murderer but (most of the time) a man of virtue, and since he is always prepared for defeat, he retains his inner invulnerability and his story need not end with his death (and usually does not); but what we finally respond to is not his victory but his defeat.

Up to a point, it is plain that the deeper seriousness of the good Western films comes from the introduction of a realism, both physical and psychological, that was missing with Tom Mix and William S. Hart. As lines of age have come into Gary Cooper's face since *The Virginian*, so the outlines of the Western movie in general have become less smooth, its background more drab. The sun still beats upon the town, but the camera is likely now to take advantage of this illumination to seek out more closely the shabbiness of buildings and furniture, the loose, worn hang of clothing, the wrinkles and dirt of the faces. Once it has been discovered that the true theme of the Western movie is not the freedom and expansiveness of frontier life, but its limitations, its material bareness, the pressures of obligation, then even the landscape itself ceases to be quite the arena of free movement it once was, but becomes instead a great empty waste, cutting down more often than it exaggerates the stature of the horseman who rides across it. We are more likely now to see the Westerner struggling against the obstacles of the physical world (as in the wonderful scenes on the desert and among the rocks in *The Last Posse*) than carelessly surmounting them. Even the horses, no longer the "friends" of man or the inspired chargers of knight-errantry, have lost much of the moral significance that once seemed to belong to them in their careering across the screen. It seems to me the horses grow tired and stumble more often than they did, and that we see them less frequently at the gallop.

In *The Gunfighter*, a remarkable film of a couple of years ago, the landscape has virtually disappeared. Most of the action takes place indoors, in a cheerless saloon where a tired "bad man" (Gregory Peck) contemplates the waste of his life, to be senselessly killed at the end by a vicious youngster setting off on the same futile path. The movie is done in cold, quiet tones of gray, and every object in it—faces, clothing, a table, the hero's heavy mustache—is given an air of uncompromising authenticity, suggesting those dim photographs of the nineteenth-century West in which Wyatt Earp, say, turns out to be a blank untidy figure posing awkwardly before some uninteresting building. This "authenticy," to be sure, is only aesthetic; the chief fact about nineteenth-century photographs, to my eyes at any rate, is how stonily they refuse to yield up the truth. But that limitation is just what is needed: by preserving some hint of the rigidity of archaic photography (only in tone and decor, never in composition), *The Gunfighter* can permit us to feel that we are looking at a more "real" West than the one the movies have accustomed us to—harder, duller, less "romantic"—and yet without forcing us outside the boundaries which give the Western movie its validity.

We come upon the hero of *The Gunfighter* at the end of a career in which he has never upheld justice and order, and has been at times, apparently, an actual criminal; in this case, it is clear that the hero has been wrong and the woman who has rejected his way of life has been right. He is thus without any of the larger justifications, and knows himself a ruined man. There can be no question of his "redeeming" himself in any socially constructive way. He is too much the victim of his own reputation to turn marshal as one of his old friends has done, and he is not offered the sentimental solution of a chance to give up his life for some good end; the whole point is that he exists outside the field of social value. Indeed, if we were once allowed to see him in the days of his "success," he might become a figure like the gangster, for his career has been aggressively "anti-social" and the practical problem he faces is the gangster's problem: there will always be somebody trying to kill him. Yet it is obviously absurd to speak of him as "anti-social," not only because we do not see him acting as a criminal, but more fundamentally because we do not see his milieu as a society. Of course it has its "social problems" and a kind of static history: civilization is always just at the point of driving out the old freedom; there are women and children to represent the possibility of a settled life; and there is the marshal, a bad man turned good, determined to keep at least his area of jurisdiction at peace. But these elements are not, in fact, a part of the film's "realism," even though they come out of the real history of the West; they belong to the conventions of the form, to that accepted framework which makes the film possible in the first place, and they exist not to provide a standard by which the gunfighter can be judged, but only to set him off. The true "civilization" of the Western movie is always embodied in an individual, good or bad is more a matter of personal bearing than of social consequences, and the conflict of good and bad is a duel between two men. Deeply troubled and obviously doomed, the gunfighter is the Western hero still, perhaps all the more because his value must express itself entirely in his own being—in his presence, the way he holds our eyes—and in contradiction to the facts. No matter what he has done, he *looks* right, and he remains invulnerable because, without acknowledging anyone else's right to judge him, he has judged his own failure and has already assimilated it, understanding—as no one else understands except the marshal and the bar-room girl—that he can do nothing but play out the drama of the gun fight again and again until the time comes when it will be he who gets killed. What "redeems" him is that he no longer believes in this drama and nevertheless will continue to play his role perfectly: the pattern is all.

The proper function of realism in the Western movie can only be to deepen the lines of that pattern. It is an art form for connoisseurs where the spectator derives his pleasure from the appreciation of minor variations within the working out of a pre-established order. One does not want too much novelty: it comes as a shock, for instance, when the hero is made to operate without a gun, as has been done in several pictures (e.g., *Destry Rides Again*), and our uneasiness is allayed only when he is finally compelled to put his "pacifism" aside. If the hero can be shown to be troubled, complex, fallible, even eccentric, or the villain given some psychological taint or, better, some evocative physical mannerism, to shade the colors of his villainy, that is all to the good. Indeed, that kind of variation is absolutely necessary to keep the type from becoming sterile; we do not want to see the same movie over and over again, only the same form. But when the impulse toward realism is extended into a "reinterpretation" of the West as a developed society, drawing our eyes away from the hero if only to the extent of showing him as the one dominant figure in a complex social order, then the pattern is broken and the West itself begins to be uninteresting. If the "social problems" of the frontier are to be the movie's chief concern, there is no longer any point in re-examining these problems twenty times a year; they have been solved, and the people for whom they once were real are dead. Moreover, the hero himself, still the film's central figure, now tends to become its one unassimilable element, since he is the most "unreal."

The Ox-Bow Incident, by denying the convention of the lynching, presents us with a modern "social drama" and evokes a corresponding response, but in doing so it almost makes the Western setting irrelevant, a mere backdrop of beautiful scenery. (It is significant that The Ox-Bow Incident has no hero; a hero would have to stop the lynching or be killed in trying to stop it, and then the "problem" of lynching would no longer be central.) Even in The Gunfighter the women and children are a little too much in evidence, threatening constantly to become a real focus of concern instead of simply part of the given framework; and the young tough who kills the hero has too much the air of juvenile criminality: the hero himself could never have been like that, and the idea of a cycle being repeated therefore loses its sharpness. But the most striking example of the confusion created by a too conscientious "social" realism is in the celebrated High Noon.

In High Noon we find Gary Cooper still the upholder of order that he was in The Virginian, but twenty-four years older, stooped, slower moving, awkward, his face lined, the flesh sagging, a less beautiful and weaker figure, but with the suggestion of greater depth that belongs almost automatically to age. Like the hero of The Gunfighter, he no longer has to assert his character and is no longer interested in the drama of combat; it is hard to imagine that he might once have been so youthful as to say, "When you call me that— smile!" In fact, when we come upon him he is hanging up his guns and his marshal's badge in order to begin a new, peaceful life with his bride, who is a Quaker. But then the news comes that a man he had sent to prison has been pardoned and will get to town on the noon train; three friends of this man have come to wait for him at the station, and when the freed convict arrives the four of them will come to kill the marshal. He is thus trapped; the bride will object, the hero himself will waver much more than he would have done twenty-four years ago, but in the end he will play out the drama because it is what he "has to do." All this belongs to the established form (there is even the "fallen woman" who understands the marshal's position as his wife does not). Leaving aside the crudity of building up suspense by means of the clock, the actual Western drama of High Noon is well handled and forms a good companion piece to The Virginian showing in both conception and technique the ways in which the Western movie has naturally developed.

But there is a second drama along with the first. As the marshal sets out to find deputies to help him deal with the four gunmen, we are taken through the various social strata of the town, each group in turn refusing its assistance out of cowardice, malice, irresponsibility, or venality. With this we are in the field of "social drama"—of a very low order, incidentally, altogether unconvincing and displaying a vulgar anti-populism that has marred some other movies of Stanley Kramer's. But the falsity of the "social drama" is less important than the fact that it does not belong in the movie to begin with. The technical problem was to make it necessary for the marshal to face his enemies alone; to explain *why* the other townspeople are not at his side is to raise a question which does not exist in the proper frame of the Western movie, where the hero is "naturally" alone and it is only necessary to contrive the physical absence of those who might be his allies, if any contrivance is needed at all. In addition, though the hero of *High Noon* proves himself a better man than all around him the actual effect of this contrast is to lessen his stature: he becomes only a rejected man of virtue. In our final glimpse of him, as he rides away through the town where he has spent most of his life without really imposing himself on it, he is a pathetic rather than a tragic figure. And his departure has another meaning as well; the "social drama" has no place for him.

But there is also a different way of violating the Western form. This is to yield entirely to its static quality as legend and to the "cinematic" temptations of its landscape, the horses, the quiet men. John Ford's famous *Stagecoach* (1938) had much of this unhappy preoccupation with style, and the same director's *My Darling Clementine* (1946), a soft and beautiful movie about Wyatt Earp, goes further along the same path, offering indeed a superficial accuracy of historical reconstruction, but so loving in execution as to destroy the outlines of the Western legend, assimilating it to the more sentimental legend of rural America and making the hero a more dangerous Mr. Deeds. (*Powder River*, a recent "routine" Western shamelessly copied from *My Darling Clementine*, is in most ways a better film; lacking the benefit of a serious director, it is necessarily more concerned with drama than with style.)

The highest expression of this aestheticizing tendency is in George Stevens' *Shane*, where the legend of the West is virtually reduced to its essentials and then fixed in the dreamy clarity of a fairy tale. There never was so broad and bare and lovely a landscape as Stevens puts before us, or so unimaginably comfortless a "town" as the little group of buildings on the prairie to which the settlers must come for their supplies and to buy a drink. The mere physical progress of the film, following the style of A *Place in the Sun*, is so deliberately graceful that everything seems to be happening at the bottom of a clear lake. The hero (Alan Ladd) is hardly a man at all, but something like the Spirit of the West, beautiful in fringed buckskins. He emerges mysteriously from the plains, breathing sweetness and a melancholy which is no longer simply the Westerner's natural response to experience but has taken on spirituality; and when he has accomplished his mission, meeting and destroying in the black figure of Jack Palance a Spirit of Evil just as metaphysical as his own embodiment of virtue, he fades away again into the more distant West, a man whose "day is over," leaving behind the wondering little boy who might have imagined the whole story. The choice of Alan Ladd to play the leading role is alone an indication of this film's tendency. Actors like Gary Cooper or Gregory Peck are in themselves, as material objects, "realistic," seeming to bear in their bodies and their faces mortality, limitation, the knowledge of good and evil. Ladd is a more "aesthetic" object, with some of the "universality" of a piece of sculpture; his special quality is in his physical smoothness and serenity, unworldly and yet not innocent, but suggesting that no experience can really touch him. Stevens has tried to freeze the Western myth once and for all in the immobility of Alan Ladd's countenance. If *Shane* were "right," and fully successful, it might be possible to say there was no point in making any more Western movies; once the hero is apotheosized, variation and development are closed off.

Shane is not "right," but it is still true that the possibilities of fruitful variation in the Western movie are limited. The form can keep its freshness through endless repetitions only because of the special character of the film medium, where the physical difference between one object and another—above all, between one actor and another—is of such enormous importance, serving the function that is served by the variety of language in the perpetuation of literary types. In this sense, the "vocabulary" of films is much larger than that of literature and falls more readily into pleasing and significant arrangements. (That may explain why the middle levels of excellence are more easily reached in the movies than in literary forms, and perhaps also why the status of the movies as art is constantly being called into question.) But the advantage of this almost automatic particularity belongs to all films alike. Why does the Western movie especially have such a hold on our imagination?

Chiefly, I think, because it offers a serious orientation to the problem of violence such as can be found almost nowhere else in our culture. One of the well-known pecularities of modern civilized opinion is its refusal to acknowledge the value of violence. This refusal is a virtue, but like many virtues it involves a certain willful blindness and it encourages hypocrisy. We train ourselves to be shocked or bored by cultural images of violence, and our very concept of heroism tends to be a passive one: we are less drawn to the brave young men who kill large numbers of our enemies than to the heroic prisoners who endure torture without capitulating. In art, though we may still be able to understand and participate in the values of the *Iliad*, a modern writer like Ernest Hemingway we find somewhat embarrassing; there is no doubt that he stirs us, but we cannot help recognizing also that he is a little childish. And in the criticism of popular culture, where the educated observer is usually under the illusion that he has nothing at stake, the presence of images of violence is often assumed to be in itself a sufficient ground for condemnation.

These attitudes, however, have not reduced the element of violence in our culture but, if anything, have helped to free it from moral control by letting it take on the aura of "emancipation." The celebration of acts of violence is left more and more to the irresponsible: on the higher cultural levels to writers like Céline, and lower down to Mickey Spillane or Horace McCoy, or to the comic books, television, and the movies. The gangster movie, with its numerous variations, belongs to this cultural "underground" which sets forth the attractions of violence in the face of all our higher social attitudes. It is a more "modern" genre than the Western, perhaps even more profound, because it confronts industrial society on its own ground—the city—and because, like much of our advanced art, it gains its effects by a gross insistence on its own narrow logic. But it is anti-social, resting on fantasies of irresponsible freedom. If we are brought finally to acquiesce in the denial of the fantasies, it is only because they have been shown to be dangerous, not because they have given way to a better vision of behavior.[1]

In war movies, to be sure, it is possible to present the uses of violence within a framework of responsibility. But there is the disadvantage that modern war is a co-operative enterprise; its violence is largely impersonal, and heroism belongs to the group more than to the individual. The hero of a war movie is most often simply a leader, and his superiority is likely to be expressed in a denial of the heroic: you are not supposed to be brave, you are supposed to get the job done and stay alive (this too, of course, is a kind of heroic posture, but a new—and "practical"—one). At its best, the war movie may

---

[1] I am not concerned here with the actual social consequences of gangster movies, though I suspect they could not have been so pernicious as they were thought to be. Some of the compromises introduced to avoid the supposed bad effects of the old gangster movies may be, if anything, more dangerous, for the sadistic violence that once belonged only to the gangster is now commonly enlisted on the side of the law and thus goes undefeated, allowing us (if we wish) to find in the movies a sort of "confirmation" of our fantasies.

represent a more civilized point of view than the Western, and if it were not continually marred by ideological sentimentality we might hope to find it developing into a higher form of drama. But it cannot supply the values we seek in the Western.

Those values are in the image of a single man who wears a gun on his thigh. The gun tells us that he lives in a world of violence, and even that he "believes in violence." But the drama is one of self-restraint: the moment of violence must come in its own time and according to its special laws, or else it is valueless. There is little cruelty in Western movies, and little sentimentality; our eyes are not focused on the sufferings of the defeated but on the deportment of the hero. Really, it is not violence at all which is the "point" of the Western movie, but a certain image of man, a style, which expresses itself most clearly in violence. Watch a child with his toy guns and you will see: what most interests him is not (as we so much fear) the fantasy of hurting others, but to work out how a man might look when he shoots or is shot. A hero is one who looks like a hero.

Whatever the limitations of such an idea in experience, it has always been valid in art, and has a special validity in an art where appearances are everything. The Western hero is necessarily an archaic figure; we do not really believe in him and would not have him step out of his rigidly conventionalized background. But his archaicism does not take away from his power; on the contrary, it adds to it by keeping him just a little beyond the reach of common sense and of absolutized emotion, the two usual impulses of our art. And he has, after all, his own kind of relevance. He is there to remind us of the possibility of style in an age which has put on itself the burden of pretending that style has no meaning, and, in the midst of our anxieties over the problem of violence, to suggest that even in killing or being killed we are not freed from the necessity of establishing satisfactory modes of behavior. Above all, the movies in which the Westerner plays out his role preserve for us the pleasure of a complete and self-contained drama—and one which still effortlessly crosses the boundaries which divide our culture—in a time when other, more consciously serious art forms are increasingly complex, uncertain, and ill-defined.

QUESTIONS

1. This essay was first published in the 1950s, and it deals primarily with Western films made then. Do you think that Warshow's generalizations are equally applicable to Western movies made during the last five years? Why, or why not?

2. "In the American mind, refinement, virtue, civilization, Christianity itself, are seen as feminine, and therefore women are often portrayed as possessing some kind of deeper wisdom, while the men, for all their apparent self-assurance, are fundamentally childish. But the West, lacking the graces of civilization, is the place 'where men are men'; in Western movies, men have the deeper wisdom and the women are children." Using "Canyon Walls" (p. 143) and "Stampede" (p. 250), illustrate the truth or falsity of these statements.

3. Why is the Western story unique among all forms of popular fiction in consistently making prostitutes sympathetic as well as sometimes making them wise?

4. "The Westerner is the last gentleman." Explain.

5. What does Warshow mean by saying of the Western hero, "He is there to remind us of the possibility of style in an age which has put on itself the burden of pretending that style has no meaning"?

Suggestions for
Discussion and Writing

Below, you will find a list of possible subjects for papers based on this source book. Many of them can be explored using only *The Western Story: Fact, Fiction, and Myth* for reference. Others will require library research or extended reading.

In choosing and developing a paper or report on one of these topics—or on one of the many topics suggested by the questions at the end of each selection—consult your instructor for guidance. Some topics will be best suited to themes or class reports; others will lend themselves to the development of longer essays or research papers.

1. Write a paper in which you define the Western story, distinguishing it from a story merely taking place in the American West.

2. Analyze two Western stories and show how the plot is developed in each. What circumstances or situations are introduced to force the hero to act or react?

3. Make a study of the lawman—sheriff or marshal—in the Western story. How does he differ from a modern policeman or detective?

4. Western stories are frequently love stories as well as adventure stories. Why is this combination rare in detective fiction?

5. Are many Western stories really "juveniles," as many critics have charged? Why do Western stories tend to have a special appeal for younger readers?

6. Readers and writers of Western fiction are usually "conservatives" —distrustful of strong government, welfare measures, and social reformers. How is this attitude reflected in many of the stories they read or write?

7. In classic Western stories, the hero is a "good guy." In "adult" Westerns the characters are more complex and motives are mixed. Compare the characterization in "Top Hand" with that in "The Trap." Which is more nearly an "adult" Western?

8. After you have seen a Western picture (*Stagecoach, High Noon,* or *Shane,* for instance), read the story or novel on which it was based. Explain how the story was modified for the screen and attempt to explain the changes.

9. Why is the game of poker so prominent in the plots or in the language of many Western stories? How does the nature of the game resemble the plots of many stories?

10. Read several novels by Ernest Haycox. Why is this author so widely admired by almost all other Western writers?

11. How is the experience of watching a Western motion picture different from that of reading a Western novel? What are the special advantages of film? Of the novel?

12. Many Western stories deal with cattle drives north from Texas. Using some of the suggested readings listed in this book, write a paper describing the trails followed by cowboys during the thirty years after the Civil War.

13. Many women have written successful detective stories, but few have written Westerns. How can this be explained?

14. Read an historical account of the development of Dodge City as a cowtown. Then compare the television program "Gunsmoke" to what you believe were the actual historical conditions in the old West.

15. "The typical Western story is a fantasy representing itself as history." Comment.

16. Why do children play as cowboys more often than as policemen? Consider the explanation offered by Robert Warshow in "The Westerner."

17. Read one of James Fenimore Cooper's Leatherstocking Tales and compare its hero with the hero of one of the stories in this book.

18. Write a research paper in which you describe the development of the Colt revolver and explain why this weapon was important in the West.

19. Why was the invention of barbed wire peculiarly important in Western history? How did its use affect the cattle business?

20. Popular literature often reflects the values and aspirations of its readers. What do Western stories reveal about the ideals and desires of the American public?

21. Discuss the treatment of foreigners and non-whites in Western fiction. How has their treatment been influenced by the actual history of the West? By the attitudes of society at the time the fiction was written?

22. Almost all Westerns are set in the past. Why do Americans who

read almost no other historical fiction enjoy so many stories about the nineteenth-century West?

23. Why does the introduction of telephones, automobiles, and airplanes drastically change the nature of a Western story?

24. Read Zane Grey's *Riders of the Purple Sage* and any novel by Sinclair Lewis. How do the two books differ in their stories and their attitudes toward their characters?

25. Owen Wister dedicated *The Virginian* to Theodore Roosevelt with the statement that one page "stands new-written because you blamed it." What was rewritten, and why?

Suggestions
for Further Reading

FACT

Abbot, Edward Charles ("Teddy Blue"), and Helena Huntington
Smith. *We Pointed Them North: Recollections of a Cow-
puncher.* 1939.
Adams, Ramon F., ed. *The Best of the American Cowboy.* 1957.
————. *Come and Get It: The Story of the Old Cowboy Cook.*
1952.
————. *The Old-Time Cowhand.* 1961.
————. *Western Words: A Dictionary of the American West.* 1968.
Athearn, Robert G. *High Country Empire.* 1960.
Atherton, Lewis Eldon. *The Cattle Kings.* 1961.
Bard, Floyd C. *Horse Wrangler: Sixty Years in the Saddle in
Wyoming and Montana.* 1960.
Billington, Ray Allen. *The Far Western Frontier: 1830–1860.* 1956.
————. *Westward Expansion: A History of the American Frontier.*
1949.
Blasingame, Ike. *Dakota Cowboy: My Life in the Old Days.* 1958.
Bolds, George. *Across the Cimarron,* as told to James D. Horan.
1956.
Branch, Douglas. *The Cowboy and His Interpreters.* 1926.
————. *Westward: The Romance of the American Frontier.* 1930.
Brandon, William. *The Men and the Mountain: Fremont's Fourth
Expedition.* 1955.
Bronson, Edgar Beecher. *Cowboy Life on the Western Plains: The
Reminiscences of a Ranchman.* 1910.
Browne, John Ross. *A Tour through Arizona, 1864: or, Adventures in
Apache Country.* 1869.
Burroughs, John Rolfe. *Where the Old West Stayed Young.* 1962.
Canton, Frank M. *Frontier Trails: The Autobiography of Frank M.
Canton,* ed. Edward Everett Dale. 1930.
Chrisman, Harry E. *Lost Trails of the Cimarron.* 1961.
Cleland, Robert Glass. *This Reckless Breed of Men: The Trappers
and Fur Traders of the Southwest.* 1950.
Coe, George W. *Frontier Fighter: The Autobiography of George W.
Coe, Who Fought and Rode with Billy the Kid,* as told to Nan
Hilary Harrison. 1951.

Collings, Ellsworth, and Alma Miller England. *The 101 Ranch.* 1938.

Collins, Hubert E. *Warpath and Cattle Trail.* 1928.

Cook, James H. *Fifty Years on the Old Frontier, as Cowboy, Hunter, Guide, Scout, and Ranchman.* 1925.

Coolidge, Dane. *Fighting Men of the West.* 1932.

Cox, William R. *Luke Short and His Era.* 1961.

Culley, John H. *Cattle Horses and Men of the Western Range.* 1940.

Dale, Edward Everett. *Frontier Ways: Sketches of Life in the Old West.* 1959.

———. *The Range Cattle Industry: Ranching on the Great Plains from 1865 to 1925.* 1930.

———, and Morris L. Wardell. *History of Oklahoma.* 1948.

Debo, Angie. *Oklahoma, Foot-loose and Fancy-free.* 1949.

Dick, Everett. *The Sod-House Frontier, 1854–1890.* 1937.

———. *Vanguards of the Frontier.* 1941.

Dobie, J. Frank. *Coronado's Children: Tales of Lost Mines and Buried Treasures of the Southwest.* 1931.

———, ed. *Legends of Texas.* 1924.

———. *The Longhorns.* 1941.

———. *The Mustangs.* 1952.

———. *A Vaquero of the Brush Country: Partly from the Reminiscences of John Young.* 1929.

———, and others, eds. *Mustangs and Cow Horses.* 1940.

Duke, Cordia Sloan, and Joe B. Frantz. *6,000 Miles of Fence: Life on the XIT Ranch of Texas.* 1961.

Durham, Philip, and Everett L. Jones. *The Negro Cowboys.* 1965.

———. *The Adventures of the Negro Cowboys.* 1966.

Eaton, Frank. *Pistol Pete, Veteran of the Old West.*1953.

Emmett, Chris. *Shanghai Pearce: A Fair Likeness.* 1953.

Fergusson, Erna. *New Mexico: A Pageant of Three Peoples.* 1951.

Frink, Maurice, W. Turrentine Jackson, and Agnes Wright Spring. *When Grass Was King: Contributions to the Western Range Cattle Industry Study.* 1956.

Furlong, Charles Wellington. *Let'er Buck: A Story of the Passing of the Old West.* 1921.

Gard, Wayne. *The Chisholm Trail.* 1954.

———. *Frontier Justice.* 1949.

Gardiner, Dorothy. *West of the River.* 1941.

Gillett, James B. *Six Years with the Texas Rangers: 1875–1881,* ed. M. M. Qualife. 1921.

Gipson, Frederick Benjamin. *Cowhand: The Story of a Working Cowboy.* 1958.

———. *Fabulous Empire: Colonel Zack Miller's Story.* 1946.

Haley, James Evetts. *Charles Goodnight, Cowman and Plainsman.* 1936.

Hoig, Stan. *The Humor of the American Cowboy.* 1958.

Hollon, William Eugene. *The Southwest, Old and New.* 1961.

Horan, James D., and Paul Sann. *Pictorial History of the Wild West: A True Account of the Bad Men, Desperadoes, Rustlers and Outlaws of the Old West—and the Men Who Fought Them to Establish Law and Order.* 1954.

Hough, Emerson. *The Story of the Cowboy.* 1897.

Hunter, John Marvin, ed. *The Trail Drivers of Texas.* 2d ed., rev. 1925.

Katz, William Loren, ed. *The Black West.* 1971.

Keleher, William A. *Violence in Lincoln County, 1869–1881: A New Mexico Item.* 1957.

King, Frank M. *Pioneer Western Empire Builders: A True Story of the Men and Women of Pioneer Days.* 1946.

———. *Wranglin' the Past.* 1935.

Krakel, Dean F. *The Saga of Tom Horn: The Story of a Cattleman's War, with Personal Narrative, Newspaper Accounts and Official Documents and Testimonies.* 1954.

La Farge, Oliver. *Santa Fe: The Autobiography of a Southwestern Town.* 1959.

Lang, Lincoln A. *Ranching with Roosevelt.* 1926.

Lea, Tom. *The King Ranch.* 2 vols. 1957.

Leakey, John. *The West That Was, from Texas to Montana,* as told to Nellie Snyder Yost. 1958.

McCoy, Joseph G. *Historic Sketches of the Cattle Trade of the West and Southwest.* 1874.

Mercer, Asa S. *The Banditti of the Plains; or, The Cattlemen's Invasion of Wyoming in 1892.* 1894.

Mora, Joseph Jacinto. *Trail Dust and Saddle Leather.* 1946.

Osgood, Ernest Staples. *The Day of the Cattleman.* 1929.

Pelzer, Louis. *The Cattlemen's Frontier.* 1936.

Roosevelt, Theodore. *An Autobiography.* 1913.

———. *Ranch Life and the Hunting Trail.* 1888.

Remington, Frederick. *Frederick Remington's Own West,* ed. Harold McCracken. 1960.

Rollins, Philip Ashton. *The Cowboy: His Characteristics, His Equipment, and His Part in the Development of the West.* 1922.

Sandoz, Mari. *The Cattleman: From the Rio Grande across the Far Marias.* 1958.

Santee, Ross. *Cowboy.* 1928.

———. *The Lost Pony Tracks.* 1953.

Sharp, Paul F. *Whoop-Up Country.* 1955.

Shirley, Glenn. *Buckskin and Spurs: A Gallery of Frontier Rogues and Heroes.* 1958.

Siringo, Charles A. *Riata and Spurs.* 1927.

———. *A Texas Cowboy; or, Fifteen Years on the Hurricane Deck of a Spanish Pony.* 1885.

Sonnischen, C. L. *Cowboys and Cattle Kings: Life on the Range Today.* 1950.

Stuart, Granville. *Forty Years on the Frontier,* ed. Paul C. Phillips. 2 vols. 1925.

Thorp, Nathan Howard. *Pardners of the Wind,* as told to Neil M. Clark. 1945.

Towne, Charles Wayland, and Edward Norris Wentworth. *Cattle and Men.* 1955.

Turner, Frederick Jackson. *The Frontier in American History.* 1921.

Twain, Mark. *Autobiography.* 1924.

———. *Roughing It.* 1872.

Vestal, Stanley. *Dodge City, Queen of Cowtowns.* 1952.

———. *The Old Santa Fe Trail.* 1939.

Webb, Walter Prescott. *The Great Plains.* 1931.

Westermeier, Clifford P., ed. *Trailing the Cowboy: His Life and Lore as Told by Frontier Journalists.* 1955.

Wister, Owen. *Owen Wister Out West: His Journals and Letters,* ed. Fanny Kemble Wister. 1958.

FICTION

Abbey, Edward. *The Brave Cowboy.* 1956.

Adams, Andy. *The Log of a Cowboy.* 1903.

Berger, Thomas. *Little Big Man.* 1964.

Blackman, Tom W. *A Good Day to Die.* 1967.

Bower, B. M. *Chip of the Flying U.* 1906.

Brand, Max (Frederick Faust). *Destry Rides Again.* 1930.

———. *Singin' Guns.* 1938.

Cather, Willa. *The Professor's House.* 1925.

Chase, Borden. *Red River.* 1949.

Clark, Walter Van Tilburg. *The Ox-Bow Incident.* 1940.

———. *The Track of the Cat.* 1949.

Crane, Stephen. *The Open Boat.* 1898.

Davis, H. L. *Honey in the Horn.* 1935.

Fisher, Clay (Henry Allen). *The Tall Men.* 1954.

Fisher, Vardis. *Mountain Man.* 1965.

Frazee, Steve. *Desert Guns.* 1957.

Grey, Zane. *The Heritage of the Desert.* 1910.

———. *Lone Star Ranger.* 1915.

———. *Nevada.* 1928.

————. *Riders of the Purple Sage.* 1912.
————. *The U. P. Trail.* 1918.
Gulick, Bill. *They Came to a Valley.* 1966.
Guthrie, A. B., Jr. *These Thousand Hills.* 1956.
————. *The Way West.* 1949.
Haycox, Ernest. *Bugles in the Afternoon.* 1944.
————. *Saddle and Ride.* 1940.
Henry, Will (Henry Allen). *One More River to Cross.* 1967.
Herlihy, James Leo. *The Midnight Cowboy.* 1965.
Hoffman, Lee. *The Valdez Horses.* 1967.
Hough, Emerson. *The Covered Wagon.* 1922.
————. *North of 36.* 1923.
Johnson, Dorothy. *The Hanging Tree.* 1957.
Kelton, Elmer. *Donovan.* 1961.
L'Amour, Louis. *Hondo.* 1953.
Manfred, Frederick. *Lord Grizzly.* 1944.
McMurtry, Larry. *Horseman Pass By.* 1961.
Mulford, Clarence. *Hopalong Cassidy.* 1910.
Nye, Nelson C. *Rider of the Roan.* 1967.
Olsen, T. V. *Bitter Grass.* 1967.
Overholser, Wayne D. *North to Deadwood.* 1968.
Patten, Lewis B. *Death of a Gunfighter.* 1968.
Portis, Charles. *True Grit.* 1968.
Purdum, Herbert. *My Brother John.* 1966.
Raine, William McLeod. *Oh, You Tex!* 1920.
————. *Sons of the Saddle.* 1938.
Rhodes, Eugene Manlove. *Good Men and True.* 1910.
————. *West Is West.* 1917.
Richter, Conrad. *The Sea of Grass.* 1937.
Schaefer, Jack. *Shane.* 1949.
————. *Monte Walsh.* 1963.
Short, Luke (Frederick D. Glidden). *Ramrod.* 1943.
Spearman, Frank H. *Whispering Smith.* 1906.
Waters, Frank. *The Man Who Killed the Deer.* 1942.
Wister, Owen. *Lin McLean.* 1898.
————. *The Virginian.* 1902.
Wright, Harold Bell. *The Winning of Barbara Worth.* 1911.

MYTH

Agnew, S. M. "Destry Goes on Riding—or—Working the Six-Gun
    Lode." *Publishers Weekly,* 23 August 1952, pp. 746–51.
Barker, Warren J., MD. "The Stereotyped Western Story; Its Latent
    Meaning and Psychoeconomic Function." *Psychoanalytic Quar-
    terly,* April 1955, pp. 270–80.

Blacker, Irwin R., ed. *The Old West in Fiction.* 1961.

Boatright, Mody C. "The American Myth Rides the Range: Owen Wister's Man on Horseback." *Southwest Review,* Summer 1951, pp. 157–63.

————. "On the Nature of Myth." *Southwest Review,* Spring 1954, pp. 131–36.

Bode, Carl. "Henry James and Owen Wister." *American Literature,* May 1954, pp. 250–52.

Bosworth, A. R. "The Golden Age of Pulps." *Atlantic Monthly,* July 1961, pp. 57–60.

Carpenter, Frederic I. "The West of Walter Van Tilburg Clark." *College English,* February 1952, pp. 243–48.

Cawelti, John. *The Six-Gun Mystique.* 1971.

Davidson, L. J. "Fact or Formula in 'Western' Fiction." *Colorado Quarterly,* Winter 1955, pp. 278–87.

DeVoto, Bernard. "Always Different, Always the Same." *Saturday Review of Literature,* 29 May 1937, pp. 3–4.

————. "Phaëthon on Gunsmoke Trail." *Harper's Magazine,* December 1954, pp. 10–11, 14, 16.

Dobie, J. Frank. "Andy Adams, Cowboy Chronicler." *Southwest Review,* January 1926, pp. 92–101.

————. "Gene Rhodes; Cowboy Novelist." *Atlantic Monthly,* June 1949, pp. 75–77.

Durham, Philip, and Everett L. Jones, eds. *The Frontier in American Literature.* 1969.

Fiedler, Leslie. *Love and Death in the American Novel.* 1960.

————. *The Return of the Vanishing American.* 1968.

Fishwick, Marshall. "The Cowboy: America's Contribution to the World's Mythology." *Western Folklore,* April 1952, pp. 77–92.

————. "Diagnosing the American Dream." *Western Folklore,* 21 December 1963, pp. 8–11.

Folsom, James C. *The American Western Novel.* 1966.

Frantz, Joe B., and Julian E. Choate, Jr. *The American Cowboy: The Myth and Reality.* 1955.

————. "Behind the Cowboy Myth." *Saturday Review,* 16 June 1956, p. 9.

Fussell, Edwin. *Frontier: American Literature and the American West.* 1965.

Gruber, Frank. *The Pulp Jungle.* 1967.

Homans, Peter. "Puritanism Revisited: An Analysis of the Contemporary Screen-Image Western." *Studies in Public Communication,* Summer 1961, pp. 73–84.

Huffman, L. A. "The Last Busting at the Bow-Gun." *Scribner's Magazine,* July 1907, pp. 75–87.

Hutchinson, W. H. *A Bar Cross Man: The Life & Personal Writings of Eugene Manlove Rhodes.* 1956.

———. "Virgins, Villains, and Varmints." *Huntington Library Quarterly,* Fall 1953, pp. 381–92.

Lyon, P. "Wild, Wild West." *American Heritage,* August 1960, pp. 32–47.

———. "Writers of the Purple Prose." *American Heritage,* August 1960, pp. 81–84.

McWilliams, Carey. "Myths of the West." *North American Review,* November 1931, pp. 424–32.

Milton, John R. "The Western Attitude: Walter Van Tilburg Clark." *Critique,* Winter 1959, pp. 57–73.

———. "The Western Novel: Sources and Forms." *Chicago Review,* Summer 1963, pp. 74–100.

Portz, John. "Idea and Symbol in Walter Van Tilburg Clark." *Accents,* Spring 1957, pp. 112–28.

Rosenberg, Betty. "Poor, Lonesome, Unreviewed Cowboy." *Library Journal,* 15 December 1960, pp. 4432–33.

Rush, N. Orwin. "Fifty Years of *The Virginian.*" *The Papers of the Bibliographical Society of America,* 1952, pp. 99–117.

Sisk, J. P. "The Western Hero." *Commonweal,* 12 July 1957, pp. 367–69.

Smith, Henry Nash. *Virgin Land: The American West as Symbol and Myth.* 1950.

Steckmesser, Kent L. *The Western Hero in History and Legend.* 1965.

Waldmeir, Joseph L. "The Cowboy, the Knight, and Popular Taste." *Southern Folklore Quarterly,* September 1958, pp. 113–20.

Walker, Don D. "Wister, Roosevelt and James: A Note on the Western." *American Quarterly,* Fall 1960, pp. 358–66.

Warshow, Robert. *The Immediate Experience.* 1962.

Weaver, J. D. "Destry Rides Again and Again and Again." *Holiday,* August 1963, pp. 77–80.

Webb, Walter Prescott. "The Great Frontier and Modern Literature." *Southwest Review,* Spring 1952, pp. 85–100.

Westermeser, C. P. "The Cowboy—Sinner or Saint!" *New Mexico Historical Review,* April 1950, pp. 89–108.

Whipple, T. K. *Study Out the Land.* 1943.

Williams, John. "The 'Western': Definition of the Myth." *The Nation,* 18 November 1961, pp. 401–06.

Contributors

ALLAN R. BOSWORTH (b. 1901), a California newspaperman and freelance writer, has written more than fifteen books, among them *Bury Me Not* (1947), *Sancho of the Long Long Horns* (1947), *Ladd of the Lone Star* (1951), and *New Country* (1962).

DOUGLAS BRANCH (1905–1954) was a scholar and historian. His first book, *The Cowboy and His Interpreters* (1926), was published when he was twenty-one; at that time he had probably never been on a ranch. Among his other books is *The Hunting of the Buffalo* (1929).

MAX BRAND (Frederick Faust, 1900–1944) was an enormously popular writer who published more than eighty-five books, most of them Westerns. He has been translated into every European language, and he wrote in other genres and under other pseudonyms (Evan Evans, George Owen Baxter, Peter Henry Moreland). One of his best known Western works is *Destry Rides Again* (1930), and he created the character of Dr. Kildare for Hollywood.

WALTER VAN TILBURG CLARK (b. 1909) was born in Maine but grew up and went to college in Nevada. His working life has been divided between writing and teaching at San Francisco State University. He is best known to the public for such novels as *The Ox-Bow Incident* (1940) and *The Track of the Cat* (1949).

STEPHEN CRANE (1871–1900) was an Eastern writer who went West for some of his material. Many critics believe that he spent the grown-up part of his short life trying to distinguish, in fiction, between heroism and cowardice. He is best known for two non-Western works: *Maggie: A Girl of the Streets* (1894) and *The Red Badge of Courage* (1895). Crane is now thought to be one of the most distinguished American writers of the late nineteenth century.

JOHN CUNNINGHAM (b. 1915) has written some fine novels—*Starfall* (1960), for example—but he is best known for his short story "The Tin Star," because it was made into the famous film *High Noon*.

CLAY FISHER (Henry Allen, b. 1912) is a master of the Western. Under the name of Will Henry he has written such novels as *From Where the Sun Now Stands* (1959), *The Gates of the Mountains* (1962), and *Mackenna's Gold* (1963). From the Western Writers of America he has won five Spur Awards and the Levi Strauss Golden Saddleman Award.

VARDIS FISHER (1895–1968) was an Idaho author, a superb writer who spent long years teaching English at the University of Utah and at New York University while he learned to write. He is best known for such novels as *In Tragic Life* (1932), *Passions Spin the Plot* (1934), and *We Are Betrayed* (1935).

ZANE GREY (1875–1939) wrote more than fifty novels after first being a minor league baseball player and a dentist. When he began to devote all his time to writing, his popular Western novels, such as *Riders of the Purple Sage*, made him the best known writer in the genre.

DONALD HAMILTON (b. 1916) is a freelance writer and photographer. In addition to articles on hunting and photography, he has published many Westerns and detective stories. Among his books are *Smoky Valley* (1954), *The Big Country* (1957), and *Texas Fever* (1960).

BRET HARTE (1836–1902) arrived in California from New York in 1854, in time to try mining in the Mother Lode country of the Sierra Nevada. He settled in San Francisco in 1860 and soon became editor of *Overland Monthly*, in which he published a number of his own stories. Some of these, including "The Luck of Roaring Camp" and "The Outcasts of Poker Flat," are among the most popular American short stories ever written. He continued to write about the American West for years after he had retired to England, but his later work never achieved the success of his first stories.

ERNEST HAYCOX (1899–1950), one of the most talented of all Western writers, published his first novel, *Free Grass*, in 1929. He had many devoted readers, and there were few afficionados who missed such novels as *Alder Gulch* (1942), *Bugles in the Afternoon* (1944), and *Canyon Passage* (1945).

EMERSON HOUGH (1857–1923) was one of the first to write of the West. He loved the outdoors and was an ardent conservationist. Among the best known of his many books are *The Covered Wagon* (1922) and *North of 36* (1923).

DONALD JACKSON (b. 1919) began a long career as editor of the University of Illinois Press in 1948. A member of the American Historical Association and the Western History Association, his specialty is trans-Mississippi exploration. He won the Missouri Historical Society award for *Letters of the Lewis and Clark Expedition* in 1965.

JACK LONDON (1876–1916) was born in San Francisco and grew up on the Oakland waterfront. When he became a writer at the turn of the century, the influence of his youthful struggles was evident in his work. His characters, human and animal, are invariably divided between the weak and the strong, and in *The Son of the Wolf* (1900), his first collection of short stories, he shows his concern with violence, brutality, and survival as they are manifested in nature on a frontier.

ALEXANDER MILLER (1908–1960) was a writer on Christian sociology and a professor of religion in Stanford University's humanities program. His books include *The Christian Significance of Karl Marx* (1946) and *The Renewal of Man* (1955).

CLARENCE MULFORD (1883–1956) began writing Western fiction seventeen years before he made his first trip to the West. His most famous creation is Hopalong Cassidy, who made his first book appearance in 1907 in a collection of Mulford's short stories, *Bar 20*.

FRANK NORRIS (1870–1902) was born in Chicago and moved to San Francisco in 1884. During his time at the University of California, Berkeley (1890–94), he wrote short stories, sketches, and poetry. Becoming an admirer of the French novelist Emile Zola, Norris wrote his first naturalistic novel, *McTeague* (1899). He is best known for his projected trilogy, of which he lived to write only the first two novels: *The Octopus* (1901) and *The Pit* (1903). These books described the growing of wheat in California and the activities of grain speculators in Chicago; the unfinished third novel was to have described the use of wheat to save and sustain life in Europe.

THEODORE ROOSEVELT (1858–1919), twenty-sixth President of the United States, lived a vigorous life in the outdoors. An enthusiastic big game hunter in Africa and the West, he was a conservationist as well. He also found time to write more than twenty-five books during his busy life, including *Ranch Life and Hunting Trails* (1888) and *The Winning of the West* (1896).

JACK SCHAEFER (b. 1907), a newspaper man and novelist, quickly became famous after the publication of his first book, *Shane* (1949). Schaefer once wrote to a friend in Wyoming: "Probably if I had been really aware of the constant flood of westerns drugging the market, I would have shied away from that field. But I had for many years been collecting and reading all authentic material on western history I could find."

HARRY SCHEIN (b. 1924), a native of Sweden, has been active in both business and the arts. He has been president of the Swedish Film Institute (1963–70) and chairman of the Dramatic Institute (1969–70), and is married to the famous Swedish actress Ingrid Thulin. He has been the film critic for a Scandinavian literary magazine and is the author of many books and articles.

LUKE SHORT (Frederick D. Glidden, b. 1908) is considered one of the finest writers of Western fiction. His stories and novels have been praised for their clever plots, swift action, suspense, and liveliness.

THOMAS THOMPSON (b. 1913) grew up on ranches in California, where he began writing in 1944. He has published eighteen books and approximately five hundred magazine stories, and has written more than a hundred television scripts.

ROBERT WARSHOW (1917–1955) was an American writer and critic who contributed articles to many periodicals. Before his untimely death he had already won widespread recognition for his original criticism of literature and films.

T. K. WHIPPLE (1890–1939) was professor of English literature at the University of California, Berkeley, and author of *Spokesmen* (1928), a critical study of modern writers and American life.

OWEN WISTER (1860–1938) was a Pennsylvania lawyer and writer who created the archetypal Western story. *The Virginian* (1920) has been the inspiration for thousands of "Westerns"—good and bad—some published, some filmed for motion picture or television audiences. Wister was a Harvard classmate and lifelong friend of Theodore Roosevelt, with whom he shared a great love of the West.